CW00519598

THE HARBINGER (

BOOK TWO

THE FINAL SIX DAYS

Copyright © 2022 Howard Sargent

All rights reserved.

ISBN: 9798394369087

HARBINGER OF THE DEAD

In the midst of a restless sea sits a remote, rocky island. Susceptible to the vagaries of wind and weather it is a hostile place, and yet, a small community of people call this island home. Some of them are artisans; labourers responsible for the day to day running of the colossal, monolithic black stone building in which they dwell. Others are soldiers, knights charged with maintaining order and discipline on the island. The majority of the residents though are far more dangerous, feared and shunned by everyday society they are condemned to live and die in this place, never again to see the land of their birth. For they possess the power of gods and demons, a perilous gift that makes them pariahs in any civilised society.

For all of them are gifted with magic.

Gytha is one such person, a sorceress brought to the island as a child she is reluctantly accepting of her fate, content to live her life as generations before her have lived it, in study, scholarship, and isolation. Her life is already planned, as it is with all mages of middling abilities, she has routine, she has order, she has stultifying conformity...

Then though, people start to die.

Their bodies bear the trace of a hand burning with cold, causing the superstitious to believe that the god of the dead is walking amongst them, killing at random. Sir Steven, captain of the knights who maintain discipline on the island believes that the culprit is more of this earth though, and recruits Gytha to assist him; together they begin a desperate search for a murderer who is intelligent, resourceful, and can seemingly call up a spirit of death to do their murderous bidding.

Yet catch this culprit both Steven and Gytha must, before fear overwhelms the island, discipline collapses, and the prospect of imminent death affects everybody that call the Isle of Tears their home.

CONTENTS

FOR HELEN

HARBINGER OF THE DEAD

DAY SEVEN
27
A tantalising breeze

She had fallen asleep. Hardly surprising considering she had been chasing through caves all night but yes, despite the perceived sense of danger she had fallen asleep. The first thing she noticed as she flickered into wakefulness was that of course her light orb had gone out, well sleep was ideal for breaking one's concentration she supposed. She was about to summon the wisp once more but at the last moment she hesitated. By all the Gods she had not a stitch on, summon the light and the man next to her could see her in all her underwhelming glory. The man next to her? She put out her hand to touch him, he was both sleeping and barely dressed too. Then at last everything came flooding back and Miriam remembered what she had just done. She had a thousand questions to ask herself but her shock at her own behaviour meant that she neither finished asking or answering any of them.

"Did I really...?"

"How could I possibly...?"

"Am I nothing more than a common...?"

"Am I as sad and desperate...?"

"Ashamed, why aren't I feeling...?"

"Should I have enjoyed it as much as...?"

Her head was turning in circles. Finally she stood up and stretched. There was something rather guiltily liberating about feeling cool air on her bare skin. Gingerly, feeling with her toes she took a few tentative steps forward, then a few more. It all felt rather thrilling and somehow her guilt and embarrassment only served to heighten her excitement. She felt a little like Saint Ethelberta who had renounced all things worldly, including her clothes and lived for thirty years in a cave halfway up a mountain somewhere. Oh Elissa but she wanted him again, she really was beyond shame, some fumbling in the dark and she had cast all her morals and principles completely to one side, yet had they served to do anything but to hold her back? Perhaps this was the real her, a woman with no inhibitions, one who obeyed her passions, whims, and desires instead of stifling them. Maybe she should have been a priestess of Jhuna, dancing naked in wooded glades under the full moon, taking lovers by the score, indulging in all the carnal desires that a woman could possibly imagine, and to feel no shame. What a way to live that would be, if she could but embrace it she could become a different person, free, uncaring of other opinions, living the life she wanted to lead rather than...

"If you are going to wander off shouldn't you conjure some light first?"

It was like jumping in that lake again, being doused head to toe in ice cold water, reality was snapping at her as sharply as a pane of shattered glass. Instinctively she crossed her arms over her chest, a ridiculous gesture because a) She was in near total darkness, b) She had her back to him and c) She had nothing that was worth hiding anyway. She just knew that as he was making love to her he was imagining she was someone else, Gytha maybe or petite little Elsa or any of a dozen other girls, he would hardly want her like that now could he?

"Umm, can I get dressed first?"

He was at her shoulder in seconds and handed her her robes which, thankfully, were almost dry. To her surprise he leaned close and kissed her on her shoulder. "You don't want to do the whole thing again?"

She did. She really, really did. She wanted to take his strong hand and move it over her, over all of her, everywhere, over and over again. She wanted to so badly...

She took the robes off him and tried to figure out how best to dress in the dark. "We need to go back; it cannot be far from dawn now."

"Go back?" there was a hint of mild surprise in Nikolaj's voice. "You don't want to find the source of that breeze?"

Sex turned the brain to mush it seemed. And it wasn't the only reason her skin had felt so alive, not the only reason she had been tingling from nose to toes. The slightest murmur of fresh air, clean air was swirling through the cave, though she felt it most strongly against her face. "Of course," she said softly, "there must be an exit ahead, and quite close by."

Within a couple of minutes both were fully dressed, and her light wisp floated over her hand, as of course her staff had vanished into the pool next to her. She felt the slightest frisson of tension between them, too much still remained unsaid, so she tried to get it out of the way before they moved on.

"Look," she said firmly, "I am not normally like that. I don't just...you know..."

"I know," he said, "I do know you quite well Miriam, even if you think otherwise."

"Yes," she said awkwardly; "I suppose so. What I am trying to say is that I know men have needs and all that and that down here you weren't exactly spoilt for choice, I mean it was me or Gideon, and it would be a difficult choice if he was still here and...I am rambling aren't I? and making no sense at all. I mean that I would hardly be your first choice but given current circumstances...and it has been a long time for me and I just…and I am still making no sense at all. Flustered, I am flustered, I need…" she felt around the pockets in her robes and finally found a rather soggy piece of mint that she popped into her mouth. It did not taste like it normally did. She sighed and was about to speak again in another attempt to clarify herself. Nikolaj though beat her to it. "You are saying that I seduced you because I am a man and have no self-control and that I chose you because you are the only creature around that goes in and out in all the right places."

She was surprised. He was proving far more eloquent and perceptive than her. She nodded. "Basically, yes, though I have a higher opinion of you than you seem to think."

"And I, mage Miriam, have a higher opinion of you than you seem to think. Can you possibly envisage a scenario where you can be perceived as, dare I say it, desirable?"

She shook her head firmly. "No, not really."

"Then you still have much to learn about yourself, I think you are rather lovely, and your manner, your uncertainties and your constant over analysis of everything just makes you all the more endearing."

"Oh," she said, not a little stunned by his comment. "I don't know how genuine those words are Sir Nikolaj but thank you anyway, they are kind words. I…I…when I was in my final year in the children's college, in my very early teens a couple of knights came to give us a talk, about what to expect when we moved to the big college, the rules and regulations and all that. Well when they had finished I had some questions to ask and I put up my hand, and do you know what the knight said? "We have a question, he announced proudly, from the boy at the front." The boy, Sir Nikolaj, that was what he called me. Nearly everybody burst out laughing, even the knight when he realised his mistake. I keep my hair short because it curls terribly and is difficult to manage and with these robes, my small chest and narrow hips and everything, well the robes swallow all that up somehow. The boy. At my age now I suppose I would shrug it off but back then I was devastated, humiliated. And I was teased relentlessly for years. So no, I will never see myself as anything other than what I am. A plain girl who tries to compensate for her physical deficiencies through education, and learning. No." She put her finger to his lips. "No more words on the subject. We may still be in danger after all, and we have things to do. We have talked away enough time."

"Come on then," he said; "but I have not given up on trying to show you your worth, my attempts have merely been postponed. The breeze it seems is coming from the main tunnel at the end of the cavern. Let's start there."

Nikolaj may have referred to it as, "the main tunnel," but even Miriam had to stoop to negotiate it. Soon afterwards Nikolaj was almost forced on to his knees as the walls narrowed even further. Miriam's claustrophobia was beginning to manifest itself again, she started chewing her lip and fidgeting. And chattering inanely.

"How far do you think we have come?" she asked. "I mean, what part of the island is directly over our heads right now? the animal pens? the casting circles? or maybe somewhere else? Maybe a patch of waste ground or a series of rabbit burrows. Perhaps a rabbit will tunnel through the walls here and land on our head! Imagine that! To be killed by a falling rabbit! Xhenafa does move in some very odd ways after all...I"

Nikolaj was ahead of her and stopped her talking by raising his hand. "Two tunnels ahead," he said, "and both appear to be going uphill. Any ideas?"

Miriam managed to squeeze alongside him, the intimacy involved in pressing close to him, an intimacy that would have embarrassed her some hours ago no longer seemed relevant. He WAS strong, she could certainly feel that. "Can you tell which passage the breeze is coming through?"

Of the two tunnel entrances facing them, one was straight ahead but narrow, the other was wider but was directly to their left, heading due south. She pressed her face close to both, the air was cold here and at first it was difficult to tell where the source of the breeze was. Suddenly though, there was a fresh gust of air hitting her directly on the face. It made her mind up for her.

She indicated the south tunnel. "Here," she said, "try this way first."

"Agreed," said Nikolaj. "Me first, you second. Only because I am more expendable than you. Besides, if we do find a way out of here Sir Beverley will probably kill me anyway." And with that he plunged into the tunnel, with Miriam hoping against hope that this would be the final darkling little hole she would have to clamber through in her lifetime.

****

The knights face the music as Gytha slips away

Back in the entry chamber, the first cave following the descent from the rope ladder, Gytha and Edgar ran into Welton again. He was there, with two other knights, all of them carrying torches that billowed smoke, stinging Gytha's already dry eyes. Her head throbbed terribly, she still tasted blood in her throat and felt hard crusts of it congealing in her nostrils. And Tola was dead. She would never see, speak to him again. The last fact was still to properly register with her, for an emotional person she felt strangely numbed in mind and body. Too much had happened too quickly for her. She would cry, long and sorrowfully, she knew that. She just wouldn't be doing it right now.

She spoke to Welton, her voice little more than a fractured croak. "You found us! How did you manage that?"

Welton was uncharacteristically surly, obviously that was what a few hours in Beverley's company could do to a man. "It took some scratching around," he said, "a lot of knights spreading out whilst the Commander...rests. We are here now anyway."

Gytha looked warily behind her, as though expecting to see spectres emerge from the shadows. "We all need to leave here and get back to the college. The spirit is supposed to attack intruders to the caves, and she could do this anytime. We need to get out...now."

"Where is everybody else?" Welton sounded puzzled, and with good cause.

"Tola is dead," Edgar said bluntly; "both myself and Gytha are carrying injuries. We will tell you more when we are out of here."

"And the others?"

Edgar shook his head. "Nikolaj and Miriam went after the prisoner. He has escaped."

"What!" Welton choked.

"He saw a side passage and scarpered before we could stop him. The others went after him."

"Have any of them turned up yet?" Gytha asked.

"No," said Welton, his annoyance obvious. "This is the first we have heard of any of this."

"Oh." Where could Miriam be? How deep did these caves go? The spirit had not mentioned them. Were they already dead? Was her good friend dead? Now her emotions were starting to kick in. She had to swallow hard to keep control. "We need to get out of here," she repeated, "and we need to find Miriam and the others. And I need to go and see Steven. Things happened down there that he needs to know about. From me."

Welton nodded. "Come on then. Back to the chapter house. You can tell me what happened then one of these boys can escort you to the other island."

Any attempt to leave there and then though was halted as, from the passage entrance that Miriam and Nikolaj had gone into to chase Gideon, both Eubolo and Kas the staff mage emerged. Eubolo was beaming from ear to ear.

"This is some place," he beamed excitedly; "there is a chamber through there that holds an artefact...well I have no idea who has been keeping this place secret, but we need everyone to know about it. We need to organise a thorough expedition, knights and mages mapping chamber by chamber..." he then saw Gytha for the first time.

"What has happened to you my dear, you look terrible!"

"Not as terrible as I feel," she replied, "but we need to leave here now, you can sense the power in this place, right?"

"Indeed I can," Kas said, "there is real danger here, an aura of power few of us could counter."

"It has claimed Tola," Gytha said breathily; "now for the last time let us leave before it claims anybody else."

She looked at the two mages as she broke the news. Eubolo looked mortified, Kas was more inscrutable but then she would not have had the day to day dealings with Tola that Eubolo would have had. "Where is he?" Eubolo asked quietly, "where is his body?"

"Beyond our reach for the present." Edgar spoke perfunctorily, as if to forestall further questions. "We will return for him but now is not the time."

To Gytha, the time taken for seven people to scramble back up the rope ladder was absolutely interminable. She expected Sinotaneh to appear through one of the passageways at any second, though now she would be vengeful and beyond reason, ready to slay them all where they stood. Would the college be any safer though? The spirit could strike anywhere after all, past events proved that. Yet this time she felt that the college would be a refuge for them for there were three different things at play here. The first was that the caves were Sinotaneh's realm, the one she had pledged to guard. Summoned by intruders into this place she would act of her own volition, this was the place she had sacrificed her life to protect.

The second thing was that outside here, in the college itself she was being controlled, being called to murder against her own will. Whoever was summoning her needed to prepare, needed to plan, and their incursion into the caves would not have afforded the killer the luxury of the time required. Yet the longer they lingered the more time this person would have. Things could change in an instant and so there was no more relieved person than herself when they were all out of the caves and back in the college passageways again. The final thing of course was that both Caswell and Raiman were alone when they died, taking on a company of seven may just be beyond the will and the capabilities of this particular murderer.

The journey through the college passages, which had seemingly taken so long and were so daunting to Gytha earlier that evening, now seemed like little more than a summer jaunt and in no time they were back at the slightly ajar doorway that led into the reception room at the foot of the stairs. The familiarity of the surroundings she would soon be in again filled Gytha's heart with the sort of joy she had never thought to experience at returning to such normally mundane surroundings. That emotion was strangled pretty quickly though when she heard a voice, a voice of a man waiting there for them, Sir Beverley was awake it seemed and was apparently berating some unfortunate knight just for being on duty.

"You are a slack jawed one are you not?" Gytha could not hear the mumbled reply.

"Look to your uniform sir, ever heard the word polish? That breastplate is a disgrace. And what are you doing staring out of the door like that? Guard duty eh, guard duty you say. What are you guarding then eh? Some ornamental hangings? Need a beating more than a hanging I say, see that dust, eh boy? Now, tell me, where is Walton? Walton, Walton, that is what I said boy, don't correct me. Where is he? I have heard you lot gossiping I have, that he is on some futile mission chasing his own arse in the passages. He needs my permission to do that, and I have not given it. So I say again, where is he? He had better have a powerful reason for going behind my back, now come on, tell me where he is, and I will forgive your slovenly appearance."

There was nothing else for it. Welton stepped through the door followed by the torch bearing knights, then Eubolo and Kas. Edgar though, stayed where he was and restrained Gytha with his hand when she attempted to pass him. She heard the outraged uproar from Sir Beverley but not his words, for Edgar was speaking to her. "Wait here till he goes. They will be off to the chapter house in a moment. I will have to go and report too but you, you can get to Steven and commander Shadan, for he is at the Isle of Healing also. I have a feeling we will need their sense before the day is out."

"I really wanted to see Miriam first," she whispered in reply.

"Well if we could have everything we wanted I would now be being carried to my palace on a gold litter where twenty dusky concubines would be waiting for me in a bath strewn with rose petals. Instead I have to grovel to that great steaming bear and, once he finds out everything he will be after you too. This will be the only chance you will get."

Gytha nodded slowly. "Gods look after you Sir Edgar. All of them hopefully. You may need them all to deal with...him."

The voices were receding, evidently they were leaving the room, hopefully going up the stairs. It was just Sir Beverley she could hear, blustering away as ever, his bombast occasionally interspersed by the odd apologetic mumble from Welton. Edgar seemed pleased by the development. "Sounds like he has let the other mages go for now. Maybe the sergeant convinced him they have barely been involved. Come on, the way is as clear as it will ever be."

He pushed the door open gently and stepped through, Gytha following. Sir Beverley was at the top of the first flight of stairs, out of their line of sight. Eubolo and Kas were whispering animatedly to each other in the centre of the hall. The great entrance doors of the college were open, just wide enough for two people to pass through simultaneously. The fog was still squatting outside and though it was still dark there was a hint of faintest magenta to the velvet blackness that hinted that dawn was not far off. She had been awake all night.

Kas looked up at Gytha, then up at the stairs, ensuring that Sir Beverley was out of earshot. "Is he in charge now? None of us seniors have been told anything! This situation is intolerable! And there is still no sign of Arbagast."

"He is in charge yes, while Steven is with his sick daughter, but the chain of command is…"

"Confused." Edgar finished her sentence, "but hopefully we will all know where we stand by the end of the day. Gytha, take a torch. Gytha will be seeing Sir Steven now senior, the sooner he can return here the better."

And a minute later that was where she was headed, descending the great steps, torch in hand, for she would not be allowed to make her own light out here. After the passages and caves the chill of the fog and dawn air was sharper, more barbed than she was used to, but she needed the freshness to give her mind the clarity she required. For she was bone weary, covered in grime and worse than that her nerves were taut, strained, and frayed. Her emotions were freeing themselves at last; she kept thinking of Tola, and of the tortured spirit, and wondering where in the name of the Gods Miriam was. She herself had been so close to death this night, so close, and now she would probably have to answer to Sir Beverley, and he appeared to be a man who listened to no one but himself. So much had happened, so many terrible things and now, for the first time that night, as she finally cleared the steps and started along the path, tears began to sting her eyes.

****

The welcome sight of the sea

It was no longer a thin breeze, as they climbed the narrow tunnel it had become so much more than a thin breeze. It was now a deep, refreshing draught of pure, frigid air, a full goblet to be downed in one gulp rather than parsimoniously sipped. And it was making Miriam shiver.

"Elissa's braid but this climb is so wearing on the thighs," she moaned,

13

"this surface is so punishing, every step jars me up to the arms."

"That is why they call it rock," Nikolaj replied. "The clue is in the name you see."

"You are truly awful at sarcasm," she said archly; "stick to what you're good at, whatever that is."

He smiled and let her get a little ahead of him before smacking her, not too harshly, on the backside. "Am I good at that then?" he asked her.

She stopped and stared at him, open mouthed and horrified. "You just...you just."

He then put his arm around her, pulled her to him and kissed her, sensitively, sweetly, most definitely unexpectedly. After he had released her she just looked at him as though he was deranged. For once in her life she was struggling for words. "Mad." She could only gasp. "Mad."

"Ordinarily," he said, "right now I would be tearing your robes off with my bare hands. But alas, we have more pressing issues at this particular time."

She was still unable to speak. She just nodded her head and continued to climb. Soon though, as well as cold, clammy air they became aware of something else, the sound of the sea and the taste of salt on their lips. And ahead there was no longer total darkness, there was the merest glimmer of something pale and silvery, a tantalising sliver of light, fragile as a maiden's fingers, appearing almost directly ahead of them.

Miriam doused her own light, and the outline of the cave mouth became even more pronounced. It was just a few feet away; it was just a question of whether Nikolaj or Miriam would get there first.

It was Miriam. And she was in yet another cave. This one though was different. Some twenty feet square this one opened out not into a tunnel, or another chamber, but onto the world outside, with its fog, stars, and sinking moon.

"Where are we?" Miriam was confused, "I do not know this place."

"My guess?" Nikolaj sounded smug, he had an answer whilst Miriam didn't. "This is one of the caves that open directly onto the south cliff face. There are several, but they can only be viewed from the sea."

"So we are still trapped then, stuck in a sea facing cave. Do we really have to traipse all the way back again?" The thought made Miriam groan inside.

"I don't know." Nikolaj strolled up to the cave mouth and attempted to peer through the fog. "Come here though, please." He added the last word after a pause, as though aware that he sounded like he was ordering her about. She came towards him but stopped a foot short.

"Artorus' beard man, you are right on the edge there, one gust of wind and you could be pulled over!...Phew, smell that damp earth!" she wrinkled her nose at the surprising odour.

"It is all right, there is no strong wind here. And no birds in the cave. You would expect nests and ...other evidence of them here. Not even a discarded feather."

It was lovely to feel the air on her face again, even if it was clammy, and strangely ominous. The song of the sea though was soothing to her, and she needed soothing right now. "You think somebody is keeping the birds out, or at least cleaning up after them?"

"Yes," Nikolaj said; "but why? And you are right about the earth, the smell is strong, and you know what that means I hope."

"That the island surface is just a few feet away, up there." She pointed in the appropriate direction, then looked around the cave again, her eyes were used to the gloom by now and she thought she had noticed something. She returned to the back of the cave once more, past the passage they had walked through earlier. There was something there, against the wall, something that was definitely not rock. She went over to it and touched it before whooping excitedly. "Here Nikolaj! Here!"

It was a flap of hide, lightly coated in pitch, presumably to try and camouflage it, and it was situated low enough against the wall to be brushing the cave floor. Nikolaj crouched on his haunches and pulled it back, letting Miriam press close so that they could both peer inside.

On the face of it, it was just another tunnel, albeit a pretty low one. But it didn't take long for both of them to see the difference. For this was a tunnel that bored through earth, not rock and it was most definitely man-made, for wooden pilings and supports ran along its length as far as the eye could see. It climbed gently, without twists and turns, though how far it went neither of them could see from here. Ordinarily it would be just about the least inviting place in the world for one such as Miriam to have to negotiate, now however, for her it seemed like a path to the golden hall of the Gods themselves.

"Me first?" Nikolaj said with little enthusiasm.

"No. It is narrow, and I am smaller. I will summon the light again; it can only help."

"As you wish."

She crouched low and prepared to duck under the flap. "Before I go can I just say something?"

"Of course."

15

She swallowed and held him firmly with her deep brown eyes. Her chin jutted out a little, as it always did when she felt she was saying something important, and possibly contentious.

"Sorry to mention it again but what happened earlier. I don't know if it will happen again or if you wish to maintain a degree of familiarity with me. If you do though then, well I rather you wouldn't...lay your hands on me like you did earlier."

"You mean when I spanked you?"

She winced. "Horrible word but yes. I would rather you didn't do it again. I just find it well...a little..."

"Demeaning?"

She nodded.

"Sorry. Some women do like it you know."

"I know. Gytha likes it, she told me once."

"But you are not Gytha."

"No. I am not nearly as much fun I am afraid."

"I disagree. Is there anything women don't discuss when they are alone together?"

She thought for a moment. "The first war of Chiran succession?"

Nikolaj laughed, "nobody talks about the first war of Chiran succession. Not even the Chirans. You had better get moving, for all we know we are still not out of danger yet."

She scuttled into the tunnel on her hands and knees. Then she stopped for a moment and turned her head to look at Nikolaj. With a little laugh she shook her backside at him daring him to do his worst. He raised his hands as far from her as he could; they both laughed in unison, then she was gone, moving up the tunnel as fast as her legs could take her.

Whoever had dug it knew what they were doing. Joists, supports and all other practical things that Miriam had little idea about were in evidence as she climbed. It must have taken a great sacrifice in both time and effort to construct such a thing. At first she wondered how it could be done with nobody noticing but, if this was a remote part of the island, and if the work, all that sawing and dirt removal was done in the cave, with the spoil being thrown into the sea, then yes, a careful man could keep such a task secret. Why was it here though? What purpose did it serve? If a man wanted to get into or out of the college without the knights seeing them then it would be perfect for the task, if a mage wanted to do the same and they had a similarly secret entrance in the college they could move from college to island and back again completely untraced. If one knew the route then they could do this journey in under an hour. But why? Why?

Journey's end. Overhead a wooden hatch painted black again barred the way. She stopped and let Nikolaj catch up with her. This tunnel was not as long as she feared, she had been climbing for less than two minutes. She let her light play over the scene a moment. There was a handle, an iron ring on the frame and a step ladder under it. She would have to stand on it and haul herself up. Nikolaj though moved to do it without speaking to her and for once, she was happy to let him have his way.   The hatch opened upwards, into darkness. She groaned at that, surely it was not another tunnel. Carefully Nikolaj eased himself upwards, through the new opening. Then to her surprise he laughed. He put out both hands to help Miriam up and again, she let him lift her and set her down on a piece of hard earth covered in damp straw.

She was in a small, circular house. It was beehive shaped and made from pieces of sharp stone interlocked together without any form of mortar. Light flooded through a hundred tiny chinks where the stone didn't lock together completely. And there was an opening into fresh air, or rather fresh fog. It was a little odd because it was not large enough for a man to walk through without crouching on hands and knees. Nikolaj, still laughing, did such a thing, Miriam followed and stood, stretching to her full height with a grimace. She was outside, back in the world again, her sigh of relief was heartfelt.

The fog was still everywhere, yet to her it seemed perhaps a little thinner than it had been, she could look further than she expected, just far enough to see exactly where they were.

They were in a gated enclosure, four stone walls that came up just past her midriff. It adjoined a similar enclosure, which in turn joined onto another, and another. And from these other enclosures came a sound, a familiar sound. She guessed it was dawn now, for there was a pinkish light permeating the fog over her head and the inhabitants of these surrounding enclosures were beginning to wake for the new day. She was grateful that the enclosure they inhabited seemed to be unoccupied for the smell in her nostrils was pungent, and very animal.

For they appeared to be surrounded by the sound of snuffling pigs.

****

Coincidence! Serendipity!

Gytha had little belief in coincidence and no belief whatsoever in happy coincidence and so just about the last thing she expected to see as she plodded the well-worn gravel lined path through the fog and the cold was her friend Miriam coming the other way. Yet perhaps it was not so much a coincidence after all for there was only one main path running the length of the island and all those who wished to cross it at speed had little option but to use it. Perhaps the only coincidence was one of time rather than place, for, as Gytha passed the gardens to her left and started to approach the animal pens it was Miriam that she met, Miriam and Nikolaj coming in the other direction.

Miriam was looking drawn, pale, bedraggled, and not a little grubby, Artorus only knew what she herself looked like in return, but such trivialities barely mattered as they hugged and cried whilst Nikolaj took the torch and retired to a respectful distance. Gytha had been trying so hard to stem the flow of tears but the relief at seeing her friend alive and relatively unscathed was the final crack in the dam. Long and hard she wept into Miriam's shoulder and when at last she stopped she felt so drained, so tired, the prospect of the walk to the Isle of Healing seemed beyond daunting.

But she had to continue. She had already considered the possibility of meeting Steven's wife and was not exactly relishing the thought, or indeed the feelings it might provoke in her. But she felt she had no choice. If she did not go Sir Beverley might end up arresting them all, or botching the investigation, or both.

Anyway, after the tears, it was time for dissemination. Quickly, falteringly, yet trying not to leave any details out both Gytha and Miriam swapped their news. Miriam spoke of Gideon, of the artefact, of the letter, and of the tunnel leading to the pig pens. Gytha told Miriam of Sinotaneh, of Tola, of the elven dead, everything she could recall in a hurry. Finally she told Miriam to be wary of Sir Beverley, a man who seemed to have little respect for novice mages. The only thing that Miriam left out in turn was news of her tryst with Nikolaj, she considered that information was best left for a more suitable time.

Gytha wanted to stay longer, she did not want to say goodbye to a friendly face, did not want to push on into this cloying gloom but then, how many times in life was one compelled to do that which seemed most unpalatable to one's nature? Miriam promised her that she would go to her cell and sleep and then they parted, Gytha resuming her journey to the other isle once more.

Soon afterwards she was in the wilder part of the island, great tumps of thick, wiry grass sprouted forth from the shadows either side of the path. The path was sloping downwards now and soon she was being hemmed in by great banks of earth as it cut into the body of the island the nearer she got to the bridge. Before long, these banks needed to be shored up by bricks and sharp stones. She stopped for a moment, moving her sputtering torch around. This was quite a familiar spot for her, she noted the lichen clinging grimly on to the brickwork and the thin, straggly weeds pushing through the cracks between the stones. She always felt quite sorry for them, the initial burst of excitement as they burst free of their seeds towards the light, their total embrace of life and all the possibilities it held only for them to encounter poor nutrients, shadows, and withering disappointment. They were yellowing, sickly, they belonged in this place just as much as she probably did.

The path started to drop sharply, she heartily wished that there was no fog because soon she would have had one of the best views the island had to offer. She used to come here quite a lot, in her teens, shortly after transferring from the Childs' college. Whenever she had a problem adjusting to her new life as an adult novice she would come here to think, to be alone, to hear the birds and the sea, to let it soothe her rather than remind her of her isolation. It brought back good memories of calm and serenity, she remembered coming here during her brief pregnancy when, in the turmoil and terror torturing her every moment, she saw how small she was, how insignificant her problems were in the context of the world around her and, just for the most fleeting period in that terrible time, she had a modicum of peace.

Finally it was down some steps, just broad and shallow enough for a well-trained horse to traverse and she was here, at the bridge. It was a span of stone that crossed the narrow gorge between islands, under it the sea was little more than a constant angry foam as it was funnelled through a space far too small to cope with its untrammelled power. Here the wind, when it blew, was at its most primal, the rain when it fell was at its most violent and the hail and lightning could kill a man, if he was in the wrong place at the wrong time.

She strolled to the centre of the bridge and stopped. The torch by now was little more than smoke and embers so she threw it over the parapet and into the sea. The path was wide and flat on the Isle of Healing, and she would not need it there. Another reason she saw, as she put her elbows on the parapet and let the breeze tug her hair, was that the fog was beginning to thin at some pace. There was a breeze, and it was strengthening, she could pick out the great stone bulwarks of the glowering cliffs up to the point where they curved away from south to west. And behind that fog she could discern a morning sky, streaked with jagged clouds the colour of sage.

The fog was dispersing, and she really had to get a move on.

****

A dishevelled woman has an unhappy surprise

She expected Steven to see her privately in an ante room somewhere.

The hospital was a confusing rabbit warren to her, she had only visited a handful of times and so, when she announced herself to the lay sister at the gate, she had asked for an escort, a service that the sister provided herself. She did not expect to be shown into a room where Steven was sitting next to his wife, with their little girl tucked up in bed in front of them.

"I am terribly sorry," Gytha coloured in embarrassment, "I did not mean to intrude."

She was pretty, Steven's wife, dispiritingly pretty, though there was a certain vapid quality to her eyes. Steven she sensed was pleased to see her though he did not smile, yet to her surprise it was little Edith that made the strongest impression on her.

And why wouldn't she? Children on the island were usually six or seven at the youngest, she had not seen such a small girl since she was a child herself. She was tiny, perfect, with a little snub nose and hair the colour of dark honey. Would her child have been a girl? She didn't even know that. Would she have looked so...so sweet, so innocent? What would her own life had been like if she were now a mother? Would she trade her gift for the chance to find this out? She knew the answer but forced herself not to dwell on it. Little Edith was sick after all and both parents must be under terrible strain, she had to remember that, she really did.

Steven and Fedrica both stood, he came over to her and now he did smile, albeit weakly.

"You are not, do not worry," he said. "Fedrica, this is Gytha, my liaison officer during the investigation I was telling you about. Gytha, this is the lady Fedrica, my wife."

A truly beautiful dress Gytha noted, she had never seen the like before. Gytha curtsied as best she could, bowing her head slightly. "Pleased to meet you my lady."

"Pleased to meet you too," Fedrica said, a little stiffly. "Have you walked all the way from the other college?"

"Yes my lady. Might I ask after the condition of the lady Edith?"

"She sleeps, as you can see," Steven replied, "but the healers are encouraged. She appears to be responding to treatment at least though it is too early to hope our prayers to Meriel have been answered."

"I will pray for her; as soon as I get a chance I will pray for her. Maybe I can see her when the Gods grant her recovery."

"If the Gods grant it then of course you may," Fedrica answered her, "but I take it my daughter was not the reason for your visit."

Gytha nodded. "You are right my lady, I was hoping for a private interview with your husband, if he can spare the time."

"It would be churlish to deny your request considering the distance you have come," Fedrica sat down again, "but I would beg you not to detain him too long."

"She will not," Steven said. "Come with me Gytha, Sir Beverley's office is free at the moment, now follow me."

It was a small room, Sir Beverley's office, a desk uncluttered by papers, a wide chair that sagged in the middle, a couple of stools, a long, low sedan, a modest bookshelf, and little else. It was well swept and looked barely used. Gytha knew that if she sat down she would probably fall asleep, so she remained on her feet as she recounted the events of the evening just past, both hers and Miriam's. Steven remained stern faced and stoic all the while, only asking questions when they were pertinent, only stopping Gytha a couple of times when he needed clarification. When she had finished he looked grimmer than ever, so grim she just started babbling.

"I am so sorry for calling on you like this when you are under so much strain, but I felt...Keth take it I don't know what I felt, you need to know that is all. Sir Beverley frightens me, he is so unpredictable, he has removed me from my position so when he finds out that I have continued working for you I might be arrested, imprisoned, anything. Some knights have mages whipped for such crimes...I really don't want to be whipped."

"Do not fear Gytha, no one is having you hurt. I will speak to Shadan, there may be a solution, but it might take a day or two to implement. Also Fedrica will have to agree. Well actually I could just order her, but I really don't want to do that..." he trailed off, obviously thinking about this "solution" of his.

"She is quite a lady, Fedrica, petite and beautiful. I wonder how I could possibly compare to her in your eyes, I suppose it must be because you have been away from her for a long time, if the prize destrier is not available any old mule will do."

For the first time during their meeting Steven actually laughed. He went over to the desk and pulled something from a draw, a small silver mirror, beautifully polished. He handed it to her. "Have a look," he said cordially.

She took it warily, ran her hand through her hair and looked, expecting the worst.

It was worse than the worst. She had never looked rougher in her life. She was covered in streaks of sooty grime apart from two patches close to her nose that had been cleaned by tears. Her eyes were red raw, her hair was a

21

tangled thatch, there were flakes of crusted blood under her nostrils. And this was how she had presented herself to lady Fedrica. "What a mess," she breathed; "I belong in the cheapest, nastiest tavern in Tanaren. Please tell the lady that I have looked better."

"Beauty is not determined by perfumes, jewels, and fancy clothes," Steven spoke warmly; "some need none of those things to glow and you are one such lady. Did I really just say that? I am getting soft. Now, when was the last time you slept?"

"Oh, not last night, the night before. Come to think of it I was with Beni, and I didn't sleep that much then either. No wonder I am all over the place."

He handed her something. "The key to this room. I will have a bed moved in here and a bath run. You can wash and sleep in here. Food too, I will have this all organised within the hour."

"Thank you Steven, thank you. Your little girl is adorable."

"Yes she is."

"We should never have contemplated..."

"Maybe not. My guilt has been rather overpowering..."

"Enough of that for now. We can talk another time. I will pray for little Edith before I sleep."

"You have a good heart, Gytha."

She shook her coppery tresses. "And a frightened one. And now Sir Beverley will probably let our new suspect carry on completely unchallenged."

"Our new suspect?" Steven looked surprised. "We have one?"

"Yes you idiot. I suppose I have had longer to think on it than you. The spirit said that the mage controlling her through the soul jewel had changed her, given her the power of ice. So it is without doubt a frost mage and a very powerful one to boot. The other clue is the letter Miriam found, that is the real clincher, it was written to a woman with the initial M."

"Oh, of course, how did I miss that."

"Lipshin," they said in unison; "Margawse Lipshin."

****

Steven was as good as his word. In less than an hour Sir Beverley's room boasted a warm bath, a plate of bread, meat, cheese, and pottage, a goblet of fruity wine and a low bed, bolster, and thick blanket. Steven had returned to Fedrica and so Gytha locked the door, ate, drank, bathed, ate some more, used the mirror to examine her cuts and bruises before putting on her shift and climbing under the blanket. She had told Steven to wake her before noon, but he had just grunted, given her a circumspect smile, and left her to her own devices.

Her mind was still a swirling maelstrom, but she was drifting, drifting, so tired, warm at last and as secure as she could be given what was going on around her.

Gytha slept, as the fog finally dissipated, and a cold sun moved towards its zenith.

****

Edith was still sleeping when Steven returned. Fedrica was adjusting an imaginary kink in her pillow. "No change?" he asked her.

"No. the healers are due in soon, to check on her."

Steven took his seat once more and yawned involuntarily. There was no talking for a while.

"Plain little thing, isn't she?" Fedrica broke the silence, her tone light, conversational.

"Sorry?"

"The mage. The redhead. Plain. Don't you think?"

"Gytha? No, I wouldn't agree with that. She was hardly at her best when you saw her."

"Really?" Fedrica harrumphed. "You think her pretty?"

"I don't think of her as anything. She is Gytha, she is a friend. A man can have female friends without judging them on their looks."

"If you say so."

"I do."

Fedrica found another kink and started to smooth it. "Do you ever get tempted when you are here? There are a lot of young women around and some must surely attract a roving eye."

"Looking is not philandering Fedrica. I have fornicated with no one other than you since our marriage."

"Please do not say that "f" word. It is so crude."

"Sorry, I could not think of an alternative."

She sat down, stood, then sat again. "You are attracted to me aren't you? Since being here you have barely had the inclination to kiss me, much less anything else."

Steven sighed. "My mind has been on Edith my dear. Once she is out of danger I will be tearing your dress off with my teeth."

"Oh." Fedrica fanned her face; "if you say so."

The silence between them resumed.

****

The worst job on the island

Aldo and Carnley. Carnley and Aldo. To many people on the island they were like bread and pottage, pastry and honey, fruit and game, best when together, diminished when separated. For over twenty years they had served on the island, one of those group of lay brothers who could turn their hands to anything. They built fences for the animals, cut the grass in the gardens, repaired walls, fetched and carried, dug and planted, assisted the smithy, the cooks, anybody that needed help to keep the wheels turning, keep the island running. They were indispensable, as much a part of the island's fabric as the rocks, the grass, and the gulls. Aldo was a thin, sinewy man with muscular, knotted arms and skin as brown as ancient bark. He was almost bald, the hair that remained was silver, long, and wispy, blowing in the direction of the prevailing winds. His eyesight was not so good, he had developed a permanent squint in his brown eyes and seemed to be constantly peering at his large, hooked nose, as though it was the only aspect of his surroundings that merited attention.

Carnley was a different sort altogether, broad and squat, with saturnine looks that were only enhanced by his crop of thick black hair and the untamed beard which extended under his ruddy, cracked lips and square jaw like a badly hung portrait. He too was brown and weathered and moved with a slight limp, the result of some old, half remembered accident; for one did not spend most of one's life working outdoors without risking both life and limb many times over. He smiled rarely, whereas Aldo smiled often, in many ways they were opposites, but, like the docile fish that cleans the skin of the shark, both were totally dependent on each other. And so it was that when, in the evening just past, lots were drawn for the couple who had to perform the worst task of the week, as soon as Carnley's name was selected that was that. The second name was not drawn for if Carnley had to do it, so did Aldo. It was just the way things were.

Not that either of them welcomed being given such a horrible job. So they had spent the remainder of the evening imbibing as much rough spirit as their bodies could cope with, and both of them could cope with quite a lot. So now, as the thinning mist wafted about their arms and ankles they strolled, somewhat uncertainly, from the lay brother's dormitory that lay south of the college, along a thin, winding path heading west, past the gardens and then the animal pens. Both men carried shovels, Carnley balanced his over his shoulder leaving an arm free to hold the lantern. Morning may have been here for a few hours, the fog may be dispersing as they walked but the gloom had still to be fully banished entirely, light was still required to negotiate the islands twists and turns, especially if one was not using the main path.

"Well, that was the oddest tasting grain liquor I have ever sampled," Aldo spat into the long grass as if still trying to take the taste away. "Tasted of hay or something."

"No," Carnley gave a disapproving shake of his head, "not hay. Hay was too good. Straw I would say, something not even the pigs would eat."

"Straw," Aldo nodded; "straw. Not that I eat straw as a rule."

"It tasted like straw smells. Rebo the cook always says smell is as important as taste when it comes to food."

Aldo put his hand to his stomach. "And as Artorus sees all, am I paying the price this morning. Arse like a ripe plum it is, and even more tender."

"Aha!" Carnley roared, "you mean like a Fashtani blood orange! I think I have left half my guts back in the dormitory!"

Aldo patted the other man's stomach. "Pity it doesn't show on you my friend. How was it Lofty Padrag described you? Rotund, that was it, and Padrag has a smart word for every occasion."

"His half a year with the monks taught him that they say."

"Half a year?" Aldo spoke with scorn, "you've been listening to him too much. Two weeks at the most so I've heard."

"Well it is still two weeks more education than either of us have ever had. "Follicley bereft" is the way he described your absence of hair. That man has a word for every occasion, even if he makes half of them up. Mind you, that was two words...I think."

"Sounds like a disease," Aldo muttered; "Aldo of Redthorn suffers from foliclybereft, or so Padrag tells it."

"Really?" Carnley grinned for the first time showing a row of uneven teeth, many of which were missing. "I thought you called it the shits."

Aldo roared with laughter as they continued their walk. They had passed the gardens and were close to the animal pens but instead of going towards them they turned south, passed a stranded rock and some straggly clumps of bracken before coming to a clearing where the grass had been cut back deliberately. As Aldo looked to his right he could see the looming stone circles the mages used to practice their spells. The cliffs were close by, but they would have to climb a steep, bracken strewn ridge to get there. But that was not held their attention right now.

"Well," Carnley said gloomily, "if either of us have the shits we have come to the right place."

In the clearing ahead stood a wide structure of seasoned hide supported by a wicker frame. The side facing them was protected by cloth hangings which could be pushed aside to enter the structure. It was secured by ropes and tent poles, a shelter that afforded privacy and protection from the elements. Inside was a long low bench into which several holes had been cut, spaced at regular intervals. It stood over a trench, a deep trench which, following complaints about the smell, needed to be filled in with earth and a fresh trench dug close by. Then the shelter, which was relatively light could be lifted and moved over this new trench.

Aldo and Carnley had been given the one job nobody on the island wanted. Filling in and digging a new latrine.

"You know," Aldo said as he stuck his shovel into the earth, noting its softness with some satisfaction. "At times like these I wish I had gone to sea like my brother. He has seen some sights I can tell you, traded in silver, silks, and spices in Fash for the most part, married one of their girls too, one of those Egoulian dancers, the ones that wear barely a stitch bar a few beads and feathers. Whenever I meet him he tells me about all of his journeys, drones on for hours he does, tis why my hair has all gone, yet, never once does he mention having to dig a stinking sewer trench. Come on, let's get this canopy moved."

He loosened one of the support ropes as Carnley set his lantern down and started to do the same with the opposite one. "Going to sea sounds good," he said briskly, "but your brother is probably telling you all the good bits whilst leaving out the rubbish. No maggot riddled sea biscuits, no chucking your guts up in a storm, and why have an exotic wife if you never see her? And aren't those dancers supposed to be spies and assassins on the side?"

"It is the rumour," Aldo said, "I have never seen him disagree with her at any rate. If he did he would be having a foxglove soup for his supper."

Carnley grunted, as though he thought no good could come from having an exotic wife. "Well give me my Magda any day. Washer woman she may be but a least she is always here when I need her, if you know what I mean." He gave his companion a dirty snigger.

"Phew, don't," Aldo said with distaste. "The smell alone here is bad enough without the image of your rutting to turn me even further. What do you do when you have finished? Count your teeth? See who has the most left? I reckon it is something like four to three in her favour."

"Four to three?" Carnley enquired. "Are we talking about my teeth or your hair?"

"Hey! No digs at my hair fellow." Aldo threw down the now untethered rope and pulled a few loose strands of hair across his bald dome from left to right, so that they sat atop it rather like six gold leaf filaments over a bare page of vellum, noticeable, but their only real effect was to emphasise the emptiness of the page. "There you go, all intelligent men are bald, it's a known fact."

Carnley huffed through his cheeks. "All intelligent men may be bald but are all bald men intelligent? You might be the exception to the rule. Right, before we move this cursed thing put some of this under your nose."

He went over to Aldo holding a small box into which he dipped his finger before smearing it under Aldo's nose. "From Magda, lavender oil. Help keep the smell away. Not too much though or you will smell like a tart's pomade."

Aldo grunted in gratitude and together the two of them heaved the canopy free of the grassy earth before carrying it a good fifteen feet to the south and setting it down again. As they hoisted it up a cloud of droning blue backed flies were released, buzzing around drunkenly, flying into the faces and hair of the two men. Aldo spat in disgust for he could do nothing else until his hands were free. Once they were he batted them away with a growl.

They walked up to the trench. Many flies still hovered over it and the stench of ammonia and putrefying excrement set their eyes to stinging. The well-worn bench sat there on two support blocks. Nearby was a pile of earth that was rapidly greening over, the spoil from the trench's construction. They would need to move the bench, fill the trench in with the earth then dig a fresh trench nearby. Then they would line the new trench with wood, replace the bench and re tie the canopy before going back to their quarters for a much-needed drink.

Aldo bent down and grabbed one end of the bench firmly with both hands, Carnley did the same at the other end. "Right," Aldo said, "heave to, after three, just think of your teeth if you can't count that far. One...two...three!"

It was not that heavy in truth, a solid piece of wood indeed but the holes made the job easier than Aldo anticipated. They set it down near the canopy and whilst Aldo stood and rubbed his back with an affected groan Carnley took up his shovel and returned to the trench.

Then he froze, standing as still as the statues in the great hall of the college. "Aldo," he said through clenched teeth; "come here."

Aldo shuffled towards him. "What is it?" Stench knocked you dead?"

"No," Carnley muttered, "not me, not me."

Aldo moved up next to him and peered at the trench through bleary eyes. And there, poking out of the semi liquid pool of thick, treacly, acrid slurry he saw it. Fingers, fingers pushing through the noisome mess, clawing at the sky. The hand of a man that had been dead for some time.

"And there is another one, up at this end." Carnley pointed at the vague outline of a human body, coated with maggots and filth. "Xhenafa guide them safely, if there was one way to get out of doing this job I never wanted it to be this."

Both men stood and stared for a while, this time oblivious of the great fat flies as they returned to the trench to feed.

28
The storm begins to build

Everyone was lifted by the disappearance of the mist and the freshness of the emerging breeze but no one on both islands was as exultant at this change as Sir Vargo. At last, he could leave this hateful place, he did not belong here, nobody wanted him here, it was only one of the orders more intractable rules that insisted he be here in the first place. More than ten knights required a commanding officer and, as the gods willed it, he was the only available one at the time. He was about to be seconded to the Eagle claw knights and sent back to fight in the war against the Arshumans when he was diverted to this island and reduced to sitting here, like a sparring dummy, dumb and impotent in the middle of this fog. Some rules were hard to fathom, and the one that had so neutralized him in this way was the hardest one to fathom of all. Over the years war had become his provenance, not playing nursemaid to these coddled sorcerers, he needed to be back there, his horse caked in the mud and the blood of the battlefield, his sword notched, his helm dented, a film of sweat and grime coating his skin and turning his woollen undershirt sodden. That was the way for a man to live, and die, for there was no better way to die than with a sword in one's hand. He was a warrior, a simple man, he had no concerns with life's frivolities, money, women, property, what use were they once you were dead? Glory, however, was eternal. Sir Vargo wanted glory and there was none to be had stuck here.

But he wouldn't be here for much longer. Already the sailors were working, preparing the ship for departure, sealing holes with pitch, stitching sails, mopping decks, and singing as they worked. Captain Fuller was there, shouting orders one moment, cajoling and guffawing the next. He had a good relationship with his men, laughing with them, exchanging banter with them, for he had a good line in banter did the captain. Vargo could not but help feel a little jealous in truth, there was a warmth to him, an openness, that Vargo would never have. He shook his head even as the captain came over to talk to him, camaraderie was for fools.

"Good to be able to see the sun again, is it not sir knight? Though granted it could do with giving us a little more warmth. Still, the sun is Artorus responsibility so a couple of handy prayers before we sail might just do the trick."

"And when exactly do we sail captain?" No, Vargo could just not do warmth, the harder he tried the more artificial it felt. "As you know I am eager to leave here, I have a war to go to, Arshumans to drive back behind the eastern rivers, my blade chafes for their blood, as do I."

Fuller blew air through his cheeks and clucked his tongue. "Fair comment sir knight, a brave man such as yourself is needed out there by all accounts." He looked out beyond the jetty to the sea where the foam tipped breakers were rising as the wind grew in strength and confidence. "I would ordinarily try and be out of here this afternoon to take advantage of the hours of sunlight that remain but alas, the likelihood is that we will be leaving at first light in the morning."

"What?" Sir Vargo gave an acid hiss. "Why wait so long, we could be gone within the hour!"

Fuller gave a non-committal shrug. "A couple of reasons. Firstly, the healers want us to take a couple of patients back to the city and I am told that it will take some hours before they are ready to leave. Secondly, if we leave in the morning, we will get a full day's sailing in. Looking at the skies and the waves I think we will be getting a squally crosswind till about nightfall; it might be strong enough out there to drive us off course. Such things do not last long though and conditions by morning will, like as not, be a lot more favourable. In fact, we will probably get to the capital at exactly the same time whether we leave today or tomorrow. Trust me, ten years doing this run teaches you a few things. It will only be one more night sir, if you can endure a field of battle then surely you can suffer one more evening here. At least you will be able to see the stars for a change, eh?"

He gave the other man a cordial laugh then left to return to his men.

"Master Scrivens, those ropes on the foredeck, they are idle man, idle! And we do not have idlers on this ship!"

"Apart from you captain!" came the good humoured reply. Many men laughed but Sir Vargo was not one of them. From a pouch at his waist he produced his ball of clay and slowly, deliberately, he began to knead.

****

A time to cleanse, and to think

No mint left. Miriam was having to cope with all this going on around her without any mint. She had instinctively reached for it in her waist pouch, found nothing, and so compensated by running her hands through her hair so many times she suspected that she had a bird's nest sitting on her head. And with good reason, Nikolaj had to see Sir Beverley sometime, he would have to mention her, ergo she could be summoned for an interview at any moment, and from Sir Beverley's reputation, it was something she was not looking forward to at all.

So, she had not returned to her cell, not as yet. Instead, as soon as she had parted from Nikolaj she had headed for the bathhouse, it made sense, she needed a wash anyway. She had not bothered looking for a private cubicle, she would probably have to ask a lay sister to fill a tub anyway and right now she wanted to speak to nobody, all she wanted to do was think, to reflect on the turmoil of the last few hours, on what had happened to her, what Gytha had told her, everything. She had never felt so confused.

She climbed into the great bath about halfway along its length. It was not level; one end was deeper than the other. She did not want the shallow end because she would be exposed above the navel and Miriam was not a proponent of the, "it's all girls anyway so it doesn't matter," school of thought which nearly every other woman in the college seemed to subscribe to. She always covered herself with a white linen drying cloth when she had to walk in the bathhouse, most of the others didn't bother with anything at all including Gytha and Kestine who would trot around here bare as a babe, brazen as you like. Cheris was almost as prim as herself, something they both put down to having come from a more moneyed background than the other girls, if people lived eight or ten to a room then they would have no concept of privacy after all. Still, at least she wasn't a man, apparently their behavior in the bathhouse was even worse.

As for the deep end, she didn't go there because the water came up to her nose and inevitably at some point, she would swallow some of it. One day a week the bathhouse was shut for a water change but it was such a big job for the lay brothers, water brought up from the sea using a bucket and pulley system, the water boiled to remove salt and then transported by barrel on a wagon pulled by oxen to its destination she always doubted that the water was replaced wholly. Under her toes the bath always felt grainy, she suspected that it was always dark here because if the bathers actually saw the colour of the water none of them would dare enter it.

So halfway along it was, the water up to her shoulders. The water was cold today, the hot stones under the bath that gave it a degree of tepid warmth had obviously not been fired yet. So she would not be able to stay here for as long as she wanted, she was basically hiding after all.

She was not alone here either, a group of three seniors were sat chatting near the deep end. She knew them by sight, but they studied different fields of power to her, so they were passing acquaintances at best. They studiously ignored her, and she was grateful for that. There were two other girls here, younger than her, Emonie and Lissa and they did stop for a brief chat before diving into the shallow end with an excited squeak. All lectures and tutorials had been suspended by Sir Beverley; they had told her. People were restricted to the libraries or their cells, the refectory, here, or the house of Artorus. Emonie mentioned a rumour that other bodies had been discovered; they were obviously trying to wrest some information from Miriam, but she gave them nothing other than saying that she had heard the rumour too. Seeing that Miriam was not forthcoming the girls soon got bored and left her alone.

She stood there, eyes half shut, letting both water and recent events seep slowly into her skin. Gytha had thanked her for giving her the name of the spirit, for she believed it had saved her life. It was only sinking in now, Gytha thought that she had saved her life. To her surprise she felt tears welling up behind her eyes, had she really done such a thing, something to feel proud of? She sniffed and dashed the tears away with bath water. But Tola was dead. He was not her mentor, but Gytha was close to him, and she knew it would hit her hard in the days to come. She had to be there for her.

As for the murderer she had her own theories; well actually she didn't, she was too tired to think clearly, abstractly. Her only sleep had been that brief one on the cave floor, after Nikolaj had made love to her. She needed her cell, she needed her bed, but was too scared to return there.

The three seniors clambered out of the bath and made for the toweling cloths where they could dry and dress. They didn't cover themselves she thought and in truth, at least two of them had the sort of bodies that could only be enhanced by being swathed in robes. A bit like her she supposed, she was physically unimpressive, scrawny, bony, pigeon chested, at least that was what she had always thought. Yet Nikolaj had thought differently, and he supposedly admired her intelligence. She smiled at that; how could she have fallen for such a ridiculous line? She knew she would be analyzing and over analyzing her behavior towards him for months to come, had she been stupid, impetuous, immoral? She would settle on one of the three by turns only to change her mind the following day, procrastination and vacillation were at the very core of the person she was. And she would never change, she knew it, she was a prisoner of her own personality, no wonder she truly hated herself at times. In her teens, when she had struggled with the confines of the college, the workload, the less sympathetic people around her she had even contemplated taking her own life, but such thoughts never went far, she was a coward and hated pain. For one such as her suicide would only be an option if she reached a certain level of desperation that she never had, and probably never would, attain. Her thoughts could be deep grey, but never truly black.

She waited for the seniors to dress and leave before levering herself out of the bath and wrapping her towel close to her. She dried herself vigorously and quickly before throwing on her shift. Her body was still damp, and the shift clung to her, an unpleasant sensation that made her shudder. There were benches against the wall closest to her and she sat there for a while until her body was dry. The damp atmosphere though was not conducive to total dryness, and she soon gave up and pulled on her shoes and robe, leaving the bathhouse to Lissa and Emonie who were laughing as they splashed water over each other.

The water had been cold so, now in the open air, she actually felt warm as her robe retained the natural warmth of her body. The fog was almost gone, and she blinked at the pale sun. Newly revealed its light gave the grass next to the path a brilliant lustre that she rarely saw in it, a rich, glossy vibrancy that made her surroundings deep and lush, the air pungent, the roaring sea a timeless balm to her senses. Pulling her cowl over her head she plodded towards the college, her feet feeling like lead weights, this was the last place on earth she wanted to be in yet at times the power, the serenity of these surroundings overwhelmed her. Sometimes it was just beautiful here. Gaining the great steps, she started to trudge up them only to stop momentarily. There were voices behind her and ahead, male voices, deep throated, urgent, concerned. She wheeled around to see a group of knights behind her and at the top of the steps there was another staring at them. For a moment she thought she was the focus of their attention and froze, but no, they were not interested in her at all. She stopped for a moment and listened.

"We need a wagon," one of them said; "there are two of them."

"I will have to tell Sir Beverley," the knight at the top of the steps replied. "Artorus help us all, the panic will be difficult to quell this time."

The knights were still ignoring her, so she took the opportunity to almost hop up the remaining steps, past the guard and into the college's reception room. She had decided to seek out Kestine at her cell, and if that was not possible, she would see Warran. Actually Warran might be a better idea, she was supposed to be helping him with his work after all. Yes, she would try there first. Cowl still up she darted through the great hall, refectory, and library, trying desperately to get to his cell before any of the knights called her back. And as she half walked, half trotted she realized that in her chat with Emonie they had been at cross purposes. Emonie had mentioned deaths, Miriam had assumed that she was talking about Tola and that her information was inaccurate. But the knight had been emphatic; two of them he had said. So others had died then, others she knew nothing about at present. This meant two things to her, firstly that any thoughts on the killer she had were probably wrong, and secondly, it had made her keener than ever to avoid Sir Beverley for as long as she could, she just prayed fervently that Warran would be where she wanted him to be. She needed time, time to collect her thoughts and regain her composure. She reached into her waist pouch once more, and still there was no mint to be found.

****

The Red Plague

As it so happened, shortly after Miriam had ghosted past the reception room towards the refectory somebody else entered it from the stairs on its wing. Sir Beverley was also in a reflective mood, and he made for the great doors then stepped outside, standing at the top of the steps, feeling the freshening wind on his face. His eyes were not so good now, but he still managed to behold enough of the green sward of the isle to pique his interest. To some the isolation made this place a trap, a prison, something to stifle the will and crush the soul. They could not see the beauty, the purity, that such isolation could bring. It offered an escape for one thing, an escape from the cruelty and hardship that life on the mainland could deal to even the most ardent supplicant of Artorus. And no one knew the fact of that last statement more than Sir Beverley.

Was it fifteen years ago? Or maybe twenty? The Sir Beverley of that time was strong, vigorous, one of the most promising men of his order. He was even being tipped as a future grand master, but such lofty talk and promotions held little interest for him. For he had the lady Arla, his wife of six years, and three children, they were his world, his promotion, nothing else mattered except his family and his devotion to the Gods. Then the red plague came.

He had held all four of them as they died, all four of them. His youngest daughter first, the lady Arla last, all had coughed and choked blood in his arms, life blood soaking his sleeves as they grew weaker and weaker, their rasping breath growing fainter, their eyes glazed and unseeing until finally their light went out entirely. He had cried then, for the last time in his life, cried as they were sent to the flames, turned to smoke and ash as he watched. And as he watched he could think of only one thing, one simple thing, surely it would be his turn next. He welcomed the prospect as he waited for the plague to infect him, so that at least he could be delivered to them in death, that they could be a family again in the next world. But the plague had never touched him, death and the embrace of his family had been postponed indefinitely. And even now he was still waiting.

His response, a long and heavy relationship with the chapter's wine butteries had been a fairly predictable one. Every passing day he tried to remember them, their faces, their voices, the way they laughed in the sunshine; as he did this the pain at his loss became unbearable and the only antidote to the pain was to be found in the nearest numbing goblet. He also grew to hate intrusions upon his reflections, people interrupting his memories with questions, problems, requests for this, bills for that, meaningless intrusions all. His responses grew increasingly bellicose, he would rant and rave at trivialities, shout and berate those underlings who had pricked him so. He was aware of his behavior but was powerless to stop it and it had come as no surprise to him when he was transferred to the Isle of Healing, the cushiest, most out of the way job in the chapter, the place to send officers that had become something of an embarrassment to the order. Yet he had accepted the posting gladly, for here he could be left alone for most of the time, left alone to think and yet, with every passing day the memories of his family had become more and more fragmented, more illusory, they were fading, just like fog in a breeze. And he was still waiting for the red plague to take him.

He knew that he commanded little respect amongst the younger knights, ordinarily he wouldn't care, they were all just faces to him anyway. But now their insouciance had put him in an invidious position. He did not want this new responsibility, the workload on the Isle of Tears was many times that of his usual position. He had hoped this business of the murderer was already done and dusted, a suspect in custody, one victim burned and the other on its way to the mainland. Now though the suspect had escaped, the knights were telling him stories about tunnels and spirits buried under their feet and two more bodies had been discovered, disposed of in the latrines of all places, presumably as some sort of sick joke. He hoped Sir Steven would return soon to reclaim this shambles for his own. And there was another source of guilt for him, when he had heard that Steven's daughter was seriously ill part of him, an infinitesimally small part admittedly but a part of him nonetheless, had wished for the little girl's demise just so that someone, anyone, could understand how he had felt these past years. What a terrible thing to think, no wonder he had drunk himself senseless last night. Now though, standing in the breeze with the smells of grass, bracken, and sea purging the fumes from his brain he wished fervently that Steven would return because his little girl was better, the way any normal person would think, a normal person with a shred of empathy, the sort of person he used to be.

"There you are." The voice came from behind and to his right. He turned his head slightly to see Chief Magister Greville shuffle nervously into the watery daylight. "Your messenger has given me the most alarming news, albeit in a somewhat cursory manner. I think it only proper that I receive a full briefing from the man in charge, once this news gets out to the mages there is going to be uproar."

"I was just taking the air Chief Magister." Sir Beverley was unperturbed by the other man's urgent tone. "Then I would have gone straight to your chambers to give you the report. No matter, you are here now. Three more deaths have been reported, two of them substantiated. They were found in the outdoor latrine of all the foul places. The third victim is supposed to have died in the tunnels under the college though as yet we have no proof and no body."

"And the victims, do they have names? The only one I was given was that of Senior Tola. I am praying that it isn't so, the man has been part of the core of this college for many years."

Sir Beverley remained matter of fact. "Yes, that was the name, but his is the body we have still to recover. The others were another senior mage by the name of Arbagast and a lay brother who had the unfortunate moniker of Havel the pig."

"Arbagast?" Greville gasped, "who would kill such a gentle man as he? He had not one enemy in the entire world. Is it known how they died? Is it the same way as...as...?"

"We do not know yet. They require a deal of ...cleaning up. They are in the House of Xhenafa being prepared for examination. All the windows have had to be opened so I have been told."

Greville was silent for a moment as he digested this new information. "I suppose it lets the suspect you have in jail off the rope then."

"No," Sir Beverley groaned, "thanks to some breathtaking incompetence from my juniors he has escaped. At first, I suspended the officers responsible but have since reinstated them on the proviso they hunt this man down. He is still my only suspect. Tola died after his escape, the two others probably died before his imprisonment. I am looking for no one else at the moment. The sealed tunnels under the college have been opened by persons unknown, he may be running around in them somewhere. It might take a while to recapture him."

"A while?" Greville was shocked, "no, that will not do at all, not at all, we need this matter resolved in the next few days."

"It will take as long as it takes," Beverley said wearily. "This suspect, this boy Gideon is a slippery customer by all accounts, a wily one, we need to be patient, starving him out might be the best option."

"No, you do not understand," Greville spoke gravely. "I have had a letter from the capital, from the palace no less, it arrived with that last ship. The Grand Duke is coming to visit us here, the ducal barge will be arriving in a week or so. We cannot have a murderer on the loose when he is here. He is not to know anything of our current troubles, do you understand?"

This was just getting better and better. "The Grand Duke? Why now? He hardly ever visits here."

"I cannot divulge his reasons directly; his letter is rather vague," Greville replied. "Suffice to say it is probably related to the war against Arshuma. I need to tell Shadan, is he still with the healers?"

"The fog kept him there, you know he won't risk his horse if the weather is bad. Still, I am hoping now it has cleared that he will return within the hour. When he gets here, we will to your chambers immediately, there will obviously be much to discuss."

Greville nodded." If he continues to be delayed, I will speak to you alone, the gossips will have got the rumors of these deaths already. I will need to get the mages together soon, to tell them something, to try and allay their fears. It was difficult enough to do when only two were dead, but with five...?"

"I understand," Beverley was remarkably low on bluster at the moment, "but I will ensure the knights are all fully armoured, it can only take one mage going hysterical to cause all sorts of problems. I will see you at the first bell after noon, by all means call a meeting sometime after that."

"I will Sir Beverley, I will. Keth's teeth I wanted to retire from this position before the year was out, but with all this going on..." he shook his head in frustration.

"Do you have a successor? Or are we to expect the usual dog fight between the likely candidates?"

"Oh, it will be a dog fight," Greville gave a weary sigh. "Each magical discipline will want its own head in the job. Right now though such matters are less than relevant. First bell after noon it is then, I will see you in my chambers." Greville gave the knight the slightest formal bow and was gone.

Sir Beverley tried scanning the path to the other island. He could not see Shadan but then his eyes were not really up to the task anyway. He had of course not mentioned the elven spirit the one knight had claimed to see, nor had he mentioned the novice mages that had been running amok without his permission. He had sent a knight to fetch each of them but as yet they had not reported back. If he was being thorough and diligent, he should right now travel to the house of Xhenafa to examine the bodies but in truth he had no real interest in doing so. He had his murderer, and he was on the run. He prayed that the knights would catch him very soon or the disciplinary hearings that would follow would surpass the judgements of the Gods in their brutality and it would be his head likely to fall first. He turned, strode back into the college, and started to make his way up the stairs to the chapter house, surprised that for the first time in an age he had no interest in taking a drink.

****

A thinly veiled threat

Her mother was singing to her. It had been so long since she had heard her voice, yet she recognized it instantly. Her voice was husky, like Gytha's own, and the accent was strong, the crisp yet lilting accent of the people of Kibil. It had been her accent once, but her life in exile had softened it considerably. She still had a little of it, her friends would sometimes pick up on some of her inflections, usually the way she pronounced her "o's" and "u's". But by and large the way she spoke was different now, more refined, for people at the college were amongst the best educated in the world and the way they spoke tended to reflect that. Gytha though resented it, she disliked the idea of being homogenized. She so wanted to retain her proud roots and the diluting of her true voice was symptomatic of the way she had been torn from her home and changed into something she did not reject totally, but was something she was never fully comfortable with. So, to hear her mother singing again made her somnolent form stretch like a cat, all contented luxurious bliss.

"Lissa so loves the child
Syvukha shields from the rain
peaceful, gentle and mild
A balm easing all pain..."

It was a long song, asking for the God's protection, usually sung when a newborn child was introduced to the world during the ritual of earth and water. Mothers often sang it to their younger children, especially if that child was crying or upset. Lissa was Elissa of course, Syvukha was the Kibilese name for Artorus. Her people had different names for many of the Gods and retained a lot of older beliefs deemed passé by the church elite. Nattan the god of night featured prominently amongst her people, traversing the sky with the moon as his shield, yet here, at the college she had barely heard his name since her arrival.

She was homesick again and dreaming. Of course, she was dreaming. Her mother was not here singing to her at all, she was sleeping in Sir Beverley's room on the Isle of Healing. She needed more sleep she knew it but for now, for this moment, her eyes flickered open tentatively.

There was a window just above her, a small one and it was glazed, the knights could afford to glaze all their rooms here. It faced south so the sun did not shine through it directly, rather its light struck through it at an angle, a singular beam of it illuminating her legs which were poking out of the blanket, for it seemed that she had pulled it upwards to almost cover her head. She realised that the strength of the light meant that the fog must have surely disappeared, it illuminated that one strip of the dark room from her legs over to the west wall. It must be late in the morning then. She peered around the room blearily and was about to tuck her head under the blanket again when she checked herself. The room was a myriad of shadows, some dark as night, some greyer, more formless and yet there was one shadow that was different again. For it was not a shadow at all, it was an outline. Somebody was sitting close by, on a stool, watching her. Thinking it was Steven, she swivelled herself swiftly until she was sitting upright, blanket still held close, facing the visitor. Then she caught her breath for this person was way too slight to be a gallant knight. The figure leaned forward a little and the shaft of light caught it at last, picking out the delicate features of the Lady Fedrica. She clasped her thin, pale hands together and gave Gytha the sort of smile that purported to be friendly but was in truth as brittle and hostile as a biting frost.

"My Lady?" Gytha blurted, feeling both uneasy and underdressed.

"Hello," Fedrica replied. "Do not fear, I have not been here for long. I was about to wake you. In truth I was just looking at your ankles and toes."

"My...ankles?" Gytha still had no reason to relax.

"Yes. I do believe they are whiter than mine, something I thought barely possible until a few moments ago."

"Well my Lady, I suppose they never get exposed to the sun."

"The same with mine. It is said that those with hair your colour have fairer complexions than their peers."

"And we burn in the sun far more easily too."

"Quite." Fedrica licked her lips and paused as though weighing carefully exactly what she wanted to say next. For some reason though Gytha felt the need to forestall her, somehow, she knew that Fedrica wanted to say something, something she wouldn't like. "How is the Lady Edith?" she asked, hoping to sound both friendly and concerned.

"She is awake," Fedrica smiled genuinely this time, "and talking. I have let Steven have a little time with her on his own. He sees so little of her as it is."

"Meriel be praised," Gytha gladly returned the smile;" all of our prayers have been answered. And so quickly too."

"She has her father's strength. But she is not there yet. She is very weak and still has the cough though it is nowhere near as ghastly as it was two days ago. The healers say that full recovery will still take weeks. So, we will not be leaving here for some time yet. In fact, you may be seeing a lot more of us than originally envisaged."

Gytha's ears pricked. "Really? how so?"

"Commander Shadan, or is it Benedict? I have heard both names here."

"Benedict is his formal name, his less "Chiran" name. The knights all call him Shadan though."

"Ah, I see. Well, Commander Shadan has spoken to us both and obtained consent from us, though that consent was reluctantly given, at least on my part. Tomorrow Edith will be taken by litter to the college on the Isle of Tears. She will be accompanied by two healers and myself. Shadan wishes for Steven to resume this investigative matter that you are both undertaking. You two will be working together again. Does that please you?"

There was an edge to the question that Gytha could not possibly miss. "If it means that Sir Beverley returns here then yes, I am pleased. I feel we are very close to catching the culprit and the change of personnel has only obstructed things. From what I am given to understand his view on the matter differs greatly to our own."

"That was not quite what I asked. Do you enjoy working with my husband? he is handsome, is he not?"

Gytha pursed her lips and tried to keep the tetchiness out of her reply.

"My lady, last night I was almost murdered in the same way as the previous victims of this killer. I am tired, and still shaken by the experience. So, if you think I have been spending the last few days ogling men then you are very much mistaken. Too many other things are happening around me for me to concentrate on such trivial matters."

The reply was icy. "Again, you evade the question. You may be busy, but you cannot tell me that it prohibits you from making the most basic judgement of all, something that takes but a fleeting moment. So, I ask again, are you attracted to my husband?"

"The question changes with each asking it seems. But, as you think it important, I will say yes, your husband is a handsome man. And I am hardly the only woman here who holds this view."

"Thank you," Fedrica said curtly, "answering was not that difficult now was it." She looked Gytha up and down. Gytha was covered in a blanket and dressed in her shift, only her feet were exposed and yet she felt more under dressed and vulnerable than ever. "He has told me that you are rather a plain girl, that your features lack a certain...delicacy, the sort of refinement that only the highest born ladies tend to possess. You do have a certain handsomeness though, a sort of honesty in your face commonly found in the better-bred peasant stock. You have the beauty of the farmer's wife, rather than the aristocrat."

Despite herself, Gytha started to bristle; who did this callow child, for she was a few years younger than Gytha, think she was? "Thank you for your assessment. I must admit I am unused to be spoken of like some sort of prize cow at market."

Fedrica gave a little laugh at that. "If you were such a beast, I doubt somehow that you would be in the prize winning category. I have a problem though. Your hair is truly beautiful. And the colour..."

"The colour?"

"Yes. You are a redhead. And my Steven likes redheads. He likes them a lot," Fedrica sighed and folded her arms over her chest. "These last few months I have spent most of my time in the knights' tower in Tanaren city, mixing with the wives of other knights who are serving away, on these islands. Amongst them there is a certain tacit acceptance that men, away from their wives for months on end, will stray, that it is in their nature to behave in this way. And that on these islands there are many unattached women only too happy to receive what a knight can give them. It is however a view to which I do not subscribe. Marriage is for life, between one man and one woman. If a woman cannot stray, then I do not see why a man should."

"You think there is something..."

"Please let me finish. Whilst I was pregnant, heavily pregnant there were rumours that my Steven was...dallying with one of the chamber servants, a pretty girl with red hair, about my age."

Suddenly Gytha was curious, "go on."

"I acted decisively once this rumour reached my ears. I had her transferred out of the tower immediately. She is now a lay sister with the order of Camille."

Gytha frowned, she could not help but be derisive in her reply. "Rumours are nothing but a more respectable form of gossip. I am sure there was no foundation to them."

"You are missing the point Gytha. A rumour alone is enough to tarnish a reputation. And I will not have my reputation tarnished by anybody or anything.

41

Understand?"

Gytha nodded, "I can see what you are implying, and I can assure you that nothing has happened between the two of us. I have only known Sir Steven for a matter of days."

"Ah." Fedrica uncrossed her arms and started playing with an ear lobe. "Though I am pleased to hear that nothing has happened I wonder whether it is because the two of you have a solely professional relationship or whether the opportunity for indiscretion has yet to present itself."

Gytha thought back to the library storeroom, of their hot kisses, of his hand under her robe, searching and finding her most intimate places. "What exactly are you trying to say?" she asked. She was going to finish the question with a "my lady," but decided not to bother, Fedrica did not deserve such a formal epithet.

"I have agreed with Commander Shadan that my daughter and I will go where he wishes, but he is aware that he owes me, that I can request a favour if needs be. All I shall say is that if I hear rumours of anything going on between my husband and yourself then I will have you sent to another college. A Chiran college many hundreds of miles from here. Have I made myself clear?"

"Clear as palace glass," was the clipped reply; "but the college is awash with gossip and tittle tattle. I would ask that any rumour is substantiated with proof before you pursue such a punitive response."

To her surprise, Fedrica did soften a little at this. "Very well. For Steven's sake. I will not act without proof, I swear by Artorus that I will not. "She touched a small marble icon of the god hanging from the silk purse at her waist.

"Thank you, my lady." Gytha's tone was snide, especially the last two words. Then she yawned affectedly. Rude she knew, but then she was a peasant girl, what did she know of manners?

Fedrica took the hint. She stood and patted down her dress. "I want no hostility between us," she said, "I just want us to reach an understanding. I will leave you to your sleep and wish you Gods' luck with your investigation." She left, shutting the door behind her with a soft click.

"What an absolute…" Gytha fumed softly to herself, before reassuming her prone position and smothering herself with the blanket once more. She had all but ended things with Steven but now, with Edith seemingly recovering she was determined that, as soon as opportunity arose, when they were in a place where proof could not be obtained, she would lick every part of his naked body. And she would let him do the same to her. No arrogant little teenager spoke to her like that and got away with, no matter whose wife she was.

A lovelorn young man

"But it doesn't say that! Not specifically. When I read something on this matter I want facts, not something vague that I have to interpret for myself!"

"But it does tell you Warran. Look at this page here...and this one here. Third paragraph. It does set things out specifically for you. Write it down for yourself so you have it all set out in front of you." Miriam yawned for the twentieth time that hour, she had given up trying to disguise them.

Warran looked at the page she had indicated and shook his head. "It is still not clear to me but yes, I will write it down and re-read it later."

"Good. You are so negative Warran. You always start at the bottom and work down. From what I have seen you should pass any test on the subject easily."

Warran set his pen down, turned to Miriam and smiled. "You are really good at this, are you going to mentor others when you become a senior?"

Miriam returned the smile, "I would prefer do some research rather than teach, but thanks, it is nice to know that I might have other options open to me."

She was still grateful that her prayers had been answered. She had gently pushed open Warran's cell door to see him sat there, reading up on the very subjects she had promised to help him out on when they had last spoken to each other. She was now sitting next to him at his table, candle lit, books and papers everywhere.

"I work in a mess, don't I," he admitted sheepishly.

"Compared to me? Most certainly. But we cannot all be the same."

"Well yes," Warran grinned; "for example, I do not have any knights on the hunt for me. You on the other hand..."

"Sssssshhhhh... They could be outside at this very moment. They will find me eventually of course but just keep the door slightly ajar till they do. It doesn't look suspicious that way."

He continued to grin. "You are full of surprises lady Miriam. I never saw you as a fugitive before, you have always been so...so, staid!"

She rolled her eyes. "I am by nature. Blame your girlfriend for dragging me into this unholy mess."

His grin faltered a little. "She is no longer my girlfriend. I don't know if she has told you."

"She has," Miriam frowned, "sorry, I shouldn't have said that. Mind you, I still don't really know why you finished with her. You are friends and I always

43

thought you looked good together."

"Because I wanted more than she was prepared to give."

"How so?" Miriam's eyes narrowed a little.

Warran rested his chin in his hands before speaking again. "A few days ago, I was reading in the garden of silence. Whilst I was there Gudrun came and sat next to me. You know Gudrun, yes?"

"Of course, she is a year older than me. Nice girl, if a little bit dull when it comes to conversation."

"True. A bit hard faced as well; she needs to smile more. Anyway, we had just been to the same tutorial, and it was obvious that she wanted to discuss it with me. So, we left the garden and started to walk the north coastal path. Well, you know what is there, don't you?"

She nodded. "The kissing rock?"

"Exactly. We got to the little side path that leads off to it and she pointed out that the stones there had not been arranged into the signal, that the rock was unoccupied, and we could take advantage of it if we so wanted."

"So, she wanted a little more than just a discussion." The path to the kissing rock skirted the cliffs and led downward from the main path. The rock was at the end of the path, shaped like a giant incisor tooth it protected a small grassy hollow. The rock concealed the hollow totally, anybody standing in it could see the long path and anyone walking along it, but intruders could not see what was going on in the hollow until they got to the rock itself. Furthermore, an overhang in the cliffs above meant that anybody trying to stand on the cliffs and look down could also not see the hollow. It was totally hidden and so perfect for quick, informal trysts because any knight trying to spoil things would be seen long before they got there. It was therefore highly popular and so, before any would be lovers started along the path to the rock, they would arrange the loose stones around the path into a shape, informally agreed between the mages, that would indicate occupation. Once their time in the hollow was done the stones would be scattered again, indicating a vacancy. Nearly all the young mages had their first experience of physical gratification at the kissing rock, it held special memories, ranging from ecstatic happiness to excruciating embarrassment for all who went there.

"Yes," Warran said resignedly, "she wanted more than a discussion. She took my hand and started to lead me there, looking around for stones so she could leave the signal. But all I could see in my mind was Gytha. Gudrun was holding my hand but when I looked at her, it was Gytha looking back at me."

"But Gytha wouldn't have minded if you had gone there. She knows the way things work here."

"I know," Warran ground his teeth in frustration, "but don't you see? I WANT her to mind. I want her to mind very much. Anyway, I apologised to Gudrun and pretty much ran back to the college. I realised then that for me, it is Gytha or nobody. Gytha unfortunately, cannot make the same commitment."

Miriam stood and put a consoling arm around Warran's shoulder. His musculature seemed puny after Nikolaj. "Poor Warran," she sympathised, "you really are suffering with this love thing, aren't you?"

He just nodded.

"Look, I think the two of you need to get together and talk things through."

"We have. She is not interested."

"But she is Warran, she is," Miriam sighed. "Look, talk to her again but not just right now. She has an awful lot to cope with right now. The last thing she needs at this time is some in depth discussion of feelings and emotions and all those finer things that a girl from Kibil probably thinks are for weaklings. Let this terrible business get resolved first, then speak to her. If you want, I will talk to her first, try and smooth things over, that sort of thing. Only if you want me too of course."

His soulful eyes brimmed over with gratitude. "Would you? you are a special sort; you know that don't you?"

"Thank you Warran." She yawned again, vainly trying to conceal the act with her hand this time, a miserable failure. "Sorry, I have had very little sleep this last day or so, I will try not to yawn again."

Warran though was already standing, now he looked horrified. "I am so sorry, what a terrible host you must think me. Look I will carry on with this work while you avail yourself of the bed there. Sleep as long as you want, I will be quiet as a mouse in a house of Artorus."

She was numbingly weary; she felt her eyes closing as she spoke. "Thank you Warran, I might just do that for a while, wake me if the knights come in. Actually, you will not need to do that, they are hardly quiet at the best of times."

She clambered onto the bed and under the solitary, thick blanket. As she did so she felt into her waist pouch again. "Ach, no mint," she said ruefully.

"Oh, your mint thing," Warran obviously knew of her habit. "Have you run out?"

She nodded, "sorry Warran, I am so tired I don't think I can talk anymore."

She had kicked off her shoes and a couple of toes appeared exposed at the bottom of the blanket. Warran adjusted it so that they were covered. "Do you think it was Xhenafa?" he asked her. "We have had so little news it is hardly surprising that people are getting scared and looking to the Gods for answers. Fear is everywhere at the moment and now..."

He stopped and looked at her. She was already asleep. He smiled and returned to the desk, shuffling papers, and groaning.

She slept heavily, but she did not know for how long. Someone was shaking her shoulder. It was Warran.

"Miriam!" he said urgently, "Miriam! The knights are here!"

She shot up with a start. It was true, two knights were in the cell, gazing at her dispassionately. She slid out of bed and started to put on her shoes.

"Lady Miriam," the one said, "Sir Beverley wants to..."

"I know, I know," she said impatiently, standing and stretching, blinking sleep from her eyes. "You had better take me there then, hadn't you?" She turned to Warran, "thank you for looking after me."

He did not reply, just smiled at her. She let the knights lead her out of the cell and towards the library and halls to the reception room, where the stairs to the chapter house were sited. She instinctively put her hand in her pouch again and, to her surprise, felt something there. She pulled her hand out and sniffed her fingers. Mint.

Warran must have nipped out to the kitchens and got some for her as she slept. She shook her head, thinking to herself, "Gytha, you have absolutely no idea how lucky you are."

29
A proposition to those in charge

Chief Magister Greville had two rooms, not including his personal quarters. The first was plush, quite small but full of elegantly carved wooden furniture, rich wall hangings, a bookcase in which each book was bound in leather and embossed in gold and several small marble busts of previous magisters. It was a formal room but neither oppressive nor intimidating. Any visitor to it would feel relaxed, sleepy even as they sank into a cushioned chair and listened to Greville's smooth, softly enunciated tones. It was the room he used nearly all the time; the other room, larger, more spacious but bereft of any trappings was kept for significant meetings or visits from important people. Miriam had never visited it and yet she knew instinctively that this was the place she was going to be shown into right now.

And of course, she was right.

She was made to stand at the room's centre, flanked by both knights and circled by a series of chairs occupied by various island luminaries. Greville was in the middle, Shadan and Sir Beverley next to him. She also spotted Father Ambrose of the Artoran church and Father Krieg of the priests of Xhenafa. She noted wryly and with just a hint of bitterness that all of those facing her were men. Apart from the sisters of Camille and Meriel on the mainland the mage college system was the only other one where women could hold all the top positions. The knights and priests were all male orders of course but she noted that Greville's deputies here, and there were three or four of them were men. The annoyance that this engendered perked her up a little. She would not be cowed by this particular cabal, after all, if the Gods were good to her, she might be occupying one of their chairs in decades to come.

It was Greville who spoke first. "Right then Miriam, I am sure you can guess that we are all here to try and establish exactly what happened last night, and to try and pin down the cause of all the terrible events that have plunged this college into its current...crisis. You are not on trial or anything, we simply want to know what you saw and experienced so that we can better assess the situation."

"Leave nothing out," Shadan said to her, "we have heard Sir Nikolaj's account already and we know you spent most of the evening with him."

"So, you had better not lie child," Sir Beverley growled at her; "tell us everything, and nothing but the truth or it will go badly for you."

"Now now Sir Beverley, "Greville gently chided him, "no need to use threats, novice Miriam is a bright and promising student, well aware of the current situation. Please Miriam, speak now, there is no need to fear."

Just for the briefest moment as Shadan was talking to her, she thought that Nikolaj might have told them everything, absolutely everything. Her heart was held in a grip of ice until she realized that any admission by the knight would put him in far more trouble than she would find herself in. Once she had put that fear behind her she spoke, slowly, clearly, and carefully, recounting everything she could remember, the artifact, the letter, the tunnel layout, the disappearance of Gideon, she spoke about all of it, all the time surprising herself with her lack of nerves. Finally, she finished by telling of the tunnel entrance hidden in the unused pigsty. "It is such a remote part of the island anybody could climb in or out whenever they wanted entirely unseen. So, if one was to know of a tunnel entrance within the college itself, they could travel in and out of the place with a degree of impunity and little fear of detection. The tunnel looked as though it was fairly recently dug, maybe just a year or two old. It would have taken a while to complete but again, if it was the pig keeper doing the digging no one would ever have seen him. I am sure that Havel the pig...er...keeper is involved in this somehow."

"Then it is rather a shame that he was found dead today," Sir Beverley observed drily. "Found in the outdoor latrine with another victim, Arbagast, an old fellow that worked here..."

"Brother Arbagast is dead Miriam," Greville interrupted. "With Caswell, Raiman, Havel and Tola we now have five victims, though it is a shame that we have such limited knowledge of Tola's passing. Sir Edgar was there but he was knocked out when it happened and novice Gytha is still to be found, as far as we know they were the only two witnesses to the incident."

"And, thanks to you," Sir Beverley bristled at her, "along with the unauthorised incompetence that occurred last night our suspect is on the run again...."

"No Sir Beverley," Father Krieg interrupted him. "I cannot accept that Gideon is capable of such things. He is a callow, lecherous boy I give you that, but he barely has it in him to swat the flies that linger around the bodies of the dead."

"But he is not always Gideon," Sir Beverley harrumphed. "I believe we are dealing with a case of possession here. The boy is weak willed and so is vulnerable to such things. Xhenafa possesses him and uses his body to perpetrate these murderous acts. I have seen such things before, people collapsing and frothing at the mouth, speaking in foul demonic languages and they can be violent yes, violent without reason, often against those that care for them the most."

"But he has been in prison," Miriam said. "How could he kill Arbagast from there? and Tola died in another cave, far away from where we were chasing Gideon."

"You know these caves?" Beverley enquired haughtily, "you are certain that Gideon did not double back and pass you, maybe through a tunnel you know nothing of? And the two victims found today died days ago, before he was imprisoned."

"But the spirit...?" Miriam faltered.

"Xhenafa again. He can change the form of anybody that he possesses for the duration of that possession. You are all digging around, trying to find complications in what is a remarkably simple case. The boy did it. He needs to be found and purged of that which possesses him, even if his life become forfeit in the process."

To Miriam's surprise, Sir Beverley was emphatic, utterly without self-doubt and consequently rather convincing. Perhaps they had all been looking at the wrong clues after all. She did not really believe in possession but, looking around her at the others in the room she could see that they were all harbouring the same doubts as her. Perhaps it was Xhenafa after all, though why a god would see Gideon as a vessel through which to bring about havoc to the world was something that eluded her.

"Xhenafa needs no earthly body to take a soul from this world," Father Ambrose pointed out. "Those due to pass into the realm of the Gods see the god himself, right at the moment of their demise, he has no need to possess a living being to fulfil his divine purpose."

"But those that die in ordinary circumstances, they are all people whose time has ended as divined by Artorus," Beverley argued. "What if he, that is Xhenafa, is acting of his own volition, taking the lives of those who ordinarily still had some time to live? Then he may need to possess a body to undertake this work. It is all outlined in the book of the possessed by Angelus of Codona. I suggest you read it."

"That is a highly speculative work," Ambrose countered disdainfully. "Full of guesses and conjecture it is merely a vehicle for his own prejudices. And even if Xhenafa is killing here, even if he is acting without the will of Artorus the question is why? What purpose do these terrible crimes serve? Why is a god choosing to directly intervene in the affairs of man here, of all places, an island shut off from the rest of the world?"

"You above all others," Sir Beverley rumbled, "should know it is beyond our capacity to understand the purpose and will of the Gods."

"Please gentleman," Greville was at his most placatory, his voice a soothing unguent to fractured nerves. "This is a debate for another time. We are holding this inquiry because there are hundreds of mages and lay brothers looking to us for answers. We need to tell them something and need to tell them something soon."

"Yes, we do." Knight Commander Shadan had been little more than an observer up to this point, but it was he who was ultimately responsible for order on the island and he who would make the final decision here. "I wish we had the testament of the mage who purportedly interacted with this spirit, but the man sent to fetch her has not yet returned and will probably not be here till tomorrow when Sir Steven arrives. We need to find this boy, that much is obvious, but we have to accept that we may not get our hands on him for some while yet. And so, we need to come up with a form of words that will calm the frayed nerves of the mages and lay brothers out there. We need..."

They had all but forgotten Miriam. She had assumed that they should have dismissed her by now, but as yet they had not, and she couldn't really leave until they did. So, she had stepped back a few paces, trying to let the shadowed parts of the room (of which there were many) claim her for their own. The indecision on display here surprised her, she had always seen men such as Shadan as firm and direct in their actions, untroubled by the merest vestige of self-doubt. It seemed the present situation, unique as it was, had wrong footed the great men of the island as much as the lowliest novice. And the matter was not about to improve.

The door ground open on its ancient hinges and a knight strode in, his steps faltering. He bowed to those present before speaking as rapidly as he could, presumably in order to forestall any awkward questions.

His words were directed primarily to Shadan. "My apologies Commander but there is a senior mage outside who insists on addressing this meeting. He states that he is a representative for a group calling itself "the concerned". Who they are I do not know myself, but he says they number in their dozens, and they have genuine grievances that they wish to air before your presence."

"And we have a solution as well." Senior Oskum breezed past the knight's shoulder to stand before the Knight Commander. He was a stocky man of medium height with a pale, waxy complexion and grey eyes that were constantly on the move. "Sorry for my impropriety but I could not be certain that you would allow my admittance."

"And you would be right too," Shadan regarded the man with eyes that were smouldering angrily; "but you are here now so say what you have to say and begone. As you may know I am a great admirer of brevity and of those that display it."

"Very well." Oskum seemed both nervous and excited, he seemed to be rather enjoying being the centre of attention. Miriam did not know him well, he was a decade or more older than her and did not teach, he was a researcher of some sort, she wasn't even sure what field he specialised in. "As your knight has already stated I have been elected spokesman for a group of people who are somewhat...dissatisfied with the response to the crisis that appears to be engulfing us all."

"Dissatisfied?" Shadan raised an eyebrow.

"With all due respect sir but yes. Most of us have barely been given any information at all apart of course from the "there is nothing to fear" platitudes whenever we have the temerity to ask a question. Yet people are dying here, they are continuing to die, and we get nothing in return but silence. And so the concerned among us wish to know firstly, if you think Xhenafa is loose among us, and secondly, if you think he isn't then do you know who is committing these crimes and has he been arrested or not. And if not why not?" he added as an afterthought with an affirmative shake of the head.

Shadan, Greville, and Beverley exchanged glances. None of them seemed keen to reply first and Oskum took his cue from their uncertainty.

"None of you know what is happening I take it?"

"Senior Oskum," Greville's voice was grave, "you are right to assume that we do not have precise answers to your questions. The investigation is still ongoing..."

"Ongoing!" Oskum interrupted, an edge of shrill panic in his voice. "For how long? Until we are all dead? What were you going to tell us in this meeting you have called?"

"We were currently in the process of deciding that." Shadan kept the disapproving tone in his voice, neither he nor Greville were used to being upbraided by a mage of such middling status. Sir Beverley though was not prepared to display their apparent tolerance.

"Boy, you are addressing your seniors here, if you have a point to make then make it with respect or it will be a night in the prison for you."

Oskum started to flush. "The prison might be safer than our cells but..." he raised an apologetic hand, "you are right, and I apologise if my concern has offended. However, both I and the people I represent have a possible solution to the current crisis, a compromise that may satisfy all of us."

Eyebrows were raised at this, including Miriam's who was by now thoroughly enjoying her status as the room's forgotten inhabitant. "Go on," said Shadan cautiously.

Oskum stood up stiffly, putting his arms straight at his sides like a child reciting a party piece. "The construction of this college took many years, well over a decade in fact. At first it was decided to move us mages here and house us in tents or in a stockade until it was completed but it was then decided by the knights that watching us and watching the construction was a risk they were not prepared to take. One mage with a grudge could seriously hamper or indeed sabotage any work going on under his nose. So, what happened then was that all the mages were housed in a hastily constructed stone fortress on the island of Sunbank some miles west of here. The fortress in itself was a pale facsimile of this college, apparently about a tenth of its size and built of inferior local stone, it was not very secure but that did not matter, for it was just as isolated as this place and it was that which made it such a good choice. It was not a viable place in the long term because there was no real water supply and little land for crops or storage, the island is much smaller than this one I believe. But as a temporary location it is fine. So, the suggestion is for those of us who do not wish to remain here to be moved there until matters are concluded, hopefully in an equitable manner. There is a ship on the Isle of Healing, it could take us as soon as tomorrow if all parties are agreeable." Oskum stopped to wipe a bead of sweat off his brow. It was a big bead and he had to wipe his brow several times before he was satisfied.

Greville regarded the younger man with a degree of sympathy. "I am gratified to see that your criticism of us is at least constructive, and it ill behoves me to be so dismissive of your suggestion but there are several problems with the idea."

Oskum gasped in frustration but let Greville continue. "Firstly, the ship you mention could only take a handful of mages at a time, maybe a dozen at best. So, several journeys may be needed, and knights would need to be spared for each journey, knights that might be difficult to find at present. The whole process could take many days and in truth I am hopeful that things here will be resolved in far less time than that. Secondly, the buildings at Sunbank are little more than ruins now. There is no infrastructure there, no food, no water, no place to sleep. To prepare it would require an investment of resources that again, would take far more time to achieve than should be required to stop the tragedies that are occurring here."

"We would be happy to sleep in tents…" Oskum blurted out.

"But what would you eat? Drink?"

"We could hunt, gather rainwater…"

"Hunt?" Beverley snorted; "you mages couldn't hunt your own arse. And as for rainwater, what if there is no rain?"

"We are happy to take our chances…"

"But my knights are not," Shadan said firmly, "and you would need knights with you whether you like it or not."

"Besides," Greville added, still trying to sound like the voice of reason here, "if Xhenafa is walking amongst us then he could jump islands far more easily than we could. He would not need a ship. Moving islands would not save you from him."

"There you are," Sir Beverley smacked his lips. "You have had your hearing and your suggestion is rejected. There will be a meeting at the great hall later, you can attend that to hear our final words. In the meantime, you can leave us. Now!"

Shoulders sagging and red of face, an open mouthed Oskum filed out of the room. Only Miriam of all those left could see the burning anger in his eyes. But Sir Beverley was not yet finished. Miriam looked up to see his pudgy finger pointed directly at her.

"And you should have left here long ago. Get out!"

Miriam assayed a semi ironic sort of curtsey before effecting a hasty departure. As the door closed behind her Sir Beverley's words followed her out of the room.

"And not a word to anybody about what you have seen and heard. Any leaked information and you know who I will be arresting first!"

****

Pilgrims, empire, and the people of Kibil

Steven had removed the mirror in Sir Beverley's room and so Gytha could only try and put her hair in order by running her fingers through it time and time again, until at last it had some body, though a couple of loose russet curls still hung limply over her eye. She had been awake some time now and, judging from the sun through her window there was maybe one hour of daylight left. She had asked Steven to wake her but in truth she knew that he would let her sleep till she was ready, and it seemed that in this case her intuition had been correct. She felt good now, refreshed, and clean and she was just about to leave the room and brazen it out with Steven and Fedrica when the door opened and Steven himself walked in, alone.

"You let me sleep," she said brightly, smiling as sweetly as she could given her surprise at his appearance.

"You needed it I think. Still, I could not leave you here forever. Besides, I need to update you, things have been happening whilst you slept." He sat behind the desk in Sir Beverley's well used chair.

She went and perched herself on the desk close to him, shaking her hair once more, though whether she did it because it needed it or whether she did it because she thought it made her more appealing, she could not really answer. "Enlighten me then," she said quietly.

"Well, Sir Leuring has returned, he has been sent by Sir Beverley with the specific instruction to take you to the college for questioning. He wanted you to go immediately but Leuring's loyalty is to me rather than Beverley and I talked him into returning in the morning. With me. So you will be spared the singular experience of an interview with the big man. I expect your eternal gratitude."

"You have it."

"There is other news though," his voice took on a more sombre tone. "The bodies of Senior Arbagast and Havel the lay brother have been discovered. In the outdoor latrine of all places. We have five dead now, five. I cannot get back to the college quickly enough, though having said that this latest event has me more confused than ever."

"But why?" Gytha queried. "We are pretty certain that Havel and Raiman were working for the order of Jedrael, that it was they who excavated the entrance to the caves and that they had ensorcelled objects in their possession, possibly to let the order keep track of them or possibly because they were used as messengers and these objects acted as signals of some sort."

"Or possibly both," Steven said.

"Exactly. Now maybe they had outlived their usefulness, or maybe they had got greedy, they both had money on them when they died, perhaps they were blackmailing somebody, threatening to expose them. As for the other victims, well I saw Tola die, Xhenafa guide him, he was just in the wrong place at the wrong time. Caswell I am sure knew something too, remember that note she had written about the arrogance of mages? and something was definitely troubling her at the end, I was with her remember, she was far more …reflective than I had ever seen her before. So maybe she needed to be silenced also. And as for Arbagast…" she drummed her fingers on the desk trying to think of a connection. "Well, if he died with Havel maybe even he had a secret to keep, perhaps he was in the Order of Jedrael too."

Steven's response was sceptical. "You are saying that people in the

Order of Jedrael are killing to keep their order secret? Why? It is a crime to belong to the order, but it is not punishable by death whereas murder most definitely is. I think there is something else, something we are missing. Why use an elven spirit to kill? Surely poison or even magic could do the job just as well? And if the order has been using these caves regularly why has the spirit not been attacking them?"

"Blue fire. Some sort of fire with power. It masks them from the spirit. It is something I need to find out more about. The librarian would be a good place to start."

"If she is not involved."

"Stop it," Gytha sounded playful, "she is a friend. I think they have used this fire to protect themselves whilst turning Sinotaneh into their slave. And as for the thing we are missing, well the letter Miriam saw alluded to an escape attempt. Perhaps the Order of Jedrael is seeking to set up independently, on some remote island, one they can defend from the knights. Perhaps Caswell and Arbagast had found out about it and were going to the authorities. Escape from a mage college can be punishable by death I believe."

"In some cases, yes. Tomorrow we arrest Lipshin and Mattris, I don't care how hard-nosed she is, I am getting answers from her. And from him."

She nodded, surreptitiously dragging her forefinger over Steven's right hand. He looked up at her, she looked away. "Does Edith continue to recover?"

"Slowly," he sighed; "she is awake but still coughs and is still quite weak. Children can ail very quickly; she still has to be watched. Ideally, she should remain on this island, but I am a knight, I have my duty and I cannot stay here. I am surprised that Fedi agreed to the transfer, but she has. So tomorrow we all move back to the chapter house. As for the here and now, the healers and Fedi are poring over and prodding my little girl. It is why I am here; I just feel useless when the healers start to work on her."

"She came to see me earlier," Gytha said through pursed lips.

"Did she? I wondered where she had gone."

"She suspects...something is going on between us. She threatened me, said she would get me transferred to Chira. She didn't specify which college, but I am sure Manucco went through her mind. It certainly did mine." Gytha then grasped Steven's hand, softly, and this time she did look at him. "I really do not want to go anywhere in Chira, she does not have the power to do this does she?" her last few words were practically pleading to him.

"Shadan would have to authorise it and he has my ear. Fedrica is a very...insecure young lady, very possessive and prone to jealousy." Steven spoke in as soothing a voice as he could muster, trying to reassure her, however she could not help but feel he was trying too hard. "She has a good heart and is a good mother, but she does live on her nerves somewhat. I hope she wasn't too insulting."

"She said that you said I was plain and unattractive."

"I said nothing of the sort."

"She said that you like redheads and had a thing with a chambermaid on the mainland."

Steven laughed. "Oh that! There was a girl yes but nothing like that happened. I caught her crying as she was sweeping my room. She had family problems, I tried to help, soon afterwards she moved to another job. That was it."

"She said that she had her forcibly transferred."

"Really?" Steven's eyes widened in surprise. "She might have I suppose, she never told me though. She really did have a go at you didn't she. I am not putting up with that, I will have a few sharp words with her later on."

"No," Gytha shook her head; "don't do that. Let us just avoid giving her reason to carry out her threats in the first place."

He smiled at her. "I thought we had decided not to take things further."

A sliver of light filtered through the window to shine on Gytha's fiery hair. She appeared to be surrounded by a corona of coppery flame. She could smell Steven; she was that close to him. He smelled clean but with the faintest aroma of scented incense. Was it the burners in the chapter house or was he using expensive scented soap? Perhaps Fedrica had brought some with her. Either way with his black uncombed hair and dark eyes deep and thoughtful her feelings for him were beginning to stir again. She strengthened her grip on his hand.

"It is your decision," she said, "but I cannot deny my feelings for you, or should that be my longing? I must admit I would like to see you out of that uniform of yours."

"Is that so?"

She giggled and swung her legs around the desk so that she was facing him, their legs brushing each other. "You have no idea what you have got here have you? A passionate, intelligent woman, one who has to constantly rein in her desires, so much so that they are rather like, oh I don't know. How about a swollen lake pressing against the walls of a dam, how does that sound?"

"Tortuous," he said; "still, am I to be the one who gets to burst the walls of that dam?"

"If you wish." She slid off the desk, leaned forwards and kissed him lightly on the forehead. "In your marital bed you have to entertain the whims of a child," she whispered, "perhaps it is time for you to remember what a real woman can do for you, and I'll wager I can do far, far more than she would ever countenance. Why, I bet she waits until total darkness before she even considers satisfying your joint needs." She kissed him again, surprised at her own libidinous tone.

He stroked her face, her cheek, her soft skin. She pressed herself into his strong hand. "You are quite the lady, Gytha of the college but we cannot continue this here, not at this time. My wife and child are but yards away."

She breathed on his hand and shut her eyes. He was right of course, and she hated it when he was right. She pulled her face clear of him. "Later then," she demurred.

"Yes later. The risk of discovery you know, there is a window there, anybody could pass it."

She nodded.

"I am not saying no. I just do not want anyone to have a tangible reason to send you to Chira."

She nodded again, more accepting this time.

"Not that Chira is as bad as you seem to think it is."

She opened her eyes, her smile had returned, even if it was a little forced. "And how would you know that exactly? been there have you?"

"I certainly have." Steven was pleased to see her smile again. She had perfect teeth, though her lips were always a little pale. "I went as a child of about nine or ten. It was before the war with Arshuma, a group of about twenty members of the Aarlen family went there on a pilgrimage. Started in early spring, got back here late in the autumn. We saw Ygfal and Crotabas, two great cities on the giant lakes, Chira city itself, and of course the holy city of Codona."

"Where Saint Abo first brought the word of Artorus," Gytha finished the sentence. "Tell me about it, I am aware that I talk far more than you, yet I like listening to you speak. So, let me listen now."

She returned to the bed on which she had slept and sat down, arranging her robe neatly around her knees and legs. Steven suspected that she, after her traumatic night and long rest needed a little felicitous company, at least for a while. In that, he was happy to oblige her.

"After you travel through Arshuma and the pass in the Derannen mountains you reach the pilgrim path, a stone surfaced road wide enough to accommodate horses and wagons. There are pilgrim's inns and offering shrines dotted along the trail with no end of hawkers selling trinkets, icons, and other badly made tat at ridiculous prices. We were on the trail for about three weeks before we got to Ygfal, on Lake Febrey. The lake is enormous, I cannot begin to describe its size to you apart from saying that it was only at night, when you could see the minute fires from towns on the other side that you actually realized that it had another side. Directly to the north are the Hagasus, the jagged mountain range where the rivers that create the lakes spring from. In the mountains themselves are other lakes, smaller ones, surrounded by forests and supposedly full of monsters. They are said to be haunted and wild elves, never conquered by the empire are said to live in hidden glades there. We spent many nights listening to ghost stories from the locals, fantastical ones I am sure, but ones guaranteed to chill the marrow of any ten-year-old boy.

Anyway, Ygfal sits between mountains and lake. It is built on giant rocky spurs that jut into the waters and is fed by tiny mountain streams. We stayed there for about a week before taking a boat across the lake to Crotabas on the other side. It took us two and a half days to cross it, the lake is often choppy. Crotabas is the biggest city on the lake but not perhaps the prettiest. Fishing is at its heart and by Artorus it certainly smelled that way most of the time. Most of its buildings are of wood, many of them built out on the lake itself, on long wooden jetties connected by bridges. The centre of the city, built on the land out of stone is quite beautiful with many small gardens around an elegant house of Artorus, the rest of the place though is a sprawl.

We stayed there for a couple of days before carrying on along the trail. It skirted Lake Coteku which is supposedly the biggest lake of all and then, some days later we arrived at the city of Chira itself. You know much about the city?"

"I have read a little," she said quietly, "but I would rather you told me."

"Okay," he replied with a slow drawl. "We stayed in the inner city and on our first day climbed the Tower of the Dawn in the city walls. From its top you can see the whole place spread out both below, and above you. I was young then and when you are young everything is bigger but even now, I would hazard an estimate that it is over five times the size of Tanaren City, maybe as much as ten. I could not begin to guess the number of people that live there. Anyway, it is built around a mountain and river, both called the Chir, with the river running through the entire city. The lower part of the mountain has been carved into three flat terraces by human hands. The first has the river pouring into a man-made circular lake, ringed by a marble surround that holds many statues supposedly of old emperors, though in truth I was too far away to make them out. Apparently either side of the waterfall there are two great sheets of sapphire crystal that turn the falls blue when the sun is in the right direction but again, I was too far away to see it properly. In the middle of the lake is the Imperial palace, an edifice of marble, silver, and lapis lazuli. Its silver topped towers are designed to catch the sun so that even the lowliest beggar can look up, see it, and feel that the emperor is protecting him. At least that is what some of the locals said, others though said otherwise, they saw it as a reminder that the emperor was watching them, constantly, and to oppose him was futile.

The river is then diverted into two falls which spill on to the second terrace. There are two lakes here, similar in style but slightly smaller than the first. At the centre of one is the house of the Ke, where the Ke'dashu, the city governors meet to run the empire. The other lake holds the grand cathedral, where the great men and women of the city go to worship. After this the river becomes a single torrent again running through the centre of the third terrace, which houses the walled inner city, the original city limits. The river and a causeway that crosses it divide the city into roughly four equal quarters. The army is run from one, the market is in another, the peoples house of Artorus in another still and the last is known for its...er, fleshpots, I was too young to be allowed to go THERE, my father told me that the sights in that quarter even made him blush.

Space is at a premium in the inner city and only the relatively wealthy can live there. We stayed in the market quarter, an amazing place, people from every corner of the world hemmed into just a couple of square miles. The inner city is walled, the walls are thick enough to house the army and the watch. The city of Chira was supposed to begin and end at its great gates, but of course, that is not the case anymore. For another city has grown up outside it, under the terraces, the dust city they call it, and it is many times larger than the original city limits. It is protected, by a ditch and sharpened stakes but each year the ditch has to be filled in and re dug, and the stakes moved for the city expands with each passing season.

The dust city has its squares and great buildings but most of it is not planned at all, it smells of fires and manure, of sweat and iron, straw and animal hide, it is a mélange of chaos, fleas, rats and people. Its only original buildings were the dregg houses, built for the conquered elves who are banned from the main city itself, but they have long been swamped by thousands of people moving in to make their fortune. Any problems Tanaren City has, Chira has fifty times over. It is both fascinating and frightening, at least it was for an impressionable child. Anyway, a week there and we were off to Codona and the end of the pilgrimage."

"Did you do the pilgrim's walk, up into the mountains?"

Steven nodded. "Of course. You don't travel all that way and not do the mountain walk or leave an offering at the celestial shrine at the end of that walk. Codona is not really a city, rather a collection of holy houses each dedicated to a single god, with the citadel of Artorus in a plaza at the centre. All the dwellings, all the trade there is geared to service the needs of the church and the pilgrims that go there."

"I would imagine so. Do people do the walk naked? To prove their faith, I believe that is what you are supposed to do is it not?"

"Yes, but most people keep a thin shirt and breeches on, only the truly devotional wear nothing at all. The wind that tears through the mountain passes is absolutely bitter, I can still recall it even now. Of my family only auntie Ermintrude disrobed completely, and the sight of her wobbly arse turned purple by the wind is another thing I can still remember, though in truth I really wish I couldn't. A lot of men stripped completely, out of bravura I suppose but a freezing wind does nothing to flatter a man."

Gytha burst out laughing at that, raising her hand, and waggling her little finger.

"Exactly," Steven concurred.

She continued to laugh, "my faith is nowhere near strong enough to do that. I would like to do the pilgrimage once though, when the war is over. The college allows a select few to go every year in peace times..."

"Guarded by us knights of course."

"Of course," she nodded. "It is the only reason I would ever have to go to Chira. The ONLY reason."

"Don't worry," he assured her, "you won't be forced to. Why the hatred for Chira anyway? Tanaren was founded by Chirans."

She did not reply, contenting herself with giving him an arch look instead. "Oh!" he said finally, "the Kibil thing."

"The Kibil thing," she nodded.

"Can't you let it pass?" he asked tentatively, "it is old history and besides, you have never actually been to Kibil anyway. And you have been at the college for most of your life, are your roots really that strong?"

"They are," she asserted; "my formative years were not spent here, they were spent with my family in a village with strong traditions and memories of our past, of where we came from. We all knew our history by the time we were five."

"Ah, but can you remember it now?" he teased her.

She pretended to be affronted. "Of course! some things you do not forget, and you already know I have an interest in many aspects of history."

"Aren't you all descended from mercenaries? Men who fought for General Tolmareon in his northern wars?"

"We were not and never were simple mercenaries," she said pointedly.

"What were you then? Come on, I have made myself hoarse through talking, now it should be your turn."

"If you so desire." Gytha arched her back, stretching her arms to the ceiling. "This is rather traditional in itself, telling stories and talking history as it gets dark outside. Well, after Tolmareon had defeated the elves at the battle of Shefom exactly seven hundred and seventy-four years ago;" she pulled a smug face at his impressed expression, "he led his army north, into lands of mountains, ice, tundra, and permanent snow seeking to expand the empire. But he met fierce resistance and his army slowly became mutinous, they were homesick and weary of years of unending war. So, he sent many of them home and sought instead to recruit local tribes to his cause, ones who would see the Chiran army as a powerful ally who could only expand their own influence amongst their fellows. And it was a strategy that worked. Tolmareon conquered a vast territory for the empire, the only land they have ever controlled north of the Red Mountains. In the pass of Lokka that wound through the mountains he constructed three high stone fortresses, known as the sisters, the likes of which the locals had never seen before and it was through these that he exercised the control of the northlands, which had also been named Tolmareon in his honour. But he knew that his new fiefdom relied greatly on those fierce barbarous tribes that were fighting for him. They were expecting booty and he had to give it to them. He had not the coin for this, the tribesman at the time used little coin anyway but he did have something else, land. And so, he started parceling some out for them.

He chose the former elf lands immediately south of the mountains, lands sandwiched between the three sisters and the new territory of Tanaren. It was a green land, fertile, land far richer than the cold northlands the tribesmen were used to eking out an existence from. They accepted it gladly and though the tribes were still rivals to each other, in their new home they found that far more united them than divided them. So, they called their new territory Kibil, or brothers in their language. And they brought their wives and children there and started to settle, building villages, herding cattle, raising crops. For a brief time, things were promising, things were good, then Tolmareon died, and it all changed."

"Have I lost you yet?" she enquired pertly, staring at his face which had become unusually blank.

"Not at all," he became expressive again, smiling at her; "you must think I have a child's capacity for easy distraction. Tolmareon died in suspicious circumstances, it was rumoured that Emperor Parnassan was jealous of his popularity and the way he commanded his new territories like they were his own and not the emperor's. Either way it precipitated the first war of Imperial succession."

"Which lasted nearly two decades and ended with a new dynasty, the Leuconids, seizing the Imperial throne, you will have to do better than that to throw me. As for Kibil though, its people were loyal to Tolmareon and him alone, his death meant that ties to the empire were cut, Kibil became its own country, and the lands between Kibil and the empire became known as Kibilchira, it would see much fighting over the ensuing centuries. For Kibil had something the empire wanted, a port.

It was one of the great port cities of the elves, Atem Lasprazhil, the city of the silver bird, though we just know it as Old City these days. The city was largely abandoned once the elves fled the empire, but it was a port, with a great natural harbour. The empire was largely landlocked, but it did have a couple of southern ports and would soon have the port of Tanaren city. Old City though was another northern port that it coveted. So, the scene was set for five centuries of struggle between Kibil and the empire. Ultimately though it was an uneven contest.

Old City was finally taken by the empire after two centuries of control switching back and forth between both sides. The sisters, and the lands north of the Red Mountains were retaken after three. Kibil's fortunes depended on the quality of its commanders, in bad years it held little more than a few scattered villages, in good years though, under men like Magnus Cragbrow, Hrolf Bearstrider and Finn the Bold, Old City was little more than an island, alone in a sea of hostile enemies. By the way, I am supposed to be directly descended from Hrolf, though I can hardly say I have his same affinity with bears."

Steven's sardonic tone was unmistakeable. "You are descended from someone called the bear strider?"

"So, I have been told," she replied in clipped tones. "He was supposed to have had about thirty children, so it is not an impossibility. He did have red hair and blue eyes too, just like me, I believe that it makes us unique in the whole world, I have never heard of such a combination amongst any other people.

Anyway, after years of struggle the Chirans finally overran our lands and

Kibil became fully incorporated into the empire. Some of us accepted it, others didn't. They took to their ships and sailed away looking for a life free from Chiran control. Some went north, back to the frozen lands, others went far to the south, Mothravia or Fash. Most though settled in western Tanaren which was then ostensibly under Chiran control with a puppet Grand Duke. But the Grand Duke was a desperate man, the west of his country was underpopulated and said to be full of pirates and rebels. We help him out he said, and the lands were ours, we could live there with a degree of autonomy. We accepted and so, just over two hundred and fifty years ago the people of Kibil became Tanarese for the first time."

"And you have been trouble ever since," Steven smiled.

"Not so!" she affected an indignant pout, "we played our part in the battles to make Tanaren independent. Granted since then there have been several minor rebellions and two major ones, the last less than a century ago. My forefathers were in both of them you know," she added cheekily.

"As I said, trouble."

She narrowed her eyes a little, her voice purred like a cat's. "If I was real trouble I would sit here and say that you are a very attractive man and that, if I were to think of you tonight I would be squeezing my thighs together very tightly indeed."

Steven's reply was choked. "Artorus help us! I have absolutely no..."

She cackled at him, "Artorus help us indeed, you should see your face! Are you like this every time a woman acts just a little bit provocatively? I am only teasing you Steven, sometimes I like to tease just to provoke a reaction. At least you aren't as bad as Warran, when I do the same with him, he practically dissolves on the spot."

There was a scraping, creaking sound behind Steven as the door was eased open. Gytha got to her feet at the sight of the petite figure of Lady Fedrica in the doorway. She continued to smile.

Fedrica's eyes burned into Steven. "I am relieved to hear that the plight of our daughter has not precluded laughter between the two of you. The healers have finished with her, she is ready to sleep but wishes to see you first."

Steven eased himself out of his chair. "Then I had best not keep the Lady Edith waiting. We shall say a prayer of Meriel together, or more than likely I will be forced to sing it."

""Send me safely to my bed, keep the agues from my head"? "Gytha enquired.

"Just the one I was thinking of," Steven winked at her.

The easy familiarity between the two of them was impossible to ignore. Fedrica stood still as a statue, her face a frozen grimace. "I have been wondering," she said stiffly, her voice slightly stuttering, "that maybe, now Edith is recovering, we could seek permission to spend winter or spring in a warmer clime. It has been recommended by the healers; sunlight is very beneficial to those with Edith's condition. It should make her stronger and ensure that she never succumbs to this sickness again. I was thinking of southern Chira, I wonder if you agree."

As she said the word "Chira", she glared directly at Gytha, just to ensure that the implied threat hit home. Gytha though kept smiling at her, apparently her barbed words were just floating over her head.

"Southern Chira?" Steven frowned, "it is a possibility I suppose though this war makes travel there difficult. A ship to Vylanta and then on to northern Fash or Hlety, I suppose we could do that. Or maybe we could go to Crown Haven though it would be a long voyage for a little girl. I will speak to Shadan about it, anything that helps Edith has to be considered." He started to shepherd Fedrica out of the door. "Oh, and Gytha bear strider," he added with a grin, "I will have more food sent in for you. But remember you are technically being held for interrogation so you are not allowed to leave the room till dawn, when we will all be on our way from here. Sneak out and I will have to put a guard on the door."

Gytha assayed an elaborate curtsey. "As you command sir. A pleasant eve to you all and please convey my good wishes to Lady Edith."

"We will do so," Fedrica said curtly before shutting the door with a flourish.

Gytha stood there for the moment before going to Beverley's scant bookshelf to find something to read. She felt good; she had flirted outrageously with Steven and successfully aggravated Lady Fedrica, though in truth she also felt a little sorry for her. She was so young; her child was ill, and it was so obvious that Steven did not love her that any victory she had over the girl could only ever be a qualified one. Still, she felt good. The terrors of the night before had diminished considerably after a few hours of rest and recovery. What was this one? "The code of the knights and the code of the mages, can they ever be reconciled?" It was more a polemic than a logically presented argument. Still, it was not too long, more than enough to pass an hour or two by. She returned to her couch and started to read.

When truculence becomes rebellion

The sun was dipping into the west and the kissing rock was occupied. The stones had been arranged into a crescent next to the path, the signal that it was being used; because of the time no one else would be going there that day at least. Yet all was not as it seemed. For this was no lover's tryst.

The hidden space between rock and cliff side could hold two people with ease, four people with some comfort, eight people with a bit of a squeeze. Now though the occupants numbered more than a dozen, maybe even twice that. They had arrived secretly, in ones or twos so as not to attract attention and now they huddled nervously, shoulder to shoulder, gossiping amongst themselves in loud whispers. They were all mages, a mix of white robed novices and blue robed seniors, they were all quite young, for all the seniors were relatively newly qualified, more importantly than that though they were all by varying degrees frightened. Gytha would have known all of them had she been there, amongst them was the girl Iska whom she had had to warn about fraternising with Mattris. Some she was on very friendly terms with, others were study partners, others she just knew well enough to nod to should they pass in a corridor, yet had she been there amongst them now she would have been horrified at what they were about to contemplate.

And finally, the last member of the company joined them. Senior Oskum half trotted down the path to the rock glancing furtively and frequently behind him until finally he was amongst them and relatively safe. Putting his back against the cold, clammy stone of the kissing rock he started to speak, for he was the reason for them gathering here in the first place.

"It is everything that I feared," he said to them. "I did as we agreed, I met with the senior knights and the Chief Magister and put our proposal to them. Now they are in the great hall, speaking to everybody else, lying to them about the peril they are in. The one good thing about this is that the knights are all there, they are not looking here, and their eyes are not yet upon us."

"And how did they respond to the proposal?" one of the men asked him.

"Rejected. Utterly." There was a collective groan at this. "Furthermore," Oskum added, "it was obvious that not one amongst them know what is happening. They do not know if Xhenafa walks among us or whether it is some human murderer who can strike whenever and wherever he pleases. This killer acts with impunity, and they have no idea of how to stop him."

A young woman's voice this time. "Is it true they have a suspect? I mean if they have a suspect, and he is at large, then surely it is only a matter of time before they catch him. We need do nothing more than wait until that happens. Don't we?"

Oskum shook his head, "I have been hearing mixed messages about this. Some say a suspect has escaped, some say that there is no suspect at all. But right at this moment they have no one for these crimes and as I said they laughed off our request to transfer to another island. We are expected to sit here like obedient children waiting for our turn to die. Well, I for one am not prepared to passively accept being dictated to by people who are groping in the dark."

"What are you suggesting then?" the man who had spoken earlier asked him.

Oskum swallowed nervously. "Well Dicken, there is a ship in harbour on the Isle of Healing. I propose that we seize it and sail to this island ourselves. You, as the only healer here, would form an integral part of my plan."

Now there was an incredulous gasp from all present. "We cannot do that!" one of the men articulated finally. "We would be disobeying the knights! We do not know how to sail, and we would be caught."

"And we have no food!" said another, "and once the killer is caught, we would have to return here, it would be arrest for all of us!"

"A whipping!" said one.

"Or even death!" said another.

They were getting loud. Too loud for voices carry easily on the wind. Oskum put out both arms to try and calm them down, but it was still a few minutes before order had fully returned and he was able to continue.

"The way I see it," he said; "it is like a game of dice, or bones. You balance the odds, stay here and possibly lose your life or break a few rules and live. You are right in that there will be a punishment for those that return here but it would probably be a period of imprisonment for most of you. Any worse punishment would fall on me as the leader of us all, but I am frightened out of my wits and would happily bear a few lashes of the whip if it meant keeping Xhenafa at bay. Besides, what is prison to any of us, forced to live out our lives in this exile?"

This time there was silence as they dwelled on his words. Then Dicken spoke out once more. "What is this plan of yours exactly?"

Oskum smiled at him. "There is not much light left. My plan involves seizing the ship now so that we can sail out and weigh anchor, away from any pursuers who could not set out in the dark. The knights' ships are small and light, not built for lengthy spells at sea so once dawn arrives tomorrow and we set sail again, we shall already be too far out for them to catch us. So, you see my plan involves acting now, seizing the initiative before darkness falls."

Heads nodded, heads shook, the audience appeared undecided, so Oskum continued.

"The ship is due to sail tomorrow, anyway, isn't that right Dicken?"

"Yes, it is."

"So, it will have taken on food, water, and supplies."

"Yes. And the body of the dead lay brother."

"We can give him a funeral ourselves. Now, we leave here as we arrived, by ones and twos, this time though we go to the bridge and reconvene there. As we then walk to the harbour Dicken will go to the hospital where the sailors are lodging and speak with their captain, telling him of some crisis that he and his crew have to attend immediately."

"What crisis?" Dicken looked horrified.

"I do not know!" Oskum retorted, "make something up, you know more about ships than I do! Just get enough of them to the vessel so that it can be crewed. Then I am afraid we will have to threaten them to take us away from here. I am not happy with this, but I can see no other option. Threaten to use our power on them, that is usually enough to cow those without the gift."

"So, they have to stay on the island with us!" several voices gasped.

"We can decide that later, between us. Once we are away from here, we vote on everything. We have to accept that we will either be recaptured at some point or that we will have to return here of our own volition, so whether we let the sailors leave when we get to the island or force them to stay with us is not that important. As long as we take the food and supplies that they have first, that is what really matters, we don't really know how much food the island will provide."

People started muttering to themselves, Oskum looked unhappy. He decided to make one final plea. "It is a big step, I know it is a big step but as I said, I am not sitting around waiting to die. If you are with me then meet me at the bridge as fast as you can get there, if not, then I beg you not to tell the knights of our plan, just go back to your cells, throw the dice and pray to Artorus you do not get a double one. Now we have to move, I will go first, you all follow at a respectful distance."

He did not look at their faces as he left. He knew he had not carried all of them, that their fear of the discipline of the knights bizarrely outweighed their fear of possible death but he did not care. He only needed a handful of them to join him, the sailors' fear of magic would do the rest. The fewer that joined him the better in truth for it meant less mouths to feed and if he was being honest, he had no idea how much food they would have to live on upon their arrival. But he had been chewing this plan over and over again for days and the deaths of two more people today, and his perceived humiliation in front of the knights and Greville had tipped him over the precipice. He would be making a stand of principle, showing them that the voices of the humblest on the island should be listened to. And he was showing them that he was not a nobody, a mediocrity saddled with a humdrum job that mattered to no one except himself. His name was Oskum and tonight, for the first time in his life, he would be listened to.

Order crumbles and Kestine is wearily imposed upon

The meeting in the great hall degenerated rather quickly. It started with an address by Greville and by Knight Commander Shadan with both saying that they had a suspect, that he was trapped in a tunnel under the island and that it was just a matter of time before he was intercepted. A few days ago this would have been accepted, albeit grudgingly. Now though people were frightened and angry, and not in the mood for platitudes. The authority that the knights and senior mages had cultivated over centuries was disintegrating like a pillar of dry sand in the teeth of a northerly gale. Things might have turned out extremely badly had not Sir Beverley ringed the hall with fully armoured, sword drawn knights but even with these, the addresses by those in power were soon shouted over or ignored. People started to talk amongst themselves, the noise generated coming to resemble that of a nest of giant wasps preparing to go out to feed. It took Father Ambrose to prick a response from his audience, suggesting that they move next door to the House of Artorus to offer up prayers for the dead. Slowly, the hall began to clear as people obeyed the request, filtering through the double doors where the sweet yet smoky aroma of incense reminded all of them that, should the secular authorities fail them, their faith would always be there.

Kestine was stood near the back of the hall with Soma, who was shaking her head and smiling wryly at the mayhem unfolding around her. "Is it always like this?" she asked the younger woman.

"No," Kessie said quietly, "everything is falling apart. Prayers?"

"You want to?"

She nodded. "It seems the right thing to do, to show our respect for those that have left us."

Soma gave her a warm smile. "You have a good heart Kessie, I could do with thinking more of others and less of myself a lot more often. I suppose being a fugitive for most of your life makes you selfish. Come on then, let us commend their souls to the gods, pray that they are kept from the furnace and all that sort of thing."

They started to follow the others into the holy house but stopped when they heard somebody hailing them.

"Novice Kestine! I need a word! Just wait there a moment!"

It was Eubolo. He had evidently missed the meeting for he had just come through the doorway dividing hall from reception room and now was waving at them with no little urgency. Kessie and Soma exchanged glances and waited for him to catch up with them.

"Meeting over already?" he cast a sardonic eye over the now nearly empty hall. "Then I am guessing it didn't go too well."

Both women shook their heads. Eubolo continued to talk.

"Thought as much. I have just come from Goodbern, she gave me a potted update on matters. You can only feed people banalities for so long before they get angry, frightful, or suspicious, or even all three as I suspect most of them are by now."

"Yet you do not seem so worried by it all," Soma observed.

"You are both right and wrong there," he replied. "I am frightened, but I tend to feel that matters pertaining to my own survival are out of my hands. Let me tell you a tale. When I was a child, five or maybe six years old I was walking along the verge of a dirt road when I saw something on the other side of that road, stuck in a bush of some sort. It was shiny, unusual. Without thinking I pulled away from my parents and started to cross the road to see what it was. I was so absorbed by what I had seen, it is the way of children I suppose, that I failed to notice my impending doom. For a soldier on a giant destrier was pounding down the road in one direction and a wagon of all things was coming in the other. Either of them could have squashed me like a beetle in seconds. My mother screamed and I looked up, saw the trouble I was in and froze in terror. Well almost froze for I shut my eyes, convinced that in a few short seconds mother would be scraping what remained of me out of the dirt. There was this terrible noise, pounding hooves, jangling metal, churning wheels, men calling out...I smelled leather and sweat and tried to picture Xhenafa in front of me, pulling me away from this world. Then the noise subsided, and I opened my eyes. Both horsemen and wagon had passed me with inches to spare and I was untouched. Well apart from being covered in mud that is. Next thing I remember was mother scooping me up in her arms and shouting at me. Since then I have been more inclined to accept what fate has in store for me than most people. What will happen will happen and there is nothing the likes of me can do to change things."

"And the shiny object?" Soma enquired.

"Never got to see it. Thinking back though I reckon it was just a particularly large dewdrop that caught the sun at the very moment I chose to look at it. When I first saw it I thought it might be a diamond or something and believed that our fortunes were made. As I said, I was very young."

"Maybe your faith protected you," Kessie suggested.

"Maybe," Eubolo smiled showing his dazzlingly white, perfectly even teeth. "It was certainly stronger then than it is now."

"You have doubts?"

He gave Kessie an arch look. "All intelligent people have doubts," he replied. "Questioning everything is what makes us what we are, what makes people collectively improve, civilisation improve. Nothing should ever be taken at face value. For example, ever wonder why those condemned by the Gods are sent through the void to work on the furnace, forging demons who may one day be sent to destroy those very same Gods that sent them there in the first place? It seems rather counterproductive, no? Why can't the souls of the damned be put in a prison or something, well away from the clutches of Keth? Seems an eminently more sensible solution don't you think? Surely divine beings must have thought of THAT before?"

Kessie lifted a finger. "Ah, now that argument has been long refuted. The fact is that they have no choice, that they need Keth, the other condemned Gods and the furnace, otherwise all their creations would exist without balance. Without balance none of us would die, we would never need food or water, the world would be as it is now but would never change, like a water droplet frozen in time. The same thing, forever. But all the Gods know that the world needs change, it needs death and turmoil for out of it comes new growth, new life, a world reborn. Sterility means atrophy, you cannot have joy without knowing suffering and so Keth is just as important a God as Artorus, in a way, just as long as we are not condemned to serve him I suppose."

"You are right of course," Eubolo agreed with little enthusiasm; "but I sometimes wonder if the church sees these anomalies and makes up any old shit to serve their own ends." He saw Kessie's startled face and decided to change the subject. "Anyway, I am here to ask you a favour. I have just come from the charging room. Kas, as I am sure you can guess, is rather inconsolable. Goodbern is with her trying to do what she can which to be honest, isn't much at the moment. But we have a pressing problem. An entire college, hundreds of people and only one mage who can charge our staves. Greville has already arranged for a mage to join us from another college but until he or she arrives we are in a quandary. No other senior wants the job you see, it is seen as a little...tedious. So the powers that be have seen a training opportunity, have some juniors sit with Kas, learn the basics of the job, and assist her. If anybody takes to it, well it could mean an early graduation for somebody."

"A graduation?" Soma sounded doubtful, "is this a pretty lure to catch an unwilling fish?"

"In a way I suppose. Anyhow Kessie, can you guess the name of the very first person selected to do this training?"

Kessie groaned, "Miriam?"

"No."

"Gytha?"

"No."

"Cheris?"

"No."

"Elsa?"

"Ummmm, let me see...no."

Kessie shrugged her shoulders. "When do you want me to start?" she said resignedly.

Eubolo clapped her shoulder. "Excellent! There is nothing I like more than a willing volunteer. You can start as soon as Kas feels up to it. It might even be tomorrow as far as I can see."

Soma gave a shrill, piercing laugh, throwing her head back and letting her ragged curls fall behind her. "Is anything wrong?" Kessie asked.

"No," Soma said, "but you know why you have been chosen don't you?" Kessie shook her head.

"To get you away from me. I am probably being seen as a malign influence on an innocent young girl. Is that correct?" she cocked her head at Eubolo.

"Perfectly," he answered in as blithe a manner as possible; "in the meantime Soma, you are stuck with me for the next few days, is there anything in particular you want to get up to?"

He offered her his arm, which she took immediately. "Well for one thing, you can show me where the best looking men all are, I have been sadly disappointed at the fare on offer so far."

"Well you are staring at the best looking man," he countered with a wicked smile. "Alas the rest of the table is rather bare. Having said that I am sure there are some places in the college you have yet to visit, seeing what lurks there might keep us both engaged for a few days. Shall we all attend prayers?"

Soma nodded and the three of them went on their way. At the last moment though Eubolo took a brief look behind him to see Sir Beverley involved in an animated conversation with Sir Nikolaj. "I wonder what those two are on about?" he pondered, as at last they left the great hall behind.

****

Potential sedition finally gets noticed

Sir Nikolaj was not at his best. Red eyed and tired he was, and his chain mail, cloak and tabard were covered in mud and grass stains, the legacy of having spent most of the day outside, searching for the fugitive Gideon. But Gideon was not the reason he had travelled to the great hall.

Not that Sir Beverley wanted to discuss anything else. "So you still haven't found him," was his brusque opening comment.

"No sir. We are pretty sure he is still in the tunnels; we have scoured every blade of grass on the surface, and he is nowhere to be seen. We are rather loath to explore the tunnels fully, they are guarded by spirits after all and are extremely dangerous as well as being a labyrinth that a cunning man could hide in forever. So our best hope is to starve him out. We have two men in the sea cave, a further two at the entrance in the pigsty and another three in the entry cave reached by the rope ladder in the college. We are even considering putting food out, in the manner of a man hunting a beast, but I am afraid we are looking at an operation that will not be concluded for some days."

For once, Sir Beverley managed to keep his voice down although his whisper was still as fulsome as an ordinary speaking voice. "Not good enough Sir Nikley, not good enough. I may be leaving this post tomorrow, you may have been lucky enough to escape my full censure but my last order to you is to grab him, and to grab him within the next three days. Put food out now, and if that doesn't work you will have to risk the tunnels. We have to take the risk; this man has to be found."

Sir Nikolaj had endured a severe browbeating from Sir Beverley earlier that day, with his commander blaming him, probably correctly, for the disappearance of Gideon. Despite that though he was still prepared to raise an objection. "The spirit sir, it is guarding these tunnels, or at least some of them, we cannot fight…"

"The Grand Duke is coming here!" Sir Beverley replied in a spittle flecked hiss; "this matter must be resolved before he gets here, and he may be here within the week. Understand!"

Sir Nikolaj saluted, putting his fist to his chest. "As you command sir. We will put out food tonight and if that doesn't work I will personally command a detail charged with sweeping the tunnels."

"Good." Sir Beverley's imminent blustering rant was rather nipped in the bud, "perhaps there is some merit in you after all. Now get back to work."

Sir Nikolaj hesitated. "There is another matter sir, one I came here to tell you about."

"Gods preserve us, what is it now?"

"My men on the island, they have been reporting some odd behaviour amongst the mages."

"Nonsense! All the mages were at this meeting, not that anyone benefited from it."

Sir Nikolaj shook his head. "That is it sir, not all of them were at the meeting, we have spotted several mages strolling around the island, generally around the main path. Even worse they never congregate in groups larger than two or three and you know how mages like to gossip, you always see them gather in larger numbers, especially if they think their lives are in danger. After receiving a couple of reports regarding these stray mages I had them followed at a distance. They all seem to be heading west, to the bridge or even the Isle of Healing. They are up to something sir, perhaps a clandestine meeting or something, they obviously didn't even want to hear their own Chief Magister speak to them. I think it bodes ill somehow."

Sir Beverley did not reply at first, to Sir Nikolaj's surprise he actually appeared to be thinking things over, his nose was practically scarlet.

"A mage troublemaker barged into our earlier enquiry, after you had gone. Before I threw him out he mentioned taking a ship to Sunbank Island, to hide there till the murderer was found. His suggestion was dismissed. I doubt he was happy about it."

"You surely don't think...?"

"I surely do think Sir Nikley, I surely do think. I will get Walton and some other stout fellows, you get the hay wagon ready, it will get us to the bridge faster than anything else. If some fool brain mages think they can take the law into their own hands then they have another thing coming!"

****

Steven asks a favour

It had to happen, the sun was not yet down and Gytha was bored. Sir Beverley's "library" had little or nothing to recommend it, just a series of warnings, in publications ranging from a few meagre pages, to dusty, never thumbed tomes inches thick on how dangerous mages could be. Gytha of course knew that already. She had spent nearly her entire life being told about how "dangerous" she was. She was well past the point of mental stimulation on THAT particular issue.

So, what does a healthy, intelligent, curious, and passionate twenty-three-year-old woman do when she is all alone and bored? Food. She looked over at the desk on which sat a pewter plate and goblet, the goblet drained, the plate sporting a mere crust of hard bread, a browning apple core and a tiny fragment of hard cheese the lay brothers had forgotten to scrape the mould off.

No, she had done food and now she was bored again, she needed something else.

Sleep, she could try that. She lay prone on the couch, pulled the blanket over her head, and shut her eyes. Problem was of course that she had slept most of the day already. Her body's synchronisation with the rhythms of nature was now totally out of kilter, sleeping till dawn would be difficult. She needed to do something to tire herself out, maybe going over the investigation would help somehow.

So Lipshin was their prime suspect, based solely on the strength of the letter Miriam had discovered in the tunnels. Was she talented enough a mage to control a sprit, get it to do her bidding? Most certainly. Was she arrogant enough, ambitious enough to believe in the Order of Jedrael, in the intrinsic superiority of mages to rule over others? Most certainly again. Yet something didn't quite ring true to Gytha, she couldn't pin down exactly why they still weren't seeing the whole picture, but she was sure there was something, something they were missing. She chewed her lip in frustration, this was not something she could just find in a book. Thinking about this Keth cursed affair was just irritating her. And now she was discovering that irritation was even worse than boredom.

She stood up, throwing the blanket onto the couch. Demons burn her but she was going to go for a walk, she would rather have a guard spy on her all night than slowly go insane. She crept across the room and slowly opened the door, peering cautiously into the corridor.

Darkness was close now; the candles and lamps had just been lit judging from the lack of melt in the wax. There was nobody about now though, so she inched herself out of the room and stretched her arms over her head. To her left was Steven's room, to her right was the labyrinth that the hospital had become over the years, a labyrinth that Gytha did not know the first way around. So even now she really had nowhere to walk to anyway. She pressed her back against the nearest wall, raised her head to the heavens and sighed so extravagantly wisps of hair fluttered above her half-closed eyes.

"Gytha?" It was Steven, she hadn't seen him in the half light, she snapped to attention in an instant, her eyes wide and staring. She started to babble, "I was only leaving my room for a minute, I was going mad stuck inside! It..."

"Doesn't matter. I was coming to see you anyway. I need a favour."

He sounded worried. "Is Edith alright?" she asked quickly.

"Yes, yes, she is awake and seems a little stronger with every passing

75

hour. No, all it is, is that I have been called away, something strange is happening. A mage just visited the sailors lodging here and told them that there was a fire of some sort on their ship. The captain and some of his men have made their way to the harbour but nobody up here can see any smoke. So the fire, if it even exists is too small to be seen, so how did the mage know about it? I am going to take a look with a couple of the boys. I won't be long. In the meantime there is no one free to watch you so I would like you to sit with Fedrica for a while."

She half choked. "You want me to sit with...but why?"

"Because somebody is supposed to be keeping an eye on you. Fedi is happy to do so. I have had a word with her about her earlier behaviour and she should be a little more...reasonable now. Anyway, I need to leave. Right now, so get down there for me,...please."

She saw he was in no mood for an argument, so she just nodded and headed towards Steven's room. At least boredom would no longer be a problem now anyway...

****

In way over her head

Iska, the junior mage, had reached the point where she no longer had control over her own life, her own destiny. She was a fool to match Uba, the God of fools and, as she trod the gravelly path leading to the harbour and the ship berthed there she constantly reviewed her current situation and wondered if there was any way, any conceivable solution for her to extricate herself from the mess her own idiocy had placed her in.

She stepped off the path, onto the verge of thick, clumpy grass, letting the moisture wet her feet and ankles, hoping the sensation would speed her mind up somehow, but alas without success. Panic had her in its grip, locking her jaw tight as a vice, clenching her hands so rigidly her nails were digging into her palms. Fool Iska, you are a fool. Fool, fool, fool, and soon you will be a dead fool. And you have no one to blame but yourself.

She was sixteen years old, barely, though she looked much older. This was her second full year in the college, after six in the Childs' college and she was accounted a decent student, with above average ability which was however dragged down by a lack of application to her studies. Her problem was that she was accounted quite pretty, and a pretty young girl often drew the wrong sort of attention, especially in the limited environs of the college, and she was not yet experienced enough to distinguish which attention was worth cultivating and which attention should be dismissed out of hand. In fact she seemed to have a gift for choosing the latter over the former, a talent that had led her here, into this desperate situation. She supposed that every fool ended up in a dark place such as this, not through their own volition, but through their inherent inconstancy of nature.

When she had been caught with Mattris, she had already been secretly seeing him for some months. As for poor Emonie, it really had been her first time when they were caught in the tower. Mattris had told Iska to pretend it was her first time too and she had complied, she always complied with Mattris' wishes. He had said it was her job to lead Emonie into a little indiscretion, it would be educational for her, all mages here needed a grounding in matters of flesh and passion, oh he did so like playing his games. He had a long term woman, the senior with the facial blemish, but on the occasions where they had argued or she had rebuffed his advances he came down the stairs, to her, for she never refused him.

And how could she? He was a senior, worldly, over twice her age, a real man, not the spotty boys most of her peers had to put up with. She had visions of them being together forever, of him throwing the senior with the mole to one side in favour of her. She was young, fit, enthusiastic when she visited his chambers, willing to give him whatever he desired. Granted they talked little but they certainly filled the time they had together. She would have done most anything for him and yet, and yet, the morning after they had been caught together by the knight he had finished with her. She remembered his words. "It has gone too far and has to end. I love Senior Lipshin. You should return to your cell and finish that project I set you. I know you are behind with it."

Not even a sorry. Not even an admittance that he had enjoyed their company. Nothing. The bastard. Angry, hurt and upset she had fled to the rose garden, one of the quietest places on the island, at least there she could cry and not be noticed. But she was noticed, even when putting her head in her hands to hide her sobs she was noticed.

He came over and sat on the bench next to her. He said his name was Oskum and he understood how harsh this place could be on gentle people. He was kind, sympathetic, and he listened as she poured her heart out to him. That was her problem, she was an emotional torrent, she had no control over her feelings at all, and she was so...needy, so willing to trust others, especially if they were older than her. The very definition of a fool.

She had heard of women, jilted women, turning almost immediately to the arms of another in a quest for solace, or comfort, or maybe it was just understanding. They needed someone to share their pain, so that in the sharing it could be soothed somehow. That was the hope that Oskum had given her. That very afternoon she had ended up in his room. And the day after they were at the kissing rock. And it was there that he unburdened himself to her and told her his plans for the first time. Only yesterday, yet it felt like it was years ago.

She had not really understood why the murders had caused so much consternation in the college. People died all the time, the lay brother had drowned, the half blind old woman had missed her footing and fallen to her doom. She did not believe the nonsense about the mark of Xhenafa, people just saw what they wanted to see, something her old guardian had told her many times as a child. Oskum though was genuinely terrified, and she felt it her duty as his new lover to support him. So right there and then as she pulled on her clothes behind the kissing rock she had pledged herself to him. At the time she thought the whole thing would blow over. As only a fool could.

Now two (or was it three?) more people were dead and Oskum had decided that the time for words was over. He had stormed (his words) the mage/knight enquiry and had been rebuffed. He had stood in front of her afterwards, as she voiced her scepticism, practically in tears, begging, almost pleading with her to stay at his side, to help him as he tried to achieve his vision (his words again). So what could she do, he had helped her, surely she should do the same in return? She still had half a mind to tell him that they had only been together two days but before such words could escape from her lips he had told her that he loved her. Loved her, a veritable two day romance, it was ridiculous. And yet nobody had ever said such a thing to her before, at least not with his sincerity. So she had nodded and told him that she would be at his side. Only now, as the butterflies chewed up her stomach and the cool evening breeze goose pimpled her exposed skin was she realising that whereas he had helped patch up her bleeding heart, he was now expecting her to put her life in his hands.

Her feeling of dread only increased when they all gathered at the bridge. At the kissing rock there were about twenty of them, all gathered to hear her lover speak. Somehow, by the time they reached the bridge that number had shrunk to nine. Just nine of them against the Knights of the Thorn. In her heart she hoped that the rest of them so assembled would turn against Oskum, persuade him to abandon this fool plan but no. These were his hardened followers, they all thought as he did. She was the only dissenter and yet she did not raise a word against him. It would wound him grievously, how could she twist the knife against one who had shown her such kindness?

He was standing in front of her right now, hand to his face to shield his eyes against the setting sun. It splashed the darkening seas in shades of orange and crimson, streaky clouds of similar shades set the sky aflame. He was looking at the harbour and the ship that rocked peacefully there, then he was looking at the path that led from harbour to hospital and it was here that he saw what he wanted to see.

Oskum turned to her, she had never seen his eyes so animated. He gave her a feverish smile.

"Dicken has done it!" he said to her, to them all. "He is leading the sailors to the ship. Come on, we need to move quickly if we are to intercept them!"

He started to trot towards the small huddle of people she could now see strolling along the path. All the other mages were keeping up with him. Then he stopped and turned, turned to look at her where she was still rooted to the spot.

"Come on!" he exhorted, "no time to lose!"

Turn you fool girl, turn. Turn and run, get away from here, this is just another man using you for his own ends. See sense girl, for once in your life obey reason over your heart! The voice in her head was like a series of clanging bells, each infinitely louder than the great college one. She choked and looked behind her, then she looked ahead, at Oskum and his wide imploring eyes.

Meekly she smiled back at him, picked up her lead heavy legs and started to trot, following the path he was leading them by, scattering the rabbits close by as they quietly fed.

****

A sorceress reborn

It was dark in the seniors' library; the only light came from a single candle at the desk. The windows were shuttered, the door was shut. It should have been open of course, at least for another hour, but all the mages were in the great hall, and with things as they were nobody wanted to read at the moment anyway, shutting the place seemed the prudent thing to do.

One mage, as always, was not at the meeting. Librarian Beneshiel sat at the desk staring into the semi darkness. She never went to meetings, even the compulsory ones, and no knights or other mages ever considered forcing her to attend. She was forgotten, as a librarian she was more often thought of as a lay sister than a mage and, for most of her time here that was how she liked it. Now though, as a succession of myriad disorderly thoughts tumbled through her mind, she was just starting to wonder if this status quo was really worth maintaining.

She was still feeling ashamed of herself. That night (was it really only

LAST night?), after she had sensed the malevolence stirring underneath them she had been asked to render assistance, Gytha might have been in trouble, the girl who had taken time and trouble to try and befriend her may have been in mortal peril. And her response? She had told them to fetch Eubolo and then she had fled. She had returned to her chambers and let others deal with the situation. She had come here, climbed into her bed, pulled her blanket over her head, and cursed herself, again and again. And once she had finished cursing she still felt no better.

Eubolo had come to her, late in the morning, to tell her that Gytha was alive, but that Tola was not, otherwise even now she would still not know what happened. And that was the problem was it not? She had run, partly out of fear, partly out of cowardice but mostly she did not want the collection of junior mages, knights, and lay brothers that she was bound to bump into if she had stayed, she did not want them to see her face, her scars. Her desire for concealment was now so strong it was destroying her morality; she would rather have let a friend die than have some moon-faced novice gawp at her.

It just had to stop.

She had always felt some disdain for those that revelled in self-pity, those maudlin sorts that shook their fist at the world, often through an alcoholic haze and yet now, after what life and the Gods had thrown at her she had become its monument, its own living saint. Statues could be carved of her fit to adorn the hall of the saints at Codona; Beneshiel, the patron of self-pity, paragon of those who wandered through life feeling sorry for themselves, what a pathetic parody of a human being she had become. People lost children, watched helplessly as they slipped away in front of them, and they still carried on. They had to. What gave her the right to play martyr, the only person to ever really hurt her was her own self. Well no, this could not continue. She could not live like this anymore. It all had to change and there was only one person who could affect that change. She had lived for nearly a third of her life this way and it was suffocating her. She had told Gytha that she would try and end her exile within an exile and that she would do so in a series of small steps.

Well, now was the time to take that first step. She stood and walked to her room, returning a few moments later with a large heavy book which she placed on one of the reading lecterns. A second trip and she returned with an oil lamp, a candle, and a small copper bowl. The bowl was placed above the book, the candle and lamp were both lit and placed either side. Then she opened the book at a page marked by a strip of black cloth and felt in her waist pouch, pulling out a couple of dried leaves which she crumbled into the bowl. That done she took a deep breath, found the relevant passage in the book, and started to read aloud.

For that evening, for the first time in a decade, Beni the librarian was going to attempt a major spell.

She was not worried about being detected, everybody else had more important things on their minds, besides, should another mage sense that someone was drawing power from the magical plane then the last person they would think responsible for it was her. She was a nobody these days, an image she was solely liable for. An image that she now wanted to shatter into a thousand pieces.

She continued to read, passing her hand over the shallow bowl before finally keeping it there, her palm turned upwards. Shortly after a nimbus of pale blue energy started to coalesce above her hand.

Beni smiled. So far it had been easy.

Now her chanting became firmer, more confident. "Tashin lakasianta, tashin kolathne, tashika lorosome, tashtra motomne…" she chanted, and all the time the ball of light grew. And as it grew it seemed to solidify, become more intense. And from it tendrils of white mist started to float. Beni now knew that if she put her hand into that blue sphere it would freeze solid and that if she directed that same ball to pass through the body of a man, or of several men, it would shatter their hearts in place. She changed its shape a little, stretching it, then compressing it. She moved it here and there, to the centre of the library, then so that it floated over her desk, then the far bookshelves before having it stand not ten feet away from her, hovering at a level slightly higher than her head. The globe of freezing death, an advanced frost mage spell only a true master of battle could conjure. And after a decade's abstinence she had summoned it, the thought almost made her salivate.

"Denadathran!" she finally commanded, clapping her hands together with a small triumphal giggle.

The ball shrunk to the size of an apple, turned blacker than a starless night, before disappearing completely. Then, with the ring of a thousand tiny silver bells, countless fragments of ice, the largest no bigger than her fingernail, fell the floor in front of her.

Then Beni really did laugh, a sweet, full bodied musical sound that had become totally alien in this sterile space, a sound she had barely uttered in all her years of isolation.

"Well what do you know?" she finally said, "you never, ever lose it."

Beni, mistress of frost magic, had returned.

A knight is reborn also

Sir Beverley was on the chase, and he had never felt more elated. He had thought that his veins had atrophied, the blood congealed within his body but no, he had been wrong. A long dormant spark within him had flared into life again, brighter than a thousand suns. He had ridden the wagon across the Isle of Tears with six other knights, Sir Welton and Sir Nikolaj amongst them. It had bounced and careered along the main path, jarring their bones, throwing them around like dice in a cup before depositing them next to the bridge, this after a skidding halt that almost pitched all of them into the sea. The other knights, the younger men, were moaning like washer women but not Sir Beverley. He was awake, alive, the journey and the clear salt air whipping past his ears had done something that a buttery full of wine casks could not.

He leapt off the wagon and tore over the bridge as fast as his long limbs could carry him leaving the others behind. Granted, they were for the most part in full armour whereas he was wearing his padded black shirt with the silver thorn emblem stitched into it, but no matter. He was giving them over twenty years each and yet was still leading them.

Once on the Isle of Healing they had to ascend a long, gently sloping ridge before starting a barely discernible decline that lead them down, slowly down, to the harbour and the hospital. Once atop that ridge the whole island would be there for them to see. The island and any of its mages that were up to no good.

"Come on lads!" Sir Beverley exhorted his followers, "can't you keep up with an old man?" He started to lumber uphill with his loping strides, sword swinging from the belt at his side. Behind him he could hear them, cursing, swearing, sweating, armour clanking, leather creaking, mail clinking, the cream of the order, they were gaining on him, but he would still breast the ridge first.

And he did. His face was red and damp, his shirt was sticking to his skin, the cool early evening breeze off the sea made him shiver. He had beaten his lads and his tearing lungs were a price well worth paying.

Sir Welton joined him finally, almost sweating as much as he was. It took Sir Beverley a few moments before he could speak, give orders.

"Sir Walton, you have a young man's eyes, is there anything to see down there?"

Sir Welton shielded his eyes and stared at the vista, a gentle green land amongst an endless grey sea. He looked at the hospital, he looked at the harbour and the sand beach nearby, he looked at the path between them. Then at last he spoke.

"There!" he shouted. "A group of people, walking to the harbour, maybe a dozen, maybe two."

Sir Nikolaj had joined them. "About eighteen people, half in mage robes, a mixture of men and women. Looks like they are making for the ship. They will be there in minutes. We will have to move quickly if we are to cut them off."

"The silly sods," Sir Beverley said between ragged gasps; "they really are going to do it."

He looked around at the expectant faces of the knights. "Well you heard the man," he encouraged them. "We need to move. Now! And Keth burn any of you who stops for breath before we catch them!"

****

The hound sees the hare

"You whoreson dog!" Captain Fuller snarled at Oskum; "I will remember your face son, don't you worry, I will remember it." He held the mage with a glare that could shatter steel.

Oskum though seemed completely unperturbed. He was smiling, though to Iska, it seemed a fixed expression, a wax facsimile. She felt sure that she could tear that face off so she could see the real expression underneath, the one the other mages held, the expression of uncertainty, the fear that they had stepped over that boundary, that no matter what happened now their transgressions would warrant punishment of some sort.

Oskum seemed to sense this. "Fan out!" he ordered his followers. "Surround the sailors and lead them to the ship. We cannot go back now, we cannot surrender, at the very least it will be the whipping post for all of us."

There were a mere eight sailors there, not enough to crew the rowing stations should the wind fail. Another part of the plan that now depended on the caprice of the gods, hopefully the current breeze would not let up till they were well away from here. The sailors were a rugged, grizzled bunch, they had all drawn their dirks when Oskum had first approached them and told them of his plan. He had had to quell them, and he did so the only way he knew how, the way he was still doing. His right arm was outstretched, palm open towards the sailors. And that palm glowed green, a deep rich green darker than emerald. Thin, snaking tendrils the colour of coal moved and shifted around it. He was using his power, his magic as the superstitious called it, for it was the only thing he had to subdue the sailors, men far stronger, tougher, and worldly than either he or his companions.

And to his relief, it worked. The men had thrown down their weapons and so far had allowed themselves to be led to the harbour. But the captain of the men was not so easily cowed. He had growled and threatened Oskum all the way, to the extent that Oskum had now ordered the sailors surrounded, and had allowed the green fire to increase, the power to swell, so that it now clouded his entire arm.

Iska was quite alarmed by this, as she stood between Oskum and Dicken in the surrounding circle. Unlike the sailors she could sense the power Oskum was using. Initially it was of little concern, a light show designed to cow the ignorant. But, as the captain continued to bait him he had increased the power by degrees, it was fuelled by his anger and fear and was now a malign and dangerous force, one that would not be controlled easily. She tried to catch his eyes, to see whether madness or reason was in control of his mind, but in that she failed, Oskum it seemed was too wrapped up in his own strategies to pay her heed. However, she was finally noticed, but this time it was by another man entirely.

"You!" Captain Fuller shouted, "you, you silly girl! What are you doing with this bunch of Uba touched lunatics? You know you will all be caught, and all of you will be punished, probably executed. You are too young for that girl, don't you think? Besides, even if you get to this island of yours, what then? A girl like you surrounded by lustful men with no knights to control them? A few days of that and I'll wager you will barely be able to walk..."

"Enough!" Oskum shouted at him, the magic flaring dangerously around his arm and head. "Shut up and keep walking!"

"Oho!" Fuller did not shut up. "I think I have landed on something. She is your little strumpet then, yours and soon to be everybody else's..."

"Enough!" Oskum screamed at him. He stopped walking, as did everybody else, then turned to face Fuller, the green light about him swirling wildly. Iska saw his eyes then, his blazing eyes and she saw that there was no reason there at all.

"Oskum!" she found her voice at last. "Don't do it! don't hurt him! we need him, and he knows it. He is trying to provoke you, can't you see?"

She looked at him imploringly and at last his anger, and the power about him, started to subside. "Keep walking," he finally said to Fuller; "and I will remember you too captain, and you will be punished for your recalcitrance, when the time is right, you will be punished."

They started to walk again but had trod barely a handful of steps before one of the mages at the head of the circle let out a cry of terror.

"The knights!" he pointed to the top of the ridge to the east. "The knights have found us!"

They all looked and saw the truth in the mage's words. Over half a dozen armed and armoured men running towards them, low sun glinting off armour as they descended the east ridge, running towards them at speed.

Oskum spat into the grass and exchanged glances with Iska. At last she could see that he was as fearful as her. But it was too late. Too late for all of them. A few words and the power around him started to flare up again.

"To the ship!" he called to all of them, "to the ship, as fast as your legs can carry you!"

****

Seeing the good in all things

It would be maybe half an hour before the sun went down. On the Isle of Tears the sun bathed the wind blasted grass with its darkling fire, covering the landscape in a hundred shades of ochre. On the Isles northern coast, just past they base of the great college steps a few stone benches had been set into the grass and mud next to the monolithic cliffs, where the mages could sit and stare at the sea, and just maybe, on a good day, the distant purple-black shorelines of Tanaren, a great country that from here, looked as though it could sit in the palm of one's hand.

Kessie and Soma occupied one of these benches now, the fog of that morning already a distant memory. For once Soma wasn't talking, preferring to gaze at the wheeling gulls as they rode on cushions of air, spying the shifting seas for signs of silvery fish.

"Most people here hate them you know," Kessie said, with a certain absent detachment.

"Sorry?" Soma replied.

"The gulls. They are just seen as noisy, aggressive, vermin here, not even good to eat, though most would happily consume one of their eggs without complaining."

"And you see them differently?"

"I do," Kessie nodded. "The first thing is people lump them all in to one collective group and just call them "the gulls". But there are many different sorts you see. Everyone knows the big grey and white ones but there are similar ones that are smaller and whose head feathers in the summer are totally black. Then there are the ones with two pronged tail feathers, little black and white ones with red beaks, others with long necks with yellow feathers, the list is almost endless. And when you study one close up, even one of the big ones you are struck by how beautiful they are and that they are masterpieces, true creations of the Gods every bit as much as we are."

"They can be very cruel to each other."

"And people can't?"

Soma nodded at that statement. They were both silent again for a brief time until Kessie felt something brush against her legs. It was a cat, a stocky black and white one with greying whiskers and just one eye. Kessie smiled and leaned forward to stroke it, eliciting an instant purr.

"Hello One-eye," she cooed at the animal, "Elsa fed you yet?"

The cat continued to purr before transferring its attentions to Soma who also stroked it, though with slightly less enthusiasm. "Imaginative name," she quipped.

"Cheris gave it to him," Kessie stated, "she used to fuss over them terribly. There were four of them she looked after but one died a year or two back. Cheris was so upset, she even cried. It is why I feed them but try not to get too close. They don't live long, and I know that, if I did get too attached, that when they died, I would be really...choked. I would rather not have to go through that in truth. Besides, it is equating animals with people, you must think our priorities are all over the place. Silly mages and their misplaced affections."

"Not at all," Soma stopped stroking the cat who swiftly returned to Kessie. "But I think you are wrong in your assertion. You want to withhold affection from something because you are afeard about the day it dies? Let me tell you something, it is not the day before you meet the thing you love that matters, nor is it the day you lose that self-same thing. What is really important is the bit in between, however long, or short it may be. There are water flies that hatch, love, and lay their eggs all in one day. Then they all die. It is terrible to think that they die so soon but by the Gods, what a day that one day must be! Do not look at the beautiful clear lake without ever diving in and do not regard the decorated cake for fearing to bite it and spoil that decoration. Participate Kessie; you may suffer pain, you may suffer loss and sadness, but you will also feel joy and wonder, your heart will soar like one of those birds. Participate sweetie, you will never regret it."

Kessie smiled, reached down, and stroked the cat even more vigorously. "You are being more wise than mad today," she said, "though I think a lot of what you say and do is a pretence, something to make you seem a lot less clever than you actually are."

"So says somebody who has just revealed her own innate wisdom maybe." Soma stood and stretched as two great gulls, feathers cerise in the sunset glow, swooped just a few feet over her head. "And her passion for nature of course, who would have thought you a lover of all those screaming birds?"

Kessie stood too, giving the cat a final tickle under the chin. She stared at the streaky sky and the tiny sliver of moon, barely discernible at the moment, a minute silver tear in a face the size of infinity.

"Night will be here soon," she said to Soma, "and the evening bell. Come on, let's see if there is anything left to eat."

They began climbing the steps; through the college windows the fires of the chandeliers were beginning to flicker and behind them the cat set to licking its haunches before it too set to finding a warm place to sleep.

****

Nerves tighter than harp strings

"Hold right there! You can run no further! Surrender yourselves and we may yet be merciful!"

Nobody could bellow like Sir Beverley. His voice carried over the grass to the fleeing mages and their captives, before carrying on to the nearby ship and the ocean beyond. Above it the sky was close to purple, the stars were beginning to blink in and out, senior mage Oskum's hope of an hours sailing before night fall was appearing more fanciful by the minute. Dragging the reluctant sailors with them had slowed their march exponentially. And by now Iska was truly frightened.

The mages were maybe just one minute from the wooden jetty, where the galley rose and fell on a sea which was getting choppier as the wind increased in proportion to the darkness. And it was a cold wind, an autumnal wind, a keen wind, a wind that caused sweating skin to shiver and bile to rise in dry, nervous throats. They were a minute away from the jetty, but the knights were gaining fast.

The harbour was a wide, shallow bay, with a beach of pale sand at its sheltered west side. They were heading for the eastern side, where the curving stretch of land was clothed in long, thick, grass, and uneven ground that could easily turn the ankle of the unwary. Several wooden jetties were built out into the sea with the nearest being the longest, the one that accommodated the largest ships. As the sea was so shallow here it was, of necessity, a lengthy construction, planking secured on to wooden piles, with nets, barrels and storage sacks obstructing its entire length. And at its end was their goal, the ship, a twin masted galley, their goal, their escape, their final hope.

Oskum looked ahead to the ship, then to his right, where the knights were closing in, running over the long grass, close enough now for him to hear the sound of their mail. He had to make a judgement, and he had to make it now.

He called to Dicken, who dropped back to listen to him, Iska also being close enough to hear their words. "By the time we get everybody into the ship, get the oars set or the sails up AND free the moorings they will be upon us. Take everybody to the ship Dicken, keep Iska close to you, I will stand between you and the knights, offer myself up as bait."

"You will let them take you?" Dicken said in shock.

Oskum gave him a knowing smile. "No, my friend, I have a plan. Trust in Lucan and in me." He held up a pouch at his waist, "the stuff in here should help put them off. Now go, we have no time to talk!"

"What are you going to do?" Iska's large eyes were shining lamps. "Lissa's blood Oskum, please don't do anything stupid."

Oskum briefly put his hand out to softly caress her cheek. "Just trust me and get to the ship. Oh and if the sailors cause trouble, show them the power you can wield."

Iska did not reply, letting Dicken lead her away without protest. Oskum allowed himself the indulgence of gazing after her for a moment before leaving the path to tread onto the yielding grass, heading towards the knights, who seemed if anything to be picking up speed as they ran.

As Iska continued to look back she saw him start to chant and walk in a circle, scattering some silver grey powder from the pouch on to the ground as he did so. She sensed the power he was starting to unlock, a lot of power, he was pushing himself to his limit, maybe even beyond it, but what exactly was he trying to achieve?

Then she felt something different under her feet. Planking, wooden planking. She was on the jetty. Ahead of her was the ship, one last spurt and they would be there, one last spurt with the sea lapping either side of her and the spray soaking the hem of her robe and soft shoes, which were already stained green by the grass. Dicken smiled at her, she could hear the sailors behind her grumble and threaten, but she only had eyes for Oskum.

He had finished his chanting and was no longer scattering the contents of the pouch. He started to run towards the jetty, his face was yellow and sweating, sickly and weak, she had been right about him overexerting himself. But his eyes were burning, a fire of passion, desire, or madness, he seemed delighted with what he had just done.

Then he stopped and turned to face the knights. They would be upon him in a matter of moments. To her surprise he started to wave his arms and shout at them, making sure they could see him in the encroaching darkness.

"I am here!" he called, "I am the leader of the rebels and I defy you! Come and take me captive if you dare! I am here, come and get me!"

Iska shook her head and bit her lip. She could see the leader of the knights, he was close enough now for her to see that his face was sweating, that his eyes were cold and triumphal, and then he turned towards Oskum and pulled his sword from its scabbard...

****

A sweet song and a coarse rejoinder

A watery sunlight filtered through the sole window and onto the cooking pot under the fire. It was late afternoon, a little cold, the door, and shutters would be closed soon. It would leave the house in a despondent sort of gloom, a gloom that fortunately would be somewhat alleviated by both the fire and the light filtering through the chimney hole above her. Gytha looked up at it, seeing the tendrils of blue smoke dissipating through it, smelling the burning wood and the pottage, which was now almost heated. She was hungry, her stomach rumbled, and for once there was meat in the pottage, rabbit, nearly cooked rabbit, she salivated, she was so hungry. She shook her head, shook her fiery curls to get the burrs out of them. She had been playing in the bracken with her brothers and sisters, the ones too young to work. They were with her now, blond Sigurd with his runny nose, Lyofa with his grazed knees and slender little Frya, as red haired as Gytha but nowhere near as robust. It was Gytha who protected her, fought, and beat the boys who teased her. Nobody bullied Gytha, no one dared, and how old was she? Six? Maybe seven. No older certainly.

They were all excited, garrulous, high, reedy voices competing with each other until mother silenced them the way only a mother could.

"If you want food you will have to be quiet first!"

She looked at them all in turn, but Gytha only recalled it when she looked at her. She smiled, a warm smile in that drawn face, a smile Gytha returned in kind. Mother had long hair, fair and grey in equal part, and piercing blue eyes, an attribute her daughter had inherited. She seemed aware that the silence would not last and so pre-empted it by bursting into song, a song all her children lustily sang along with.

"As the sun shines brightly in the sky
The men let work fall idly by
And leave the fields go brown and die
To dance the reel at Thetta
O, they danced till their feet were sore

O, they pranced both rich and poor
Dance they did till they could no more
All at the reel at Thetta

As the sun shines brightly in the sky
The girls let work fall idly by
The cook fires just go cold and die
As they dance the reel at Thetta
O, they danced till their feet were sore
O, they pranced both rich and poor
Dance they did till they could no more
All at the reel at Thetta

Now the night fires they are glowing
Meals need cooking, fields sowing
So tired and happy all are going
From the reel at Thetta
O, they had danced till their feet were sore
O, they had pranced both rich and poor
Dance they had and could do no more
All at the reel at Thetta. "

The memories of her past had never felt more tangible as Gytha finished singing to little Edith. She didn't know why she had chosen such a happy, boisterous song but she had loved it as a child and though Edith was younger now than she was then, she obviously hoped the little girl would feel the same way about it.

And she seemed to. She smiled at Gytha and put her tiny arms out for a hug, a hug that Gytha gladly gave her. She held the tiny body close and was surprised to find tears stinging the corner of her eyes. Such a sweet little girl, how could the Gods even think of tearing her from this world? But they could of course, and it would not be the first time. Consumption had been the way they had done it to Frya, just two years after Gytha came to the island. She had heard about the death of her sister some four months after the occurrence, from a knight who had been in the area, her family being illiterate and unable to write to her. How the Gods decided these things was beyond her understanding, they could be so cruel, so very cruel, she would gladly have died in Frya's place.

"Did you enjoy the song my sweet darling?" Fedrica was standing just behind her and spoke over her shoulder.

Edith nodded. "Yes mother," she replied in her tiny voice.

Gytha stood back and let the child's mother tuck her in, pulling the coverlet up to her chin. The two women then sat in silence for a while until they could hear the little girl breathing softly in her sleep. It was, after the events of the day, an uncomfortable silence finally broken when Fedrica leaned over to whisper to her. "You have a good way with children."

"I do?" Gytha was surprised.

"Yes. You are a natural. Do you teach the children here?"

She shook her head. "No. My friend Miriam does though. She enjoys it. She says that she enjoys being bossy with them."

"Why don't you join her."

"No," she said firmly, "I would just indulge them. They are all older than Edith and well, I would just...I wouldn't be suitable, that is all."

"You would want to be a mother to them."

Caswell's hand on her stomach, her head swimming with the drug, the smell of blood, the fear, the cold fear, one less child to be buffeted by the whims of the Gods. Do not think of it, push it out of your mind Gytha, push it out.

"Maybe," Gytha nodded, "maybe."

"Does it bother you, not being able to have children?" Fedrica was applying her usual bluntness, though whether her intent this time was borne out of curiosity or malice Gytha could not tell.

"Yes, I suppose it does. I came from a big family and mother loved children; I suppose I have inherited some of those feelings from her. But the Gods had other plans for me, few people get touched by Lucan after all, and because I am one of those few I never want for food, and I have had an education any noblewomen would be envious of. We only have limited control of our destinies it seems."

"Indeed. It does seem unfair though, if Lucan touches you with magic surely it would be reasonable for him to remove all your carnal lusts and desires at the same time. Yet he does not."

"No he does not. We are the same as you in every respect bar the one."

"Yes." Fedrica had a habit of either fidgeting with her ear or some part of her dress before asking an awkward question. She was fidgeting with her dress right now.

"And fornication is banned here. This place must be seething with suppressed...longing, must it not?"

"You are possibly overstating it. We are used to the way things work in

91

this place. When the sun goes down we are confined to our cells till dawn. It is the perfect time to deal with any such…longing… we might have."

Fedrica gave a tiny laugh. "That is refreshingly honest of you."

"Well I am a peasant girl; obfuscation does not come naturally to me."

"I suppose not. Surely though there must be times when you desire the intimate company of others?"

It was Gytha's turn to laugh. "Of course, and there are ways of dealing with that too. But my lady there is really no need for you to make a second attempt to warn me off your husband. You made your point perfectly clearly the first time. Not that any warning needed to be made," she added hastily, and untruthfully, though lying to Fedrica troubled her conscience but little.

Fedrica though persisted. "Yes, but if intimacy…"

And, like a dry twig under a heavy boot, Gytha felt her patience snap at last. She had tried, for Steven's sake she had tried but Fedrica had made one attempt too many to rile her. And at last she had succeeded. As she spoke Gytha's only surprise was that she kept her voice low enough so that Lady Edith would not be woken by her.

"As you seem so keen to know the details of my personal intimacies I shall have to oblige you. Am I a virgin? No. Do I love the salt taste of a man's hot secretions on my tongue? Yes. Do I love sticking my rump in the air as I am pounded from behind, serviced as the mare is by the stallion? Yes. Do I scream like a dog at the moon when I take pleasure from a man? Definitely. Have I done any of these things with your husband? No, no, and no again. I hope my answers satisfy your curiosity and fear not, I will not prevail upon you to confide your own personal predilections on this subject. Common stock I may be, but I know when a question crosses the bounds of polite enquiry. And that my lady is how a peasant girl talks of fornication, I hope your ears have not melted in the telling."

"Er…quite." It was dark now, the room lit only by one lamp and two candles, but Gytha did not need to see Fedrica's face. She could feel it burning even from where she was sitting.

"Quite," Fedrica said again before falling silent. She fidgeted with her dress, then with her ear, then her dress again. And finally Gytha afforded herself the slightest of smiles.

At last, at long last, she had shut the Lady Fedrica up.

****

A deadly and terrible power

Iska was shivering. The sun had all but disappeared and the temperature next to the choppy seas was dropping sharply. As she stood on the jetty the swirling wind tugged at her robe, pulling it tight around her legs before whipping it away again. She could not feel her fingers and there was a metallic taste in her mouth that had nothing to do with the cold but everything to do with the fear that was rising inexorably inside her. She looked across to where Oskum had been preparing whatever sorcery he felt was necessary to keep the knights at bay. What had he planned she wondered? He had told her nothing in their short acquaintance, nothing past his own desire to get away from here. He had not confided in her, she had no idea as to his ability as a mage, she had noticed nothing outstanding about him in that respect at all. They had both needed somebody to draw comfort from, that was as far as things had gone with them. Maybe he was trying to protect her by keeping things from her, but why?

He had finished baiting the knights and was now turning to run towards the jetty. She had large eyes, keen eyes, and despite the encroachment of night upon the land she could see enough of him to trouble her even further.

He was ashen pale, sweaty, his pallor sickly, the strain of the spell he had prepared had exhausted him. He half staggered towards them and as he did so he wiped something away from his nose. She knew instinctively that it was blood, a sign that he had pushed himself beyond his capabilities. They all did it at some point, all of them had experienced the mages bleed, a haemorrhage borne of overestimating their own abilities. Most knew the signs and knew when to stop but, in some cases the bleed could be fatal. Oskum did not look like there was blood coming from his eyes or ears, so it seemed he had not gone too far in his conjuring. But he had cast something powerful, something dangerous, and the knights were heading for the patch of ground he had ensorcelled.

How could they be so stupid? She wondered. But of course they didn't know, they couldn't sense a mages power, all they had seen was Oskum running around in a circle and shouting at them. They probably thought he had gone mad, that their parlous situation had pushed him over the edge, in truth she had been thinking the same this last half hour so why would not they? Oskum was their target, and they were gaining on him, and that patch of ground lay directly between them and him. To Iska it felt like watching a blind man at a cliff edge, she knew something terrible was about to happen, but she was completely incapable of doing anything to stop it. She could only watch, impotent, helpless, as Oskum's trap was finally sprung.

The lead knight, an older man, was at the head of the pursuers. One other knight was close to him with the remainder being a few feet behind. And it was that distance that probably saved their lives.

She heard the lead knight bellow at them again. "Hold still! All of you!

Your plan has failed!" She heard Oskum calling to Dicken. "Get to the ship! Get Iska to the ship!" She heard the other knights shouting, their words unintelligible, they could be telling the mages to stop, they could have been warning the commander. But she had no time to try and understand them, to consider things rationally.

For at the same time the earth under the lead knight's feet erupted in a pillar of green fire.

Soil and grass were ripped from the ground and thrown twenty, thirty feet into the air. There was a loud crack and a shockwave that caused them all to stop their ears. Iska then realised that the second knight, the one just behind the commander had also been catapulted to the skies, thrown upwards just as easily as the soil had been, she heard his cry of shock and horror as he plummeted back to earth, landing with a crash of armour and a crack of bone, rolling over a couple of times before lying still.

Iska gasped, the mages around her gasped, even the sailors gasped as the implications of Oskum's trap dawned on them. A knight was grievously injured, possibly even dead, what had been a bold, foolhardy, maybe naïve escape attempt was suddenly so much more, possibly treason, possibly murder. The mages needed to get to the ship right now, the wrath of the knights was too terrible to contemplate, but there was still more to come.

The pillar of sickly green fire was diminishing rapidly, soon it would be nothing but embers and a circular patch of scorched, lifeless earth. But right now it was still there, coruscating, somehow swirling independently of the wind, a bilious, writhing inferno, a column of twisting, tormented power. And then, from its heart, something terrible emerged.

It took Iska a second or two to realise that this was the commander of the knights, Oskum's closest pursuer. Yet now he was something else, barely a man at all, more like a vision from a painting of Keth's underworld. From head to toe he was charred and black, clothes indistinguishable from flesh, like a statue carved from polished coal. But the statue was smoking, the flesh shrivelling, the skull and bones were slowly exposed under this unholy fire. He continued toward Oskum with his arm outstretched, and as Iska watched she saw the arm wither under the clinging flame, the flesh disintegrate as limb became little more than a series of blackened bones, muscle vaporised, skin turned to powder. Now the man was little more than a shambling skeleton, by all the laws of the gods he should be dead, yet still he came towards Oskum, still he reached out for him, though his eyes had gone, and he had no throat, lips, or gums to call out from. This ghastly spectacle persisted, time seemed to freeze around them, even

Oskum had stopped to watch, transfixed by the horror he had unleashed. The blackened knight got closer and closer to him before he finally collapsed at his feet, a pile of smoking corpse bones, all clothes, blood, flesh, and hair burned clean off and turned to ash, ash sent billowing around them by the persisting wind.

Then, at last, the green fire died and finally, finally, after years of hoping and waiting, Sir Beverley was with his family once more.

****

The wolf enters the fold

"Gods help us, Artorus protect us, Elissa preserve our souls..." Iska was praying like she had never prayed before. Oskum was running again, half bent with exhaustion, loping over the long grass till he finally gained the jetty. But the knights were still there. They had stopped, stopped to look at the havoc the mage had wreaked, to look at the bodies of the dead, or dying. But their gaze had soon shifted, from their fallen to the mage who had caused them to fall. Their weapons were drawn, and they were screaming at Oskum, close enough now for Iska to hear their words.

"You murdering bastard! Stop and face our justice! You and your fanatics are doomed!"

The mages, including Iska, had been frozen in place as the tragedy unfolded before them. Now though it was they who were in peril, they who were in line for retribution, and there was no greater spur to haste than naked terror.

Iska, and her fellows, turned and ran.

She looked to her left, to her relief she saw she was there, that the prow of the galley, painted with the eye of Hytha, was right next to her. Dicken, the only mage ahead of her, was lifting the gangplank and placing it over the water and onto the ship. The ship was rocking markedly, the sea under the piles and planking of the jetty was foaming white, the traverse from jetty to ship would be a precarious one but right now Iska didn't care, she just wanted to get on board. She would burn away the mooring ropes herself if she had to, anything, anything, to keep the knights away from her.

The plank was as secure as it could be, Dicken turned to face the approaching mages and sailors, ready to exhort them into one final burst of speed. He opened his mouth to call out to them, but the words never came. For two things happened almost simultaneously; firstly he heard an impact behind him, something had jumped onto the jetty with a heavy thud and a ring of tempered steel, secondly he saw Iska's face, her huge eyes, her dark eyes,

95

betraying a degree of horror that was even surpassing his own.

Something was behind him.

He turned to see what it was.

Sir Vargo was standing there. He was smiling. His sword was raised high in the air. There was just a couple of feet between the two men and Dicken thought, as he gazed into those pitiless eyes, that if Xhenafa was possessing anybody it was possessing the man standing before him. He contemplated using his power but there was no time to think of a suitable spell, let alone cast it, he was utterly at the mercy of this armoured knight.

But Sir Vargo was not known for being merciful.

He was part of an aristocratic family was Sir Vargo, and his sword reflected this. It was forged from Derannen steel, the blade folded dozens of times so that it bore an intricate mesh pattern across its entire length. The guard was studded with small rubies and the head of the pommel bore a single white diamond, a family heirloom indeed. In the Edrington family for centuries, it had vanquished the occupying Chirans, destroyed the rebels at the battle of the Blood-Soaked Banner and, most recently, sent the Arshuman invaders running for their very lives. And it was sharp, sharp as only a true weapon of war could be, and Sir Vargo whetted it every day.

A year or two ago a man had made a wager with him. They had taken four Arshuman prisoners to one side, so that their own men could not see what they were doing and put their money down. Could they, with one blow, divide a man in half from head to pelvis. Four men, two attempts each, a bag of coin for the winner. But for Sir Vargo the money was not important, the thrill was in the challenge, in the attempt rather than in the outcome. Nevertheless he had won the money.

He thought of that wager now, as he brought his sword down, passing it through air, through Dicken's skull, through his throat and diaphragm, separating the lungs until he felt it shear into the hip bone, at which point he twisted it and pulled it free. Not a complete division this time, but that hardly mattered.

Iska watched Dicken's body shatter into a spray of blood, bone, and brain. She saw the spilling of his viscera onto the jetty, and she stood helplessly as she was drenched in a shower of tissue and ordure, her face and the top of her robe becoming caked in the remains of the dead man. She touched her face, as the twitching, pulped corpse crashed on to the jetty, then looked at her hands, heard the blood dripping from the tips of her hair, felt the ooze sticking her robe to her skin. And then, she passed the point of final endurance.

She gazed unseeingly at her bloody hands and screamed. She emptied her lungs with her screaming. She screamed fit to shatter the wind and boil away the sea, she screamed at the shivering moon and the fitful stars, and she screamed most of all at the figure of death that was approaching her.

Sir Vargo too had a bloodied face, but this did not seem to trouble him at all. He stepped over the heap of twitching flesh till he was right next to Iska. She still screamed though, even as he tilted her face upwards to look at his, forcing her eyes, her white, terror strewn eyes to look into his own.

Then Sir Vargo smiled at her.

The zealot metes out his justice

Sir Vargo looked down. He was off the ship. For the first time in days he was standing on something that did not move and sway as Hytha, Goddess of the seas, willed. He was of course breaking an order, he was forbidden to set foot on either island but then he had just thwarted an escape attempt, surely he would be given some latitude, maybe it would be seen at last that he was no pariah, he was a hero.

And that silly girl was still screaming.

She did not know him of course, she did not though that he obeyed the knights' code scrupulously, and part of the code called for a fair and proportionate treatment of women. So he was hardly going to kill her now, was he?

Instead he reversed his grip on his gore streaked sword and smashed her full in the face with both pommel and iron gloved fist. She crumpled on to the jetty with both hands covering her face and now some of the blood oozing between her fingers was no longer Dicken's, it was her own. For Sir Vargo this tactic worked, the girl stopped her infernal screaming, replacing it with some sort of tearful whimper that was much easier on the ears.

He forgot her in an instant, stepping past her to view the rest of the mages. They were a sorry rabble, utterly cowed by his bloody dispatch of one of their number and now they had no will to escape at all. He stood at one end of the jetty and the other knights were at last crowding on to the other end. The mages could either jump into the sea or try and go through him, and Sir Vargo surmised that they had no fight left in them to take him on. He had to seize the moment.

"All of you," he spoke in clear, calculating tones, "both hands in the air where I can see them, and no talking. Any attempt to cast and I will separate your head from your shoulders. I am Sir Vargo, Magebane, disobey me and I will introduce you to Xhenafa personally."

All hands shot up, though a couple of them hazarded a glance at their leader for clarification. They got none though for the man was exhausted, he could barely stand and now the knights were on him, Vargo saw a fist hit his ribcage before he was dragged off the jetty and thrown onto the neighbouring grass. It seemed that these knights were also in no mood to be merciful either.

He looked past the jetty and up the sloping headland where the lights of the hospital, its lanterns, candles, and chandeliers were showing softly through cracks in the shutters or the thick glass panels of the windows. Closer than that though, he could see flaming torches moving on the path between hospital and harbour. Though quite small at the moment he knew that they would grow quickly, for they were coming nearer and the path they were now on led in only one direction. Here. Other knights, they had to be and yet, before they arrived he was senior officer here, the situation was still his to control.

The remaining mages were shepherded off the jetty and on to the grass next to Oskum. Vargo separated them by sex then commanded them to lay face down on the ground with their hands stretched out behind them, over their back. The knights stood around them, swords drawn, pointing at their prostrate figures. Only one knight did not do so, he stepped off the jetty with his hands on the shoulders of the young girl Vargo had floored. Her face was still covered in blood.

"Sir Nikolaj, sir," the knight introduced himself. "I don't think this one can lie face down, her nose is broken, she will probably just choke on the blood. She may have lost a couple of teeth as well. Really I should get her to the healers."

"Not yet," Vargo replied, "put her on her knees, hands behind her. They all have to hear their sentence first."

Sir Nikolaj did not reply, contenting himself with leading the whimpering girl off to join her companions where she knelt without complaint. Four men, including the shivering Oskum and four women, including Iska, all of them utterly helpless under the blades of the knights and all knights were now looking at Vargo, to see what he would say, or do next.

"You all saw what they did to Sir Beverley," he started to growl before Sir Nikolaj chanced an interruption. "And Sergeant Welton sir, we all knew him better than Sir Beverley."

"Is he dead?"

Sir Nikolaj nodded.

"I am sorry. I did not know him myself, though I did know Sir Beverley. They both died as a knight should, in the pursuit of their holy calling and thanks to their sacrifice we have the miscreants captive. The question now is what to do with them and as the commanding officer here the judgement shall be mine." He looked to his left where four men lay face down in the grass, he looked to his right where three women lay face down with one other on her knees. He saw her spit some blood out of her mouth before shutting his dark eyes for a moment, inhaling the crisp, clear air, the aromas of grass, salt, and sea. Then he opened them again.

"The women can be put in chains and thrown in the cells, as can the injured one once the healers stop the bleeding. I would have their forefingers broken, a warning against future transgressions. As for the men…" he walked slowly past them before prodding Oskum with an iron shod toe. Oskum continued to shiver.

"The men are to be executed. We can do it now. Leave the leader to the end so he can see where his folly has led him."

With that a couple of the male mages started to stir in horror, to try and right themselves, to defend themselves now their fate was laid out so starkly before them. The knights responded by flooring them with the flats of their blades, adding a few stamps and kicks for good measure. Some of the women were sobbing, tears mingling with black, dense earth. Vargo waited till they were subdued before continuing.

"We will be civilised, make it quick, a heart thrust for each of them, even the murderer. Anyone here wish to carry out the sentence or will I have to do it myself?"

To Sir Nikolaj's surprise a couple of the knights nodded in the affirmative. They were all still in shock, they were all angry, but to have his friends succumb to primal blood lust so easily was something he had not expected. Nobody became a knight to partake in cold blooded execution after all. Or at least that was what he had thought. He was closer to Sir Welton than any of them and yet it was they who were afflicted by the thirst for revenge whereas he…he just felt utterly divorced from reality, as though he was watching a mummers play on Trageshnight, when the spirits of the dead broke through the void to walk the earth one more time. Sir Welton was dead, Sir Welton was dead, Sir Welton was dead, words, just words, no meaning, no impact, not yet, it would take time to hit him, as the deaths of close friends or family always did.

At the moment though he just felt numb, clasping his sword with nerveless fingers, a numbness that was not caused by the cold. He reached out and put his free hand on the bloodied girl's shoulder. She was still spitting blood on to the grass, but her body was now heaving less and shivering more. He could not keep her from punishment, but he could see her treated, cleaned up, her nose set, her scarred gums closed. She was old enough to know better than join this idiot escapade but even so, she was the youngest one here and he would do what he could for her. It would be important, he felt, to keep in touch with that human part of him over the days to come.

And maybe never more so than at this very moment. For the knights had selected their first victim. It was a senior mage in his early thirties, a lumpish, clumsy fellow of middling abilities called Ebden. He, like Oskum, was one of those mages who, once seniority was attained, just disappeared into the bowels of the college, assigned menial study task after menial study task, a man doomed to spend a lifetime copying other people's work, preparing and assisting in the experiments and castings of those with true ability. A mediocrity made flesh, an addendum to a footnote in the annals of college history, yet still a man, nonetheless. And there was no man or woman alive that did not dream, that did not hope, that did not aspire, that did not want for something else. It was easy to see what had brought him to this position.

For now though he was being dragged up off the ground like an over filled sack of grain. Hauled to his knees by three knights, hands still clasped behind his back. His head turned and bobbed drunkenly as he stared at each knight in turn with wild brown eyes stricken with panic. He wriggled and tugged against their iron gauntlets but was pinned in place soon enough. He felt rather than saw a knight move behind him, he knew what that knight was going to do and at last, at long last, despite the threats and orders of earlier that night he finally found his voice, though it was hoarse and incoherent. For he was a man trying to buy time, any time before his heart was split by a sliver of cruel steel.

"No!" he called out to all that would listen. "No! don't kill me! I have hurt nobody! I have threatened nobody! I did not know that power would be used on you! I would not have come if I had known that! And we weren't escaping, we were going to come back! I swear by Artorus and every god in the Pantheon! Spare me! In the name of mercy, spare me!"

Sir Vargo rolled his eyes, one of the knights placed his sword tip vertically behind the left shoulder ready to thrust it through the body, the heart specifically. Ebden felt the sharp point of the blade, the heavy force behind it ready to push, push. He screamed out one final "no!" in the hope the Gods would answer, but all he could hear was the thin wind, the swaying grass, the drunken waves, what did the Gods care for such as he?

The Gods may have been deaf to him, but somebody else, closer, more human, definitely was not. The command to kill had formed on Sir Vargo's lips, the knight, both hands on the sword hilt, stood, poised, frozen, waiting for it. Yet it was not Sir Vargo's command that he heard next.

"Hold sir! Put that sword down! I have given no order to end that man's life!"

Sir Steven was there at last. Flanked by two other knights each bearing a torch he fairly bounded over the tussocks, tumps, and tangling grass to get to them before any further mayhem could occur. He looked at the mages on the ground, he looked at the ship that was now tugging at its moorings in the teeth of the resurgent wind, he looked at the pile of blackened smouldering bones that had once been a knight and at the prone, unmoving body close by, and then he looked at the glittering eyes of Sir Vargo. He read the excitement, the malice, the unquenchable desire for vengeance, and then he finally spoke.

"Stand down Sir Roban and tell me what in the name of the furnace is going on here."

"The mages, the male ones, have been sentenced to death." Sir Vargo said dispassionately. "The evidence is there for all to see." He nodded towards the still smoking remains of Sir Beverley.

"Who are the dead?" Steven enquired of Nikolaj.

"Sir Beverley and...Sir Welton." The reply was subdued.

"What?" Steven gasped, his pale complexion becoming almost ghostly, "Nikolaj, come with me, tell me everything and you," he pointed at Sir Vargo, "no more killing, not till we talk."

"Of course, once you know everything, I am sure you will see my way of thinking."

Steven said nothing, striding up to where Welton lay as Nikolaj talked to him in frantic tones.

****

A battle of opposing wills

And Sir Welton was not dead. He lay still, eyes staring glassily at the enfolding sky. Steven crouched next to him, eased his helm off, then laid his sweat bathed head gently on to the soft grass. Welton choked a little, sending a fine spray of blood from his half opened mouth, then he twisted his face slightly and with great effort, started to speak.

"Sorry sir, one mistake too many eh. I saw the mage, I saw him circling, I knew he had done something bad but I still...I still..." He started to choke again. Steven lifted his head slightly till the coughing eased before settling him down once more.

"No my friend," Steven replied, "it is I who needs to apologise. I have never given you the credit you were due for your hard work and loyalty. We will get you to the healers, see what they can do for you."

Welton gave a choking laugh. "Nothing sir, they can do nothing. I cannot see the stars anymore; I cannot see you...or are you Xhenafa? There is something there...something...something."

Steven continued to kneel close to him until he was certain there was no life left in Welton's body. "Xhenafa guide you my friend and may the Gods give you peace," he said quietly before easing himself back to his feet and fixing

Nikolaj with a steely glare.

"Oskum did this?"

Nikolaj nodded.

"But no others were involved."

"No sir."

"Why were they trying to steal a ship? Where did they want to go?"

Nikolaj shrugged, "according to the fellow facing execution they were going to come back here eventually."

Steven looked to where the sailors stood next to their ship. He strode past Vargo and on to the jetty to speak to them. Captain Fuller told him what he knew; that they were being forced to sail to Sunbank Island.

"And they threatened you if you did not obey?"

"Yes sir," Fuller said; "well the one in charge did, he conjured a green fire in his hands. The others barely said a word."

"Thank you captain. It may be best if you spend the night in your ship. Apart from that everything is unchanged, you may leave in the morning, weather permitting."

"Thank you sir. What about...that, though."

He nodded towards the bloody carcass of mage Dicken. The planking of the jetty was soaked with gore and viscera and some gulls were already showing an interest, alighting at a safe distance from the men but close enough to both see and smell the prize any scavenger would want to claim.

"I will organise a detail to transport all of the bodies to the house of Xhenafa." Steven shook his head at the terrible sight. Unsurprisingly, the Isle of Healing also had one of these establishments, even mage healers had their failures. "In the meantime, get someone to keep the birds away." He looked up; Sir Vargo was staring right at him. "I am afraid though that I have other matters to attend to right now."

He returned to the knights and captive mages. As he did Sir Nikolaj went over to a much calmer Iska, placing a hand on her shoulder. The blood on her face, nose and hair had largely congealed but her nose and mouth were hurting as much as ever, a situation the dropping temperature did little to alleviate. They were also swelling nastily. Steven finally recognised her as one of the girls Mattris was trying to seduce the other day and committed the fact to memory. Now though he had orders to issue, and maybe, just maybe, a confrontation that he was not relishing the prospect of.

"Bind the hands of the prisoners," he said firmly; "then take them to the college cells. Nikolaj, take the prisoner Iska to the healers. Once they have seen her though she has to go to the cells also. This is a matter Knight Commander Shadan should decide upon."

He sensed a certain reluctance among the knights to comply with his orders, but that was as nothing compared to the reaction of Sir Vargo.

"I have already given an order," he said in granite hard tones, "and on this island, I am the senior officer, I certainly attained my rank long before you Steven, did I not?"

"You did," Steven agreed, "but Shadan has jurisdiction over both islands."

"Technically yes, but I believe in emergency situations the commanding officer in the field is allowed to make the key decisions. Shadan is one for delegation is he not?"

He smiled at Steven who did reciprocate, though his smile was utterly devoid of mirth. "He is like all senior officers yes. But what we have here is a situation that is now under control and so, as far as I am concerned, the fate of these mages is in his hands. Whatever he decides will have to be acted on swiftly, a situation like this cannot be allowed to fester."

Sir Vargo's smile vanished. "But I have been decisive. The men are to die, the women imprisoned, with a finger broken. We do it now and no mage will dare consider taking such treacherous action in the future."

"Have you forgotten Sir Vargo that just by standing on that patch of grass you are breaking the long standing order that you should never set foot on these islands? I am afraid that any order you issue here has no validity at all. Therefore it is I who is senior officer here and it is my orders that will be adhered to."

"Without my intervention Sir Steven," Vargo hissed like a spitting snake, "these sorry excuses for sorcerers would already be at sea by now and you would be having to explain to Shadan how they all disappeared on your watch!"

"On Sir Beverley's watch," Steven corrected him; "and he has already paid the price for his laxity. And do not think that I am not grateful for your part in this affair, I certainly am, but that part has been played out now. You should return to the ship, and I shall take over from here. I thank you for your "intervention"".

"Pup!" Sir Vargo scowled. "You are seeking to dismiss me? You are saying that I am good enough to slaughter Arshumans by the score yet somehow am incapable of being nursemaid to a mob of spoiled, cosseted, children! What right have you to send me skulking back to my kennel! You are inferior to me in seniority, in honours gained on the field, and in bloodline. Go back to your wet nurse's teat boy, your indulgence of these people has led to this crisis, and I am resolving it. In the only way it can be resolved, by making an example of those who laugh at our laws!"

Steven kept his reply cool and composed. "Nobody has been indulged on these islands Vargo, nobody. We have a unique situation here; a killer is running loose, striking whenever it pleases them, and these mages have allowed their fear to displace common sense. That is all. As for the personal insults, I could fling far harsher words at you, there is a reason after all that you are usually kept as far away from mages as can be contrived. There will be no more killing tonight, and none at all until Shadan has made his decision."

Sir Vargo smacked his lips, his sword was still drawn, and he ran his maimed free hand up and down the blood smeared blade, steel gauntlet sliding against steel. He regarded his sword for a moment, a look that Steven deemed to be affectionate, almost loving. "This place..." Vargo said finally, "you know what many people think of this...college, and the healers up yonder? They think it a sea of pestilence, a sink of moral depravity, they say the mages here are lazy, afforded every luxury and that they spend their days gorging on foods they have never laboured for, fornicating with anybody that catches their eye, writing thesis after thesis on how the world should be run for their benefit. People wonder if there is any need for mages, whether they should all be strangled once their power manifests itself. They are seen as the children of Keth, demons in human guise, sent to infiltrate this world, heralds for the final invasion of the God of the damned. And after witnessing the events of this terrible eve, I myself have some difficulty countering these arguments."

Steven shook his head and half laughed. "But counter them you would, for you are a Knight of the Thorn, sworn to protect these people from such base ignorance. You fight such prejudices with reason, do you really think that these people laying on the grass before us are demonic? That that girl whose face is coated in her own blood works for Keth? Utter fallacy Vargo, these are flesh and blood just as we are, just as you proved with your sword earlier, and we are their guardians, whether you like the idea or not. As for criticising them for their indolence, just remember that right now three of them are fighting in the Arshuman war, they can be as brave as you and me Vargo, and would any demon truly fight for our cause like they are?"

"Yet the deceiver takes many forms," Vargo said curtly.

"Indeed he does!" Steven held up his arms in a grandiose gesture. "Perhaps I am the deceiver, or, more likely at this moment perhaps you are. Perhaps we are all demons on these blighted isles, or perhaps, just perhaps, your words resemble something that has been passed by a bilious cow."

"Do not rile me Steven," Vargo warned. "It is your regime that has led us to this terrible outcome. Three men dead Steven, because of these "people". If you ran this place like the more stringent Chiran colleges…"

"What!" Steven was incredulous. "Like Manucco! Over a hundred dead on both sides! I do not fear fighting in a full scale war but I would rather that it did not take place here."

"You are ignorant about Manucco. I have spoken to knights that were there. The whole thing started because the mages were given the hour before nightfall to exercise in the courtyard. When that privilege was suspended the mages rioted. My argument is that the riot would never have occurred not if such rights had been curtailed, but rather if they were never given in the first place."

"You espouse treating all mages like prisoners then? Stick them in a cell for the rest of their lives and forget about them? Vargo, until tonight these people had committed no crime. And yes, I would agree with you in one respect, that they have been touched by the Gods, but the god in question is Lucan, not Keth. Lucan, Artorus brother, who sits at his right hand, an invaluable ally to him. Yes he is capricious, unpredictable, dangerous even, but no god does more to keep the forces of the underworld at bay than he."

Sir Vargo shook his head, pacing round in a small circle before replying.

"It appears Steven, that we are at an impasse. I have given my order, you have given yours, now all we need to do is see which orders are to be obeyed. Have you given any thought to that? These knights…" he pointed to them with his blade, "have seen two of their number cut down in cold blood tonight. Do you not think they want vengeance? That they see your supposedly merciful and reasonable words for what they are? They are the mewlings of a milksop, of a man yet to be fully honed upon the field of battle. Perhaps they would rather obey my orders than yours. Why don't you ask them? Why not see what their true feelings really are towards these "special" people?"

His tone may have been sneering, but Steven was astute enough to see that Vargo was setting a trap. Steven's men were angry, they did want vengeance, but their minds had been clouded by events, by the next morning they, like as not would see things very differently. Vargo though was daring him to ask his men what they wanted right now, and when they answered that they wanted bloodshed, a request he could not possibly grant, then his authority on these islands would be fatally undermined, perhaps for good. He would lose respect in those he commanded; they would see him as a weak man. But then Vargo was a man who admired strength of purpose, would he ever seek the opinions of those he commanded? Of course he wouldn't; and in that certainty lay Steven's answer.

"They are my men Vargo. They do as I command. I am not required to ask their opinion unless I specifically want it."

Vargo nodded slowly, he seemed impressed by the reply. "So then we are turning circles here, it seems all that this comes down to is who has authority here. I say it is me because I am senior, you say it is you because, well, you say I should not be here in the first place. Any proposals on who we resolve this...thorny issue?"

"There is no issue Vargo. I command here, yet I fear you have a proposal in mind. As a fellow knight it is my duty to hear it. So speak and let me respond."

At last Vargo started to wipe his sword on the grass. Once clean he lifted it where it caught the light of a nearby torch, the slick steel glittering like a faceted gemstone. "Disputes between knights of the same rank are honoured in a very traditional way, a tradition as old as the order itself."

"A duel." Steven said flatly.

"A duel," Vargo concurred; "to second blooding. If you receive a second wound these men are to die, if I receive it then do what you will with them, they are your cattle from then on and any consequences of your mercy will be yours to deal with. Agreed?"

Steven thought for a moment. He was, as were all the knights, an accomplished swordsman but Vargo was older, with much more experience in the field. He knew that Vargo thought he could best him easily, yet to refuse an honour duel would again be a disgrace he would never be free of. He had been backed into a corner.

"Agreed," he said, "but if I win then you return to the ship immediately and never set foot on these isles again. In fact, I personally do not think you should be a Knight of the Thorn at all so should you lose you are to resign from the order completely. I am sure that your family can buy you a place elsewhere, the order of the Scarlet Hammer or the Twin Serpents always need recruits. In my report on tonight's events I will emphasise your bravery and your role in stopping this escape attempt, I will say nothing as to what happened afterwards. As for your report, well put whatever you like in it. Now Vargo, are we in agreement?"

It was his turn to demand a concession. All previous attempts to get Vargo out of the order had been thwarted by his powerful and influential family. They could however do nothing if he resigned voluntarily. And as for the two other knightly orders Steven had mentioned, prestigious orders they certainly were but they were considered a step beneath the Knights of the Thorn by the aristocracy. The Silver knights, the Grand Dukes bodyguard were the greatest order, then the Knights of the Thorn, then all the other orders. If Vargo lost this duel, he would effectively have to demote himself, so now both men had been backed into a corner. "You ask a heavy price," he said slowly.

"Yet I do ask it. The alternative is not to duel at all and to put this dispute before the Knight Commander, and the Knight Commander will usually back his serving officer over the other complainant. Your choice Vargo, your choice."

Vargo's eyes burned with an intensity that could cause steam to rise from soil.

"A torch man in each corner, let us measure out the field of honour."

"One more thing…"

"State it!" Vargo hissed.

"You are armoured, I am not even wearing mail."

"Of course," Vargo growled; "of course." He sheathed his sword and slowly, deliberately started to loosen the straps on his breastplate. As he did so Steven went over to Nikolaj and Iska, who was still kneeling with her hands behind her back. "Get the girl to the hospital, let the healers look at her. Once they are happy with her though she is to be taken to the cells and put with the other women. I can do no more for her than that."

Nikolaj nodded and eased Iska to her feet. "Come on girl, you heard the officer."

"And Nikolaj, not a word to my wife about this, understood?"

"Understood sir."

"Good."

Steven watched the two of them, the tall knight, and the slight girl, walk towards the main path to the hospital. The last thing he wanted was for Fedrica and Gytha to know about the events that had unfolded and indeed, were about to unfold. He wanted to tell them both in his own time and in his own way.

Yet, not for the first time and certainly not for the last, the Gods had other ideas entirely.

****

A bloodied victim helps deliver bad news

Edith was sleeping, and over her one of the white clad healers was hovering with a warm cloth soaked in water, unguents, and herbs, which she was about to place on her forehead. Gytha and Fedrica were sitting in silence still. Both women were somewhat embarrassed, discomfited, Fedrica because of the frank and explicit way Gytha had spoken to her, Gytha because she still could not believe exactly what she had said. Speaking without thinking again Gytha, it is a curse that will haunt you to your pyre, so she thought. She was not by nature a vulgarian, but she knew how to use the power of words to shock. Yet it was her intemperate nature that had caused her to speak thus and as she replayed her words in her head she was getting increasingly mortified at her lack of manners. And so it came as a surprising relief to her when Fedrica finally said something.

"Do you wish to take the air for a few moments Gytha? The healer will stay with Edith until we return."

Well, the company could be better, but she could do with stretching her legs. "Of course my Lady, I would be honoured."

The house of healing would always be a serpentine mystery to Gytha, a shifting maze of snaking corridors each holding innumerable featureless polished oak doors. She knew where some of them led; the House of Meriel where offerings to the Goddess were left, the chapter house of the knights, a door that stood apart from the others leading to the longest corridor of all, the one that led to the asylum, a building connected, yet separate from the main bulk of the hospital. It annoyed Gytha even more that Fedrica already seemed to know her way around instinctively. She led them both unerringly to the main doors, double doors carved with the heart and blood drop, symbols of the healing goddess, and once they were there they walked straight through them into the night air, eager for it to blow away their cobwebs.

To their right, to the east, the rugged cliffs of the Isle of Tears could be vaguely discerned, an inky silhouette against a deep mauve sky. The Isle of Healing did not have the craggy heights and uneven gradients of its larger sister, yet the hospital was situated on its highest point, and from it the land sloped gently down to the sea, to the harbour and beaches of the north and the stony outcrops of the south. From the main doors a broad, white, chalky path meandered towards the harbour with a side fork branching off towards the connecting bridge between both islands. The harbour path was broad and well maintained, but it did twist and turn frequently on its way. It reminded Gytha of the rocky white-water streams that flowed from Mount Talman far away, through stony valleys thick with scrub and spidery silver barked trees, streams that ran past her home village, back in Tanaren, a long time ago now. Furthermore, though the lower part of the island was thick and grassy its higher reaches sported brakes of heather and yellow bracken high enough to obscure the harbour view completely. From where both women stood, part of the harbour was visible by day, now though all they could see was the occasional orange pinprick signifying a burning torch.

Gytha could smell the heather now, fresh and fragrant, blown her way by a wind that always seemed softer on this island. Indeed she often saw the Isle of Healing as the younger, gentler, more nurturing cousin to the Isle of Tears, where wind and rain were harsher, the cold more penetrating, the conditions altogether more savage. Yet something in her nature led her to prefer the Isle that was her home now, its ferocity and unbridled passion struck something primal inside her, she could identify with it somehow, its storms, its tempests, the driving winds and rain, nature untrammelled. How could one prefer soft breezes and gentle soothing sunshine to such raw power? She could try and remember Tanaren till her face turned blue, yet it was no longer her home, the college was, and she had little choice than to both observe and recognise its unique beauty, and those aspects of it that connected them both.

Tiny birds were trilling in the nearby bushes, a droning insect brushed her hand, it was being careless, made groggy by the seasonal change, the poor thing was not much longer for this world. Gytha could taste the air, early autumn was becoming late autumn, the temperature would be dropping imminently, a precursor to winter, when things would get truly wild. And there was still no sign that the novices would be getting braziers for their cells, the next few nights could be very chilly indeed.

Fedrica clasped her hands together and inhaled audibly.

"The night smells here are invigorating," she said brightly, "and the quiet! Tanaren city has many attractions, but peace and tranquillity are not among them. And the streets can be quite noisome in hot weather. When we are able I would like Steven to purchase a manor in the country, somewhere to escape to when city life becomes unbearable."

"Does he earn enough?" Gytha asked bluntly.

"No, not yet. But he will be commander one day and both of us have private means. Add that to the connections that we have then maybe in a few years it will happen for us."

"I wish you well with that," Gytha spoke with surprising sincerity, "a change of airs can only help the lady Edith too."

"Yes, that is a good point. Of course by the time we move I hope she will have a little brother or two, or maybe a sister..."

"Or maybe both."

"Yes!" Fedrica chirruped excitedly, "that would be wonderful!"

"I will add your wishes to my prayers tonight," was the dry response. "Shall we go inside now; it is colder than I thought."

Fedrica nodded and turned to leave. But they were interrupted by the sound of footsteps coming up the path. It was not so much the footsteps that bothered them so, rather it was clear that one of the walkers (there was too much noise for it to be just a single person) was in some discomfort. It was a woman, and she was choking and spluttering as she walked. Gytha was all for getting back to her room and leaving the poor creature to the healers but as she started to head for the door Fedrica tugged at her sleeve.

"Who is that?" she asked concernedly. They could see shapes now, two shadows engulfed by shadow. It was a man and a woman, the man had to be a knight, the sound of the armour gave that away but the girl? She knew almost everybody from the college, hardly anybody from the hospital, but she knew this girl, she was a fellow novice surely.

It was dark and the lamps still had to be lit so Gytha moved forward until both people were fully visible to her. And once she did that her jaw dropped like a stone.

"Iska! in the name of Elissa what has happened to you? what bastard hurt you in this way? tell me and I will make sure they regret it."

"Sir Vargo," Nikolaj answered for her. It was a name that caused both women's' eyes to widen. "But I thought he was not allowed to leave his ship," Gytha said softly.

Behind them a lay sister was finally lighting the lamps that hung from brackets either side of the main doors. They walked towards them, the better to see each other clearly and as they walked Nikolaj told them about Oskum, the escape attempt and Sir Vargo's intervention. Both Gytha and Fedrica listened in silence.

"Can you fetch a healer for the girl?" Nikolaj finally asked the lay sister. As she nodded and disappeared through the doors Iska's injuries were assessed by all three of them.

"Well the bleeding has stopped, "Fedrica said encouragingly.

"But the nose is broken," Nikolaj added; "it will probably still show when it heals."

"Cheekbone is ok by the look of it," Gytha was peering intently. "Open your mouth sweetie...oooh, you have lost a couple of teeth. How could this man do this to you? I should freeze him dead where he stands."

"It is my own fault," Iska spoke finally, and with some difficulty. "Oskum and me, we are...we were...close..."

"I understand," Gytha said.

"I felt I had to support him, I didn't know all this would happen, I didn't think..."

"Don't worry about it now, just let the healers look at you."

"She will have to be punished I am afraid," Nikolaj sounded sheepish. "I just don't know what that punishment will be. Steven and Vargo were arguing about it when I left."

"Steven will sort him out," Fedrica's jaw jutted determinedly. "No matter what the crimes were this girl did not deserve...this." She gestured at Iska's bloodied and swollen features

"What is it?" Gytha asked. She had noticed the crestfallen look on Nikolaj's face.

"Vargo wants to kill the men and throw the women in chains after breaking a finger on each of them," Nikolaj sighed. "Steven wants Commander Shadan to make the decision. Neither man was budging so..." he looked at Fedrica with weary eyes, "they are going to duel for it."

"What!" both women were aghast.

"Not to the death," Nikolaj added hastily; "to second blood, as is tradition.

"Accidents happen though," Fedrica could barely talk. "And Vargo is...not right somehow."

At that point, several healers in their red and white robes came out to take Iska from them. A couple of them were carrying simple rushlights in metal holders. Gytha asked to borrow one of them. "Lady Fedrica," she asked, "are you coming?"

"Most definitely," came the reply.

And so, as Nikolaj followed the healers and Iska into the hospital, a tiny bobbing flame went in the opposite direction, along the harbour path, in double quick time.

31
A battle of tempered steel

Two men standing at the centre, an improvised arena marked out by torch bearing knights, their fires guttering in the wind, slick grass glittering under flame light and star light, moon rising over the Isle of Tears. The scents were sharper at nightfall, the acrid smell of smoke was stinging the nose and drying the eyes, though it was not strong enough to mask the aroma of the churning white surf rolling over the harbour and beach.

A duel was in the offing.

Steven wore his black shirt and leather breeches of the same hue as he circled his opponent side on, sword swinging loosely in his right hand. Vargo had on his woollen undershirt, maimed hand hidden by a leather gauntlet, he had not removed the mail skirt that protected his legs, nor his iron sheathed boots that bruised the grass as he paced the bounds of the arena. Steven could have laboured the point and forced him to change but felt that it would just be nit-picking, and something not worthy of two men of honour.

"Taste the air Steven," Vargo spoke almost exultantly; "smell the steel and the leather, the very essence of battle. Do you not miss it man? Your true calling as a knight is not here but out there," he gestured with his free hand in the vague direction of Tanaren. "Do you not agree!" this last statement was half shouted for there was an audience for the proceedings, the sailors had come over to watch and now lined the imaginary bounds of the arena. The mages still lay on their bellies not a stone's throw away, though the two knights standing over them were also being distracted by the duellists, both of whom were staring intently at each other, absorbed in nothing else than the way their opponent carried their blade.

"Nothing to say?" Vargo taunted Steven's silence. "You know I am right that is why, you know that spending years in this place dulls your senses, makes you lazy, makes you rusty..."

And with that he sprang at Steven, sword raised, eyes keen as a raptor's claw. Steven raised his own blade to parry, there was a spark and a ringing of sharpened steel, yet his defensive alignment was slightly askew, Steven felt a draught whoosh past his ear as both weapons fell then felt a sharp stinging sensation on his right cheek. Then in a blur Vargo was past him, Steven spun round to block a further attack, but none was forthcoming. Vargo just stood there, lips curled in a cruelly satisfied smile. Steven felt blood sticking to his face and soaking into his high collar. His neck felt sticky, Vargo had drawn first blood.

"See what I mean?" Vargo was gloating, he could barely keep the triumphal tone from his voice. The lives of the four men lying on the grass hung by the thinnest of silken threads.

"You have achieved nothing yet," Steven replied coolly, "second blood not first, remember?" Yet he felt his words had little substance to them. For of course Vargo was right, though he trained every day it was no substitute to the cut and thrust of battle. And when it came to battle Vargo was vastly more experienced than he. Steven was an orthodox swordsman, schooled from childhood by the finest tutors whereas Vargo was more the street brawler, he did what it took to win and ultimately, nothing mattered more than winning. So what advantages did Steven have? Youth, that was the first thing, Vargo was more powerful, but Steven was quicker on his feet. He had to keep moving, disorientate his foe, wear him down. The other thing was that Vargo had a temper, he could let anger suborn cold precision. Perhaps Steven could exploit that somehow.

He moved forward a little, towards the centre ground which meant that Vargo had to use his feet more than he, to circle him more to find an advantage.

"A Knight of the Thorn Vargo, an honour for both of us to serve eh?"

"Indeed." Vargo was tight lipped, studying Stevens's movements, noticing he held his sword a little too low, leaving his left shoulder relatively unprotected.

"And no knightly order has the many and varied duties we have, to be keen in battle, to protect the weak, especially the children, or more specifically, the child mages. It is dangerous is it not, striking out to near deserted parts of the country, dealing with superstitious locals on one's own, taking the child to a place of safety before the barbarous fools throw him to the flames, you must agree, surely."

Vargo swung at him, a blow to test his guard only, Steven blocked it assuredly enough, though he was a little late with his parry. He continued to talk.

"I have done it many times myself, hoping the child has been given to the House of Artorus where he has sanctuary rather than taking to horse to try and rescue the poor terrified creature from a terrible death." Steven stopped talking to swing at Vargo's midriff, expecting the blow to be countered easily, which it was. He kept talking, relieved that the blood on his cheek was at last beginning to congeal.

"Of course the worst thing, when you reach the child and scatter his would be killers is trying to win that child's trust. He or she could be what, five, maybe six years old and experiencing nothing less than utter terror, why should not they see you as just one other maniac trying to end their life?"

"Go on," Vargo replied, "just say it." Steven looked at the way he was carrying himself, far too tense now, far too stiff, his history was about to be laid out in front of an audience, and he didn't like it one bit.

"A while ago I spoke to your squire at the time, he told me pretty much everything that happened to you. A girl wasn't it, about seven? You caught the villagers as they were carrying her screaming to her pyre. And then in front of her eyes you beheaded two men and ran the very same sword you wield now through the face of the man carrying her. And after that, after she had wriggled free of the dead man and wiped his blood from her face you ran up to her and erm...what did you say exactly? What measure of empathy did you extend to a little girl frightened beyond her wits?"

Vargo said nothing. He was barely moving now.

"Ah yes that was it, feel free to correct me if I am wrong but wasn't it, "Gods fuck it, the arse end of nowhere for another snotty brat. Come here if you know what's good for you or I will whip your arse raw." Was that right? And was it then that she screamed out and burned you?"

Vargo spat on to the grass, the knights and sailors watching started to whisper amongst themselves.

"It must have hurt you terribly, the child mage's fire, I suppose that was why you killed her."

The whispering grew in volume.

"Murdering a frightened seven-year-old girl, one you went there to protect. We can see here that you like killing. Did it give you a thrill then, stopping a little girl's heart? Did you tell the mother, no, I remember what your squire said now, you just rode away, you were in agony so I can accept that, but did you go back when you were better, did you face a grieving woman and tell her that you ran your sword through the body of her little daug..."

Vargo roared at him, charging forward in a mindless fury, swinging his sword wildly and with little focus at all. Steven swatted his sword away, his intention then was to slice across his opponent's chest but Vargo, blind to anything but his own anger, closed with him first. Steven grabbed Vargo's sword arm but could no longer bring his own weapon to bear. They were stood toe to toe, grappling like beasts, wrestling like two drunks in a dockside tavern. Neither could use their swords but in one respect Vargo was compromised.

His left hand was trying to pin Steven's sword arm. He was stopping him from bringing his sword to bear but the hand doing so was maimed, weak against Steven's forearm. Steven saw his chance. Using all his strength he tore his arm free and brought his elbow up into Vargo's face, hitting him in the nose.

There was a crunch of gristle and Vargo tumbled backwards falling slowly, almost comedically to land flat on his back. Steven stepped back, allowing Vargo to stand in his own time. He did so, measuredly, deliberately, then put his damaged hand to his nose. It was bleeding, not to the extent that Iska's had done earlier but the blood was running freely enough to coat his top lip. He put out his tongue, licking it away with a degree of theatricality.

"Clever," he said coldly, "very clever."

Steven waited for him to take up his sword and hold it out to face him. He did the same and the two men started to circle each other once more.

"Well," he said, "it appears that we are now even."

****

"Vargo is a very unnerving man," Fedrica was saying as she and Gytha continued to trot along the path. "He believes in the way the more extreme Chiran colleges are run, and his religion is also very...stringent. It is an unsettling combination."

"Is he a Frachter?" Gytha asked; "" all flesh is corruption," that sort of thing." She was using the slang term for the Fracht brotherhood, that branch of the Artoran faith once considered a dangerous sect but now fully subsumed into the official church. It believed in a stripped down, less grandiose form of worship, fewer offerings to the gods, fewer drunken festivals, and it was far more judgemental towards those it considered transgressors from the tenets of the faith.

"I believe so," Fedrica answered carefully. "It is very popular in the east of the country, where the war is. On top of that though I have been told that he is a devotee of the war gods, he may even be a priest of them, you know how secretive soldiers are about these things."

"A priest of Mytha?" Gytha was intrigued. "They only ever divulge their identities to fellow warriors, an oath of secrecy is taken, break it and the punishment is death. I have read about this, there are books in the lib..."

"It is rumour only," Fedrica corrected her; "but there are other rumours, that he is not a priest of Mytha but of the God of slaughter, and those people truly are insane."

Gytha shaded the near useless rushlight with her hand. "Then he would believe that killing gives him power, that it is the way to the seat of the Gods, the more that fall under his sword, the greater he becomes..."

Fedrica cut her short. "Your words are not what I want to hear right now, my husband could be his next...offering," her voice started to rise.

"Sorry," Gytha added sheepishly. "Can you trot a little faster? Keth take this useless flame, we are getting more light from the moon!"

****

The blades sliced through air, clashing with a ring that faded, but did not die, sounding in the ears of the onlookers for a long time afterwards. Vargo's nose had stopped bleeding, but Steven's cheek had still not fully closed. The cut was burning him, and his blood continued to soak into his shirt. It would probably leave a scar, and that annoyed Steven, he was quite proud of his dark good looks and was not happy having them spoiled, especially by the man facing him.

A slash and thrust from Vargo, Steven switched his weight from left foot to right and part evaded, part deflected the blow. He countered with a thrust of his own, again with no result, Vargo standing firm and blocking it. Both men it seemed were too well matched for each other, any victory would be an extremely hard fought one indeed.

The pace of the duel had slowed, both men were moving a lot more deliberately, trying to conserve their energy. Vargo's confidence, dented after Steven's verbal and physical assault had apparently returned. Indeed it seemed it was his turn to try and rattle Steven through the use of words rather than arms.

"How is your daughter?" he asked in a casual tone.

"Recovering."

"And your wife?" Vargo's concern for Edith seemed to be forgotten immediately   .

"Fine."

"Pretty little thing, and young. It is odd that she mixes so little with the other wives in the knights' tower in Tanaren. With all their husbands serving out here they tend to form their own clique, go into the city together, embroider together or whatever it is that women do when on their own. Not her though, while I was in the tower she seemed rather lonely, in need of sympathetic company. Fortunately though she did seem to find it in the end."

Laughable. A feeble attempt to try and rile him, Steven could barely believe the desperate measures Vargo was sinking to. He had to ask the obvious question just to see how pitiable the answer could be. "And whose company are we talking about exactly?"

"Young fellow. Newly promoted. Handsome. Likes to help the ladies where he can. Dylan? Yes, that was his name, Dylan. She seemed grateful for all the help he could provide, long walks along the city walls, trips to see the harbour, late night dinners in his chambers…"

Then Steven did laugh. "You really will have to do better than that Vargo, if you are trying to put me off my sword play that is. You sound like a gossiping chambermaid…"

Then Vargo came at him and this time his slashing blow was not aimed at the torso, not an attempt to merely draw blood. This time it was a high blow, arcing downwards, an attempt to slice off a good portion of Steven's head, an attempt to deal death, and it almost succeeded.

Steven took a fraction of a second to register his shock at the blow, which left him about the same amount of time to twist his body, lift his sword high and glance Vargo's sword so that it cut nothing but cold air. That he managed this with some aplomb was a testament to both his training and his reflexes. The sword sheared off and struck downwards towards the grass, a dangerous but fruitless attack. Vargo withdrew the blade, adjusted his stance, and assumed a defensive position once more.

"Don't play smart with me boy," Vargo snarled at him. "You want proof, then check the tower ledgers. Money granted for them dining together, buying medicine together, his laundry account even includes an amount for cleaning a woman's silk shift. You think I need to lie to you to defeat you in combat? It was tower gossip, whispered in all the dark corners by all of the servants all of the time. Just thought I would let you know; it cannot be nice to learn that you are something of a laughing stock on the mainland."

He was lying Steven thought. He had to be. "I find it hard to picture you ever reading a ledger Vargo, even less that you listen to tower gossip. Even if it were true what possible interest would it be to you anyway? We hardly know each other after all."

"Life in the tower is dull for a man of war Steven. An idle mind casts around for amusement, however trivial that amusement might be. I heard the gossip, thought of you, and interrogated the bookkeepers. People there think your wife is dallying with another man. Think about it, no one cares when the knights here indulge themselves with a mage or two but their wives? Nobody thinks of their wives, yet are they not subject to the same baser desires as their menfolk? Lengthy separation is hardly conducive to a happy marriage now, you surely have to admit that."

Steven bit his lip; he noticed his breathing was heavy. Fedrica was a nervy girl, one that craved affection and yet he could not envisage her ever being unfaithful to him. It was nonsense, he knew it was nonsense and yet…to his intense annoyance he realised that Vargo's words had registered with him. He was doubting, Gods confound it he was doubting and as he doubted his attention on his opponent wavered momentarily…

A flash of steel in the torchlight, Steven saw it finally, a sword thrust straight at his chest, just under the heart. Too late to block, all he could do was turn his body sideways in an attempt to avoid this potentially fatal blow. The swords razor sharp edge cut through his shirt as Steven stumbled away from the strike, staggering briefly before finally righting himself.

Vargo was ecstatic, he thrust his sword into the soft earth and whooped with delight. "Second blood Steven, I have you! Yield like an honourable man!"

Steven looked down at his ruined shirt, the torn edges of which were flapping uselessly in the breeze. It had been cut under the breastbone, a slash about five inches in length. He looked up at Vargo's face, it was eager, excited, ready to accept his submission.

Then Steven smiled at him. He pulled the lower part of the shirt up, so that Vargo could see the place where there should have been a noticeable gash in the skin.

But there was none. Vargo first looked incredulous, then his jaw set hard as Steven mocked him.

"A cut shirt does not count as second blood Vargo, unless of course shirts bleed as well. You grazed the skin that is all, you did not break it. So we are still even. Do you wish to continue?"

Vargo spat into the grass, his anger and frustration now plain to see. Without a further word he pulled his sword out of the earth and adopted his battle stance once more, pacing slowly and purposefully around the younger man, who was still smiling as he once more, held his sword out before him.

****

"Need…to…stop…a…second." Fedrica put her hand to her side and doubled over, breathing hard. Gytha stopped with her, sighing in exasperation at the delay. They had cleared the last high brake of heather and bracken and now the restless ocean, churning like liquid tar, glistening like polished jet, gloriously bejewelled under the canopy of stars and moon, was fully laid out before them, endless, yawning, permanent. More interesting to her though was the sight to her right, a rectangle of burning torches close to the sea and the black, bobbing hulk of the great ship moored there. She guessed it was the arena, the place where the duel was playing out, it was close yes, but still too far away for her to see what was going on. They needed to put a spurt on and having this hopeless dead weight gagging for air next to her was not what she needed right now.

"Enough time?" She tried not to sound too impatient. Tried and failed.

"Nearly. Not quite."

Girl had never done any physical work in her life. Gytha was getting rattled. Now was the time to raise something that Fedrica had said earlier. Something that had irked her.

"You said that this Vargo supported the Chiran colleges that employed the...harsher methods."

"Yes," Fedrica was still breathing heavily.

"So you disapprove of these methods, though I suspect, neither of us know fully what they are."

"Yes, from what I hear they basically run such places like prisons."

"Yet you are quite happy to have me transferred to such an institution."

Fedrica gave Gytha a sideways look, she was probably trying to look indignant, Gytha just thought that it made her look shrewish. "That would only have been the case if certain conditions were fulfilled. I explained this with some clarity to you earlier."

"Well," Gytha shrugged her shoulders, " that makes me feel so much better." In her own mind of course Gytha was extremely conflicted. The more she thought about Fedrica's threat against her the more outraged she was becoming. But then with the outrage came the guilt. For there was something between her and Steven, things had happened between the two of them and she was still quite happy for this to continue should the opportunity arise. Fedrica was right and Gytha was lying to her. To try and counter this she looked at Fedrica once more. She was wearing a different dress now to the one that Gytha had seen at their introduction. This was another silk dress, the overskirt red, the underskirt black which showed through the slashes in the overskirt. She was wearing a silver brooch that had a sapphire as its centrepiece, quite beautiful, very expensive. Fedrica had brought an entire wardrobe out with her it seemed. Gytha, like all novices had three robes, white, coarse enough to necessitate the wearing of an under shift, all fairly shapeless, designed to make all the young women there look like sacks. Fedrica had money, status, a husband, a child, in a few years she would have a manor in the country. She could go places, see different things, ride a horse through apple orchards, follow the course of a wide, silent river watching great silver fish break its surface, look through a window at dawn, peering past morning mists at high, frost capped mountains and dark sweeping forests. Fedrica, though she knew it not, had everything. Who could blame Gytha for borrowing a tiny piece of that for the briefest period of time, who could blame her for trying to colour her grey, constrained existence with just a hint of scandalous turquoise? Her life was here, she could never leave, her life was here, here, who could blame her for trying to

120

find a sliver of solace in the bleak, grinding, vista that made up the life of every mage on the island. Who could blame her? Who could blame her?

Well Fedrica could for one, Gytha had stopped, and her mind had drifted, the tiny rushlight was finally snuffed out by the buffeting wind. Gytha shivered as it changed direction, she smelled smoke from the torch fires below them and at last, heard the harsh voices of men shouting as they watched her erstwhile lover, the husband of her companion, fighting for his life close to the sea.

Fedrica was wrinkling her nose at her, more disapproval apparently. "You may not like it Gytha but, as I have already said, for my family, for my child, I will do anything. Our acquaintance is of but a few hours, why should I not sacrifice you to preserve that which is most precious to me?"

"Then just be assured that any antipathy is mutual. Right now though we have a common goal, to try and stop whatever madness is going on close by. Can you move now?"

Fedrica nodded and together the two women, rivals, and companions both, started the final part of their journey.

****

Both men were tiring, both were sweating and bloody, but neither of them was giving up the fight, not this fight, for this had become far more than a duel between peers. Steven's legs had long felt like they were fashioned from wet clay, he could barely lift them, and his arms were tearing and burning at him as he swung his sword, then blocked, swung, then blocked, again and again. They were like two dancers at the festival of the banishment, ritual dancers repeating the same moves for hours as the audience watched in a trance. Which God was his dance representing though, Artorus or Keth?

Vargo too was suffering. A solid, powerful man built for stamina Steven assumed that by now he would have the advantage, but no, he too seemed weighed down by fatigue, fighting on through will and determination alone. His face seemed now to have just one expression, a sort of wild eyed atavistic grimace. He was sweating copiously, his skin was covered in a glistening sheen and so it came as a surprise when he broke the silence, speaking in a forced growl between almost clenched teeth.

"Shall we dispense with the charade then Steven?"

"What charade?" Steven's reply was equally guttural. He had no idea how long they had been fighting but the moon was risen now, dominant, and it was getting cold despite his lengthy exertion.

"Second blood of course. Neither of us wants it. Let us fight until one of us submits, or until one of us is too incapacitated to continue. Or of course until one of us dies. The way it should be between men of honour. Agreed?"

"Agreed." Steven did not even think about it. Both men had long ceased trying to merely cut their foe. He had no problem at all with seeing Vargo dead and as for the other eventuality, well, he was too tired to even think about it.

"Good. You are a man of honour after all, only such a man would seek death to defend his whore of a wife."

Earlier in the evening Steven would have contemptuously dismissed such a clumsy jibe. But he was weary now, and there was nothing more guaranteed to destroy reason than fatigue. Clenching his sword, gripping the hilt with both hands he came at Vargo with a roar, a downward blow to the head, parried, a swing at the midriff, blocked, a reverse swing at the arm, blocked again. Then it was Vargo's turn. He charged into Steven shoulder first, sending him staggering. Then, he swung his sword downwards, hitting him on the side of the head with the flat of the blade. Steven crashed to the ground, rolling over and over until he stopped, face down in the grass, his sword now a foot away from his right hand. He was not moving.

"You have Uba's fortune Steven." Vargo stopped to breathe before strolling towards the prone figure, sword at the ready. "You were meant to taste the edge of the sword not the flat. Still, the inevitable is just delayed. I will now claim your soul, for Mytha, for Huaga the slaughterer, but most of all for me."

His sword was poised to run Steven through his back into his heart but in his triumph he had forgotten to be watchful. For though Steven appeared to be semi-conscious with his face in the grass it was turned just enough for him to see Vargo's every move. And Vargo's little speech had given him time to draw breath also, to give him just enough energy to do what he needed to next.

Just before Vargo could make the fatal thrust he spun on the ground and, with both hands grabbed at Vargo's iron shod foot. Using his own body weight he dragged at the leg sending Vargo spinning to the ground with a heavy crash. Vargo grunted as the impact forced the air from his lungs, he too dropped his sword but instantly reached out to retrieve it. Too late though, Steven was up, fresh, invigorated, eager to finish proceedings. He stamped on Vargo's good hand then leaned over and picked up Vargo's own sword, the irony of slaying this man with his very own blade was not lost on either of them.

Vargo had raised himself to his knees, he looked for Steven's sword, but it was too far away for him to get to in time. For Steven was now standing over him, sword tip angled at his face. Steven looked down at his bested foe, but he saw no defeatism there, no regret, only anger and maybe shock at being beaten by a man he had thought his inferior. Steven felt his own anger flare inside him, burning, incandescent hatred of the man who stood for everything he despised in the knightly order he had been part of since he was seven years old. He wanted to drive Vargo's own sword through his face, splitting the skull, sending his grey, slippery brains showering over the grass, cutting through his eyes, making this vile, murderous, fanatical killer unrecognisable on his funeral pyre. His right arm tensed as he readied to deliver this final, killing, thrust.

And it was at this juncture, this pivotal moment, that Gytha and Fedrica finally arrived at the scene of the fray.

****

Vargo spat past Steven and into the grass. Then he leaned forward placing his forehead against the tip of the sword. "Go ahead Steven, I am not afraid, I will show you all how a man can die, but have you really got it in you to make the killing thrust?"

Steven glared at him, his eyes burning with a ferocity and a pure unabashed hatred that made the knights closest to him take a step back in surprise. He pulled the sword back into a sweeping position, preparing to smite this degenerate knight's head from his shoulders.

Then he saw Fedrica and Gytha pushing past the sailors at the far end of the arena and froze where he stood.

In the briefest instant of time, a shard of a fragment of a second Gytha looked at Fedrica, waiting for her to do something. To her abiding horror though Fedrica was as immobile as her husband. She stood transfixed but the reason for this paralysis appeared to be that she seemed too ecstatic to move. Her man stood before her, he had bested Sir Vargo, he had shown his prowess to her, to all the onlookers. She seemed perfectly happy for him to take the head of his vanquished enemy. Her lips parted almost orgiastically. Gytha looked at her with distaste.

It was up to her then, she always expected it would be.

"Steven!" she shrieked at the top of her lungs. "Stay your hand! You are better than this! Do not become what the other man already is!"

All heads turned to her, but though she knew she was blushing she ignored them, the only person she needed to stare at her was Steven.

And to her eternal relief he did as she asked.

It was apparent to all, when Steven met Gytha's imploring eyes, that there was a bond between them, they saw and immediately understood each other, as a husband understands a wife. Most of all of course it was apparent to Fedrica, and not for the first time, she had seen it when she had surprised the two of them in Sir Beverley's room that afternoon. Her expression fell from elation to deflation in a trice.

Steven sagged a little, lowering the sword in his hand, Vargo looked positively amused.

"Another warrior bested by a woman; some things never change. Are you a coward Steven? Are you afraid to do what needs to be done?"

Steven beheld his kneeling enemy, the contempt both men had for each other not disguised in the slightest. For a moment anything could have happened between them but then, finally, Steven's expression finally broke.

He smiled, a twisted half smile but a smile, nevertheless. Then he threw Vargo's sword into the darkness, watching as it landed, point first, into the grass yards away from them.

And then he smashed Vargo in the face with his fist, splitting his lip.

The power of the blow knocked Vargo backwards onto the grass, when he finally righted himself and stood blood was streaming from his mouth.

"Second blood Vargo, the victory is mine. Pick up your sword and get back to the ship. When you get to the mainland you are honour bound to leave the order. I thank you for stopping the escape attempt tonight, my report to Shadan will be fulsome in its praise for you. But you are done here now, and I bid you farewell. May the Gods grant you the honour in battle you so crave."

Vargo glared, a beast brought to bay. His reply was as a blizzard howling through a cave of ice. "We will cross paths again Steven, the whims of the Gods guarantee it, and when it happens things may not turn out as well as it has for you tonight."

Steven ignored him. He did not even look at the man anymore. Striding past him and massaging his bruised knuckles he called the knights up to him.

"Get the mages to the cells on the other island. Keep the one who started all this in a cell on his own, how is he?"

A knight standing over Oskum tried to lift him, it was obvious that the mage was still groggy. "Still all over the place sir," he told him.

"Right. One of you get to the hospital, ask for a healer to cross the bridge and take a look at him, once he has been imprisoned that is. Also get Nikolaj to bring the other mage girl over when she has been cleaned up. We are all going back to the college, right now. Gytha, you are coming with me. Oh, and Sir Roban..."

"Yes sir?" Steven was speaking to the knight who earlier had been poised to execute one of the mages, before Steven had stopped him.

"I will be seeing Commander Shadan immediately. He will be passing judgement on the prisoners. If any of them are to be executed then it will be you who will be performing the execution. Let's see how enthusiastic you are about the matter after a night's sleep. Now get going."

The sailors and Sir Vargo started to stroll down to the harbour, Vargo did not look back, but Steven could almost feel the hatred for him oozing from the other man's pores, somehow that gave him a grim sense of satisfaction. The remaining knights busied themselves getting the mages to stand before binding their wrists and, as they did so, Steven finally found time to talk to the two women. Fedrica was all smothering concern.

"Your face!" she cooed, "your poor face." She touched his wounded cheek and the stream of sticky blood that ran from it, down into his torn shirt. "We must get you to the healers!"

"No. No time for that. It looks far worse than it is. For you, the plan is unchanged, come over with Edith and the healers in the morning. I want you both to get a good night's sleep in the meantime. I have much to do before dawn. Edith fares well?"

"Tolerably," Fedrica nodded. "Why do you want the lady Gytha to accompany you now?"

"Because the ramifications of tonight's events will last over many days, maybe over weeks, or even months. She is a mage and needs to be there to see exactly what will happen next."

Fedrica seemed to accept this, nodding quietly as he spoke. "I will return to my lodgings then. Steven, I will see you in the morning."

"Indeed you shall. Now Gytha, you come with me."

****

A return to the college, and a terrible mess

Steven waited until the healers and priests of Xhenafa arrived to take the remains of the dead away then he and Gytha started the long walk to the college on the Isle of Tears. They caught up with the main convoy of knights and mages just after crossing the bridge where the salt spray, flying skyward as echoing waves ground against unmoving cliffs, made the tips of Gytha's bronze curls stand on end. She would normally be in the library or back in her cell by now and found the night sounds of the island, or rather the paucity of them, unsettling. As they climbed the cut in the cliff side after crossing the bridge the quietude, the pungent aroma of damp, moist earth, the chirping of insects in the overhanging bracken, even the uneven stones underfoot pressing into the soles of her shoes made her feel she was somewhere unfamiliar. Fifteen years here and she thought she knew every rock, every blade of grass, every sharp pointed bramble, but not now. Now she was seeing the island as an outsider would and the thought was not a comforting one.

Once through the cut they caught up fully with the convoy. The wagon Sir Beverley had reconnoitred was still there, the ponies still tethered to it were patiently chewing the grass on the verge. So now the knights bundled Oskum and the female mages on to the back, and after some persuasion, got the ponies to start trundling homeward with it, with Steven and Gytha following closely behind.

The two of them talked little as they walked, too much had happened, there was too much to think about for any conversation to have any use somehow. Finally though Gytha did think of something, speaking quietly so that nobody else could hear her.

"Did you really need me to return here tonight?"

Steven nodded without looking at her. "Yes. Every word I said to you was true. Tonight will have consequences for all mages, it is best for you that you are there to hear them."

"You mean there will a crackdown of some sort?"

"Undoubtedly."

"Oh."

"Did you and Fedrica get on better this time?"

"Not really, no."

"Pity. Not unexpected I suppose but a pity, nonetheless. I will try and keep you apart from now on."

"It may be for the best."

"I am sure of that."

"Yes. We are two very different people I am afraid."

They walked on in silence for a little while before Gytha added, "I am sorry about Sergeant Welton. I was only speaking with him yesterday; it seems unreal somehow."

Steven did stop walking then, turning to look at her. "I never had a good word to say about him when he was alive. He was a plodder, slow but steady, it used to infuriate me at times. What a fool I was, he was the ideal man for a crisis such as this. Now he is gone, a life wasted over what? No one will benefit from tonight, no one."

"No. I am really sorry, if you need to talk to someone…"

"No, I am fine, I have many other things to do before I can grieve over a lost comrade."

They started to walk again, slowly, far enough away from the convoy to be cloaked in darkness, away from the arc of torchlight. Before she realised what she was doing Gytha slipped her hand into Steven's, squeezing it gently. She expected him to pull away immediately.

But he didn't, he squeezed her back, and that was how they walked until the lights of the college fell upon them.

DAY EIGHT
33
How time crawls in the darkness

She had no idea how late it was, she presumed it was only a few hours from dawn, all Iska really knew was that she was tired, hungry, still in some pain and very, very, frightened. Sir Nikolaj had tried to be as kind and sympathetic as he could as he walked her from island to island but ultimately he was powerless to decide her fate, he was not the Knight Commander after all.

The healers had cleaned her up, stopped the bleeding, done what they could but the left side of her face was still bruised and swollen and tender to the touch. That would heal in a few days though, what wouldn't be returning however were the two teeth she had spat into the sea after the knight had struck her. Two molars on the left side of her mouth that would never grow back, she ran her tongue over her bloody gums for the umpteenth time, it would take some getting used to. As for her nose though, the break would always be obvious, she was told not to touch it, it could move the cartilage and make it worse but even if she obeyed these instructions the bridge of her nose would always be bent out of shape even when it healed. It would not be hugely disfiguring, but to a girl of sixteen it felt she had turned into a withered old hag overnight.

And now she was sharing a cell with the three other women. She had never seen the cells before, underground, sited in the tongue of land projecting from under the college's east wall and, if she had known it, the cell Gideon had occupied two days ago. The slab of rock that covered the grille in the ceiling had been put back, leaving the cell in near total darkness, Iska only had her ears to fall back on. Before she had been locked inside the knight had told her that not only were these cells warded, they were also alarmed and any magical attempt to destroy the door would have explosive results. Their own power would be turned against them, alerting the knights, and possibly killing the caster in the process. She had accepted his words with a shrug of her shoulders, using her power had never even occurred to her.

All the other women were around ten years older than her, maybe even more. There was Brytta, a dumpy, sour faced novice, a long-time friend of Oskum not too far away from her graduation exams; then there was Karel, a peer of Oskum newly into her seniority, she was thin, sickly, and very religious. She was praying now, praying to Artorus, begging him to show them mercy. Finally there was Asitaigne, closest to Iska in terms of age, a striking, statuesque blonde with piercing ice blue eyes. Iska had no idea why she would have got involved with Oskum at all. She was praying too, to Elissa this time but her prayers were barely mouthed, a tiny whisper Iska was only hearing because she was sitting next to her. There was no bed in the cell, the table had been moved out, just four rush pallets on the floor and a latrine bucket. They all sat on their pallets though none of them could sleep and as for the bucket, Iska needed to use it but was far too reserved to try, she felt that the other girls were feeling the same.

"Artorus, both savage and merciful, extend your clemency to your errant children, for they understand that they have lapsed from the tenets of the faith and now seek redress for their foolishness. Let them show their supplication to you..." Karel spoke slowly, evenly, her pitch never altering.

"Elissa protect us, Elissa forgive us, we have been so, so stupid..." Asitaigne stopped whispering and started to sob softly, Iska then realised that Brytta too was crying, she was snuffling softly into her robes, Iska was too tired, her eyes too dry for tears to come, and her throat was hoarse with all the screaming she had done earlier. She had a brief image of Dicken, head split in half right in front of her and dug her nails into her palms.

"Did any of you know Oskum had planned that spell?" she asked timorously, eager to break the suffocating melange of prayers and tears that felt like it was making her already throbbing head burst.

"I didn't," Brytta said tearfully. "Nor me," Asitaigne croaked. "Karel?"

The prayers stopped. "He told me he had something prepared," Karel said, "should the worst come to the worst. That was all I knew; I didn't think twice about it." She was silent for a moment before starting to pray again.

"If anyone knew what he was doing it was you Iska," Brytta said accusingly.

"Yes," Asitaigne added, a note of hysteria in her voice. "You were fucking him; he would have told you before anyone else."

"He didn't though," Iska said quietly, "he just didn't, I only knew him for a couple of days."

"I was so frightened." Brytta spoke after a brief pause, she seemed more composed now, now that Iska had said she knew nothing of Oskum's plans. "The murders seemed so random, it seemed anyone could be next and when we heard Arbagast was dead, I mean who would kill old Arbagast? We all knew him, the gentlest man I have ever spoken to. Who can honestly say that they are safe here, even now?"

Karel shook her head, her tone despondent, defeated. "None of us are safe, Xhenafa is still amongst us, waiting, watching, he may even be in this cell now, judging us, preparing to make his choice as to who will follow him next. And now we are tainted by murder. If they had just accepted Oskum's proposal, just let us leave here when we asked them three people would still be alive now. Only prayers and repentance can save us."

"I only wanted to see somewhere different," Asitaigne said. "I just wanted some kind of...adventure of some sort, I wanted to go somewhere, a change from this stultifying, suffocating place. Sometimes I feel like I am dying by slow stages here..."

"And now we might all be dying together..." Karel added ghoulishly.

"No," Brytta spoke forthrightly, "not even that mad knight wanted to execute us."

"That means nothing," Karel said, "they need to make examples of us. The last thing they want is for somebody to repeat what we have done."

"But none of us wanted anybody to die!" Asitaigne pleaded.

"But two knights ARE dead Sita," Karel said. "They will want vengeance for it."

Asitaigne started to cry again. "Oh fuck it, fuck it, I don't want to die, I don't..." she broke down into a series of gasping, uncontrolled sobs. Iska went over to her, tried to hold her hand.

"Go away!" she cried. "It was your boyfriend who pulled us all in, if anyone deserves to die it is you!"

"That is unfair," Brytta said. "Iska has already gone through more than the rest of us. She hardly asked to have her nose broken, the rest of us are old enough to make our own decisions. We have no one to blame for our predicament but ourselves."

They all fell into silence again before Karel resumed her monotonous prayers. Asitaigne continued to cry and then Iska heard Brytta relieving herself in the bucket. Despite everything she had to put her hand over her mouth to stop herself sniggering. She didn't know why; she would have to do the same herself soon after all.

Then she stiffened, as did they all. There were voices outside and the sound of keys turning in a lock. "Someone is visiting the men," Brytta hissed.

"Perhaps they are being told what is going to..." Karel trailed off, Asitaigne whimpered. Minutes passed, interminable minutes, minutes that stretched into infinity, head pounding, heart thumping minutes, Iska wanted to drag her nails over the cold stone floor, beat her fists against the walls, scream at the frozen sky, anything to break the agonising tension clawing at her innards...

Then the key started to turn in their door.

All heads turned, Asitaigne put her hand over her mouth. Steven stood there with another knight holding a lamp. The warm, buttery light flooded over the four women, the four pale, gaunt women, their eyes wide with unbridled fear.

"I have spoken to the Knight Commander," Steven was obviously not interested in prevarication; "and he has passed sentence on all of you."

"Which is sir knight?" Brytta spoke for them all, the only one there whose throat had not been constricted by fear.

"Well, you have all been found guilty of sedition, of attempting to escape from the college bounds without permission and in violation of the mage treaties to which all civilised countries are signatory…"

Iska's heart skipped a beat, this sounded terrible.

"However, we have concluded that none of you either colluded in or partook thereof in the murder of either of the knights this evening, also your story that you intended to return here has been believed. So you have been spared the penalty of death. In fact the Knight Commander has been relatively merciful, you have been awarded the minimum sentence for your crimes."

All four women inhaled simultaneously, even Steven heard them, it stopped him speaking for a moment.

But only for a moment.

"You will each receive five lashes of the razor whip. Sentence will be carried out at dawn, on the funeral beach, the whipping crosses are being prepared as we speak."

"Razor whip?" Asitaigne gasped.

"Yes. I am required by law to tell you what that is. It is a long metal wire, flexible, to which a series of small steel teeth have been welded. The wire filament is then enclosed in a sheath of cured leather, through which only the teeth protrude. It was designed in the earlier days of the colleges, when such punishments were more commonplace. It was felt that sometimes the relationship between the lay brothers carrying out the sentence and the mage victims was too close, that sometimes the whipper would go easy on them. This whip is guaranteed to tear off a strip of skin with each blow, however hard that blow might be."

"Oh by all the Gods…" Asitaigne started to cry again.

"As women you have the lighter sentence, it is ten lashes for the three men…"

"And Oskum?" Iska asked.

Steven swallowed. "He has been found guilty of both murders. He is to be put to death once your sentences and that of the other men has been carried out. The college is to be turned out, so all are compelled to watch proceedings. Healers will be present with salt and balms to clean your wounds. You will be given two days to recover from your injuries, thereafter you are to resume college life as usual, you have committed a crime, you have been punished for it, no further stigma will apply to you."

"How far away is dawn sir?" Brytta asked. "We cannot see the sky from here."

"It is close, you have time to pray and prepare yourselves but not much more than that. Now I will leave you to contemplate your folly. I admit I am sorry for you but then, a close friend of mine died tonight and that is something that should not be forgotten."

The door went to close but then, on impulse, Iska called out to him.

"Sir! May I speak to Oskum, for one last time? Can I prevail upon your mercy for this one small thing?"

"Why would you want to speak to him?" Steven asked.

"We are...we were close sir; I just want to say goodbye."

"Very well," Steven sighed. "Come with me now and keep your hands where I can see them. You can have a couple of minutes with him but both I and a healer will be with you. And remember, all these cells are warded against your powers..."

"I will not try and use them I swear."

"Yes girl." His voice softened at last; "I believe you. Now get to your feet and come with me."

****

A final meeting, and a promise

Oskum's cell had a low, stone bed, a natural feature jutting out from the wall, for all the cells here were chiselled out of a long cave far older than the college itself. He was sitting on it now whilst a healer stood close by, his head over a brazier which was heating a copper bowl full of water and scented leaves, their aroma instantly clearing the passages in Iska's battered nose. Oskum looked weak, he swayed as he sat and his skin was grey, Oskum's sweat making it look waxy. His eyes too were wide, almost feverish, though when he saw Iska he broke into a wide, manic smile, however Iska noticed he did not try to stand.

"They let you see me!" he said happily. "I thought I would never speak to you again. The good lady healer here is charged with keeping me alive till morning, it would not do if the central attraction of tomorrow's performance expired before he is supposed to after all."

"Oskum," Iska said sadly, "I am sorry it has come to this."

"No! No! You must not say that. I am the one that should apologise, I led you all down this path, and I bear responsibility for your punishment."

Iska remembered Brytta's words earlier on. "That is not true, we are all adults, we make our own decisions, and we accept our own punishments. If we had not joined you, you would hardly have tried to escape, would you? For there was no way you could have escaped on your own."

"I hadn't thought of it that way. Who knows though? Maybe I would have tried on my own, mad Oskum is capable of anything, at least that is what I have been hearing."

Iska was silent for a moment, biting her lip. There did seem to be a madness in his eyes, it almost looked like there was a sort of demonic light shining from behind them. "That spell you tried…"

"The fire of Glebyne? I have been assisting a mage who was studying it. Reckoned I could do it myself. The plan was to set up a wall of flame to hold back the knights for a few seconds, a few seconds was all we needed after all. I wanted to prove myself as a mage, to show that I could cast a powerful spell but of course I failed. It all went horribly wrong, you have to believe me when I say I wanted no one to die, you know I am no murderer."

"I know," Iska nodded, "you are a good man at heart."

"I wanted to stand for something Iska!" He was almost ranting now; spittle flew from his mouth as he spoke. "I knew people were frightened, Keth's teeth I was frightened too. I wanted to help, to be the man with the radical idea. When the knights turned my proposal down I was angry, frustrated. I felt, no I knew that I was right, that I could get people away from here until all this trouble died down. I wanted to be a leader, not a…an irrelevance, you understand?"

"Yes Oskum, but you were never an irrelevance, not to any of us."

Oskum nodded. "Yes, maybe, I did lead you, you did have faith with me, I thank you for that."

There was a moment of silence, Steven took the opportunity to speak. "Right, you have seen each other now. Time to say goodbye."

"Iska," Oskum was calmer now; "could you do one thing for me tomorrow, if you can?"

"Name it."

"If you are close enough, will you look at me, at my eyes? I will refuse a hood, I would just like you to be the last thing I see, before…before."

There was a lump in her throat, she could not speak, blinking away the moistness in her eyes she just nodded to him.

He smiled again, "Gods keep you Iska, you are a special girl, have the long and happy life you deserve."

She didn't care, she couldn't help herself. She just ran forward and threw her arms around him. He smelled sweaty, sickly, and only now did she realise that the strange look in his eyes was not madness, it was terror.

"I am so frightened!" he wailed as he buried his head in her shoulder, his tears soaking into her robe. "I don't want to die, not like this, I do not want to look like a coward!"

She stroked his lank hair, buried her fingers into it. "Do not fear, I will be there, I will help you, I know how brave you are."

When she had run towards him Steven's hand had gone reflexively for his sword. But now, seeing the two of them together, the girl so young, the man who had so totally overreached himself, he let them have this one, last, tearful moment together. He waited until Iska had extricated herself from the embrace and was standing once more. "That is it," he said, "time to return to your cell."

Iska nodded, but before turning to leave she took one last look at Oskum, his red eyes in stark contrast to his ashen pallor. "Watch me," she said, "I will be there."

And she knew they would be the last words she would say to him.
****

A recalled conversation

"Sunbank Island." Steven had said to Gytha as they climbed the college steps earlier that night. "I have actually been there, when I was a squire, one of my last tests before knighthood. A Knight of the Thorn can spend a lot of time in the field and so needs to learn to live off the land. So I spent a couple of weeks there, with a handful of other squires, trying to survive."

"Trying to survive? Is it that bad?"

"The island is about a third the size of this one, much steeper, a lot of dangerous cliffs. There is a place to moor a ship but like as not any ships left there for a period of time would end up dashed to pieces by storms. It is not a safe harbour. As for the island, it does have a stone reservoir to catch the rain and a ruined tower in which the bottom two storeys are still viable as shelter. But that is about it. Lying there listening to a storm raging beyond the walls, the rain pouring over the stones outside was an amazing experience. We survived by building fish traps and catching the occasional bird. There was a type of thorny bracken that we could burn as firewood and use for those traps, without that we would have struggled. Now remember we had been trained to survive in wilderness but you mages, well you can blast a man to smithereens but left to fend for yourselves, I would suspect you would be little better than babies. I dread to think what would have happened to them had their plan succeeded."

Gytha had sounded exasperated, "if somebody had explained this clearly to them…"

"Then none of this would ever have happened. Exactly. If only I had been over here…"

"Don't. You needed to be with your family. Artorus willed it so, though I don't know why."

"Neither do I. The Gods don't exactly seem to be on our side at the moment."

"They don't, do they? I wonder what we have done to anger them so."

Steven hadn't replied as they stopped before the great doors. "So you can survive in the wild then?" she had asked him.

"Yes. One of our responsibilities is scouring the country for young mage talent and bringing them here. You can travel to all sorts of mysterious, out of the way places, just you, or just you and a squire sometimes. I did it for a couple of years in my early knighthood, there are about half a dozen in the children's college who are there because of me. If I hadn't had found them they may well have been just charred bones by now. Burned to purify them, to take them from Keth, it is one of the great horrors of the Artoran world, a true source of collective shame. I can sometimes see why the southern Kozean Empire sees us as barbaric. Anyway, this is no time to be reflective, I have to see Shadan now, it will be a difficult meeting, that much is certain."

"I am sorry about Welton," she had repeated to him.

"As am I. I will miss him. I hope you understand I am conflicted about all this. I have great sympathy for all mages and yet, because of you, a close friend is dead. I will do all I can to plead the cases of the accomplices but as for the man that killed him, my defence of him will be less…robust, I hope you understand."

"I do. Am I to be reinstated as your liaison?"

"Yes, but it might be better if you stay in your cell from now on. If I install you in lodgings in the chapter house it might end up with you and Fedi clawing lumps out of each other, and I have enough on my mind at the moment."

She had smiled. "You might be right. When will Shadan make his judgement?"

"Very soon. And it will be carried out immediately. I wouldn't be surprised if you heard something at dawn."

And then they had parted.

34
A clear and dreadful morning

Gytha returned to her cell feeling weary, despite having slept most of the day. She had climbed, fully clothed into her bed for the cell was freezing cold and, despite her swimming head, drifted off to sleep almost immediately.

Which made her forced awakening even more jarring. She sat bolt upright at an assault on her ears, somebody was walking the corridors hitting something metallic, a cymbal or a pewter plate or something. People were shouting too, male voices, knights.

"You are all to rise! Immediately!" The voice was shouting at the top of its lungs. Then her door creaked open, and a knight walked in unannounced. He was fully armoured.

"You are to get dressed and go down to the beach. Right away! No questions. We will be checking the cells to see if any remain behind!"

Then he was gone.

Well Steven said the judgement would be quick. The tone and behaviour of the knight was worrying though. He was aggressive, angry, and a knight rarely strode so brazenly into a sleeping woman's quarters. She swung her legs out of the bed and slipped on her shoes without touching the chill stone floor. Then she went to her small, grilled window and pulled back the shutter.

It was still dark.

"Artorus holy beard," she moaned through clenched teeth.

Dark it may have been, but dawn was not far away. She could hear the gulls calling, stirring themselves for a new day. By the time they all got to the beach the first rays of pallid sunlight would be twinkling off the water.

Of course only she had any idea of what was happening. The corridors were full of grumpy, bleary eyed mages, all of them clueless as to the reason for their rude awakening. She joined the milling crowd only to see one of the male novices approach a nearby knight.

"What is the meaning of this? Have you all gone mad?" he moaned.

"You have been ordered on to the beach. Now be quiet and do as you have been told. I sometimes wonder if you realise who has authority here." The reply was delivered in such terse, angry tones the mage had shut up completely and joined the procession to the great doors.

On top of the steps, almost at the same point where she had parted from Steven, she ran into Miriam and Kestine. It was a still morning, calm, but the autumnal cold penetrated to the bones.

"It is freezing!" Miriam did her best to make her teeth chatter and, to her own surprise, succeeded. She wrapped her arms around her waist, stamping her feet on the stone.

"Do you know what is happening Gytha?" Kestine's breath came out in steaming white plumes.

"Yes," Gytha said, "and no. Something happened last night, something bad, and this is part of it. We are not in trouble as individuals. As mages though, well I don't know."

"Well what happened then?" Miriam asked. "Or are you determined to remain cryptic?"

"I, I cannot say. And we cannot stand here, we need to move on, the knights are looking at us."

"So?" Miriam asked.

"Just believe me when I say this is not a good time to annoy the knights. Now let's get moving."

Both Miriam and Kestine saw her face, the mix of concern and fear written there and fell silent. The three of them joined the procession, senior and junior mages hemmed in by a line of knights carrying torches, firstly along the main path from the college, then down a side path of partly frozen mud that cut between animal pens and storage barns, until finally they descended the steep cut towards the beach. Every time a mage raised a voice or asked a question they were shouted down by the knights. Soon everybody had got the message and so that final descent to the beach was carried out in near silence.

The narrowness of the defile, the fiery torches, and the proximity of bodies to each other finally started to warm Gytha up. She smelled the sea, crisp, cold, refreshing, and breathed deeply, sand and salt grass, barnacles and rock pools, dank weed coating clusters of sharp, pitted rocks. Small green crabs scattered as they finally trod the sand, the knights corralling them, hundreds of people into a rough semicircle surrounding the raised plateau where they had recently witnessed Caswell's funeral. Several rectangular patches there were coated in black soot, a testament to past funerals but there was no pyre for them to see today, today held something different entirely.

The plateau was coated in a thin film of sand that ran all the way up to the cliff face. The cliff itself was sheer betwixt beach and headland, a climb of over one hundred feet, with only a few green fringed ledges to break its frowning visage, caliginous and impassive as a starless night sky. Where cliff met plateau stood four wooden structures, each consisting of two great sawn planks crossing each other in a giant "X", all of them leaning at an angle against the cliff.

"What in the name of the furnace are they for?" Miriam nudged Gytha.

Gytha did not reply, though she had already guessed at their purpose.

It seemed that every knight on the island was turned out for the occasion, all were in full armour, most even had their helmets on. It was obvious to even the most sleep addled mage that something was seriously wrong and so, despite ordered to silence the sound of gossiping voices soon even overpowered that of the restless sea. Then though, through the entrance of the cut strolled Knight Commander Shadan, in his full ceremonial armour, polished steel decorated with cut emeralds and rubies on the breastplate forming the image of the bloody thorn. His white cloak billowed behind him, its edge brushing the sand. He was flanked by two squires each solemnly beating a drum, a procession of knights followed behind as well as a burly lay brother clad in leathers. Shadan walked to the edge of the plateau, all the easier to address his large and fully attentive audience.

"Mages of the Isle of Tears," he began; "this is the most difficult address I have ever had to make to you. For decades, for a time long before my arrival here we have operated as a partnership, knights and mages fighting together on the field of battle, protecting each other, a relationship based on mutual trust and respect. Unlike several of the Chiran colleges there has never been any adversarial element between us, never any need to enforce discipline, never any need for a rebellion to be incited. Well now, all of that has changed."

"What?" Miriam gasped; the word was echoed by many others. People looked around at the knights as though seeking answers. They got nothing but silence, a silence broken only the sound of several knights loosening their swords in their scabbards.

"We are currently in the midst of a crisis on the island, that much I readily admit to you. However, that does not mean that any of you," he waved his arm at the mages, "should be taking the law into their own hands. Last night though a group of you decided to do exactly that."

Miriam clasped Gytha's hand, Gytha holding it firm.

"Several mages here crossed the bridge last night, attempted to seize a ship and effect their escape. In the ensuing chaos three people were killed: Sir Beverley, Knight Captain of the Island of Healing, Knight Sergeant Welton and mage Dicken the healer. The two knights killed were killed by a mage, Senior Oskum, a man I am sure most of you know.

"Artorus teeth Gytha," Miriam gasped, "Welton dead? Did you know?"

Gytha nodded, "I had no idea how to tell you."

The hum from the crowd started to swell, now the knights had to draw their swords yet still the noise grew. It took the drummers to bring back order, their drum skins pounding frenetically, that and Shadan finally losing patience and shouting the single word," Silence!" at them.

The noise finally died at that. Those at the front of the audience could see the knight's face, puce and angry. He resumed his tirade.

"You have been brought here to witness the punishment of the guilty. The male conspirators will receive ten lashes of the razor whip, the female conspirators five. Then mage Oskum will be executed in front of you. Though, thanks to our gull problem, his body will not be hung in chains from one of the towers you will all watch the execution and see the consequences of any attempted subversion. That should make you all understand."

He ploughed on, "once this matter is concluded you will all be seeing some changes in the way things are done here, at least temporarily. The Grand Duke is due to visit us within the week and we cannot take the risk of a similar event happening again. After we have finished here you will all return to your cells which will be inspected and searched, a process that will continue at least once a day. There will be no talking in the refectory, each tutorial will have a knight present to witness it. There will be a curfew, when the night bell sounds there will be no gathering in the library, you will be expected to go to your cells. Any public gathering of more than four people will be forbidden. There will be further restrictions on behaviour too, all will be written down and posted on doors and notice boards throughout the college. Ignorance of the rules will be no excuse if any transgressions are reported." He shook his head, as though he could hardly believe his own words.

"Finally I wish to express my sadness and disappointment at all of these developments. Two personal friends of mine are dead. My natural instinct is to be angry and to seek vengeance from the perpetrators. But I know that this will solve nothing. As the Gods will it hopefully in six months we will have reverted to the natural way of things and these matters will no longer be relevant, though they will never be forgotten. That is my most fervent wish. In the meantime you are all compelled to watch the punishing of the guilty. Proceed."

The drummers resumed their playing, beating a slow, melancholic tattoo as the guilty were lead from a place of concealment in the cut, out on to the plateau in full view of the observers. The men were clad in long white smocks, the women in their shifts. At some point in their procession they had been told to remove their shoes with the result that their bare feet were now cut and bloodied. Gytha listened to the increasing and urgent whispers around her for, of course, there was not one mage present who did not know the accused and only a small amount who did not have a personal friend on the plateau.

"Ebden! It is Ebden! I was looking for him last night, I had a book to return to him."

"That can't be Brytta, she would have more sense!"

"Karel isn't well enough for this, she has had a strange illness for months, she is too weak!"

"Is that Asitaigne? What has the silly cow done this time?"

"Oh Artorus be merciful, Iska? Oh poor Iska!"

The last statement was made by Emonie, her close friend who was standing just in front of Gytha, and all Gytha could think, as she listened to the angry, confused, and fearful voices around her was.

"If we had caught the culprit by now, none of this would have happened."

Her left hand was still holding Miriam's, now her right hand too was holding Kestine's.

****

The miscreants encounter the razor whip

They had ropes around their necks and cords had been tied around their waists, though Iska did not know why. She was very tired and as a consequence she felt rather displaced by the events of the last few hours, as though it was her body feeling the cold, her throat feeling the bilious nausea, her mind experiencing the unending fear and yet it somehow wasn't actually her standing there, toes bleeding into the sand, thumbnail digging into white finger, it wasn't really her, how could it be? How could she be standing here? How could it be her about to be whipped, used as an example, to instil fear and docility into her fellows?

The four women were led off to one side and made to kneel. Next to them a group of red and white robed healers set down a series of wooden buckets and earthenware jars, salt and water in the buckets, poultices in the jars, or so a knight had told her as they walked from the college. There was also a pile of clean white cloth which the knight had not talked about, it suddenly dawned on her that they might be used to mop up blood, she bit her lip and looked straight ahead of her, eyes as dead as a landed fish.

The men were led to the wooden crosspieces where the knights lowered their smocks to the waist, Iska now realised that the cords were tied there to stop the smocks falling off completely and that she would be stripped in a similar manner. Then the men were tied, arms above head, legs splayed, to the whipping cross. Iska swallowed, this was happening just yards away, she wasn't sure if watching would be worse than experiencing.

Then up stepped lay brother Muleforth. He was stripped to the waist now, a large, burly man with a scowling face sitting under a shock of wiry black hair. Few mages knew him well, for he tended the larger animals, donkeys, and cattle. He never tried to socialise with the mages and perhaps this was why, for it seemed another duty of his was to administer the punishment of the knights. And in his gloved hands he held the razor whip.

It was about six feet long, fashioned from black leather and even at this distance she could see the glint of steel as he first flexed, then straightened it. The bound men were facing the cliff and so in turn he took each man by the hair and twisted their neck slightly before saying.

"Behold the whip."

He held the thing up to their eyes before doing something else to their face (Iska could not quite see). Then he moved on to the next man.

That done he moved a few feet away from the man nearest to Iska, unfurled the whip and gave it a couple of practice swings, slapping it on to the rocky surface. The drummers stopped beating until he had finished, then Muleforth looked over to them and nodded. They resumed their playing, a single leaden beat, then a space, then another beat, Muleforth lined up the distance between him and his first victim.

And then the punishment started.

****

Every time the whip was swung, every time it impacted on unprotected flesh, the crack echoed hard and long off the cliff face. It was a sharp sound, piercing, and Gytha flinched every time she heard it. The lay brother would strike one mage, then move to the next one, then the next, one blow for each mage before resuming from the beginning again. It was time consuming, almost balletic, a slow ghastly horror play, both fascinating and repellent. Gytha was quite a distance away, her view partly obscured by bobbing heads, but she did not feel compelled to search for a better vantage.

"Oh Elissa, this is beyond bearing," Miriam was shaking her head; "I cannot watch anymore."

She started to turn away, but Gytha held her hand firm. "The knights will notice if you don't watch. Squint, squeeze your eyes to blur them, then you won't see any of it."

"The sound is worse than the sight," Kessie whispered. "Those poor men. What drove them to try and escape?"

"Fear of Xhenafa maybe, dissatisfaction with this place, a desire to wake up somewhere else with different views, who knows?" Gytha said. "Be honest, we all have felt some of that, maybe they just felt it more than us."

"Shut up and watch!" a knight reprimanded her. She obeyed and focussed once more on the "spectacle" taking place in front of her. To her relief it appeared that the whipping had finished. The men were being untied and passed on to the healers, who made them lie face down on a white cloth before kneeling over them to tend their wounds. She started to sigh with relief but soon checked herself.

For now it was the turn of the women.

****

The blood, the agony, and one brave donkey

Iska may have felt divorced from reality before, but not now, certainly not now, she had seen enough, heard enough for her throat to constrict with terror.

The men were strong, they had to be. They twisted and turned in their shackles as the blows hit home, blood spraying like rain, flesh tearing, a horrible, horrible sound. Asitaigne next to her was whimpering, Iska could not feel her own legs. She wanted to vomit but there was nothing to bring up, so she stopped looking at what was happening next to her and started to look up at the sky. It was grey, peppered with jagged strips of heavy cloud, yet there was light there too, behind it all a sun was shining, fighting to be seen. The sky held a thousand contrasting monochrome shades, such a vast distance away, such a vast distance, such a....

A knight was easing her to her feet, she looked around wildly. The men were not there...yes they were, but they were now on the ground groaning in pain. Healers were putting salt on their backs, their backs were raw, covered in slick blood just as the sand and stone next to the whipping crosses were. And now she was being led to one of them.

Brytta was first, a knight unlaced her shift, pulling it to her waist before telling her to place her arms on the cross where they were tied, roughly, with little regard to comfort. The same was done to her feet. She was ready.

Karel was next. She had spent all night praying and was doing the same now, Iska felt that she had ceased to be human, chanting the same lines over and over again like some puppet show marionette, the one they used to embody penitence on the five festival days spread throughout the year. Then it was Asitaigne, she cried openly as they undressed and tied her. As the night had passed in the cell Iska had watched her disintegrate completely, she was normally aloof, self- confident, physically beautiful, and readily dismissive of others. Even now as they undressed her Iska was aware of that, Emonie had

143

talked about her many times. In the college physical relationships between mages of the same sex were grudgingly accepted, something which caused many of the younger mages to experiment with their sexuality, and Iska and Emonie had been two such young women. They had tried intimacy with each other on a couple of occasions and it seemed that that was the course that Emonie was happiest with. She had long confided her unrequited desire for Asitaigne to Iska and Iska had oft agreed that Asitaigne was beautiful. Not now though, her face was grey, her eyes red with crying, her hair bedraggled. She even tried struggling free before she was tied but the knight was far too strong for her and tied up she was. "Please!" she called out to no one in particular. Her voice was pitiful, heart rending. "Please! I have done nothing!"

She was ignored. Instead the knight left her and walked up to Iska. Her breathing was quick, shallow, audible as the knight unlaced her shift. Instinctively she went to cover herself with her hands, but the knight prevented her, lashing her right arm to the cross. She did not resist as he did the same with the rest of her limbs and now she was tied, splayed, helpless, staring at the cliff face just a couple of feet away. It smelled dank, clumps of rotting weed spilled over the loose stones and water filled crevices nearby. How best to cope with what was going to happen? Her mind raced with alternatives but could settle on nothing. Her mouth was dry, dry as a dead twig under summer sunshine, her exposed skin was goose pimpled, white flesh marbled with blue veins, she could not think for fear...

Suddenly, she felt a gnarled, strong, heavy hand grab at her hair. Her neck was twisted to the right, and she looked into the eyes of Muleforth; black eyes, hard eyes, a predator's eyes. He opened a mouth full of rotten teeth and spoke, foul breath stinging her still tender nose.

"Behold the whip."

She looked at it again as he held it up, but it was much closer now, supple leather studded with sharp, tiny metal teeth. This time though she could smell the blood coating it. He saw her eyes widen and smiled.

"Open your mouth."

She did so and half choked as he slid a piece of wood between her teeth, it was still wet with the spittle of the man it was given to before her.

"Keep it there or you will bite off your tongue."

And then he moved on to Asitaigne.

She could only breathe through her nose and her nose was sore and still swollen. Brytta had told her to try and take herself to some other place in her mind, to detach herself, it would be the best way to deal with the pain. Brytta had always frightened her before, she seemed a joyless, severe sort and yet, last night, after some initial hostility, she had shown an almost motherly concern for her. While Karel prayed in her monotone, while Asitaigne cried and prayed with her head in her hands Brytta had put her arm around Iska, told her to be brave, told her how she would deal with the pain. She made her use the latrine bucket, something that Iska was now very grateful for, a grumbling bladder would be no help at all right now, only Asitaigne had refused to use it and Iska doubted that that was hardly helping her fragile mental state at all.

Think of something Iska. Think. But she was too frightened, her thoughts came in vivid, inchoate flashes, almost impossible to pin down. She listened to the drumming, she saw the pattern of barnacles on the cliff face in front of her, she tried to work out what shape they resembled, but she couldn't, she just couldn't.

Crack! He had started. He had started with Brytta. She could hear Brytta groan even from here. Iska struggled against her bonds. Hopeless. It just chafed her wrists.

Crack! Karel's turn. Another groan. Iska's breathing became frantic. Her battered nose ached. By Elissa, by Camille, let her endure, let her be stoic, be brave. Iska called on the saints to help her, Saint Barnaby, paragon of forbearance, Saint Ariane, whose suffering in the name of the Gods was an example to all, Saint…

Crack! Asitaigne shrieked, almost spitting out the block from her mouth. Iska could hear Muleforth's heavy boots, he was standing behind her. Oh Gods, oh Gods! It was her turn. By Saint Sarrak, banisher of demons, by Saint Erise, who stood up to an emperor and lived…

Crack! White, searing, agonising pain, like being stung by a thousand wasps, stings full of molten poison, tearing, ripping, torturous, torment. A strip of prickling fire across her lower back. Iska writhed in anguish, she never sweated normally but now there it was, beading on her forehead, her eyes moistened as her throat dried. One down, four to go, could she withstand four?

She looked over at Asitaigne who was also pulling at her bonds. Iska would love her figure, especially her full breasts, no wonder men swarmed over her.

Crack! Brytta again. Another groan. Iska looked at her own breasts, small, most flatteringly described as pert, she felt inadequate. Emonie fantasised over Asitaigne, and she had not told Emonie about her and Mattris, Emonie did not know that she preferred men, she did not want to upset her best friend, Emonie only went to Mattris that night because Iska suggested that she tried it, just for once, just in case. She had to apologise to Emonie...

Crack! A soft cry from Karel, Iska barely heard it. Why was she thinking about such stupid things right now? Because it was doing as Brytta suggested, taking her mind elsewhere. Apologise to Emonie and thank Brytta, two things to do afterwards...

Crack! Asitaigne screamed, then sobbed, slumping as much as her bonds allowed her to. Heavy boots again, coming close to her, heavy set man grunting, preparing herself, she would be a different person after this, less frivolous, more studious...

Crack! Iska's mind screamed as she bit down hard on the block. It hurt! It fucking hurt! It hurt so much, so much. You stupid cow Iska, how did you end up here, stupid, stupid...

But she would be different now, less disruptive in tutorials, she would read her books, pass her tests, be as good as mentor Marcus had told her she could be, before he had gone to war. She would fulfil her potential and make penance to the gods as any sinner should...

Crack! But Iska was not really listening to the whip now, she was thinking that she would be stronger for this, just like the way suffering made the saints what they were, she would embrace the pain, draw it into her, make it part of her, she just needed the will to endure...

Crack! She had it! Something to distract her, a story that enthralled her as a child. The tale of the explorer Lassiter and his faithful donkey, Dash. A hundred years ago he decided to cross that great natural boundary that stopped the expansion of the Chiran Empire in the south east, the colossal Rift of the Divine Axe, caused when Artorus smote the ground during his final duel with Keth. Narrow, yet too wide to bridge, too deep to see the bottom, it ran from the southern Dragonspine Mountains in a line to the mountain kingdoms of the Norvak people and had always been deemed impassable...

Crack! Asitaigne writhed, a spray of blood flew from her back, Iska continued to think of her story, trying to ignore her loud, rapid breathing. Lassiter travelled the length of the rift before finally discovering a path into the gorge. It took two years for he and Dash to climb down, cross the shadow river at the bottom and climb up the other side, where he saw the Gargantuans, a line of enormous statues so old their features had been worn smooth by the elements, statues that may or may not have depicted humans, possibly magical statues for not even the flying beasts the emperor commanded dared pass them. The boots were behind her, whip poised to strike, bite down hard Iska...

Crack! She had tried to be brave, to not cry out but she had forgotten what Brytta had told her, that screaming could help deflect the pain, so this time she emptied her lungs into the loudest shriek this block in her mouth would allow. It helped, a little, but her face was scarlet, her eyes stinging with tears, the cold trickle of blood on her back was becoming a river, she could feel it soaking into the cord at her waist. The third blow down, a sixtieth percentile suffered, only two to go, only two...

Crack! He was back with Brytta again. Where was she? Oh yes, Lassiter and Dash had crossed the rift. They spent another year wandering a parched, open desert of dust and rock until finally the peaks of the Dragonspine were to the west of them and not the east, Lassiter was the first Chiran to see them thus...

Crack! Karel was almost silent. This worried Iska more if possible, at least people that screamed were alive, she hoped the Gods answered Karel's constant invocations and protected her. Anyway, Lassiter was now in a shattered wasteland, there were few plants other than thorns, and no grass, just grey, dry earth. Here they crossed beaches where intense heat had fused the sand into glass, where the seas steamed and lakes were yellow with sulphur, where petrified forests bestrode plains of crumbling ash, until finally they met the Zmeyudi...

Crack! Asitaigne. Poor, feeble Asitaigne. And again Brytta's wisdom asserted itself. For the pain had caused the poor woman to lose control completely, her legs sagged like a drunkards' and running down her leg came a stream of dark urine which started to form a pool around her feet. Iska wondered which hurt the haughty woman most, the pain or the humiliation.

The Zmeyudi was an elven term, the dragon people Lassiter called them, the Kozeans called them the Zaa. Human... mostly, yet their eyes were yellow, they had smooth skin, some had red scales covering parts of their bodies, some had crests on their heads, some had spines, others had tails, or even horns, he was behind her again, get ready Iska, get ready for it...

Crack! She screamed again, thrashed against the ropes, a swarm of biting ants crawling over her back, spitting acid into her wounds. She had heard that the later lashes hurt less than the first, as the nerves were destroyed by the flagellation. Well she had experienced it now and in the words of the mother that had raised her, it was utter bollocks. Tears were now running freely down her face, without warning a stream of mucus spilled from her nose, she had never sweated so much, blood was dripping on to the stone.

Crack! Back with Brytta, Brytta's last lash. They were untying her already, lying her down, tending to her, it was almost over, just one lash to go, Gods be praised. Lassiter was accepted by the Zmeyudi, spent two years living with them, learning their ways, understanding them. Finally he left for home, determined to set up a trading network between them and the empire, but when he was within a few days journey of the Rift of the Divine Axe a great dust storm blew up around them, a storm that lasted for weeks...

Crack! Karel was still silent, when they untied her she flopped like doll. The healers crowded her, gave her water, mopped her brow. One more lash to go Iska, the pain was unbearable, fire, tearing fire, sharp talons rending flesh, ripping her nerves apart. Her hair was plastered to her forehead, her face throbbed with heat, her back pulsed and spasmed, flesh exposed, she wondered if the crowd could see her internal organs, well she had been told oftentimes that she had a vivid imagination.

Crack! Asitaigne. Less than a second afterwards Asitaigne spat the block out of her mouth and screamed long and hard at the blank cliff. "I hate you! I hate you! she wailed again and again as the men untied her. Muleforth's heavy tread was moving behind Iska once more. Two years after the storm began Dash strolled into a Chiran army outpost, emaciated but alive, he would later be described by the emperor as the noblest beast that had ever lived. Lassiter's journal was tied to the saddle but of Lassiter himself there was no sign...

Crack! There it was. Punishment over. All that was left was agony. She followed Asitaigne's example and spat out the wooden block. Keth curse it all, the taste of it would live with her forever. She too shrieked at the blank stone and then, energy expended, she slumped against the whipping cross as the men finally came to untie her bonds.

She wanted to collapse, faint away, let the healers take control, let them ease the pain that was causing white lights to flash behind her eyes, but she couldn't, not yet, for she had given somebody a promise, a promise that she intended to keep.

****

Executions half remembered

Miriam was shaking her head, her distress was obvious, Kestine was remembering, remembering her own ordeal by fire so many years ago, her grey eyes registering the pain she felt then, and the pain others were feeling now. Only Gytha seemed relatively unmoved, something that Miriam picked up on immediately.

"Doesn't this bother you?" she asked, keeping her voice low. "By punishing them they are punishing us, punishing all sorcerers for having the temerity to push against the rules. Aren't you angry at least?"

"It isn't that" Gytha responded, "I was just thinking that out here, in this place, how insulated we are from the world outside. We have seen nothing like this in our time here, yet I remember watching a couple of executions on the mainland. I was a child, my parents loved me yet thought nothing of letting us watch such things."

"We used to travel to the main town in our area occasionally," Kessie spoke almost absently. "The one time they were hanging a man, a thief I think it was. All of us kids watched it, I remember the man's purple face, his enormous swollen tongue sticking out of his mouth, his white eyes popping. And when he was swinging his arms and legs were jerking all over the place, he had no one to pull on his legs to make it quicker for him. It took him an age to die. Then, the following summer we returned and just outside the city gates he was there, stuck in a gibbet, or at least I think it was him, it was difficult to tell, there wasn't an awful lot left bar hair and bone. And some yellow skin. Used to give me nightmares it did. Still does sometimes."

"The difference is, is that we didn't have to watch them then," Gytha pointed out; "now we are being forced to watch."

"As I said, we are being punished," Miriam was reinforcing the point, "the actions of a few idiots and we all get the blame."

"They are not idiots," Gytha objected, "they were just frightened. And two knights are dead, one of whom we all liked, they have every right to be angry."

"I don't see Steven here," Miriam was on tiptoes, looking over the crowd. "You think he would be given the occasion."

"He is helping his wife and daughter settle in," Gytha said; "they crossed over to this island this morning."

"What is she like, his wife?" Kessie asked.

"Horrible. A rich spoilt brat."

"Oh dear," Miriam managed a half smile, despite the circumstances. "You will have to stop flirting with him now."

"I was not flirting. And I know you disapprove of us working so closely, knights and mages and all that."

Miriam bit her lip. She suddenly remembered that Gytha didn't know about her and Nikolaj. "Sorry Gytha, I need to speak to you later, when you have some free time."

"Is it important? It is just that I might be quite busy today."

"Yes. Well no, given what we are watching, I just have something to tell you, an apology if you like and you know I cannot keep secrets from either of you."

Both women turned to look at her, Miriam went red. "Kessie and me?" Gytha asked.

"Yes."

"I will see you when I can then. It looks like we have to go back to our cells first, to be inspected or searched or whatever it is they want from us."

"You will have to tell me separately," Kessie shook her straw blonde hair. "I have to spend the day with senior Kas, learning how to charge staves. Artorus only knows when I will be able to get away."

"Boring!" Gytha and Miriam spoke in unison.

"I know. The Gods know how to test a girl's patience."

At that point though, they all fell quiet, for the drums were beating and senior Oskum was being led out for them all to see.

****

The justice of the sword, and a promise kept

There was blood everywhere. Spatters of it coated the sand, it had run over the waist cord to soak into Iska's shift, the hands of the healers were stained crimson. She could smell it too, the metallic tang mingling with rotting weed and stagnating pools; she wanted to retch, but still had nothing to bring up.

And she had not realised how weak she was, she had to be supported when they lead her from the whipping cross to the sheet she was to lay face down on, she barely had the wherewithal to put her hand over her chest. She slumped onto the cloth and shut her eyes. Then she opened them, the pain was too great, every time she flexed a shoulder blade or inhaled too deeply it felt like somebody was ramming a spear into her diaphragm, a sharp, penetrating pain, sticky blood still oozing from her wracked body. She eventually found a position, propping herself up on her elbows, staring straight ahead that was reasonably bearable as the healers started to work on her.

Firstly they washed her back with salt and water, which, like a whole cherry placed on a custard pudding, merely applied the finishing touch to her agony.

"Keep still!" the healer ordered, and she tried, she tried hard, but it was impossible to stop flinching completely. She was close to sobbing uncontrollably but, with an effort of will she did not realise she was capable of, she managed to keep the tears at bay. She would cry later, once her responsibilities were fully discharged.

She looked over at the other women. Karel still seemed to be unconscious, but the healers did not seem to be as concerned as they were with her before. Brytta did notice Iska and looked at her in return, she was white as chalk but still managed to nod to her, it seemed like she was saying "well done," so Iska nodded back, a nod she hoped Brytta would read as, "thank you". Asitaigne next to her was in worse shape, she lay flat, head turned towards Iska, frost blue eyes half closed. They had pulled her soiled shift off her and were washing her naked body from head to toe. She was humming to herself, "Meriel watches over me", a childhood tune, a comforting tune. Iska was relieved when they finally covered the lower half of her body with a linen cloth, at least they had given her some dignity at last. Many of the female mages, Iska included, saw Asitaigne as something of a bitch, using her looks to her advantage, getting to the front of the queue in everything. Iska never thought she would ever feel sorry for her but now, right at this moment, she thought she had never seen anything so sad and pathetic in her life.

Then though she turned away, the drumming had changed, something was about to happen. And there he was, Oskum, hands tied, surrounded by three knights, being marched to the centre of the rocky shelf. Father Ambrose walked behind them, he was holding the book of Artorus and reading passages from it, from the final chapter, "Preparations for the great journey". Oskum was walking unassisted, but he was obviously unsteady on his feet. He tottered to the appointed place and was told to kneel and face the crowd.

But he resisted. "No!" he said, "not that way, I want to look over there. You are supposed to give me a final request and that is it."

The knights shrugged their shoulders and let him kneel the way he wanted, facing Iska. Ignoring the healers she pushed herself up on her hands, all the better to look at him.

"Do you accept Artorus into your life and do you want us to intercede with Xhenafa on his behalf?" Ambrose intoned; his voice suitably doleful.

"I do," Oskum choked. He was shaking, fear was constricting his throat.

Ambrose then said the prayer of Xhenafa. "Divine Xhenafa, whom we shall meet once and once only, I commend the soul of the condemned to thee. Guide him safely to the seat of the Gods and forgive him the sins of his miserable life. Let him be judged fairly, and, if he is required to labour in Keth's furnace for eternity, grant him the forbearance and endurance required for such a task. As it must be. For ever."

Ambrose walked away. A knight then held out a black hood for Oskum to put on, but he shook his head, swallowed, shut his eyes, then blinked them open again.

Then he looked straight at Iska.

She met his gaze without tears. She no longer covered her breasts because if he wanted them to be the last thing he saw then she was happy to oblige. She was gratified to see though that it was only her eyes, her large, dark, expressive eyes that he was interested in.

The pace of the drumming increased; a knight told him to kneel up straight and push his hands down as far as he could. Oskum complied. The knight raised his sword and placed it on top of Oskum's left shoulder, Oskum was only wearing his white linen smock, one accurate push and the sword would pass right through his heart.

"Senior Oskum!" the knight called out, more to the crowd than the condemned man. "You have been found guilty of the murder of two Knights of the Thorn and the punishment for such a crime is death. May Artorus show you the mercy we flawed mortals cannot!" The knight was hoarse, rasping, nervous, reluctant. Iska prayed that it would not affect his accuracy, she wanted more than anything for Oskum to die quickly.

The drumming continued. Oskum had stopped shaking by now, he appeared calmer, resigned, almost peaceful. To her surprise she saw a wan smile cross his face. He was smiling. At her. Thanking her for not deserting him. She smiled back, a flickering, fragile smile, she felt no pain now, all her thoughts were for him. And then the tears did start to come.

The drumming became even faster, even louder, the knight clasped the sword hilt firmly with both hands, pressing it into Oskum's skin till a drop of blood started to show on his smock. The mage did not notice, he had Iska, he had her smile, and for just a couple of days, for the first time in his life, he had felt what real love was truly like...

And then the drumming stopped.

Gytha's cell, and her person, is searched

Gytha took another look around her cell. She was not by nature an untidy person, it was just that in life one had priorities and when in her cell these priorities revolved around reading, sleeping, washing, and looking out of the window, staring wistfully into space and dreaming of a better world than this. Once all of these matters had been attended to then tidying, that is, the matters of placing her inkwell in the correct position, of ensuring her spare robes were hanging evenly, of checking that her books were stacked neatly with the most important ones on top and seeing that her notes and other papers were gathered together rather than resembling a shower of autumn leaves shaken by a brisk wind, then indeed tidying became the most important thing on her mind.

Today though, the matter of keeping her cell in immaculate order had rather escalated in importance, for today her cell was going to be searched by the knights. After witnessing the grisly and extremely deflating spectacle on the beach she had skipped back to the college as fast as her protesting legs could carry her. Once in the cell she kicked off her sand soiled shoes and replaced them with the slightly tattier second pair that she wore in emergencies. Twenty minutes of busying herself about the place and she felt that her cell, whilst not coming close to Miriam's in terms of inch perfect order, was at least presentable. It was not as though the knights needed to take long here, like all novices, outside of books and parchment her possessions were very meagre indeed.

Finished with her work she sat on the bed and at last started to think about recent events, events that she felt where beginning to overwhelm her. In two days, no, in less than two days she had seen two men die, two others fight each other almost to the death and of course been inches from the same fate herself. Oh, and she had met the lady Fedrica, or, as she had taken to calling her in her mind, that supercilious, snotty bag of bones. Perhaps facing death had not been the worst experience of the last couple of days after all.

Oskum had died immediately, the killing blow, one very difficult to execute she had been told, had been inch perfect. Once the blade had been withdrawn he had flopped to the ground like a stranded seal. The people around her had watched in a stunned, resentful silence; she had wondered if the execution had fuelled, rather than quelled, any sense of rebellion amongst her peers. In theory of course there were enough mages here, enough power within them to blast every knight into the sea. But of course as with most theories, a forensic examination of the facts soon resulted in them slowly being pulled apart at the seams.

Firstly none of them were warriors, they were a group of educated people, almost gentle people, inured to the realities of everyday life, whereas the knights were professional warriors, all of whom had dealt death at some point in their lives. Secondly, the armour of the knights and their magic resistant properties were well known, Gytha sometimes wondered if these were exaggerated somewhat, that a myth had been allowed to grow with the express purpose of intimidating the mages. Yet yesterday Sir Beverley had died without his armour and the armoured Welton had been killed by his fall, not directly by the power unleashed by Oskum. Thirdly of course any rebellion would ultimately doom them. If they expelled the knights they would all either be left to ultimately starve or, even worse, they would have to face an invasion from the Grand Duke's forces, one in which they would be hopelessly outnumbered. Also if Gytha remembered rightly the treaties held with other nations concerning the organisation of the colleges meant that they were all obligated to send troops if a rebellion started. A coalition of all the northern nations of the world against a few hundred frightened people, some of them children, some of them elderly. Any solidarity mages held would soon crumble in the face of such imminent hostility. Rebellion truly was futile.

Footsteps outside the door. Gytha got to her feet as two knights airily strolled in without knocking. They were both armoured though neither wore their helmets and to Gytha's surprise she saw that she didn't recognise either of them. The first man was thick set, fair haired with eyes that had the blue of an early spring sky. He had a small scar above his tangled eyebrows and blinked constantly, as though even the gloom of her cell was too bright for him. The second man was taller, thinner, darker, a man who seemed completely at home with his brooding nature. He had a pencil thin moustache, unusual for a knight, and a curved, high bridged nose that put Gytha in mind of an eagle poised to swoop down on some poor hapless rabbit. He held a sheet of parchment in front of him and was scanning it keenly whilst the blond man did the talking.

"Good. You are standing by your bed. Now stay there while we check the bookshelves and the drawers in your desk. My colleague has the list of proscribed items, if you have any of them they will be confiscated with a warning. If you still have one of them after a second search then the discipline may be a little more rigorous."

He went over to her desk and started to lift the items off it, scrutinising them with such efficacy it was as though he was regarding a bejewelled figurine fashioned by a master craftsman, before finally realising that he was only looking at a wood carved pen and setting it down again with a disappointed grunt.

"May I ask exactly what these proscribed items are?" Gytha queried.

"They will be posted on doors and noticeboards throughout the college." The other man had a thin, reedy voice, he spoke to Gytha without looking at her.

"It is mostly objects with sharp edges, knives and the like…" He paused for effect.

"And some books with…questionable subject matter," he continued after the pause, "and no, do not ask me what constitutes "questionable." I am only doing as instructed."

"Does that mean I cannot borrow a knife from stores? I was going to you see."

"Yes," said the blonde man, "it means exactly that. Refectory knives too are to be handed in once you have finished with them. What else would you want a knife for anyway?"

Gytha wondered if there were any group of people, anywhere on earth that had to put up with such persistent scrutiny. "A woman sometimes requires a knife for…personal reasons."

"Ha!" the dark man exclaimed, "these mages shave themselves like noblewomen!"

Gytha snorted indignantly. "It is a precaution, like everywhere else we sometimes have problems with lice, not that I have, but…"

The other man cast a baleful, blinking eye over his companion. "Mages get crabs too? I thought you could just blast them with magic. Anyway, I am afraid that until these restrictions are eased, stores have been told not to hand out knives to anybody."

"You will have to put up with a bit of itchy thatch on your nethers."

Gytha had already come to the conclusion that this dark haired knight was not one of noble birth. "Still, it might keep the parts that matter warmer this winter."

He had given her the perfect chance to change the subject. "Ah! I was wondering if you knew when we would get a brazier in our rooms. The temperature is dropping…" she trailed off as she saw the two of them shaking their heads. "Is that twenty-five times?" the blonde man asked his companion.

"Twenty-six," the other man corrected him.

"Yes. You are the twenty sixth person to ask. The answer is not yet. We are waiting for a ship bringing charcoal from the mainland. Until it arrives…"

"The senior mages have them," Darkman interrupted; "but the novices will have to wait, as will the lay brothers."

"The lay brothers sleep communally," Gytha said pointedly "They have each other's body heat at least. And they are close to the kitchens, the bread ovens can keep them warm."

"That's as maybe," said the blonde man, "but the situation is as it is."

"And you knights?" Gytha asked, "are you struggling manfully in the cold?"

"Settling in just fine thank you," the dark fellow answered, "coals burning fit to toast my toes."

"I am so happy for you," Gytha said archly. "I take it you are new arrivals here?"

"Yes. In with the last ship." The blonde fellow had pulled open the draw under her desk and was rummaging through the scant number of objects present there. He lifted one out and held it out in front of her. "What is this?" he asked, as though the answer was not obvious.

"It is a comb. My comb." Gytha emphasised the "my".

The knight removed his glove and pressed his forefinger against the bone teeth. "Quite sharp aren't they? Are such things on the list?"

"I will check." Darkman peered so closely at his parchment Gytha wondered if he could see any of it at all. Her patience was beginning to thin.

"Oh come on, you are just teasing me, I am hardly going to stab you with a comb am I? It is the only thing I have from home!"

The blonde placed the comb gently on the desk. "Let us check your books and the bed. Then we will see."

She stood to one side as he rifled through the bookshelves, checked the pockets in her spare robe and felt the mattress on the bed.

"Anything under the bed?" he asked.

"A pair of shoes, covered in sand, and a chamber pot. You want to check that?"

The dark fellow sniggered. Seeing Gytha's raised eyebrow he started to explain. "One of the Chiran colleges, in the mountains. Instead of emptying the chamber pots in the morning one of the lay brothers was collecting it, putting it into flasks and selling it in the city as a kind of tonic! "Magic water" he called it, bald men were rubbing it into their scalp to make hair grow, people were putting it on their chests to cure colds, women covered their chins to get rid of spots..."

"You are not going to say they were drinking it?" Gytha could almost feel herself ageing.

"Course they were! A rejuvenating elixir. He was adding rosemary to it to add flavour, but piss will always taste like piss. I doubt mage piss is that different somehow."

"Having drunk some Chiran beer I doubt that they would ever notice," his friend said with a knowing wink.

"He made a fortune before he was caught. Was given a public flogging but I bet he just stood there and thought of all that money..." Darkman trailed off, as though he was seeing gold coins floating in front of his eyes.

Gytha made a face. "I am sorry if you are feeling thirsty, but I am afraid my pot has already been emptied..."

Both men laughed uproariously at that. "Aha! You are a good one!" blonde man said finally. "Can hand it out just as well as you can take it."

"I hope so. Are you finished with me now?"

"Not quite I am afraid," he suddenly looked uncomfortable. "Your robe, the one you are wearing I need to check it."

She threw her arms up and rolled her eyes. Speaking through gritted teeth she asked. "How so?"

"It is better if you take it off. I need to check the pouch belt and all the internal and external pockets. The alternative is for me to pat you down and put my hands in your pockets myself and I don't really want to do that. You are wearing the full length under thing I hope. It covers as much as a robe does."

"Elissa make me saintly, just as I thought this morning couldn't get any worse." The full under shift did cover everything but forearms but even so...

She loosened the belt, pulled the robe over her head, and almost threw it at the blonde man, feeling a huge, balmy, cloud of body heat leave her never to return. She hopped from leg to leg as the two of them took an age to open each pouch, ferret through each pocket, removing the various powders and tinctures concealed within. Eventually they seemed happy with themselves and handed the robe back to her.

"Now are you done?" she asked, her voice muffled as she pulled the robe back over her head.

"Yes," said the blonde knight; "a bit disappointing really, everything in those pouches was pretty standard, the sort of stuff all the other novices have..."

"But I am a novice myself!" Gytha protested.

"Well yes," Darkman agreed, "but we were expecting a little more from you Gytha, after all we had been told."

"You know my name?" she was startled, she had never seen these men before. "How?"

"The captain mentioned you," said the blonde knight. "Tell Gytha I will meet her at the house of Xhenafa, after you have finished with her," he said. So I asked, "but sir, how will I know who she is?" "red head" he said, "has an attitude, witty, answers back". I think he summed you up rather marvellously, no?"

She did smile then. "Yes," she nodded, "I am Gytha, the description must have a slight measure of accuracy I suppose."

"Indeed," said the blonde man; "and as we are at introductions, I am Sir Borak and this, my colleague is Sir Janner. We are very pleased to meet you."

"Likewise." They were both smiling now, she realised that they had both been trying to get a rise out of her. "And I had better go, if Sir Steven needs me."

"Yes," said Sir Janner, "and just to say, we didn't see the events of the morning, too busy going through this list, but we are both sorry for what had to happen. We will be strict, we have to be, but we will be fair too. Both Borak and I came here after serving for ten years at Old City College. You mages are a decent bunch, good people, I hope we can steady things after all the trouble of late."

"Thanks, I hope you are right. So you came from Old City. Any of my people, Kibil people there?"

"Hundreds," said Sir Borak, "and every one a stroppy redhead."

"" Stroppy" is it? I would remind you that people with red hair are not a homogeneous group, we do not all think and speak in exactly the same way, and we do not all lose our tempers at the tiniest piece of provocation."

"You were close though, admit it."

"Close to being outrageously patronised do you mean? The only thing you didn't do was pat me on the head and tell me to calm down."

Sir Janner was grinning. "Point...taken" Sir Borak acknowledged.

"Glad to hear it." Gytha breezed past them and made for the door. "You can close up here when you are done. Thanks for turning the mattress by the way."

"Think nothing of it. Now catch."

Borak was throwing something at her. She caught it one handed. It was her comb.

"Better not forget that," he said to her.

"No. I never will again." She slipped it into a pocket. "See you tomorrow, if you are doing the same thing."

"We are and we will. Fare you well."

"Gods keep you," she said, surprised that she actually meant it.

And then she was gone.

****

More dead to examine

The smoke from the incense burners in the House of Xhenafa was so pungent, so eye stingingly intense, that Gytha started to choke immediately upon entry. It took her a minute to adapt to the hanging blue haze and the muted glow from the lamps. When she had done so she saw two figures laid out on separate black clothed dais, the long, thin form of senior Arbagast, alabaster skin covered in an oily film of embalming unguents, and the shorter, stockier, form of lay brother Havel, Gytha noticed his arms, thick as saplings, he must have been strong as stone in life, but then his strength counted for nothing in the end. White funeral cloth covered the lower half of each man's body, Gytha was grateful for that, seeing Arbagast naked would she felt have been an intrusion too far for her. The permanent, one pitched drone of the priest's song of the dead sat as heavily on Gytha's ears as the incense smog did on her eyes, the pervasive atmosphere sinking her spirits to the bottom of the sea. Finally there was Steven, standing, arms folded at the other end of the room. He sported a clean black shirt, he must possess dozens of the things she thought, and of course his new scar, healing but still red and angry, sat like a badge of honour on his left cheek.

"How are you?" he asked quietly, "I mean, how was it this morning?"

"Chastening," she replied, she saw no reason to lie. "I watched a man die in the freezing cold, I watched several people flogged with a…well with what exactly? Every stroke seemed to draw a gallon of blood."

"A specially designed whip," he sounded deflated, tired. She suddenly realised that he must have had hardly any sleep these last twenty-four hours. "I did what I could Gytha, the punishments you saw were the most merciful the law could allow."

"No need to explain, you lost a friend last night. I will go and see Iska, the youngest woman to get a flogging, when I can, I feel partly responsible for what happened to her."

"Why?"

Gytha opened her arms. "See where we are…again. And we are no nearer to finding the person responsible."

"No," his voice was leaden, devoid of its usual animation. "The two boys doing the cell inspections, what did you think of them?"

"Mad as Uba."

"I chose them specifically. They are veterans of the college system yet are not known here. So they can search the cells without mages trying to get familiar or resentful with them, yet they know enough to at least try and pick all of you off the floor. At least that was my theory."

She smiled for the first time since entering the room. "Well, that is one theory that just might work, they had me on their side by the end at least. Now, what do you want me to do?"

"Look at these two gentlemen, try and tell me how Xhenafa took both of them for their final judgements."

"You don't know?"

"I didn't say that, I just want your opinion."

She nodded and walked up to Arbagast, she suddenly realised the reason for the smoke and the excessive balms coating his body. "Oh by the gods, I had forgotten where the bodies were discovered, the smell close up still penetrates the incense and the oils."

"That it does. The priests had to burn their clothes and clean the bodies up outdoors. Unfortunately, shit is one of those smells you cannot eradicate completely. And ignore a lot of those tiny wounds over the body. They happened after death, things trying to nibble away at the corpse, fortunately with both men the cause of death seems quite obvious."

Gytha pointed to Arbagast's lower jaw, which was almost covered by a dark, livid bruise. Steven nodded. "Now look at the head, the back of the head."

Gytha stood behind Arbagast and crouched a little, peering through the haze. "Is that a fractured skull?" she asked. "It looks almost dented."

"No "almost" about it. He was killed by a skull fracture. It would have knocked him unconscious and being a frail old man he would have passed on soon after. His jaw has been broken too."

"So there is nothing remotely supernatural about his death?"

"Nothing whatsoever. My guess is that he was struck in the face, that the blow knocked him backwards and he hit his head on something hard, something that killed him."

"The blood Miriam found in the stone circle?"

Steven nodded. "I think he was struck there, hit his head against the stone then collapsed and died."

"But how was he found in the sewer trench?"

Steven shrugged his shoulders." You tell me. What I do know is that we have a very earthly perpetrator here. There may be no link at all between this man's death and the deaths of Raiman and Caswell."

"I wouldn't be so sure," Gytha pushed an errant curl out of her eye. "Raiman and Havel were friends, they were found with money far in excess of their regular earnings, they were keeping items ensorcelled with power they had no idea how to use and they died within days of each other. The Gods may sometimes use coincidence to tantalise us, but I think there are too many common factors here for the deaths to be entirely unrelated. Maybe the killer didn't have time to summon Sinotaneh and looking at the strength of the blow it would point to a man doing this, don't you think?"

Steven gently felt the edge of his scar. "Older people bruise easily, a strong, angry woman could do the same. My first thought was that they had somehow killed each other but then who put them in the trench? As for how the lay brother died I would love to hear what you have to say."

Gytha laughed as she moved close to the second dead man for it was fairly obvious what had caused his demise. Nearly the whole left side of his torso was blackened and bruised, bruising that extended up to his lower jaw.

"He has had several ribs broken," Steven told her, "and not just broken but splintered. His lungs have been pierced several times and again his jaw has been broken. The force required to cause these injuries must have been excessive. It must have been a large, unwieldly weapon, that or…"

"The power of a mage," Gytha sighed. "I can well guess how this damage was done."

"Excellent. Good to see knights and mages working together again. Now could you enlighten me?"

"Just one knight and one very uneasy mage working together," Gytha corrected him. "What killed this man is a spell that all mages can execute, the only one we learn as a child. We all carry a reservoir of latent power inside us, some people have a lot of it, others not so much. It is healthy for us to release it from time to time, it stops headaches, nosebleeds, that sort of thing. The way it is done is to focus it into a block of force, you have probably seen mages here standing at the cliff edge from time to time, holding an open palm out, we are sending our power out to sea."

"I have seen them," he admitted. "It just confirmed my prejudice that you are all a bit strange."

"Perhaps we are," she said, rebuffing his attempt at humour; "but it is confinement that makes us so, not our powers. A force spell, a Ptareia, can be formed and cast in seconds. It is an unwieldy club as opposed to a precise rapier, totally unsubtle and only cast in panic, anger, as a matter of last resort, or when there is no time for something a little more elegant. Its strength depends on the power of the mage. This was done by somebody with more power than I."

"A senior?"

"Probably. But not necessarily a frost mage, as I said all of us can cast such a thing."

"So the best way to find out who did this is to look at the why, not the how."

Gytha nodded.

"We are agreed then. I already have Sir Edgar enquiring amongst the lay brothers, to see if Raiman and Havel had a common enemy. Perhaps you could talk to Arbagast's colleague..."

"Kas?"

"Yes, Kas. Talk to her. See if she knows of any enemies he may have had, any reason that anyone would have to kill him."

She shook her head, the wild curl sat in front of her eye once more, "Arbagast had no enemies. He was that rarity, a lovely man. He was a fixture here, we all knew him from childhood, when others say that he was liked by all they are not lying."

"Great." Steven blew air through clenched teeth. "The nearest thing we have to a saint here and he is dead. Now, we have a problem. I am going to be busy for most of today, I need to sort out the effects of the dead men, write to their next of kin, that sort of thing. I would also, if at all possible, like to spend some time with my sick daughter. The dead, and their killers will have to wait till the morrow I am afraid."

"What about Lipshin and Mattris? Surely they are our main suspects still?"

"Detained and in separate cells. We picked them up after they saw the execution. The night Arbagast died though they were definitely in the college because I spoke to both of them. I am presuming, as "Xhenafa" was not involved, that these two killings would have to have been committed by someone close at hand. I am guessing this force spell is a close range thing?"

"It is yes. But the two of them could have sneaked out before or after speaking to you, through the tunnels, unseen."

"Yes they could. But wouldn't the spirit have stopped them?"

"Not if they had this strange blue elf fire. With your permission I will speak to the librarian, see what she knows about it. It is not something we have common knowledge about, we are not taught about it here, but somebody must have researched it at some point. The details may have been in the missing pages of the journal the elves left behind. I think it is important, if we can find out who can wield it, we have our killer. Probably."

Steven pondered her suggestion for a moment. "Speak to her by all means. We can leave our two prisoners till the morning, a night in the cells might aid their desire to assist us."

"Or hinder it. I need to speak to a couple of other people first, personal reasons, then I will speak to Beni."

"And then Kas."

"No need. Kestine is with her today, I can speak to Kessie afterwards, see if Kas mentioned anything that might help us. If she hasn't well I can always see Kas myself tomorrow, in person if need be."

There was a brief, and unusually strained silence between them, Steven came towards her and stood next to Havel's dais so that he faced her directly. "Are you angry with me?"

She shook her head. Now a second curl fell, almost directly in front of the first. "Am I angry? Yes. Am I angry with you? Not really. It will take a long time to get this morning out of my mind. When Sinotaneh almost killed me, I recovered from that in hours, what I saw done to others today..." she sighed, pushing her curls away from her forehead. Seconds later they returned. "I haven't even combed this stuff properly; I normally spend hours combing my hair."

"The weather on the beach probably did it no favours."

"No," her face softened a little; "at least I saw you best the knight Vargo last knight, even if we only saw the end of the fight."

"Bested?" he was unconvinced. "In truth I couldn't land a blade on him. Both the wounds I caused were made by my fist, my arm."

"You still beat him though."

He nodded, and a broad smile broke over his pallid face. Gytha looked him in the eye at last and smiled in return. "So I might not see you till morning then," she said. "Give my love to Edith, I hope her recovery continues."

"I will. Shall I give your love to Fedrica too?"

She spun away and headed for the door. "I need some clearer air. See you on the morrow sir knight."

"On the morrow. I will send for you. And think long and hard about anything you want to ask the two mages, they will be harder to crack than stone."

****

A reluctant trainee

"Right, you can take the cloth off your eyes now."

Kestine pulled her blindfold down and threw back the cowl of her robe, shaking her hair free. Senior Kas regarded her with bright eyes brimming with enthusiasm. She was smiling for the first time that day. "Plaudits are due novice; you have just assisted in charging your first staff."

They were sat in the Oval Room, next to the black slab of a table. On it sat a simple wooden stave, fashioned from pale ash and at its head was fixed a small orb of crystal. As Kessie looked at it she saw a small cobalt blue light flicker at its centre, always diminishing until it finally disappeared completely. She blinked away the yellow after vision at the back of her eyes and exhaled slowly.

Kas was briskly removing the metal finger coverings, setting them down neatly on the table "Well, what did you think?"

Kessie splayed her fingers on the table, noting the smudges they left on its glossy surface. "That was...interesting. Though I am not sure if I really did that much to help."

"You prepared the staff for charging, assisted in the chanting and used part of your own power to complete the process, saving me both time and energy. Not bad for your first morning. Your diligence is to be commended, at least so far."

"And this is a staff for novices? It certainly looks like one."

"It is yes. A training staff. The staves the seniors use need more power and time to process. Do two or three in a day and you really will feel tired. We will do a few more of the simple staves like this one first and then, if you are still interested, we will try one of the advanced ones. Let's see how we go."

She stood, picked the newly charged staff up and set it against the curved wall. She stopped then, looking down at it, her mind elsewhere. "We have a rack we normally put these on. The one we usually use is still in Arbagast's room. I cannot bring myself to go there and get it."

"Shall I go, senior?"

"That would be dear of you, but not now, do it after lunch." She sat again and was silent, fidgeting with the fur lining of her robe. Kessie thought it best to break the brief hush.

"If you need to be alone I can come back another time. I know how close the two of you were."

Kas shook her head. "No, no. I am sorry. I think perhaps I should have company at this difficult time."

"How long did you work with Senior Arbagast? The two of you have worked together for as long as I can remember, and I have been here thirteen or fourteen years."

"Yes," she said slowly, "it would be about fourteen years. It is about fourteen years since I graduated, and I have always worked at this job since then. But I have known Arbagast for a lot longer than that. He took me under his wing in my late teens, once I was sitting where you are now, watching him work, so it was a natural thing for me to join him once I had graduated."

Kessie found herself pricked by curiosity. "Why did he take you under his wing in the first place, if you don't mind me asking?"

"Of course not. It was quite simple. A couple of women who shall remain nameless but are now both respected seniors were pulling my hair and teasing me. Arbagast saw it happening and stopped them, not by hitting them like others might do, he just sat and talked to them, told them how their actions only demeaned them, how foolish they were making themselves look. They were quite shamefaced by the end, they never did it again. Then he started talking to me. "What is your name?" he asked. "Kassali" I replied. "An unusual name" he said, "does it hail from Fash? I know a lot of their female names end in "i". "Yes sir" I replied, "my mother is Fashtani, she settled in Tanaren after fleeing the Kedrogan purges and the ten year civil war they caused. My father is a city guardsman..." And so it started from there, I talked, he listened, and eventually he offered to part mentor me at this job. He became my father here, in this place, this room became an escape for me, I enjoyed coming here far more than doing my regular studies and the work, though sometimes prolonged and tedious, isn't so bad really. You have far more freedom than most mages, as long as you charge your expected quota, your time is your own."

"You like going on walks, don't you?"

"Yes. I try and get out for an hour or so a day, even in bad weather. Later on, I will take flowers to the House of Xhenafa and burn a candle for Arbagast. Then I will sit by the cliffs for a while, take in the air and think. It is a good way to recover after a day's work. Actually, speaking of flowers, your name..."

"Oh I know, "Kestine, the Goddess of flowers". My mother always revered her. "Imagine a world without flowers," she would tell me; "what a dull place it would be." So I have the name of a goddess, if only I had the looks..."

"I have always thought it an odd convention," Kas stood and stretched, feeling a crick in her back. "Nobody dares name a child Artorus or Elissa, or after any of the major Gods because it is disrespectful, saying your child is as a God, making a like for like comparison. Yet minor Gods are different for some reason, people get named after them all the time. Here we have a couple of Karadash's, a Mattris, several Ulian's, a Beneshiel, the list is a long one."

"Yes, a lot of people are named after Gods few people have even heard of. I tried to learn them all once, the complete pantheon. I had been taught my letters, so I wrote this big, long list, over a hundred names, the God and what they are responsible for. I could recite it from beginning to end back then. I used to be bullied too see so when it happened, when they were calling me names I would hide in a corner and read my list. The Gods help us in many ways we cannot foresee."

Kas gave her a narrow glance." It was just a couple of girls with me and it all but stopped with Arbagast's intervention. Was it bad for you?"

"For a while," Kessie admitted; "used to be called all sorts of names. Awkward, clumsy, lumpish, heavy set, fat faced, stupid, slow witted, backward, dull, just to name a few. I couldn't talk you see, as a child, because of something that happened to me. They used to pull my hair to see if I screamed. The bullies were all girls, and they are all still here. I have nothing to do with them now, I managed to find my own friends eventually and they have always come good for me. Mind you I can fight my own battles now, when I did start to talk a few of them had a go at me because I speak quite slowly and have a strong accent, one that was even stronger then. But a few sharp elbows and Kudreyan burns (she mimed the technique) shut them up eventually."

"Girls and women can be the worst. Always trying to climb on somebody else's shoulders. Perhaps that is why I like this job, away from all that maelstrom. Though it won't be the same now Arbagast..." Kas stopped and put her hand to her face, sniffing loudly. Kessie got up and put her arms around her. "You shouldn't really be working now," she said softly.

Kas wiped her reddening eyes. "Oh I should. I need to. I need to fill this...void with something." She pulled a handkerchief from her robe and wiped her face, putting on an unconvincing smile. "Come on, we will try another staff and then you can have some time off."

Kessie let her go and then, completely unexpectedly she found herself yawning, putting her hand over her mouth to shut herself up. She looked guiltily at Kas. "Sorry," she said, as humbly as she could manage.

Kas though was sporting a very knowing look. "I thought you seemed too unaffected by what we just did. Staff charging leaves you mentally tired, you get used to it but for a first timer you will find it draining. You may need a little sleep between charges."

"Oh! I didn't think it would be that bad. Will I have to go back to my cell for a bit?"

"Not at all," Kas smiled at her. "Come with me, I will show you a staff mage's little secret."

She led Kessie out of the Oval Room onto a wide stone landing lit only by a couple of stuttering lamps. A spiral staircase cut through it on the west side, climb up some fifty steps and you would enter the college's main reception room, close to the great doors. Climb down for well over a hundred steps, walk through an open archway and you would be standing on the stone pier of the college harbour. Small and relatively sheltered as it was situated in a cave this was the place smaller ships would moor if they had items specifically for the college. Scrolls, books, treaties pertaining to the way the college was run, specialised spell components, secret correspondence for the Chief Magister, most of them arrived on the island via this harbour. The broader harbour on the Isle of Healing was the place for supplies of food and other goods that needed to be transported in bulk. Given the sensitive nature of the cargo that arrived here a knight was always present and on guard, ship, or no ship. No real view, nowhere to really walk, no one to chat to it was easily the least popular posting amongst the knights, the one they all hoped wouldn't appear next to their name when the new duty roster was posted.

Picking one of the lamps off its wall bracket Kas did not head towards the stairs, instead she turned east, away from them. This surprised Kessie because all she could see was a wide alcove of faceless dark stone. However Kas was purposeful enough, stopping in front of the stone some fifteen to twenty feet away from the entrance to the Oval Room. Holding the lamp up with her left hand she rummaged in her robe for a moment before pulling out what to Kessie looked like a stone disc slightly larger than a coin. Closer inspection showed that there were a series of irregular grooves carved into its face. Puzzled, she asked Kas what exactly it was.

"A key," Kas replied.

"For what, senior?"

"For this," Kas pointed to the wall. To her surprise Kessie saw that there was an indentation in the stone. It had to have been fashioned by hand because it too was a perfect circle. Kas fitted the stone key she held into this circle. A perfect fit she then gave it a half turn by placing two fingers into a carved hole at its centre. There was a click.

"Well! Lissa's silky hair, I have never seen that here before," Kessie breathed.

"Well you wouldn't. People go up and down the stairs, sometimes they visit the Oval Room, but they never walk past its doorway. Some people know about this place, some do not, the ergonomics of the staff charging area are rarely a major conversational topic upstairs. Come on in."

She pushed against the stone. As Kessie watched she saw the outline of a doorway appear. A stone door maybe half a foot thick it creaked inwards, leaving a gap large enough for a person to fit through comfortably. Kas removed the key and walked in, Kessie right behind her.

She was in a small room, maybe fifteen feet by ten. It was very dark, no windows as they were underground but as Kas moved the lamp around Kessie saw a small, but comfortable bed, covered in blankets and cushions and a low desk at the room's end. It had a drawer and atop it sat a large, much melted, much used candle. On the floor, extending under the bed was a slightly threadbare rug, the colour of which was difficult to discern in the darkness.

"Rather than traipsing all the way to our chambers we can just come here for a cat nap when we need to," Kas explained. "Arbagast rarely used it, he found it oppressive. I suppose it is rather dark, but you get used to it. Besides, if you are tired you don't care where you sleep. Half hour here and back to work. Mind you having said that since Arbagast disappeared I have been spending the whole night here, I haven't had the will to return to the first floor, too many memories for the moment. Still, I have slept well here..." She placed something into Kessie hand. It was the key. "Have that for now. I have Arbagast's. When your duties with me end you can hand it back."

They left the room, Kas pulling the door shut with another soft click, but before they could return to the Oval Room they were halted by the sounds of tramping feet coming down the stairs. As to the identity of those feet well one of them was known to Kessie immediately, Soma had a laugh that could splinter wood.

Eubolo was with her; he, like Kas was carrying a lamp. Once the two of them had alighted on the landing they came over and enquired as to how Kessie was doing.

"Very well," Kas replied. "She is an attentive student. If she wishes I can request that she sits in for a little longer than originally planned."

"I don't mind," said Kessie. For in truth she had found the experience more enjoyable than expected, though if she was being honest with herself she hadn't been expecting much. It had taken her mind off the horrific spectacle earlier that day at least

"Had your cell searched yet?" Soma asked with a twinkle in her eye.

"Yes," Kessie said; "they were an odd pair those knights mind."

"Say that again," Eubolo piped in, "I think they fancied themselves as comedy players at the Red Drake theatre in Tanaren. Did they say anything to you?"

"" Oooooh! Haven't you got big tits!" Like I haven't noticed. "You will never drown with those two, more buoyant than a pig's bladder full of air!" Kessie's vocal impersonation of Sir Borak was not wholly successful.

"They suggested that I should eat more," Soma said. ""I like a woman with meat on her bones, something to give me leverage! "I almost gave him leverage, right over the cliff."

"It is deliberate though," Eubolo observed. "Trying to cheer us up after this morning's debacle. Anyhow, I am showing Soma around the college, down to see the harbour and then up for some lunch, maybe we will catch the two of you there. Though of course we can't talk or assemble in groups larger than four. Perhaps we can communicate by waving handkerchiefs at each other. See you later." He headed back to the stairs, going down this time. "Now that was the staff charging room, and here is the harbour, nothing like the smell of the ocean to put you off your meal..."

Kas and Kessie watched them go, looked at each other and giggled. Then they headed back to the Oval Room where another shaft of polished wood was waiting for the touch of their powers.

****

There is always time to tease a friend

"Sorry Miriam but can you hand me some cloth, I need to clean out my ears."

"Really?"

"Yes. It was just that I thought you had said that whilst I was facing down death by elven spirit you were rolling around on a cave floor somewhere on the end of a good sorting from Sir Nikolaj!"

"Oh. So you don't really need a cloth then."

Gytha spluttered. No words, just splutter.

"You are angry with me aren't you? For being a hypocrite. For warning you off Steven then doing the exact thing I was warning you against."

Words finally came out. "It is just...just...that it is you!"

Miriam's eyes narrowed. "I am as human as the next person you know."

"But wasn't the cave floor dirty?"

"It was dark. I also chose not to look too closely."

"Weren't any crawly insects nearby?"

"Mmmm, I hadn't considered that. No, insects do not thrive in darkness."

"But wasn't it uncomfortable?"

"Yes. But he made me forget my discomfort."

"I am sure he did. But Miriam, the whole thing just sounds so...spontaneous!"

"Well it was. I didn't plan it you know."

"But you have never done anything spontaneous in your life! You agonise for hours about which cheese to have on an end day! I remember once having this lengthy debate with you about which of two books you should bring to a tutorial, it went on all morning until somebody pointed out that you could actually take both…"

Miriam managed a guilty half smile; "oh yes, I remember that."

"And now you would have me believe that without any prevarication whatsoever you gladly let a knight, admittedly a very friendly, not unattractive knight, jump on you in the dark. How persuasive must he have been? What words did he use that caused you to divest yourself of both the character and personality you have hidden inside these past two decades? What in the name of Artorus did he say to you?"

"He told me how clever I was."

"Ha!" Gytha clapped her hands. "Intellectual vanity! I knew it would be your downfall!"

"I am not vain!" Miriam folded her arms defensively. "It was dark, I was frightened, he had just stopped me from drowning, I needed…something…comforting…companionship…I am sorry if it has upset you but I just…what are you doing?"

Gytha had put both hands over her face as Miriam was explaining herself, then her body started to convulse slightly. Miriam stood and started to prise Gytha's hands apart, brown eyes all concern. At least they were until Gytha voluntarily put her hands down.

She was silently laughing.

She sat on Miriam's bed, her arms clutched around her sides and continued to laugh. Eventually she had to lay on her side and draw her knees up, her laughter finally breaking into uncontrolled whooping. There were tears in her eyes. Miriam sat next to her, completely expressionless, until finally she had had enough. Getting to her feet she went to her desk and poured some fresh water from jug to goblet before returning to stand over her companion.

"You need something to drink? Or shall I just pour it over your head?"

Gytha finally managed to calm herself sufficiently to sit up, take the water and nearly drink it all in one go. "Oh my sides," she finally said, her voice huskier than ever.

"So you are not angry with me then?" despite her apparent disapproval of Gytha's actions, she sounded immensely relieved.

"No Miri, not at all. I am delighted in truth, so pleased that you came down from that plinth you keep standing on to actually enjoy yourself for once. You did enjoy it I take it?"

"On a purely physical basis I rather…"

"Oh Artorus big toe! Yes or no?"

"Yes. He was extraordinarily strong. He even managed to lift me up entirely at one point, and continue to..."

"Elissa pinch me, is the world ending or something? I am even getting all the intimate details. You are not that spirit from the old tales are you? You haven't killed the real Miriam and stolen her skin?"

Miriam pursed her lips, withdrew a tiny piece of mint from her side pouch and proceeded to chew on it fastidiously.

"I see not," Gytha said.

"It appears that once more..." Miriam swallowed the mint finally, "I am the subject of a certain degree of mockery. And it is not even the first time today."

"Go on. Someone was laughing at you? Other than me obviously, I am allowed to laugh at you after all."

"Why?"

"Because you are a best friend and I care about you. Reason enough?"

Miriam sat next to her, Gytha was still wiping her eyes. "Reason enough. No it was the two knights who searched my room earlier. They said this was the neatest, tidiest, cleanest cell they had seen and so therefore I must be the most boring woman in the whole college. I directed them to the theory espoused by Wilhelm of Anhaug, that dust and dirt congregate in places where disease is prevalent and that the probability of a correlation between dirt and disease is exponentially high, as he then went on to illustrate with a series of research articles and graphs undertaken by his students."

"And what did they say to that?"

"They thanked me for proving their assertion."

"More fool they. Boring is the last word I would use for you, something that Sir Nikolaj would no doubt agree with. In fact, you could say that he bored you, in a manner of speaking."

"Thank you. And don't be filthy."

"I bet you are a bit of a wild animal when it comes to sex, all that unleashed repression..."

"I have my moments."

"Would you do it with him again?"

Miriam sunk her head into her hands and exhaled through her fingers. "Part of me would like to. But that was in the dark, in a cave, where we could not possibly be caught. Here, especially with the current atmosphere things are different. You can be whipped for being caught with a knight and whipping

HARBINGER OF THE DEAD

seems to be rather a current theme at present. I could not stand up to what the likes of Brytta had to endure." She ran her hand through her hair, tousling it. "How is it a word can have so many meanings? Curls for example, your curls are long, loose, and elegant, with your hair colour they look nothing less than beautiful. Mine are short, tight and thick, they look like a fleece from a farmyard animal..."

"No they don't Miri, I shall use the example of Sir Nikolaj again..."

"It was dark, all I had to be was biologically correct, gaps in all the right places, and you are right, his line of patter was excruciating, only a desperate old maid could have fallen for them, which I suppose is exactly what I am..."

Gytha stood suddenly. "Right! That is it! My maudlin self-pity threshold has finally been crossed! Even if what you were saying was true, which it isn't, you are certainly seeing more action in that respect than I am. Besides, aren't all of us old maids in this place? Well, apart from Steven's wife, and if marriage makes your personality anything like hers then spinsterhood is something to be celebrated."

Miriam stood too. She poured out more water, this time into a bowl and splashed her face.

"Actually, you complaining about a lack of "action" brings me to the second thing I wanted to tell you. As my part in your investigation appears to be over and I have nothing scheduled for today I will soon be visiting Warran in his cell. He has some exams coming up and I am helping his studies. Do you mind?"

"Why should I?"

"You know why."

It was Gytha's turn to fidget. She adjusted the pouch at her waist and pulled her hair clear of her face. "He has finished with me, you can do whatever you want with him, study or otherwise. If you want me to say it then no, even if we were still together I wouldn't mind. I was never possessive with him anyway, I neither knew nor cared if he had other women and if he did, well I would rather it was you than anyone else. So, to sum up, I am very happy for what happened to you the night before last and you are welcome to teach Warran until your head falls off in frustration, which it probably will. You never really thought I would be angry with you surely?"

"No, not really, but there is always a nagging doubt..."

"No there isn't. Anyway it is my turn to thank you."

Miriam's eyes widened. "Thank me? What for?"

"For making me laugh and cheering me up. Especially on such a desperate morning. And for giving me strength to do what I want to next."

"Which is?"

"To visit Iska. To see how she is. And to remind me that I never want to see one as young as her punished that way again."

Miasma row

Iska was only a couple of years out of the Childs' college and so her accommodation reflected that status, the most novice of the novices. Her cell was situated in the corridor leading directly from the ground floor library, it was nowhere near the external walls and so had no window at all. It was smaller even than Gytha's cell, the desk was sited at the foot of the bed because there was not enough room for the two of them to be side by side. The reason the cells were regarded as the worst available though was not so much the size, but that between the library and cells, through doors that were stout, yet not stout enough, lay the novices latrines. It was not for nothing that this group of cells were referred to by the novices as miasma row. Every evening the lay brothers flushed both male and female latrines out with water but even then, especially in warm weather, the unmistakable taint of stagnating ordure was impossible to clear from the back of the nose. As an attempt to ameliorate the problem the House of Artorus issued all the novices in the row with sticks of incense but all that really meant was that on warm summer days the cells were filled with pungent blue smoke and the unconquerable smell of excrement. It was a combination that older novices and seniors, all of whom would have spent their early years here, remembered instantly the second they trod the affected corridors.

Gytha was remembering her early years too as she approached Iska's cell for once it had not belonged to Iska, it had belonged to her. Three years she had resided there, before moving to her current cell some six or seven years ago. Despite the odour she had a lot of happy memories of the place and of course some terrible ones too, for it was the one she had sat in whilst agonising with herself about what to do about the child she had carried. Yet it was also the one she had spent hours with Miriam and Cheris in, young girls setting the world to rights, forming bonds of friendship that so far had not even come close to being broken, mixed memories, yet indelible.

As she got closer to her destination one thing was becoming obvious to her, that the unease engendered by the recent spate of deaths had only been exacerbated by the events of that morning. The whole college was now operating under a pall of fear and mistrust, mages were shuffling along corridors, heads down, making little or no conversation, just furtive whispers where the shadows were strongest. The knights patrolling the hallways were ignored, mages picked up pace when they saw one, eager to pass them as quickly as they could. Just a week ago they would acknowledge each other, "Gods bless you this

174

morning", "Artorus keep you safe", "rain again, won't Uttu leave us alone for once?" such friendly interchanges seemed already to belong to a happier, more tolerant past. Now it was all viscid suspicion, the tension hanging in the corridors being thicker than the dust.

All of Gytha's impressions were of course only reinforced when she walked into Iska's cell.

The girl was lying, face down on her bed, blanket pulled up to her waist. Her back was a sight fit to make Gytha wince, the healers had cleaned up all the spilled blood and stopped the bleeding but all that had done was make her wounds, those horrible gashes, stand out in sharp relief to the pale skin on her back. Five deep scored slashes running from hip to shoulder, spanning the whole length of her back, no finer butchery had ever been carried out in the shambles of Tanaren city. In addition to these gashes were deeper indentations, punctures caused by the spikes in the razor whip, some of those wounds still oozed blood, not even the magical healers could stop all of them it seemed. Iska's head was on her bolster pillow, turned so that she could see Emonie sitting on a stool close to her, and it was Emonie that rounded on Gytha the moment she entered the room.

"What in Artorus name are you doing here? You work with those bastards that did this to her! You are just about the last person she wants to see! Why don't you get out and destroy someone else's life!"

Gytha was shocked into silence. She hadn't expected hostility like that. She was about to do as bidden but Iska managed to crane her neck slightly to see who it was. "It is alright Em. She hasn't destroyed anything. Come on in Gytha, there is a spare stool there, I have had quite a few well-wishers already this morning."

Her voice was weak, but perfectly clear. Gytha did as requested, sitting next to Emonie, who pointedly scraped her stool to move a few inches away from her. "How are you?" she asked quietly.

"Well I won't be running anywhere for the foreseeable future. But I could be worse, I could be Oskum."

"I am sorry..." Gytha started to say.

"So you should be," Emonie interrupted. Gytha ignored her.

"I am sorry for what happened," she continued, "I have been tasked with trying to find who is responsible for the murders in the college. If that person had been apprehended by now then last night would not have happened. So Emonie is partly right, I do bear a measure of responsibility for the way you are now. I am just wondering if there is anything I can do for you. You are welcome to stay in my cell while you recover, I can move in here. It used to be my old cell anyway, so it is no hardship for me."

"You used to live here?" Iska brightened at that, the thought that an older woman once lived here seemed to intrigue her.

"Yes. We all start in miasma row. You will be moved out in a year or two, depending on how many new arrivals come from the Childs' college. My cell is larger and has a window, though it is a little colder than this one. You are welcome to it if you want."

The girl thought for a moment, Gytha noticed her swollen nose, and the missing teeth once she spoke. "No, thank you but no. I actually quite like this place, I would rather recover in familiar surroundings in truth. They brought us here by cart, except for Karel who has gone to the Island of Healing and since I got back here do you know what everybody who has spoken to me has had in common?"

Gytha shook her head.

"They have all blamed somebody else for my misfortune, the evil knights, stupid old Oskum, some bad food I ate yesterday that affected my mind, everybody has been blamed except the one true culprit."

"Which is?" Emonie asked.

"Me of course. I could have said no at any time, just walked away, left everyone else to get into their own trouble. But I didn't. I stayed. And I have been punished. A punishment I probably deserve."

"Not...true," Emonie said sharply.

"Too true," Iska replied, "and the person I have lied to, the person I have deceived more than any other..."

"Yes?"

"Is you Em. I have been lying to you for a long time. The reason I joined the escapees was not because of ideals, it was because of Oskum. We were lovers you see, only briefly, but we were."

Emonie coloured a little, for the first time since Gytha had arrived she avoided Iska's gaze.

"I did suspect that, the way you looked at each other at the end."

"And before that it was Mattris. It was not my first time with him when that knight caught us. I had been seeing him in secret for months before that."

Emonie said nothing.

"I decided as I endured the lash that it would change me, that I would emerge the stronger for it. And I will, and honesty with my friends is the best place to start. I love you Em but not entirely in the way you want me to. If you wish to leave, if you wish to sever things with me I respect that, and I will understand. You are a better person than I could ever hope to be."

Gytha suddenly felt a little awkward, personal disclosures between the two girls was something else she was not expecting. She guessed that Iska was in too much pain to care, Emonie however was obviously a lot more embarrassed.

"A girl knows Iska. She just...knows. And I guessed about you and Senior Mattris a good while ago. What you are saying is not really news to me. Neither of us are perfect after all. And for my part I never want to lose your friendship. One good thing I learnt about this morning, Asitaigne, what a baby, I will have to dream about somebody else from now on."

Gytha smiled at them both. "We all have secrets, and we all make mistakes. I was younger than you when I made mine..."

Both girls looked at her with a mix of curiosity and excitement. A confession from an older woman didn't happen every day. Gytha suddenly realised she had said too much and that to stop now would mean that her concern would not really appear genuine. She had dug a hole and honesty was indeed the only way out.

"Only a handful of people know about this, so I beg you never to mention this to anybody."

Emonie pulled an icon of Elissa from her pocket, held it to her heart and said. "I swear."

So Gytha told them. What else could she do? Tell a girl that had been whipped that morning that she was not important enough for her confession? She trusted Iska as she spoke, Emonie less so but she knew her to be religious so she had to hope that faith would hold her tongue.

"You see Iska," she said finally. "What I learned was that if you like someone, if you want that friendship to endure, you don't actually have to lie with them. If they are true friends, and you say no to them, then they will understand and respect your decision. I could tell you to give up boys altogether, that would be best after all, but you would just ignore me anyway."

"Yes I would," Iska smiled.

"You are tired, aren't you?"

"Yes. No sleep last night."

"And sleep is what you need. So I will leave you now. If you need anything just ask. I will call in tomorrow if I can."

"Thank you Gytha," Iska said. "Once the pain goes all I have to worry about are the scars. I have already been called Iska Crook-nose by somebody."

"All the scars will be permanent unfortunately," Emonie said. "You are still pretty though and only your nose will be noticeable, and we will soon get used to that."

"If you are bothered by it," Gytha said, "I will speak to a friend of mine. She has scars, more than you and she may be able to help you, even if it is only by talking."

"Who is she?" Iska asked.

"A senior. A second floor senior no less. You wouldn't know her. She never visits the ground floor."

"And I never visit the second outside of tutorials. Are you sure she would even want to speak to me?"

"I am seeing her now. I will speak to her about you. Gods keep you Iska. And you Emonie."

Iska put out her arm, "wait, there is one thing. One thing you can do for me."

"Name it."

"Can you light a candle at the house of Xhenafa? For Oskum. Nobody has a good word for him, but they do not know, they didn't know him like I did. He deserves a candle, he was not a bad man, just a frightened man who wanted to help."

Emonie pulled a face, she obviously did not agree with her friend. Gytha though was not here to see Emonie.

"I will do so this afternoon. And again tomorrow if that is what you want."

She left the two girls still talking softly to each other, she guessed that she would probably be the subject of their conversation, she just hoped that anything they said would go no further than Iska's cell.

****

Gytha follows a lead

She stopped at the refectory, the eerily silent refectory where the only sound came from clacking paring knives and spoons scraping pewter bowls. A quick repast of oats, red autumn berries, and weak ale and she headed upstairs, through the wider, rug strewn hallways of the senior chambers until she stood outside the carved, oiled door of the library on the second floor.

The noon bell had sounded as she climbed the stairs and so she was not surprised to find Beni eating at her desk, scooping a milky porridge into her mouth with a broad wooden spoon. She had her cowl down to eat and had pulled her hair forward to partly hide her scars. Gytha noticed that a couple of ends of it were tipped with porridge, a surprising lapse for someone so conscious of her appearance.

She set the bowl to one side as Gytha approached her and smiled. "Reinstated by Sir Steven?" she asked.

Gytha nodded.

"Good. And you have something to ask me?"

"Yes. Privately if possible." For there were a couple of senior mages sat at desks close by, both of whom had looked both surprised and somewhat displeased at a novice barging in on their personal space.

"This way." Beni led her back to her own quarters, inviting Gytha to sit on a chair. As Gytha did so she finally noticed the porridge on her hair, wiping it off with a disgusted little grunt.

"How can I help you then Gytha? Or am I a suspect again?"

"No. You are not a suspect, well you are, just not today. Elven blue fire. People are using it to navigate the caves under the college. It keeps the spirit from attacking them. It is not something taught here so the knowledge to use it has to be acquired by other means. Now, although our killer has probably obtained it from the missing elven documents, I just wondered if any books here spoke about it, and if I could borrow them if at all possible. Ideally I would like to know how it is made."

Beni looked thoughtful, playing with her hair, pulling down a loose fold in her robe. "It is alluded to in a couple of books relating to elven lore. It is I believe called the blue fire of Istraek. Whether these books actually tell us how to make it though I really don't know. I will be annoyed if they do not."

"Why?"

"Because if they do not then the knowledge has to be in those missing documents. Documents that had been sitting in my archive room for years uncounted, unread, barely noticed. Knowledge in them that any mage..."

"Would kill for?"

"Not an appropriate phrase to use at the moment. Say rather that it is knowledge that any mage would hunger for. Other colleges and even universities could well have more about it than we do, but to find that out I would have to contact them, many dozens of them. I could write to them I suppose but it would take time that you probably haven't got."

"No, we have little time as it is. Did you see it all this morning? The punishments I mean."

"Go outside?" Beni gasped. "No! I did my usual thing. Once I heard the knights clamouring outside I left the door to my rooms open and ran upstairs into the archive room in the tower. The knights coming in would think that I had left already. Was it bad?"

Gytha nodded.

"Stupid question. Sorry. Now shall I try and find those books?"

"Please."

"Come on then. Time to test my exhaustive cataloguing system."

She returned to her desk in the library and removed from under it three tatty old ledgers, each thick as a warrior's arm. As Gytha sat quietly and patiently next to her the librarian began the painstaking task of rooting through each one, turning yellow page after yellow page, each inscribed with entries in thick black ink written by several distinct hands. Occasionally she would stop running her fingers down the page, say something like, "mmmm, perhaps that one," before writing something on a loose leaf of parchment next to her. Gytha started to feel time creak around her, felt the shortening day start to drift into darkness, felt her eyelids get heavier as Beni continued her work. Gytha wondered if she had ever seen the other woman happier, a task requiring thoroughness and diligence, all in the pursuit of knowledge, she was utterly absorbed. The other mages started to drift off, their tasks completed (either that or Gytha's presence still affronted them), until finally it was just the two of them sat in silence, with just the rustle of the pages and the flickering mustard light of the hanging lamps breaking the stillness.

"There," Beni said finally, startling Gytha into wakefulness. "I have found some eighteen or so sources that may or may not detail blue fire. If you want to know how it is made then it will be in these books or not at all..."

"Yes," Gytha said, "and when we find such a book I want to know who has taken that particular book out."

"Of course you do. Now which one will we start with, which is the most likely to give details, tum, tum, tum, let us see. How about "Reiger's compendium. A collection of essays detailing unusual manifestations of Lucan's power." The length of the title will give you an indication of the thickness of the book. It should be over here." With a speed of action Gytha was unused to see in her the librarian sprang up, disappeared behind a winding shelf piled high with books and parchment, before returning shortly afterwards with a large volume bound in dark leather pressed under her arm.

"Can I do anything?" Gytha asked.

"You don't know how to find any of them. Tell you what I will find all of them first then we can divide them between us, go through them that way. What do you think?"

Gytha nodded, realising that she might have to make the offering at the

House of Xhenafa in darkness. Still, Beni seemed rather keen to help her and she couldn't really turn such an offer down. So whilst the librarian busied herself gathering the books in her list Gytha picked up the compendium and started to read…

****

The fugitive still proves elusive

To Steven it felt like he had spent all day in the chapter house writing letters, checking documents, and reading the wills of the dead men. The scar on his cheek was throbbing and his spirits were evaporating faster than a goblet of New Perego gut rot. He had needed some peace and quiet to get this work completed but all day he had had little respite from knights, superiors, and his spouse, all of whom wanted something from him, ranging from simple orders regarding guard duty to a request for musicians to play in the women's chambers (thank you Fedrica).

And it seemed that there was to be no reprieve as somebody else rapped on his door.

"Come in," he sighed, downing the last of the small beer in the tankard on his desk.

In strode Sir Nikolaj, looking as tired as Steven was feeling.

Steven gestured to the empty chair opposite him. Once the knight had made himself comfortable Steven asked. "Bad news? it has to be, the way the day has gone so far."

Sir Nikolaj nodded. "Probably. Have you sorted Welton's details out?"

"Pretty much. Just the details of his death payment to do, and I have to see Shadan for that. He didn't leave much in truth. It is Sir Beverley who has been the problem, several distant relatives who will start to value him from the moment he ceased to live. Anyway, please distract me with your bad news, I am in the right mood for it."

"First thing sir, I would like permission to go to the other island, Welton is laid to rest there, and I would like to make an offering…"

"Permission granted. I need to do the same when I can."

"Thank you sir. Now the second thing…"

"The search for Gideon the priest? The one you let escape?" Steven gave him a quizzical smile.

"In a moment sir, I just wanted to say, if you didn't know, that seniors Mattris and Lipshin have been detained and are in separate jails. Mattris was easy to find apparently, they got him as soon as he returned from the execution, Lipshin though was more of a problem."

"I knew they had been detained hours ago. Why was she a problem?"

"She wasn't in her chambers. They had to search the entire first and second floors. They finally found her by voice, she was in Senior Goodbern's room, they were arguing about something, the noise was coming through the door."

"Is there anybody that woman doesn't argue with? I will see her in the morning, give her a night alone with her thoughts. I might enjoy locking horns with an angry, poison spitting serpent, even more than I enjoy mixing my metaphors. Now tell me about Gideon. You haven't found him I take it."

"No sir. But it could be worse than that."

Steven groaned. "Go on."

"Well, Sir Beverley ordered us to go into the tunnels to find him. So what I organised was two groups of three knights to search the tunnels with orders to run at the first sight of anything...weird. The tunnels there lead into this cave that opens onto the cliffs and from the cave a shaft has been cut leading to a secret entrance in a disused pigsty, so I stationed a further knight there. We also put some bread out, on a plate in the cave, figuring the boy would be hungry and it might draw him out." He saw Steven's pained expression, "Sir Beverley's idea."

"So what went wrong?"

"Well while that was going on I went to Sir Beverley with the rumour that some mages were up to something. Next thing I know I am being dragged over the bridge with him to stop the escape. Because of that I wasn't able to get back to the search till the morning."

"Who was left in charge while you were gone?"

"The senior knights were Sir Leuring, then Sir Beech. Good men but, well it was night and everything sir, difficult to see things properly."

"They were in caves man; it is always dark in there. What happened exactly?"

"Well they spent several hours in the caves, but the place is a honeycomb sir and the boy Gideon had had a full day to get his bearings."

"See any spirits?"

"No sir. Some strange noises, even a bobbing light at one point but no direct sighting no. The thing is that having the knights in the caves like that it was possible for a slippery eel like this boy to get past them through a side tunnel and to reach the open cave behind them."

"So that is what happened I take it. But the only way out of the cave was through this tunnel into the pig pen and we had a knight stationed there, no?"

"We did sir. But there may have been another way out of the cave. At least when I inspected it earlier on."

"What way?"

"The cliff face sir."

"I thought it was sheer, impossible to climb."

"For a knight in armour, probably. When I checked the cave opening this morning though there are handholds a cunning and desperate climber could use. I would say the odds were more than even that anybody trying them would end up falling into the sea, but this boy is wily, and we constantly underestimate him."

"It seems we do. Do you have any evidence that he escaped that way?"

"Well the bread was gone and at the top of the cliff it looked like some roots, from the overhanging trees I think had been pulled free recently, like somebody had grabbed onto them to pull himself up onto land. There had been a recent disturbance in the earth there too, it looks like the point where he might have hauled himself up."

"Could you have climbed it? Without your armour?"

"It would be risky, but I think so sir. I think you could too."

Steven checked his tankard. Empty. And he was still thirsty.

I sometimes think I have been saddled with the most hopeless bunch of men ever to submit to knighthood. Still, they are soldiers, not bloodhounds. Better call of the search then. Keep one man by the pig pen just in case. The boy isn't the killer anyway and there are only so many places to hide on the surface. Task those knights in the caves to scour the island for him in the morning. I do not give the finding of this boy the same priority Sir Beverley did."

Sir Nikolaj sighed in both gratitude and relief. "Will do sir, we will get him, it just might take a couple more days. But I haven't told you the strangest thing of all sir."

"There is more? Artorus be praised!"

"There was something else in the sea facing cave sir, when I searched it this morning, something unexpected."

"Go on."

"Senior Tola's body sir. Somebody had moved it there. And none of the knights noticed them doing it."

****

A missing book and a dubious horn

"So what do we have?" Beni closed the cover of the book she had been perusing before stacking it on the pile next to her, a pile that was fast becoming a tower.

"Eighteen books and none of them give me exactly what I wanted." Gytha pouted, her frustration obvious. "I have gone through all of them from beginning to end and I still don't know how to make this blue fire."

"Well why don't you concentrate on what we do know." The librarian still sounded upbeat; she had obviously enjoyed indulging herself in research. "We know that it can be produced by incantation or distilled, by a mage, into an oily liquid enabling those without the gift to use it. We know some of the leaves and herbs required, spitweed, blackleaf, though we don't know which variety, heartphlox, though we don't know whether it is yellow or blue, fresh Lambsfoot, Emperor's trefoil, pink verbena, that is a start surely?"

"A couple of components are missing, and we don't know any of the quantities. We only have a fragment of the incantation required and we hardly know anything about preparation, what to add and when. We cannot make blue fire given the information that we have. Yet somebody here has. Are there any other books that might help us? If not I will have to assume that the missing elven journal has what we need, and the murderer has that." Gytha had been reading for what seemed like forever, her thoughts now were bent on getting to the house of Xhenafa before the curfew bell sounded.

"Well think for a moment. A couple of those herbs are quite rare and the only source for them here is Senior Frankus the herbalist. His record keeping is patchy at best, but he should know who has requisitioned these ingredients in the last few months, no?"

Gytha nodded in agreement, perking up a little at the suggestion. "I would imagine that the murderer has been smart enough not to leave such an obvious trail. But it is a lead we shall have to pursue. So yes this hasn't been a complete waste of time."

"Sir Steven should be pleased with you."

She shook her head. "Only if I had found something. Now he will just say that I was colluding with a suspect who could easily have left the really incriminating titles on the shelves."

"Well he is right in truth." Beni placed her hands behind her head and stretched ostentatiously, "I would say the same if I was him. Oh and it is seventeen books, not eighteen, one of them is annoyingly missing."

"Really, I thought I counted eighteen."

"Well there are eighteen here, but one of them was a title I had been looking for, somebody had sneaked it back and put it on the wrong shelf."

"Sneaked it back?" Gytha enquired, "why?"

"It is probably our most popular title, but nobody wants to be caught reading it."

Gytha's blue eyes seemed to deepen in colour. "Oh stop teasing me! What is it?"

Beni handed her a relatively thin book, whose spine and cover were worn enough to indicate that it had been read many times. Gytha looked at the title and laughed.

"Oh this! We have all heard of it, but it is banned from our library, "The depravity of woman, how beauty conceals a soul of corruption." By Father Harrow of Cleshy. The temerity of the man!"

"Yes, a mad priest from the Dragonspine mountains. He hated women for some reason and devoted his life to collecting examples of the vile lusts all women possess in their heart. Want to borrow it?"

"It is not allowed."

"Oh go on, I will write a chit for you, say it has been given to the mage liaison officer for research purposes. It really is quite hilarious and terribly filthy in places. I have always found it interesting that each God seems to have a different attitude to women and sex, Artorus barely mentions it, Elissa says it should be one man for one woman, probably that is why Tanaren is so conservative, Camille says we should hump anything that moves, though their priestesses are supposed to abstain. Sarasta wants us to get pregnant every time, Hytha thinks we should copulate excessively but only in spring; no wonder we all get so confused. Tanaren actually gets in to one of the stories, one about the sisters of Camille in the capital. The chief sister there wanted her girls to get more exercise, so she hung some thick ropes from a beam there and got them to climb them. Never understood why it was so instantly popular, all those celibate young women from noble families rubbing themselves against the ropes, until finally her second in command pointed out that the yelping they were making wasn't actually being caused by rope burns. And then of course there is the tale of the Horn of Murmuur...."

"I have definitely heard of that one, though I don't know the story exactly, to have a Murmuur is slang for...for..."

"Exactly. Well the horn was taken from some desert beast and given as a gift to a mage college in Svytoia, a land in the south that faces the empire of Koze across the sea. It was about eight inches long, three or four inches in diameter and was polished smooth at the top, removing any sharpness the original horn may have had. Well one day the knights imposed restrictions on the mages, rather like it is here at the moment, anything of no practical use had to be confiscated or destroyed. So the female Chief Magister had to find a use for this horn, it was a problem, she did not even know from which animal it came. So, she gave it to one of her council, also female, and asked her to find a practical purpose for it. Then the following night she passed it to another mage, then another and so on. Finally she got these, all female, all happily smiling mages together and asked them what they had done with it. Well not one of them said exactly the same thing but they each in turn went into excruciating detail about what use they put it to, ear reddening stuff seriously. For the full details you will have to read it, all it is missing is illustrations, but they so convinced the Chief Magister of its importance that she realised she had to keep it at all costs. So she told the knights she used it to prop open a creaky door, and they believed it! They never discovered its real purpose, it obviously never occurred to them to ask their wives. However the morale amongst the female mages improved immeasurably over the ensuing months. And that, according to Father Harrow is why women are depraved, libidinous sinks of the vilest lusts. Consider yourself told."

"Right," Gytha was decided, "I will take it to my cell with me, just write me that chit first. Now, this missing book, what is the title and who has borrowed it recently?"

""The Arcane Wych. Power lost to civilisation." By Immel of Anmir. I am not sure I have ever read it and nobody else has taken it out in the last five years. I have checked. It may have even been destroyed, there was a small fire in the archive room just before I became librarian, the books destroyed were never catalogued so I have never been able to fully verify the extent of the damage. It is probable that less than twenty books were lost, and that might have been one of them. It is a very rare book too; few copies were ever made. If it has been lost then it is quite a tragedy. Though obviously not as big a tragedy as anybody losing their life," she added hastily on seeing Gytha's face.

"Your records only go back five years?"

"The ledgers I hold here, yes. Older ledgers are kept in the storeroom. I can check them if you want."

"No, no need, I think five years is quite enough." She eased herself into a stand then touched the tip of her nose, a gesture that acted as a reminder of something she had to do. "Thanks for your help but I have to go, I have to get to the House of Xhenafa before curfew."

"Think nothing of it. I owed you anyway."

"What for?"

Beni found a blank piece of parchment and started scribbling on it. "The other night, in your cell. I could tell there was something wrong, that bloom of power was extraordinary; unfocused power like that rises, just like a gas. I sensed it, I knew that you might be in danger and yet I fled, I let Eubolo go and find you just because I didn't want anybody to...see me. I am sorry Gytha, my shame burns me, you deserve better than my cowardice."

Gytha looked thoughtful. "Well, there is something else you can do for me."

"Name it."

"It involves going to the ground floor again."

Beni was deadpan. "Oh."

"You have done it once; you can do it again. One of the girls punished this morning, she also had her nose broken by a knight and she has lost some teeth. Her name is Iska, she is only a young girl, she could do with some..."

"Motherly advice?"

"Big sisterly advice."

Beni sighed, "can't she come up here?"

"Her feet are cut, and she has five lashes across her back, she won't be climbing stairs anytime soon. Also, as you have said before, novices are banned from the library."

Beni smiled sheepishly; her own rules had entrapped her. "Of course. I suppose I can keep my cowl up. Where is she?"

"Miasma row. Fourth door on the left."

Beni pulled a face. "Oh, memories. Miasma row, where a girl becomes a woman. And no...not like that, it was there I started to bleed, the pain used to be so bad I would bite my arm as a distraction. I was too shy to talk about it, it was some months before I discovered Ellen's powders from the healers, Elissa's grace but that made such a difference. Okay Gytha, as it is you asking I will try. I wouldn't do this for anybody else. Now take this, it is your permission to borrow the book."

"Where is the Horn of Murmuur story?"

"Near the end. Plenty of other interesting stuff before it."

"Right. Thank you." Gytha shook her hair, letting her curls cascade around her shoulders. "That is my evenings reading sorted, tomorrow I will try and find our killer."

"Artorus speed on that. Especially with the ducal visit imminent."

"Well yes. We must catch the perpetrator before he arrives. If we don't then presumably the Chief Magister will try and keep it all quiet till he leaves."

Beni stroked her chin thoughtfully. "So you have discounted one possibility then?"

Gytha picked up her newly acquired book. "We haven't discounted anything. What possibility are you talking about?"

"Well. The early murders, Caswell, and the lay brother. You haven't considered that the murders were not so much because the killer wanted them dead but rather that they wanted to experiment, to see if casting a spell through the body of the spirit was possible. That these murders were perhaps just rehearsals, that they were just honing their technique until the real victim arrived."

Gytha inhaled sharply, her eyes widening. "You think they are after the Grand Duke?"

"Why not?" Beni said, stifling a yawn. "If they are of the order that believes in mage supremacy what better way of proving it than by killing the Grand Duke? I hope I am wrong, that you catch the person before his arrival because if the Grand Duke is killed on this island, by a mage, then I fear for all of us. There is no knight in this world who would show us any mercy after that."

****

A still night for a change

It was not an evening for lingering outside and yet, for this island, at this time, it was special in one way at least. As soon as Gytha left the great doors behind her and started tip toeing down the broad stone steps she was struck by something immediately, or rather, struck by an absence rather than a presence. She was so used to standing on that top step and feeling the wind buffeting her cheeks ruddy, sending her hair wind milling around her face, drying her lips and creasing her eyes that the dearth of any of these sensations shocked her as surely as if she had plunged her face into a pail of freezing meltwater.

No wind. No wind at all. Utter stillness, pensive silence, Uttu the storm god was holding his breath. Gytha could hear the sighing of the long grass, the cracking of the bracken as a rabbit bolted through it to escape a predator, the susurration of a sea struck by an unfamiliar peace, even the gulls seemed to have tranquillity in their hearts as they cooed to each other instead of screaming in their ceaseless fury.

But by the Gods did it make things cold. Whenever Gytha negotiated the great steps she was in the habit of holding her robe up at ankle level to avoid tripping, now it felt that tiny imps of ice were nipping at her exposed skin. She was a frost mage, she thought, cold should hold no sway over her. But it did, perhaps that was why others were better at performing it than she. She had read that far to the south the lands bathed in permanent warmth, even at night, that the beaches ran for mile after silver mile and the sea never raised its voice in anger. She had read that it was so hot that the natives of such shores wore little by way of clothing, that their skin was tanned even deeper than Tola's had been, that fruit hung from every tree, that life was one long joyous song, but then, as Miriam of all people had told her, not everything you read is always true. It was always easy to suppose that others had things easier, yet even the nobility of Tanaren, who had never wanted for food, warmth, or clothing, seemed eternally restless with their lot. There was some lesson hidden in her musings, she thought, but the Gods alone knew what it was.

Now she was on the path to the house of Xhenafa, soft shoes kicking loose stones, fingers trailing through the high grass on the verge. She would light a candle for Oskum, but Iska had not told her what to write on the dedication. She chewed around it for a while, until she entered the covered trellis to the house, with the hooded lamp shining its crescent of pallid ghost light onto the damp earth and doorway before her. She had it at last, she would write,

"Xhenafa guide the spirit of mage Oskum to Artorus side, please judge him not by consequences but by intent, that of a good man who wanted a better life for others, who wanted his brothers and sisters to live without fear, of a man who loved and was loved and who was special to one in particular. As it must be, forever."

* * * * * * * * *

A path rarely trod

As Gytha trod the night path under its shroud of silky silence another figure, cowl drawn up so that the face was nothing more than an oval of impenetrable darkness, emerged from the library and made its way down the stairs. The figure was slight and crept noiselessly, keeping to the shadows, and acknowledging nobody should she pass them. Her gait was so smooth, so fluid that it seemed that she was floating rather than walking, a spirit in a college haunted by spirits. She glided through reception room, great hall, empty refectory, into the novices' library. There she stopped for a moment, seemingly disconcerted, for the library was quite full, novice mages gossiping quietly as the knights strolled amongst them. She picked up speed then, flitting from bookshelf to bookshelf, keeping away from the knots of humanity, paying them no heed, and receiving none in turn. Through the library she went, past the male latrines to her right, female to her left, until finally she was in the first corridor that held the novices' cells. She stopped again, whispering to herself, maybe she was counting the doors for suddenly she seemed to pick one of them, approaching and knocking softly before opening it and disappearing from general view.

"Who is there?" a girl was on the bed, face down, long glossy black hair. Her back was exposed, scored with angry cuts, only partly healed. She was in the right cell then.

The figure did not answer immediately, she had noticed something on the desk, a small bowl often used to hold lamp oil, but it was holding something else here now. The figure ran a long, slender finger around the bowl, looking at the blackened residue it left on her fingertip.

"Soot," the figure said. "To line your eyes? to make them look bigger?"

Iska turned to look at the stranger. Large brown eyes, sensitive, seductive, soot could never have been put to more productive use. She used to use soot once, get it in her eye by accident and a sooty tear would trail from eye to mouth. Time to introduce herself to the confused girl.

"My name is Beneshiel, once Beneshiel of Whiterush. I am the librarian for the senior magisters. A mutual friend asked me to come, I might be able to help you."

"Gytha?" the girl asked; "Gytha sent you?"

A stool still stood close to Iska's head, Beni sat on it, her cowl still covering her face. From a pouch at her belt she produced a small box which she opened. A smell of butter, menthol, sage, and mint tickled Iska's bruised nose.

"What is that for, senior?" she asked.

"Scars." Beni said, finally pulling back her cowl. The room was dimly lit, candlelight only, yet there was enough light for Iska to behold the librarian's face.

She reacted well, Beni thought, for a young girl. No recoiling in horror, just a slight dilating of the pupils and a bite to the lower lip. "As you can see, it is something I have to use extensively. Shall I try it on you?"

"Please," Iska said; "the scars burn, and a couple of them are starting to itch."

"Itching is good, itching is healing. You are mending already, a good thing in a strong young girl like yourself. Come, I shall start, and if the wounds are hot perhaps I can do something about that, something my peers would frown at."

She started, so, so gently, applying the salve on to the open, damaged skin. As she did so she spoke softly, words under her breath, difficult to hear. Iska knew it was an incantation, that power was being expended. And she could feel it too, a gentle, flowing wave of cool air ran from the librarian's hand to coat the tortured skin of Iska's back. The salve too eased both the itching and the hot, throbbing pain. For the first time that day Iska felt she could stretch out her arms without suffering for it. "That is very good senior, very relaxing, perhaps I might sleep tonight after all."

"I hope so. Gytha says that you endured the lash with great fortitude, that is good, and I can sense that you hold a substantial well of power inside you too. You might be one to watch in a few years Iska, I shall observe your progress with interest."

"Iska Crook-nose," the girl said; "I was called it earlier and I now realise that I quite like it, it is distinctive at least and sounds so much better than Iska of Tanaren City."

"You are from the capital? Which part? Loubian hill, Artisan's hill, the poor quarter?"

"None of those," Iska sighed, a sigh touched with resignation. "I thought everybody knew my past."

"I am very out of touch, what is wrong with coming from the capital?"

"I am Iska of the Rose district, that is why."

Beni dug out some more salve with her finger and continued to apply it, it was almost all gone by now. "The brothel district, well someone has to live there."

"No, senior, you do not understand. I was born in, and grew up in Fell house, the largest, and one of the wealthiest brothels in the city. My mother worked there; I obviously have no idea who my father was."

"Do you look like your mother?"

"Yes, almost identical."

"Then your father is of no importance."

"It didn't stop me being called Iska Whoresdaughter in the Childs' college. It is a stigma I will never fully shake off."

"Did you love your mother?"

Iska nodded. "Very much. I didn't really understand what she did back then, not until the end, but she was always kind and gentle to me. There were a few of us, the children of the girls, we were raised collectively, had our own little gang, protected each other from the name callers and the bullies. I had quite a good childhood really. Until my powers came."

"Oh yes, that special day when everybody realises what you are, when the smiles of your neighbours are replaced by fearful glances and whispers. We all go through that."

Iska sighed languorously, "so relaxing," she breathed. "It was slightly different with me, I was seven or eight and knew by then what my mother did, if not exactly what it involved. Then one day I could hear noises outside her door.

It was unlocked so I walked in to see a man hitting my mother in the face. I screamed, and my power just came out, the man was thrown backwards, I heard his jaw snap, heard him scream. I knew the man, he was one of the Kegertsa family, the owners of the brothel. His cousins wanted to kill me, till they heard that the man was abusing one of their "assets". They have a strange code of honour the criminal gangs of the Rose district. They made my mother take me to the House of Artorus, who in turn handed me over to the knights. That last hug between my mother and myself is something I will never forget."

Beni finished applying the salve, slipping the empty box back into its pouch. "Life and the Gods have seen fit to put you through many trials, Iska Crook-nose, may I suggest that with both you and your mother matters of the heart usually take precedence over cold reason."

"You mean, are we both flighty? Yes senior, I fear you are right."

"Call me Beni. And give me emotion over logic any day. Now, shall I tell you how I came by my scars? We have enough time till curfew I feel."

"Yes senior...Beni. I would like to hear that."

And so the two women talked, until the bell came.

DAY NINE
37
Refreshed, prepared, with a suspect to see

The following morning, after a night fit to chill the bones, Gytha strode to the novices' library, the laughter of Sir Borak still ringing in her ears. She had stood, freezing in her shift until they arrived, only to tell her that the search of her robes was not going to happen that day. The reason for the laughter was of course, the book Beni had loaned her which, to nobody's surprise, was near the top of the proscribed list. She had shown them the permission Beni had given her, which they had accepted gladly, but did insist on leafing through some of it to "educate" themselves. They both sniggered so much Gytha began to wonder if the past ten years of her life had been a dream and she was back in the Childs' college having to deal with some boys deep in the throes of puberty. However the search was not nearly as long or thorough today, and she was glad to wriggle free of it earlier than expected.

A doorway in the library led to the tunnel, that in turn, led to the jails under the island's eastern promontory, jails that had not seen so much use in many years. Steven and a couple of other knights were waiting there. He looked refreshed, invigorated, proffering a genuine smile as she walked towards him.

"Sleep well?" she asked him.

"As though Artorus himself had fluffed my pillow," he replied, "early night and early rise. Edith seems well and I have work to do. I have even been with Sir Edgar to look at the tunnels beneath us, and in the cave that held the letter. I have it here..." he patted a leather wallet at his belt, "and will shortly confront Senior Lipshin with it."

"You have been in the caves?" Gytha was surprised. "Wasn't that a risk? The spirit is supposed to protect them."

Steven spoke confidently. "I think our spirit is on its best behaviour. Some of the boys have been in there for a good while looking for the young priest. They have heard things, seen lights glowing in the distance but there has been no direct contact."

"She must be watching," Gytha said, "maybe waiting to see if I can help her, seeing if I can find the jewel that binds her soul."

"Well she may have to wait a little while longer yet. Shall we proceed?"

Gytha nodded and followed Steven into the corridor holding the cells. The last time she had done this she had been with Sergeant Welton, a fact she decided not to mention. Instead she determined to ask him what the cave that held the letter was like, given that she had never seen it herself.

"It was a cave," he laughed. "Dark, three or four exits, oh and some bizarre elven artefact never before seen by man. All very humdrum."

"We think it is a housing for the soul jewel," Gytha reminded him; "I would like to see it sometime myself. Miriam said it was beautiful yet totally alien, the sort of thing many a scholar would pay a duke's ransom to research."

"Weird was the word I would use. It was totally out of place in the cave. To be honest apart from that it just reminded me of a senior mage's office, desk, quill, a couple of torches with an oil flask, little else to talk about really."

Gytha stopped in her tracks a moment causing Steven to look at her bemusedly. "Are you sure it was oil?" she asked.

"What else could it be? Torches, oil..."

"It could have been a ...substance. The way our killer has avoided the spirit has been to go into the caves with the elven blue fire, Sinotaneh cannot attack anyone that wields it. It can be ignited using our power but for someone such as you, the only way to use it is in a form similar to oil. I wonder if the flask contained that substance, the means of lighting blue fire, and if so why was it there?"

"How do you mean?"

"Well Raiman and Havel were the only non-mage personnel we know of that may have worked with the killer, or with the Order of Jedrael, if the two are different. So they needed the oil to navigate the caves. So why is it in the caves and not in say, Havel's quarters, what use is it in the caves if they have to walk through them to get it? Unless..."

"Unless?"

"Unless it was in Havel's little house and his killer carried it to the cave themselves."

"Why?"

"Because it is evidence, if we had found it when we searched his house we may have shaved a day or two off the investigation. The killer left it in the cave and returned to their quarters through the tunnels." She sounded excited.

"And how does this help us? Any of the suspects could have done that."

"It doesn't really," her excitement died momentarily." At least it means that Arbagast and Havel didn't necessarily kill each other, that a third party was there. I mean we knew that anyway because somebody had to throw them into the sewer trench, but we have a partial confirmation that they returned to the college through the tunnels. It points the finger towards a member of the Order of Jedrael."

"True," Steven admitted. "If only we knew who all the members were." They were finally at the door of the cell Lipshin was occupying. "Edgar, go back to the cave and bring up the flask of oil." He turned to Gytha. "Can't do any harm."

"No," Gytha agreed; "also can someone go and see herbalist Frankus, see who has ordered these herbs in the last two months or so." She produced a scrawled list from her belt pouch.

"I can do that too." Edgar nodded to Gytha and took the list before departing. Steven watched his back recede before facing Gytha, his smile was broadening as she watched. "Maybe we are getting somewhere at long last. Now to face our chief suspect. Ready?"

"Ready," she said as he turned the key in the door.

****

Steven gains the upper hand

Gytha found senior mage Lipshin intimidating at the best of times, but these were a long way short of the best of times. She was glowering fit to melt the stone surrounding her and Gytha could feel herself quailing inside as she sat opposite her, the two of them not five feet apart. This was one interview in which she was perfectly happy to let Steven take the lead.

And he seemed perfectly happy to do so. Lipshin sat on a bench of stone hewn from the very fabric of the cave, Steven directly opposite with just a small wooden table between the two of them. Above them the stone grille in the ceiling admitted some bright, pre noon sunlight, cold but clear and far stronger than the shapeless candle on the table, which smelled far more than it illuminated.

"Senior Lipshin," Steven said cheerily, "you are here because you are the chief suspect behind the murders of two, maybe four, or maybe even five people. Before we start, would you like to admit your guilt for any of these crimes?"

Lipshin said nothing, her expression was a response in itself.

"Very well," he continued, "I shall ask you directly. Did you kill senior mage Caswell?"

Some hesitancy, before the single word "no," was spat out.

"Did you kill senior mage Arbagast?"

"No."

"Senior mage Tola?"

"No."

"Lay brother Raiman?"

"No." Lipshin rolled her eyes upwards.

"Lay brother Havel?"

"No."

"Then you maintain that you have murdered nobody these last few days?"

"Well done. It appears that I am in the company of genius."

He sounded cheerier than ever. "Then if you are so innocent do you suspect anybody of these crimes yourself?"

She narrowed her eyes. "Why would you ask that?"

"Well the murderer is a frost mage, you are a frost mage, the murderer is probably one of the Order of Jedrael and you are of the Order of Jedrael, if you didn't do the killings yourself you must have some inkling as to who the guilty party might be surely?"

Lipshin did not reply immediately, if Gytha didn't know the woman she would say that she was almost hesitant, unsure of herself. Then the reply came and Gytha realised her premise was a false one.

"A long time ago I read the law pertaining to us mages as codified by your order. A rather thick tome I remember it detailing many heinous offences and the range of punishments available for each one. Now I seem to recall that even admitting membership of this "Order of Jedrael" could lead to imprisonment, or a whipping, or, if the order had already been found guilty of fomenting unrest against the knights, execution. Given your current enthusiasm towards whippings and executions what earthly reason would I have for admitting such membership? So to answer your questions I have no idea who could have killed these people and I am not of this Order of Jedrael. The only possible suspect I can see is Xhenafa himself. May I go now, unless that is you have some "proof" of my guilt. I trust you are as honest as you are stupid and have not concocted some evidence merely to make it appear that I am guilty. Or are you that desperate by now?"

"Oh no, I am not that desperate," Steven said blithely. "All I want is the truth. Otherwise these killings could continue indefinitely. You know of the tunnels in the college walls and the caves underneath them?"

She looked puzzled at his change of tack. "The tunnels yes; the caves less so, they are alluded to in documents about this place but as far as I am aware they have never been fully mapped."

For some inexplicable reason Gytha found herself wanting to take the senior mage's side. She was as acidic as ever, but Gytha could actually detect something of a façade to her. She was nervous and for once was unable to conceal the fact completely. "He knows, senior," she finally said, "he has a letter."

"Letter?" she frowned, "what letter?"

Steven gave Gytha a sideways look, obviously less than happy that a key part of his evidence had been revealed before he was ready. Nevertheless he opened his wallet and passed the letter over to Lipshin. "Any comments?"

She took it with a brusque gesture and snorted loudly as she started to read. Then, her expression started to change and, for the briefest moment, for the first time in her life, Gytha thought she saw Lipshin frightened. Then though the usual haughty mask reasserted itself.

"This letter proves nothing. It is addressed to somebody called "M". My first name begins with that letter, but I could rattle off another half dozen mages with that letter in their name. You have obviously searched my chambers and discovered it there but that in itself does not prove that I am the recipient. I could just have been holding correspondence on behalf of another."

"But the letter was not found in…" Gytha started before a look from Steven shut her up.

"You are denying that this letter refers to or was intended for your eyes," Steven said.

"Yes." Lipshin looked from Steven to Gytha and back to Steven again. She really was unsure of herself.

"Very well," he continued, "then you will have no interest in the outcome of the little escapade detailed in the letter, I will have it back now thank you."

Lipshin practically thrust it into Steven's face. He took it with a smile. "You haven't seen it yet have you Gytha?"

"No," she said; "heard about, not read."

He passed it over to her. "Could you read it out for all of us please?"

Biting her tongue at seemingly being placed in the role of clerk, Gytha did as requested, she was after all extremely interested in its contents.

"My good friend M, if I can be allowed to call you friend for we obviously have yet to meet. I can at last confirm that I have assembled a group of likeminded people and will be proceeding with our oft discussed plans. If the Gods are with us by the time you receive this missive the journey to our rendezvous will have already been underway for some weeks. Your journey can now therefore be undertaken, as it will be of shorter duration than ours perhaps we will meet up at around the same time. They say the island is remote and can be beset by fierce storms, but these same storms make it both lush and fertile.

The lay brothers accompanying us will rebuild the derelict fortress and help make it a true refuge for us so persecuted. The life will be hard, it may be short but most importantly it will be free. As Jedrael once remarked, one day free from the impositions of the Emperor and the constraints of the knights will be worth a thousand in the fetters that our "gift" has brought down upon our shoulders. If the Gods do deliver us to our new home then at last I can marry my lady, and you your man. Think on that and the hardships awaiting us will be all the easier to bear. Gods keep you, and please accept my felicitations. In eager anticipation of our first meeting. S. "

"Married?" Gytha half gasped after she had finished. Steven said nothing, he had been scrutinising Lipshin's face the entire time, only now it was his pale eyes showing the disdain and Lipshin's that refused to meet them in return.

"But this letter means nothing to you, even though you believe it was found in your room. It wasn't by the way." Steven was coolness personified.

"No. I deny everything." Lipshin said unconvincingly.

"As you wish. Now, let me tell you a tale, one given to me by a couple of newly arrived knights, here on transfer from the mage college at Old City in northern Chira."

Lipshin shut her eyes briefly, when she opened them again they were raised no higher than the table.

"Just before they left this college, have you ever been there by the way, it is south of the city built on an island in the middle of a vast salt marsh. It can only be reached by a causeway that is only exposed at low tide. The sea is just a mile or two to the west, but the college has high walls and is surrounded by water, fen, mud, and bog, practically impossible to escape from. Nevertheless there was an escape attempt from there recently, led by a mage called Stahl; "S", Stahl, can you see the correlation with the letter? They managed it too, smuggling money out through a compliant lay brother who then hired both a small boat to traverse the marsh and a sea going vessel to take them to whatever island was alluded to in the letter."

"Sunbank Island?" Gytha asked.

"No, it would be a lot more remote, a place where recapture would be all but impossible. I reckon it is south of here, in a much warmer clime, the letter says the journey from Old City is a much lengthier one, so it would fit. Anyway, this small group of mages and two lay brothers did escape. Audacious really, I heartily commend their spirit. They crossed the marsh at night and were at ship by dawn, sailing from the great harbour of the city. The knights had no inkling of the escape till the morning, they guessed they would be headed for Old City harbour and so got there some time later, and do you know what they were told, what they found?"

He stopped, Lipshin was clasping and unclasping her hands and staring resolutely at the candle.

"Wreckage. Less than an hour after dawn a great storm blew up. The local sailors knew it was due and had not dared set out to sea. Only one ship had that morning, though they had been warned against it, and those on shore all watched it in the driving wind and rain as it was pushed onto rocks and dashed into a thousand pieces. It took days before the bodies were washed up and even then not all of them were found. A noble attempt, but a doomed one. Xhenafa guide them to the seat of the Gods. If you think about it we get sailings from the capital to here delayed all the time because of weather, and that is for a distance of less than thirty miles; these people wanted to travel hundreds. We are all in the lap of Hytha the sea goddess at such times and I am sorry to say that she wasn't merciful with these people."

Lipshin was silent, her shoulders hunched forward, her face flushed scarlet. Steven spoke again though this time he was deadly earnest, his humour gone.

"Now, we can do this several ways. I can go to Shadan and say you are part of the Order of Jedrael, I can say that you are having sex with Mattris, something you as good as admitted in front of us. I can find you guilty of these crimes and have you punished as severely as the law allows. I can have you whipped, your head shaved, or as you said yourself put to death if the order is found to be behind these murders. Indeed, given your attitude I might in normal circumstances do all of this gleefully. But I only want to punish the guilty party and if it is not you, then I want to know who it is. And I believe you can help me."

"How?" she spoke at last. Her voice was barely a whisper.

"Information. Tell me everything you know about this Order of Jedrael, whom you suspect and why. Do that and you might escape with little more than a reprimand."

She stirred at that, some of her spirit seemed to return, something Gytha was surprisingly happy to see.

"Very well," she said tersely; "I will talk if you wish but I want something first."

"What?"

"Some of my testament might be self-incriminating. I want something in writing from your commander absolving me of any punishment should everything I say be proven to be true. Get that and you will have what you wish."

Steven pushed his chair back, standing slowly. Gytha did the same. "You shall have it within the hour," he told her. And with that the two of them vacated the cell where Lipshin shut her eyes once more and started wringing her hands with some vigour.

****

And now for the second suspect...

Outside, in the corridor which itself was only lit by a ceiling grille and a couple of torches in sconces, Steven shepherded Gytha to another door. "Now we shall go and see Mattris," he said to her.

"What about getting this document from the Knight Commander?"

"All in good time. This is the way it works. We go and see Mattris and tell him that his beloved is about to tell us everything. Then we see Shadan and let Mattris have some time on his own to ponder his future. Then we interview her, then him, asking similar questions so that we can check on any discrepancies in their accounts. If they are guilty then they should trip each other up somehow, if they aren't, well hopefully they will point us in the right direction."

"But aren't you going to give Lipshin a letter absolving her of any guilt whatsoever, even murder?"

Steven sighed and stroked his chin. "In theory yes, but if she has killed, and only if she has killed, well the Grand Duke will be here soon, she can be handed over to him. His justice supersedes that of the knights, we cannot punish her, but he still can."

Gytha grimaced slightly. "That is very devious Steven, not like you at all."

"What can I say? We need a capture before the Grand Duke gets here. We need to use what means we have. Now shall we scare Senior Mattris? You can do it if you want, I know what you think of him."

She flicked her hair away from her face, it had been nothing but trouble these last days, "I will let you do it, he is a senior after all, it would feel wrong for me to threaten him. Being a senior does mean something even if that senior is like Mattris. Anyway, I am not really sure what you need me for, I have felt rather superfluous all morning. You seem to have planned everything to the last detail."

"Well I had a lot of time to think yesterday. And you are needed now more than ever, I just wish you were not so ...deferent to these people."

"It is just the way things are done here; you should know that. Novices and lay brothers are bottom of the heap, you are pretty much at the top, as is this lady coming towards us."

Gytha stepped back as senior mage Goodbern strode past the pool of light admitted by the roof grille to stand in front of Steven. She had under her arm a large book and a number of loose leafed parchments. "May I have a word sir knight?" she asked, her tone rather more curt than usual.

"Of course senior, I wanted to see you too, when I had the time. Is there a problem?"

"In a manner of speaking. You have detained two frost mages here; I would like to speak to them. I would like to remind you that I am head of the frost mage chapter in the college, so I do have that right."

"But why would you want to?" Steven beamed at her, all charm once more.

"Are you going to be accusing them of murder?"

"Possibly. Their guilt has yet to be determined though."

"If you do charge them, then they are entitled to a trial in front of the Knight Commander and Chief Magister. They can have their case put forward by somebody who has a greater awareness of the proceedings than either of them."

"You?"

"Exactly. I just want to talk to them, make them aware of the rights they have under college laws."

Steven looked thoughtful. "Very well, though I shall say it again, neither of them have been accused of anything...yet."

"But they might be, Captain."

"I cannot rule it out, no. Before you go in though just answer me this, when Lipshin was detained she was with you, you were heard arguing. What about exactly?"

Goodbern sucked in her cheeks, thought a moment, then nodded. "Lipshin was...upset and angry by the events of that morning, the execution and flagellations. She wanted me to put in a formal protest to your commander. I told her that I could not, that my hands were tied, that guilt had been determined and the punishments were entirely in keeping with college laws, indeed, many colleges would see them as unduly merciful. She disagreed, feeling that any protest, however token was worth registering. You know how she is, disagree with her and you are guaranteed a row. I was grateful your knights turned up to be honest."

Steven and Gytha nodded simultaneously. "Very well, you can see Lipshin first, she may have a few things to tell you. Sir Benet!" he called out to the knight guarding Lipshin's cell. "Senior Goodbern wants to talk to her charge.

201

Go in with them, make sure nothing untoward is said." He turned back to Goodbern. "Sorry, but the way things are..."

"Perfectly understand Captain." Goodbern smiled broadly at him, adjusted her arm and the things she was carrying and strolled to the door where Sir Benet was waiting.

"Now for Senior Mattris." Steven looked at Gytha as together, they went into their next interview.

****

Soma questions accepted orthodoxy

Another staff charged; this was becoming routine. Kessie took off her blindfold and sat back, tired but content. Kas had already done so and was positively beaming at her. "Well, you are doing this as though you were born to it. We will have a little break and if you want you can assist me with a senior's staff, two or three times the power, you will definitely need a sleep afterwards. Do you want to try?"

Kessie nodded. "If you never try you never know."

Kas stood and stretched, yawning as she did so. "Indomitable and understated, you can tell you come from the north of Tanaren, few people, but tough as they come."

"More central than north, Skonnetha and Carn were the nearest big cities, and it took a full day to travel to both, longer in bad weather."

"I was a little bit more southern than you. It does strike me though how much time all of us spend talking about our origins, even though we all probably lived on the mainland for less than ten years. The scholars all say though that our early years are the most formative, the ones that shape us as people." Her ears pricked at a noise outside, guttural laughter that could cut through the thickest fog. "It looks like it is time for our daily visit from Eubolo and Soma."

"Unmistakeable." Kessie smiled as the two people referenced strode into the Oval Room. Eubolo had had his hair cut, it was short at the back and his fringe had been trimmed, not a follicle was out of place. Soma, by way of contrast appeared to be cultivating hair that was the very definition of chaos. It seemed wilder and curlier than ever, spreading over head, neck, and shoulders like a family of tipsy octopuses. She was beaming as she came over to hug Kessie. "I swear that master Eubolo is the filthiest person I have ever met. Apart from myself that is. I don't think there is a knight on the first or second floor whose toes we haven't curled."

"Are you sure that is wise?" Kas looked warily over her shoulder as if expecting half a dozen armoured figures to appear and drag them off screaming.

"What can they do? Whip me for being too loud?"

"We have actually spent most of the morning discussing magical theory," Eubolo interjected, "and which knight has the cutest arse. Actually we have probably spent more time discussing the latter rather than the former. Soma is turning me into a terrible person. In fairness to us we have also been arguing about who has the nicest eyes. Soma reckons it is Gytha's friend Warran, though I reckon she could devour the poor man for breakfast."

"I appear to have gained a reputation even though I have only been here a few days. I am actually nothing like any of your suppositions." Soma spoke in an affectedly posh tone, as though trying to ape Tanarese nobility.

"In what way?" Eubolo asked cheerily, "are you rather more demure than your outward persona suggests? You hide it well if you are.""

"Possibly. The best thing about being mysterious is, well, being mysterious. I rather like keeping it that way." Soma pulled a hair down until it was in front of her mouth, then she blew it away from her face.

"So what theory were you both discussing?" Kas asked her.

"Not so much a theory, rather initial impressions of how this place is run." Soma looked around, "do you have a piece of blank parchment, and something to write with?"

Kessie busied herself with furnishing Soma with the required paraphernalia. "I thought you couldn't write?" she asked her.

"Oh I can, just a little, just the odd letter here and there, don't ask me to write a complete sentence though, a spider dipped in ink would make more sense, but I am not writing words now. One thing you should know about me Kessie is that I am well aware of the power of words and how they can deceive. Remember that, remember that I will say whatever is necessary to give me an advantage. You are my friend, yet there have been times when things I have said in your presence may not have been wholly accurate."

As Kessie pondered the meaning of these strange words Soma helped herself to a piece of parchment. At the top and bottom ends of the parchment she scrawled a large "X". "Now," she said, "this is the problem I see with your colleges. Imagine that, centuries ago, some sorcerer somewhere has an idea for a spell, say he or she wants to seal a wound or start a fire or something. Now say the top "X" represents the idea for the spell and the bottom "X" represents its successful execution. To get from top to bottom requires years of trial and error, experiments, and mistakes, but finally we have a happy outcome. Now this line...," she drew a long wavy line between both "X"s, "represents the journey between concept and execution. Now, what happens once success has been achieved?"

"Any innovations made in the implementation of our powers are codified and made available to all colleges," Kessie said, still wondering where Soma was going with this.

"As I thought!" Soma sounded triumphant. "So you all end up doing the same things in exactly the same way. I am not saying that as the years pass things aren't modified in any fashion but basically you all take this route," she pointed to the wavy line, "to achieve this end. But if you stick so rigidly to that which you know works then you become stale, innovation is stifled. Now, imagine, and this is always the case, that you can get from "X" to "X" using this path", she drew another wavy line between them. "Or this," this time the line was jagged, "or this, or this. You see that the truth is there are always thousands of ways to get from beginning to end, you use just one and it is probably not the best one because there is always this route, the best route, the route you hardly ever use." This time she connected both "X"s with a single, straight line.

"I think you will find," Eubolo said tartly, "that the situation is slightly more complicated than a few squiggly lines. Honestly..." he addressed all present, "we have been arguing about this all day."

"But it is!" Soma insisted. "Now, when I was being taught I was told that in the old days each Wych folk tribe operated independently, their spell casters would come up with their own ways of doing things and, every ten years or so they would meet at an appointed place to discuss what they had discovered."

"Isn't that the same thing though?" Eubolo asked her.

"No. Definitely not."

"Sounds like it to me."

"Well, you are wrong, and I am right. Simple enough really. The Wych folk would discuss things, but they were never bound to a single rigid path for eternity, nothing was ever "codified", whatever that means."

"You are missing the point. At some stage there has to be a gathering of some sort and some way of unifying practise. Without that there would be too many miscastings and too many people...or elves would die. A centralised structure is necessary, our power is too dangerous otherwise, even for us."

It was enough for Kessie. "Sorry senior but we have just charged a staff and the two of you are giving me a splitting headache. Can you go somewhere else if you want to argue about the finer points of nothing at all?"

Eubolo assayed a gracious, none too sincere bow. "Sorry my dear, we will carry this on upstairs. You can always have a lie down next door if you wish. Has Kas shown you the little bedroom?"

Kessie and Kas nodded as one.

"I have used it myself before now," he continued. "I have a key you see, was given it years ago because, and this might surprise you, I used to do some charging myself when I was younger. I am surprised old Goodbern hasn't suggested I help you out now Kas, probably because we frost mages are getting a little thin on the ground. Actually the key was useful the other night when I came to get you to look in that cave for Gytha and the knights."

"Useful?" Kas enquired.

"Well you were snoring like a seal my dear."

"I do not snore!" Kas said indignantly.

Eubolo looked to the heavens. "My mistake. The sound was that of the wind whistling up the stairs from the harbour. I think Soma, that we had better go before I offend all my present company past the point of apology. Coming?"

Soma waved at Kessie before she and Eubolo disappeared from the Oval Room, their voices continuing to float down the stairs for some time afterwards. Kas then started bustling around, leaning the finished staff against the wall then briefly disappearing from the room. Kessie sat down again, she was thinking, she had a mental itch she wanted to scratch but knew that now was not the time. Maybe later, when she saw Gytha and Miriam for a meal or in the library. In the meantime she had to concentrate on other things.

Because Kas had reappeared, and she was gripping another staff. Not a simple novice staff of ash but one that was far more aesthetically impressive, cool, gleaming dark metal whose clawed head gripped an orb of pink crystal.

"Do you need more time?" Kas asked, her face curious, "or shall we do this now?"

She was tired, but damn her to Keth if she was going to show it. "As I said before, now is as good a time as ever. Show me how it is done."

****

And Xhenafa finally takes control

Steven had left Lipshin in obvious distress, something Gytha had not expected, she had also not expected to feel sorry for the woman. It was not easy to watch somebody have their secret hopes crushed like a beetle on a well-used stone path, not easy at all. Gytha wanted to see her privately afterwards, Lipshin would probably just shout at her, but she wanted her to know that she was not antagonistic towards her, that she understood in a way a knight never could.

Mattris however was a different proposition. As soon as Steven and Gytha had seated themselves he went on the attack, with Gytha as his target.

"Ah, the redhead with the creamy tits. Gytha, so much like so many mages in the college, clever, but not too clever, pretty, but not too pretty, talented but not too talented. Destined to live, die and be forgotten in this place, the substance that turns porridge grey, that adds the odour to melted tallow. Are you here to castigate me? Do you really know how to?"

Few people got under Gytha's skin, actually that was not true, a lot of people got under Gytha's skin, but few could do it as well as Mattris.

"Actually," she bristled, "I thought you were describing yourself with those words, apart from the tits thing obviously. But then, I am a woman, I have them as a matter of course, whereas you, being a man, just are one, and a big one at that."

His supercilious tone persisted. "You had better be careful, novice. You need to be assessed by five different senior mages in order to graduate. Now just imagine if one of those seniors happened to be me? You had better start being nice to me or you just might have a lifetime of stock keeping or inventory taking to look forward to. Fetching and carrying for your betters might be your lot in life if you do not start showing me some respect, and maybe more than just respect, if the mood takes me."

She wanted to spit on him. "Well at least you make your intentions clear. How many girls will be forced to fuck you to get what is theirs by right I wonder?"

He leaned forward, elbows on the table, faced pressed as close to hers as he could manage. "Well, perhaps you just might be the first."

Now it was Steven's turn to snap, bringing a gauntleted fist down on the table with enough volume to distract their mutual loathing. "Enough! Both of you! Take your personal hatred elsewhere! Mattris, we are here for a reason, I want answers and you just might have them."

"The murders?" he sat back on his bench again; "I know nothing about these damned murders, I have told you that before."

"Maybe not," Steven said coolly, "but Senior Lipshin might know something you don't, and she is about to tell us. She is happy to tell us everything."

"She wouldn't," he sounded defensive for the first time. "She wouldn't know anything relevant that is, because she is innocent. Besides, even if she did know something she would never risk incriminating herself accidentally. We all saw on the beach yesterday how keen you knights are on guilt by association."

"And how could she incriminate herself exactly? Do you know something about her that you aren't telling us? Not that it matters now anyway, the Knight Commander is going to put something in writing absolving her of any guilt, just so long as she tells us everything that she knows. I won't be making the same arrangement for you."

Mattris shifted uneasily in his seat, Steven continued to press him. "I will let you think on that awhile, then I will be back to hear exactly what you have to say. If…"

Now, when Gytha tried to recount the events of the next few moments to Miriam and Kessie later that day she wasn't sure if she was exaggerating wildly. Then, that night, lying in bed in her cell, playing them over and over again in her mind she was still not sure if she was over embellishing things. But, as she would always remember it, while Steven was speaking to the scowling Mattris there came a noise unlike anything she had heard before, not even whilst practising her powers. It was not so much a noise but a wave of pressurised sound, one that seemed to lift both her and her chair up slightly and to pop her ears so badly that she would be partly deaf until well past noon. The percussive bang, that more conventional noise Gytha would always associate with Cheris fireball practice, came moments later, along with the sounds of splintering wood, a cacophonous impact, a mighty crash and, seconds afterwards, the hoarse and panicked shouts of men. Gytha's hair seemed to rise and stand on end as she put her hands over her ears, then clutched at the table, convinced that she was going to be blown off her legs and dashed against the unyielding black stone wall. That didn't happen but, with the noise ending as suddenly as it had burst forth she was left, sitting, gasping, eyes wide with stupefaction and fear.

Steven was the first to react, both his and Mattris face were milk white, she dreaded to think what her own was like. As she breathed deeply, legs trembling in shock he got up and ran to the door of the cell, flinging it open in a dramatic gesture.

"The wards." Mattris mouth was gaping like he no longer had control of his muscles. "Somebody has tripped the wards on the cell doors." He remained seated as Gytha finally forced herself up off her chair and staggered to join Steven in the corridor.

Mattris, it seemed, was right. A great door, bound in wood and iron lay at an angle partly on the floor of the corridor, partly against the door of the cell opposite. Splinters of wood mingled with the straw and rushes under her feet. The door had been blown completely off its hinges, the door to Lipshin's cell.

And from that doorway a figure emerged, on hands and knees, crawling, moaning, face masked in blood from a deep gash in her forehead.

"Senior Goodbern!" Steven shouted, kneeling to examine her closely. As he did so other knights emerged from the shadows at the other end of the corridor, staring open mouthed at the wreckage.

Goodbern was trying to say something, the words came slowly and thickly, her eyes in their bloody mask looked like they were going to pop out of her head.

"Had to...break wards...it...was...coming for...me!"

"What?" Steven asked, passing her limp form on to another knight. "What was coming for you?"

There was no answer as Goodbern slumped into the other man's arms. Now Steven could see that several splinters had stuck into her back, presumably from when she had instinctively turned away to protect herself from the blast. Leaving her he bounded into the now door less cell, only to find Gytha already there. Neither of them spoke as they beheld the scene before them.

The table, two chairs and the chamber pot, the only items of furniture in the cell, had all been upended, hurled, and smashed against the obdurate walls. The ammonia stink of spilled urine stung the nose. All over the floor Goodbern's papers had been scattered like chaff, stirring slightly in the breeze provided by the wind through the roof grille. And, prostrate on the floor not two feet from Steven's left boot, lay the silent form of the knight, Sir Benet. Steven stared at him, too numbed for a moment to think. Then he recovered himself and looked around wildly for the cell's other occupant. It took him but a moment to locate her.

Lying flat out along the stone bench against the far wall was the equally unmoving form of senior Lipshin, face down, arm trailing onto the cell floor where her fingertips brushed the dark pool of spreading urine, some of which was already soaking into Goodbern's upset documents.

"Benet!" Steven called, "Benet!" He turned the man over so that he could see his face. Then he looked at Gytha to check that she could see the same as he. Her expression told him that she could.

Sir Benet was dead, glassy white eyes opened, staring blindly at something, at nothing, for what could he see now? But it was not his blank eyes that drew Steven's attention so. For across his face stretched the four thin finger marks, frost seared into flesh, the hand of Xhenafa. It had seemed that the hand had grasped the face and twisted the neck, for the neck of the man had been snapped clean. Very quick, and extremely effective. He set Benet down gently and moved over to stand next to Gytha, who had partly turned Lipshin's body, so that the face could also be seen. And the marks were there too, over the face, just as they were with Sir Benet.

"Quick, much more savage, too quick even to feel nauseous. And no singing either," Gytha observed. "She was pushed hard against the stone; it broke her skull." Her hand had been gently cradling the back of Lipshin's head, when she removed it her palm and fingers were covered in sticky, dark blood. "A desperate act from someone who knows we are getting close."

Steven said nothing, but his face was white, his lips bloodless, his eyes cold with rage. He had been cheerful, confident, almost certain that this would be the day where a name could be pinned to these crimes. Now two more people were dead, and his certainty had all but dissipated.

"Fuck!" was all he said, channelling all his anger into one throaty, full voiced expletive. He turned away and punched the stone wall, hard enough to bruise his knuckles, even through his glove. Then he stormed off into the corridor, leaving Gytha alone.

But she was only alone for a moment. Gytha blearily turned her head to see Mattris standing in the doorway. His eyes scanned the room, and the stinking horror within before finally alighting on the one thing that truly mattered to him.

"Margie!" he called out. Bounding past Gytha as though she wasn't there he reached the lifeless woman and swept her up in both arms. Her bloodied head lolled sickeningly, unnaturally, before he adjusted his embrace so that it sat propped up by his forearm, where he could look at her one more time, one last time.

And then he looked up at the roof and wailed in his despair. "Fuck you Artorus! Why couldn't you punish me? Why couldn't you take me? If anyone deserves it...if anyone deserves the touch of Xhenafa..."

His voice trailed off into a grief ridden sob. He turned Gytha's way, still carrying the woman who he must had felt far more for than Gytha had realised.

Further proof of this was etched into the man's twisted face, where she saw something she had never expected to see in such an arrogant, overbearing individual.

For senior mage Mattris, was standing there, in front of a woman, and he was crying.

38
A despondent man, a consoling woman

A short while later (actually it might have been a long while later for no-one was keeping track of time anymore), and Gytha and Steven were sitting together in the modest chapter house library, the same library Miriam had used when translating the journal of the elves. While Miriam had used it, it seemed she had kept the dust in abeyance through the power of her will alone, now though, with her gone, the dust had returned in force, encroaching on every bookshelf, in every corner, on the sills of the windows and filling the cracks in the stone floor and the thin rugs covering it. They both spoke little, drained by this latest event, heads still pounding from the shockwave engendered by the explosion. Yet, of course, things had moved on and conversation between them had to happen sometime.

And it was Steven who finally broke the silence. "On the mainland, in Tanaren city the officers in the city watch have experience in catching criminals, the dregs of the city. Somebody dies and they have the knowledge required to track the killer down, on some occasions at least. Out here, there is me, pushed into the same role because of my rank. I can fight a man toe to toe, protect frightened children from a vengeful mob, ride a charger through an enemy's lines to shatter their formation but this, this is something I have never come across in my life before. This posting is seen as the easy one in the order, a couple of years break in between battles, but I have been found wanting, and people I am charged to defend have died as a consequence. I will be seeing Shadan afterwards, I will ask him to call up another captain to replace me, to take over this investigation. I will return to the mainland, do something I am better at, either hunting mages or fighting Arshumans. If there is one thing I have been shown it is that here is not my place. I have failed here. Utterly. And I can barely look these people in the face anymore."

Gytha shook her head. She had been told in the past that her natural facial features could sometimes make her look hard, uncaring, so she desperately tried to look as sympathetic as possible. "Steven, it would take days, weeks for another man to come here and replace you. He would not be here before the Grand Duke, and we have to catch this person before he arrives. We are up against something extraordinary, someone is harnessing ancient powers to further their own ends, there is no one alive who could have done more than you have. And we are getting closer. You have to have faith in yourself, and in me, this isn't over by any means."

She reached out under the table and took his large, strong hand in her own, she knew of little else that she could do.

To her surprise he managed a half-hearted smile. "Well I have faith in one of us at any rate."

"Good!" she exclaimed in an equally half-hearted manner. "Now, leave that very un-knightly self-reflection behind, we have work to do, what did Senior Goodbern tell you?"

"Very little, the healers were all over her and she was understandably in some pain. The spirit floated down through the grille and killed Lipshin first, smacking her head against the rock, Sir Benet ran to protect her, so it killed him before he could even draw his sword. Then it advanced on Goodbern. She knew that to use any of her power would trigger the wards in the cell door, so that is what she tried. The wards might kill her, but the spirit definitely would, so she took the path that gave her a slim chance of survival. I think she tried that force spell you were talking about. The rest you know."

"What did the spirit look like?"

"No idea. I didn't ask. Does it matter?"

"Probably not. She might look different when controlled by another, this person is twisting her, corrupting her. Sooner or later she may become so debased that she will cease to exist in her original form."

"What might she become?"

Gytha shook her head. "I have no idea. Yet these murders seem different somehow. There was no singing this time remember; I think this might be telling us something, though I have no idea what."

Steven looked thoughtful as he considered Gytha's words. "Interesting, I was right to seek a mage's perspective. One other thing Goodbern told me. Lipshin looked up first, saw the spirit coming for her and she did nothing. She didn't try to move, or scream, or even use her power to defend herself, she just sat there and waited for the end. Like she no longer cared, like she had nothing to live for, obviously a result of my little chat with her minutes before. I took away her will to live Gytha, I killed her before the spirit did."

"You weren't to know she would take your news that way. It surprised me, she just mentally collapsed in front of us, perhaps Mattris can tell us more. Yet maybe there was more to it than that. Think of Raiman and Caswell, they too seemed entranced by the spirit before they died. And me for that matter, when I saw her I could not run, something was rooting me to the spot, some form of bewitchment that made me accepting of my fate, it was a real struggle to break free. Perhaps Lipshin wanted to run but she just couldn't, so do not be so eager to put the blame upon yourself."

Before Steven could reply the door opened and Sir Edgar and Sir Nikolaj strolled in. Edgar was carrying something, a sheet of parchment and what looked like a standard flask for carrying oil. He set both objects down on the table in front of his captain. Gytha swiftly removed her hand from Steven's.

"Sir, the list from Senior Frankus detailing who has had what herbs in the last few weeks. And the flask from the cave, as requested."

"Thank you, Edgar, is Mattris ready to talk?"

"Yes sir," Nikolaj answered. "He has been released and a guard put on his chamber door, for his protection that is. But he told me that he is happy to talk to you because he no longer cares what happens to him. He is outside sir, awaiting your pleasure. Before you see him though there is one more thing."

"You have found Gideon?"

"No. The poor lad must be very hungry by now. No, what it is, is that I was stopped by Father Krieg, the Xhenafan priest, whilst I was outside. You know they had to burn lay brother Havel's clothes, well he noticed the lay brother doing it was acting furtively, as though trying to hide something. Krieg pressed him, threatened him with a whipping and so finally the brother coughed these up, found in Havel's clothes after he was dug out of the trench."

Sir Nikolaj opened a purse and dropped three shiny silver coins on to the table. "I am guessing that robbery was not the motive behind his death sir," he said.

Steven gazed blankly at the coins for a moment before picking up flask, parchment and money and putting them out of view on a concealed shelf. He returned to his seat. "And they still smell of shit," he said. "We will look at everything afterwards. In the meantime, let Senior Mattris in, I am sure our conversation with him will be more convivial than the last."

****

And another man who has lost it all

Senior Mattris was ashen of face and red of eye. His hair was unkempt and blood, Lipshin's blood, still stained the left sleeve of his robe. When he looked at Gytha now the fire and animosity in his face had gone completely, Gytha's expression too had no fight in it anymore, their mutual antagonism belonged in the past, at least for now.

"You two wanted to get married," she said, it was as much a statement as a question.

"Yes," He replied, his voice was flat, tired. "There was a senior mage in Old City College, name of Stahl. He had somehow persuaded an Artoran priest to his side. This Stahl wanted to marry as well, and the priest was happy to do so once..."

"Once you had escaped," Steven said.

Mattris nodded. "Once we had escaped. Both Margie and this Stahl fellow were members of this secret order, they corresponded privately, through lay brothers that secretly worked for them."

"The Order of Jedrael?" Gytha asked him. "Were you a member?"

"You have to be asked," he said bitterly. "I never was."

"So the two colleges were colluding in an escape attempt," Steven prompted him. "You have been told what happened to the others?"

"I have," he said. "Poor Margie. You see she was some five or six years older than me. A childless woman of that age, well sometimes their maternal instinct becomes overpowering."

"She wanted a child as well," Gytha felt dead inside.

"She did yes. We both did. And this was the only way it was going to happen."

"Alright," Steven wanted to press on, "you wanted to escape from here, that much I understand. But how?"

"Full tack and harness eh? If you wish. The dead lay brother, Raiman. He worked for Margie, for all of these Jedrael people. Margie was siphoning money from the college coffers, you know how rich this place is, a few silver pieces here or there would never be noticed. And they never were. Search her chambers and you will find a bag of coin salted away somewhere. Anyway, on his last trip to the mainland, he was given money with which he purchased the services of a small ship, a cog of the kind that is five a penny in the capital's harbour. The arrangement was that on three separate nights, this cog would sail up to the island, weigh anchor and wait for a signal. If the signal appeared the cog was to sail into the small harbour here on the island. We would embark and be away at the dead of night, hours before anybody would notice our absence."

"Which nights were these, and what was the signal?" Steven asked.

"Well, we have already missed the first one, too much going on here to attempt anything, too many knights prowling around."

"And when was that?"

"Sarasday just gone. Three different days the ship would wait for us, each wait being twenty-eight days apart."

"And the signal?"

Mattris closed his puffy eyes, he looked utterly broken. "We were to go onto the roof and set off a sparkfire torch. Simple as that."

"Sparkfire?" Steven queried, but it was Gytha who answered him this time.

"A low power spell, easy to cast, we learn it as children because it looks great and is quite safe. The fire is cool and changes colour, red to yellow to dark blue and back again. A torch could be seen from miles away and would look different from the torches burning in the windows. It is a cheap conjurer's trick, ingenious to use as a signal because no other mage would sense the power being used. You must have put so much time and consideration into your plan Mattris, yet how would you get from the roof to the harbour without the knights seeing you?"

Mattris opened his eyes again and looked at Gytha, again there was no malice in either expression. "These Jedrael people have a lot of secrets, a lot of knowledge. Margie knew a route through the wall passages that would take us from roof to harbour, it was only the harbour guard who would see us, and she had a plan to drug him, slip a pellet in his drink or something so that he would sleep for hours. Notice that she did not want to kill, she never wanted to kill. Her weapons were her words and that was it."

"So who would want to kill her?" Steven frowned.

Mattris shrugged his shoulders. "I don't know. Plenty of people disliked her but surely not enough to kill her. People dislike me more, yet I am still here and she…she…" he trailed off and shut his eyes again.

"One more question," Steven said, "and you will be free to go. There will be a guard on your door, but it is to protect you, no other reason. All the senior frost mages have them now."

"Fine. But as it stands I don't really care if Xhenafa comes for me or not. Ask your question."

"Senior Lipshin wanted marriage, wanted a child so badly she was prepared to risk her life to get it. But what of you? Why would you join this venture? You are well known for womanising and Lipshin had neither the youth nor looks of your usual…erm, conquests. What was in this for you?"

And then Mattris, eyes still shut, sat back in his chair, tilted his head upwards and laughed. A bitter, mirthless laugh, the laugh of a man who loathed the world he inhabited yet contrived to loath himself even more. Gytha and Steven sat in an uncomfortable silence until he had finished and had opened his lifeless eyes once again, staring at both but seeing neither.

"You really think me incapable of feeling don't you? Sure, I have had my cock in over half the girls in this place, yet I forget the experiences in a trice. It is an addiction, like spirit grass, or Kebbelan fungi, quick, intense, forgettable. I have only ever had real feelings for two women in my entire life, and Margie was one of them. She knew me, knew what I did but she accepted it, and you two knew her not at all. Now I shall take my leave, I have a flask of Vinoyen grain liquor in my chambers, a gift from family on the mainland, and I intend to drink every last drop of it."

He stood, Steven and Gytha following suit. "Sir Edgar will escort you to your chambers," Steven told him.

"No need, I know the way."

"And for what it is worth, we will get the person who did this to her."

Mattris turned on his heels, his words were laced with scepticism. "Sorry Sir Steven but if Margie had lived, she would have tried to escape, and if she had been caught, you would have run a sword through her body as happily as you did with that poor sod the other day. My grief is my own, and I want no intrusion upon it."

He strode towards the door, not looking back. Gytha wanted to ask him something, but her throat felt dry, crackly. When she did speak her voice was so hoarse it was almost inaudible.

"You said that you had feelings for two women. Who was the other?"

Mattris caustic smile returned. "Ah! A pertinent question! But I am sure you already know the answer."

"The librarian."

"Well done. Beni, sweet little Beni, everything about her is a contradiction. A painted viper. Imagine her Sir Steven, without her scars, there has never been a more beautiful girl on these islands."

Gytha felt her courage return. "The two of you argued recently. Why?"

"Because fair Gytha, my Margie was getting worried about your burgeoning friendship with her. She was worried Beni might say too much about her to you. So I went and...leaned on her a little."

"What did you do to her exactly?" it was Steven's turn to be interested.

Mattris whistled through clenched teeth. "I suppose you might as well know. Do you ever wonder Gytha, where my general disdain for your sex comes from? Think back more than ten years, think of a man hopelessly in love, devoted to only one girl. Then imagine him walking in on that same girl one day to find her riding someone else like the world was about to end, both of them naked as a spring sheep. Something like that changes a man Gytha, even one as hard as me. Anyway, the man she was bestowing her affections upon died soon afterwards in an accident. I just let Beni think that perhaps it wasn't an accident, that perhaps I helped him on his way. And if I could do it once..."

"And did you?" Steven asked.

"Keth take me for a fool. No! I worked the man over when I found them together but that was it. Give me a book of Artorus and I will happily swear on it if you wish."

Gytha looked confused. "But what did Beni know about Lipshin that could be so incriminating for her? Why did you need to threaten her to buy her silence? Silence over what exactly?"

"Well," Mattris spoke slowly, though he was obviously eager to get away; "as far as I understand it, with this Order of Jedrael there is one top person, they know all the members, but you see, all the other members do not know each other. Everything between them is done in writing with the leader co-ordinating it all. But, in such an enclosed environment like the college, people suspect, people whisper, and Margie knew that Beni knew that she was a member. This was information that obviously had to be kept quiet from both of you."

"But why would Beni know this?" Gytha asked, though again, she had already guessed the answer.

Mattris confirmed her fears with another angry laugh. "You want to know how the Order of Jedrael works? Then ask an expert. Ask Beni. I am not saying she is a member now, but she was, oh yes she was. Why don't you ask her Steven? Ask her why she thinks she is inherently superior to you and all of you folks without power? Should be an interesting conversation. Now I really have to go or there will not be enough hours left in the day for me to drink myself senseless."

The door closed with a creak of hinges and the click of an iron lock. Steven stared at it, his thoughts at odds with the silence in the room.

"Oh do not worry Senior Mattris," he spoke to no one but the air, "I fully intend to."

****

Blue fire and crimson fury

"Well, are you ready?" Steven asked her.

"Ready." Gytha replied through pursed lips.

On the table in front of them sat a small, white ceramic bowl. Steven was holding the oil flask in his hands. With a sigh he pulled out the stopper and poured the tiniest amount he could manage into the bowl.

"Interesting smell," he said, sniffing the top of the flask, "almost floral."

"More herbal than floral," Gytha corrected him. She was holding a long taper; a tiny flame was dancing at the tip. She was being very careful not to breathe on it and put it out. "Well, time to see what happens next." And with that she touched the flame to the oil, an oil that was the colour of amber and streaked with something a lot darker, almost black, and very viscous.

Instantly the oil ignited, bursting into life as a thin, twisting wisp of flame. It started to pirouette around the bowl, turning the parts that it touched a grainy black. Steven and Gytha though had eyes only for the flame, for it was the colour of sapphire, and now that fragrance of herbs and flowers started to spread around the library's dusty confines.

"Elven blue fire," Gytha breathed, "by all the Gods I never thought I would see the like."

"What makes it so different to this sparkfire of yours?" Steven asked. "Or the fire that killed Sir Beverley?"

"Sparkfire has no special properties outside of its colour. The green fire that killed the knight I am not sure about, but it was obviously just a brief, destructive blast. What we are looking at here is something else, something older. We know it confuses the elven spirits and we will not be attacked whilst wielding it. As for what else it does, who knows? The college's fire researchers will be studying this for years. And look at the flame you are getting from that miniscule drop. And it shows no sign of abating."

"And you can make this fire without the oil, just using your own power?" Steven looked over at her questioningly.

"Apparently. But I do not know how. Only one person in this college does. And the oil too, only a mage can make that for it holds power in the same way a mage's staff does. What does the list from the herbalist say? Who has been taking out the herbs used in making this…beautiful fire?" She meant it when she said "beautiful". There was something rather captivating about it, she could not tear her eyes away, blue eyes gazing into blue fire, enraptured blue eyes, it took a huge effort of will to tear herself away and concentrate on Steven's next words.

"The list from the herbalist? Well, all the frost mages have had some, or all of the ingredients out at some point in the last few months. One name though stands out, all the ingredients taken out many times over."

"Who?"

"Eubolo." He answered firmly, expecting Gytha to look triumphant as it was her idea that produced this firm lead to the killer.

Instead she just laughed. "Well, it would be I suppose."

"What does that mean?" he asked, his confusion apparent.

"Eubolo takes a lot of herbs out for other mages, we will just have to ask him I suppose."

"And why," Steven said impatiently, "would he do that?"

"You don't know?" her eyes shone in amazement. Before her, the fire still burned. "Eubolo and Frankus, the biggest pair of old women in the college."

"You mean they are...?"

Gytha nodded, "been together for as long as I can remember. Probably for as long as they remember."

Steven ran his finger along his healing scar, "I see. Of course he could be using his relationship to cover for his rather excessive requisitions. He has taken out all the herbs you put in your list, saying it is for others is a rather convenient excuse, is it not?"

"You really think it could be Eubolo?" she sounded surprised.

"Of course. I mean out of our original list of suspects we only have Eubolo, and the librarian left."

"But when Caswell was killed he was taking a tutorial. With Warran, and Warran has confirmed that to both of us."

"And the librarian has a witness to say she was at her desk working when Caswell died. I have yet to verify their whereabouts during this morning's debacle, I will do that later. But both testimonies are flawed, Eubolo did leave them for a few minutes during the tutorial and there was only one witness for the librarian, a lay sister who could have been bought easily enough. My men have questioned her twice now, they say she is both plausible and convincing, either that or she is a brilliant liar. So, which one do you think it is?"

This was uncomfortable. Gytha chewed her lip. "They are both friends. I..."

"You think it is the librarian?"

"No. I don't know. I just cannot see her doing these things, neither can I see Eubolo doing them. This is all getting too...close for me."

"And there is another possibility," Steven gazed at the tiny blue flame, which still clung resolutely to life in front of him. "That we are not looking at one killer but two. If they are both part of the order and they share the same goal, whatever that may be, then why wouldn't they collude? Eubolo gets the herbs, Beneshiel summons the spirit, that sort of thing."

He was being far too sensible, she usually prided herself on her rationality, but the events of that day had frayed her nerves too much to think properly. "Two people? it could be, we know these aren't crimes of passion, that there is a purpose to them. If that ultimate purpose is to remove the Grand Duke...you may well be right you know."

"Success!" Steven exclaimed sardonically. "You actually admit that I might be right. You know it could even be Beneshiel and Mattris, perhaps they are only pretending to hate each other, perhaps they are still lovers and Lipshin was getting in the way…"

"And now you have spoiled your little triumph. The tail end of the argument I saw between them was genuine enough, and why kill all the others if Lipshin was the only target? I am sorry, I find the possibility that it is probably Eubolo or Beni really rather upsetting." Gytha took his hand again, a strong man, a firm hand. "I have been little help today, so much has happened in so little time it is hard to take a step back and look at the whole situation objectively. Picking out the salient facts from the meaningless…noise surrounding them is far more difficult to do than I thought it would be."

He squeezed her palm gently. "My late father used to say to me, "if you come across an intractable problem, one that seems impossible to solve then the best place to start is at the beginning. See why this problem arose in the first place then everything else should follow on naturally". Perhaps it would help us if we did that, looked at the beginning of things, tried to unpick the events of the time, see if there was something we missed."

"Raiman," Gytha stated," he was the beginning of things. Why was he selected for death and who knew he would be in the aquifer that night? We have never really answered these questions. I reckon Beni had something when she said the killer was experimenting, seeing if they could use the spirit to kill somebody. I know she is a suspect but what she said makes sense, the killer chose Raiman because they knew he would be in the aquifer, alone and far from aid. What better place to try something out? To kill someone where they knew nobody else would be there to thwart them."

Steven gave a long, drawn out sigh. "Who would know he was in the aquifer that night? Well all the lay brothers for a start, but none of them were mages. We know he was working in the college that morning, that he saw several people including the librarian…"

"Yes," Gytha clutched at her chin, her keen eyes springing to life as though she was at last able to see through a thick fog. "But in all probability we are looking for someone with whom he had a protracted conversation, something like, "Artorus teeth but they have stuck me in the aquifer tonight, moan, moan, moan." It is the sort of thing somebody would only talk about if they were doing work for somebody else, if they were in their company for a decent period of time. Then the killer would be alerted, and they could tell the exact time they entered the aquifer by using the tracer, not essential, but it would give them any confirmation they needed."

Steven suddenly stood and headed for the door. Flinging it open he disappeared for a moment before she could hear him bellowing down the corridor. "Sir Beech! Come here a moment, I want a word!"

He returned to his seat as the knight, Beech, dressed in a black velvet jacket, the clothing of a man off duty, came and stood in front of them. He was holding some playing cards. "Sir?"

"You spoke to the lay brothers after Raiman died, yes?"

"Yes sir?"

"Raiman's duty roster for that day, what did it say?"

Beech pulled a guilty face and started to stare at the floor. "Well, I didn't exactly see it sir, I just went on what I was told by their clerk..."

"Why didn't you see it man?"

"Because they didn't have it. The roster is written on a scroll which is rolled up and sealed when full, and it was filled that very morning."

"And where do the completed scrolls go?"

"They are sent to the library sir. If you want to look at it now, that is where it will be."

"Thank you Beech, you can go back to your cards now."

"Thank you sir."

"Don't thank me man. I saw your hand. I hope your purse is deep enough to handle your losses."

Beech groaned and left them alone. Steven stood again and started to pace the room. "We will pursue that later; it is certainly worth following up. Now for Senior Beneshiel."

Gytha sighed loudly. "If we must. Is she in the library?"

"I am having her brought here, away from her "safe" environment. This may not be pleasant Gytha, I may have to lean on her a little. And there is something else, something I will not use unless things get truly desperate but something I should tell you about before we proceed."

A bad day sounded like it was about to get worse. "Go on," she breathed.

"Shadan is getting panicky. The Grand Duke could be here in two to three days, and he needs this matter cleared up. To that end he has authorised, should I so need it, the use of...physical interrogation methods."

"Sorry?" she said, with a bleary shake of her head, "I don't understand."

Steven sighed and scratched his head. "Torture, to put it bluntly. I have permission to torture people should I so have to. He has had the finger breakers brought out from the vaults." He saw her horror struck face and reacted hastily to placate her. "I am a knight Gytha. Such devices do not fall within my code of honour. I will not use them, I swear by all the Gods, on my Edith's life. But I am going to have them on display, just as a reminder to people of what we can do, should their answers prove to be evasive."

There was another explosion, almost as powerful as the one in the cells. Gytha's temper was to the fore again. She stood, her face flushed, her anger untrammelled. The dam had burst and was flooding the nearby villages.

"You use that on people, you threaten to use that on people, you force people to look at such things to terrify them and you lose me, you lose me for good! You really have no idea of what you are talking about, what you are implying. The best way to torture a mage is to break their fingers so they cannot cast, we used to tell each other horror stories of such things as children. They are a mage's worst nightmare; they are my worst nightmare, and I will not sit in a room with such devices. You would be threatening Eubolo and Beni for Keth's sake!"

She placed both her hands in his, her fingers splayed. "Would you use them on me? Or even threaten to use them if you had to? Look at my fingers Steven, look at them! Would you watch them being placed in that gripping thing and see them bent backwards by the lever till they snap? How could you!" To her surprise, she realised that there were tears in her eyes, a tiring, over emotional day had taken more of a toll on her than she realised. "How could you!" she said again, this time with her voice raised to a shriek, hoarse, almost incoherent.

"I am sorry," he tried to reassure her. "I am so sorry; I do not know what I was thinking. I..."

He stopped and turned his head like his neck had been snapped. Fedrica was standing at the door, looking at him, looking at him holding both the hands of a tearful, grievously upset woman. Her husband, holding the hands of another.

Gytha finally saw her too. Angrily she pulled her hands free and stalked past Fedrica to the door. "He is your husband; you talk to him!" she half shouted at her, before striding into the corridor, painfully aware of how awkward things must have looked for them both. And then the tears really did start to come.

****

A myriad of confused emotions

Cowl up, hair pulled forward to cover her face she stormed out of the chapter house, down the stairs and back to her cell. Once there she curled up onto her bed in a foetal position and, to her own not inconsiderable surprise, started to sob uncontrollably. She buried her face into her bolster so that

221

nobody could hear her, so embarrassed was she by this unexpected outpouring of raw emotion. Her body shook as her tears stained both face and pillow. Finally she burnt herself out and, throat sore and lungs aching, drifted into an uneasy sleep.

"Gytha, Gytha, are you all right? I am, I cannot tell you how sorry I am for all this."

Steven was in her cell, gently shaking her shoulder. It took a few moments for her to get her bearings, remember where she was and why she had come here. Once she had done though she pulled away from him, sitting with her back against the wall, arms clasped around her knees. "What is it?" she said defensively, "what do you want?"

"To apologise, that is all, to ask you to come back with me." He spoke softly, as though desperate not to aggravate her further.

"I have had the ...erm finger...erm instrument...returned to the vaults. It will not be seen or talked about again. We have both become rather overwrought these last days and it has affected my judgement, in this at least. I hope you can forgive me."

"Overwrought?" she could not keep the shrill edge from her voice. "Yet another knight patronising a woman! Can you just think for a moment? These last days I have had to deal with the death of my old mentor Caswell, I stood and watched as Tola, my closest mentor, a man I respected like no other, died right in front of me. Then this morning we lost Lipshin, and it was not until after she had died that I realised how I had misunderstood her...and Mattris. And then I had to sit and listen as a knight I had grown...close to, sat there and talked about threatening my friends with torture! I mean...Fuck! I don't know what I mean! I trusted you Steven, I know you said you would only use torture as a threat but just to contemplate the idea of it...and now it looks like I am going to be banished to Manucco just for holding hands with you! And you say I am overwrought! I will give you..."

Steven knelt on the bed, pulled Gytha towards him. And kissed her. A bruising kiss, hot and intense, one borne both of desire and dejection, of a need to share his despondency with another. For a moment Gytha almost pulled away from him. But she didn't, she just responded in kind. One hand was pressed against the small of her back, the other threaded its way through her hair. She smelled so clean, of clear skin and fresh air, so unlike a perfumed noblewoman who felt that an exotic southern scent could camouflage a multitude of unwanted odours. Her hand found the bottom of his shirt and moved under it, to run up the skin of his naked back, she spread her fingers, found a scar and gently caressed its edge, soft fingers, intensity pulsing through the touch. He kissed her face, her cheek, her throat, tasting the salt tears, smelling her warm breath. His hand left her hair to play with her ear, teasing the lobe. She murmured and tilted her head back, his hand slipped to her waist, then moved up to her breast, lingering there, squeezing, her hands too moved downwards, to his breeches, feeling for the fastenings...

Then came footsteps in the corridor.

Reflexively they pulled apart from each other, she remained on the bed, he stood away from it, his shadow towering over her.

The footsteps passed.

He swallowed hard as they stared at each other, fierce, pale eyes, anguished eyes, the longing within them frustrated once more.

"You see what I am," Gytha said finally, "I know I will destroy us both, yet I cannot stop, I have not the control..."

"I kissed you Gytha," he reminded her; "and it wasn't just to shut you up."

She gave a little laugh at that. "I thought of a dam bursting earlier, all those pent up waters released to flood and destroy. I think I was referring to myself, so much happening, so many terrible things, I had no other recourse than to cry like a child. You have seen me weak Steven, silly and vulnerable. It must not happen again, not till this is over."

"All forgotten. And I am still sorry. Are they creamy by the way?"

"What?"

"Your breasts. They are according to Mattris."

She was smiling again. "He was just guessing. If you really want to know then yes, I have a very pale colouration, apart from the top of my arms, which are freckled to death. I hate my arms."

"There is nothing on you to hate."

"There is plenty. What will happen to me Steven? What will Fedrica do?"

"I have spoken to her, told her why you were upset, it will go no further."

"I bet she would have the finger snappers used on me. And I know you are lying, I would rather drink hemlock than go to Manucco, it is easy enough to obtain here, that or a dozen other poisons."

Steven sighed and shook his head." It would be Old City, not Manucco, they would not go to the trouble of sending you that far away. The regime in Old City is much more like here."

"Old City, Manucco, they are both just names. I was sent here as a child, my life is here, nowhere else, I would rather die than leave for another college,

Old City college is in the middle of a swamp for Keth's sake."

He took both her hands and slowly levered her off the bed. "Leave Fedrica to me, you will be going nowhere, you have my word. Now, our librarian is getting a little testy with all the waiting, are you coming?"

Gytha was quite tall, yet Steven was half a head taller than her. She leaned forward and kissed him on the cheek. "I mess up nearly everything that I touch," she said, "and now it does seem I have to trust you after all. My face isn't too tearful is it? It isn't too red?"

It was still a little puffy, but he didn't tell her that, he just held her close and kissed her forehead. She was so warm. "You are rather special," he said. "Now come with me, together we can resolve this mess in a couple of days, I promise you that."

****

The Order of Jedrael

When they returned to the chapter house library Beneshiel was sitting at the table under guard, fidgeting ceaselessly with the sleeve of her robe. Her cowl was up but as Steven passed her he tugged it down, tousling her glossy, dark hair. She glared at him as he sat opposite her, Gytha taking her seat next to him, Beni noticed immediately how nervous she was.

"Am I in trouble again?" Beni asked her.

"Don't look at her," Steven said; "it will be me asking the questions and yes, you are in trouble, you are in serious trouble."

Beni's tongue protruded the tiniest length between her lips. "What is it this time?"

Steven looked into her dark eyes; his gaze so intense that she could not look away. "Senior Lipshin is dead. There has been no announcement yet, but she is dead. Killed this morning in the same way as Caswell and lay brother Raiman. You didn't like Lipshin, did you?"

It was with some relief that Gytha noted Beni's startled expression at Steven's news. "She didn't know," Gytha whispered to herself, "she had no idea."

Beni though was stumbling, trying to answer his question. "We did not get along…that…that much is true. But personal dislike is no motive for…murder. We two dislike each other Sir Steven, but I would never kill you." It was a lame response and only served to make Steven angry. He pounded his fist onto the table.

"I am sick of you and your bullshit! I want answers here and now or I will have you dragged down the stairs and thrown in the jail."

She closed her eyes, "if you must. I do not know what answers I can provide."

"But," Steven continued in his angry tone, Gytha could not look, shutting her eyes also; "I will have you stripped first."

Well at least it wasn't torture Gytha thought, but it might as well have been judging from Beni's response. Her eyes doubled in size, darting left and right as the two knights guarding her came to flank her on either side. "You wouldn't dare!" she hissed at him.

"I don't want a stitch left on her," Steven said. "Then drag her to the jail if you have to, we can continue the interview there, make sure that as many people as possible see her on the way."

"No!" she squealed. The knights started to lift her from the chair. Gytha stared imploringly at Steven, he steadfastly turned his shoulder to her. Beni started to wriggle as her robe was pulled over her knees, her white scars gleaming like marble under the flames of the chandelier. "Gytha! Please!" she screamed, her cries were shrill, touched by hysteria.

Gytha was about to interject, even though she all but knew he was bluffing. Fortunately, she didn't have to.

"Stop!" Steven ordered. "Sit her back down and stand back."

They knights obeyed the command. Thus released Beni slumped on to her chair, panting heavily, tears moistening her eyes, Gytha tried to catch her expression, but she was ignored again. Both Steven and Beni seemed to wish she wasn't there.

"Make no mistake, I will order it done if you do not co-operate. Understood?"

Beni was crying now, hands over her face. As she nodded to him he wondered how many women he could make cry in a day. Gytha, Beni, and Fedrica so far, he was running up quite a collection.

Finally her tears ceased. Beni sat up, straight backed, and inhaled heavily, trying to compose herself. "Begin," she said quietly.

"Have you committed, or are you complicit in any of the murders that have taken place here these last days?"

"No. I swear it, bring me the holy book and I will swear on that if you wish."

"No, I doubt your faith is strong enough for such words to have credence. Do you know who has committed these murders?"

"No. Are you going to torture me?"

"Why do you ask that?"

"I overheard a couple of your knights talking about the finger breakers.

Am I the one they are to be used on?" she tried to sound calm but there was a tangible thrill of fear in her voice.

Steven looked at Gytha. "No. No one is to be tortured under my command. I think my threats should be sufficient for the task."

Beni swallowed. "They are. You played on my biggest fear like an expert."

Steven acknowledged her words with a grunt. "Are you a member of the Order of Jedrael?"

Beni looked at Steven, then at Gytha, a knowing expression on her face.

"Is this what it is all about? The Order of Jedrael?"

"Just answer the question."

A slow, measured reply. "I was once, yes, back in the days when I used my powers."

"You believe mages are superior to the rest of us? That you should be ruling us?"

"I did. I do not think so now. I was arrogant in my youth, I saw things only in black and white, I am wiser now. At least I hope I am." To Gytha's surprise Beni turned her tearful face to look at her. "Do you think I am involved in all this Gytha? I am truly lost if you think so."

"No." Gytha said, but she hesitated before her answer, a hesitancy that was far more truthful and eloquent than her reply, and it was one that the librarian read immediately.

"I see," Beni said softly. "The girl Iska is strong, she is healing fast. She is a precocious talent, reminds me of me at that age. I will see her again, if I am allowed."

"Thank you," Gytha said, her voice guttural with emotion.

Beni turned back to Steven. "Here is what I know about the order, based on my experiences, whether any of it is relevant to your investigation I will leave it to you to decide." She took a deep breath, tugged her disarranged robe down to her feet and started to speak. And Steven and Gytha did not interrupt her till she had finished.

"I was in my twenties; in the preceding week I had just graduated to senior status. I was proud of my achievement, few people graduate at my age, I felt that the world was mine to command. I had a thousand ideas about how to use my power, a thousand ways I wanted to research it, I was drunk on my own ego, I was the best of my generation. Or so I thought.

I had transferred to my senior quarters on the first floor when I received the letter. It was sealed, a single sheet of parchment, waiting on my desk after I returned from prayers. The seal was a blank one, no insignia, I opened it nonchalantly enough, expecting nothing special.

To my utter shock the letter was an invitation. It had been written with an odd ink, like a metallic blue and all the letters had been drawn with a straight edge, making it impossible to identify the handwriting. The words went something along the lines of "We would like to congratulate you on your graduation. We feel you have promise, that you share our beliefs and can contribute to our overall objectives. Consequently we would like to invite you to join the Order of Jedrael where your talents can burgeon, flourish, where they can fulfil their true potential." There was a bit more, but that was the gist of it. Then, as I watched the letters on the parchment disappeared, it was Laedler's ink, ink laced with power. The letter gave me instructions on how to join, so I did, I became part of the order for a couple of years, and this is what I learned about it.

The Order has two people in charge, a High Thaumaturgist and a Chief Thaumaturgist. These two alone know the names of all the members and they co-ordinate the order's activities. There are two because if one of them dies, the names are still known to the other and he or she can recruit somebody else, teach them all the secrets, so the order has worked his way for centuries.

Recruits are determined not just on ability, but on any other talents they have that might be useful in some way. It is not unheard of them to accept novices into their ranks. Also of course they must believe not so much in mage supremacy, few really believe that anymore, but on whether they feel that treatment of mages is too harsh, too punitive, whether or not they believe that there is a better way than the current system, and that such a way can be found and implemented successfully. The order is in truth extremely dull, its notoriety is in name only, it is just a way for mages to communicate ideas with each other. It is little more than a discussion group though what is discussed could be considered treasonous by some. To be recruited you are given instructions in that letter, it involves giving a written reply of sorts and you are allocated a secret letter drop location, a place to put the letter, there are dozens of these drops, often little more than gaps between the stones in the walls, each member has a drop location unique to them. Now you are thinking, "but say somebody does not want to be recruited, say they go running to the knights." But with what? A piece of blank parchment? A hole in a wall that is just a hole? If you do want to join though you pen a reply, place it in the drop, and sit back and wait."

Beni asked for some water. She sipped it delicately, then continued.

"There are three or four lay brothers that work for the order. They are paid for their work and selected for their discretion. Each of them carries a simple everyday object that has been ensorcelled so that a mage can recognise it to the touch. The brother will leave it on your desk, when he does you know there is a message waiting for you, then the brother will collect it again later to pass on to the next person. The lay brothers can go anywhere in the college, they are pretty much unnoticed. They can see the High Thaumaturgist at any time and be given appropriate instructions, they are the glue that holds the order together. My guess is that Raiman started to have his own ideas, started to threaten one of the leaders, that is why he was silenced. I knew he worked for the order, he was doing so when I joined it, he was the one that passed ensorcelled objects to me, it was usually a wooden pen, if I remember rightly.

In my time in the order all I was asked to do was theorise on certain aspects of frost magic and to envisage scenarios where mages and, well everybody else, could co-exist. That is all they want, co-existence. No more fear, no more mistrust, no more child burnings, just people co-operating, they believe in the best of all of us, not the worst. I believe that the High Thaumaturgists in each college are working on a presentation to lay before the Emperor of Chira himself, expounding on such a possibility. But the ideas and the wording of these ideas has to be right, has to be sound, nobody wants the sort of mage purges we have witnessed before, just look at what has happened here of late. One badly phrased sentence could precipitate a massacre.

And that is about it. I was active in the order for a couple of years then I had an idea for a powerful battle spell which I wanted to share with them. My scars were its only outcome, I have had no involvement with them since."

There was a brief and solemn silence as Steven and Gytha digested her words. Finally Steven scraped back his chair, stood, and started to circle round her. Beni remained staring resolutely ahead, not even looking at Gytha.

"You knew Lipshin was in the order?" he asked her.

"Yes," she replied, "though our identities are supposedly secret you get suspicions about other people. Being young and gauche back then I went up to her one day and flat out asked her. She was very unhappy with me, but she did admit it."

"And she was worried you might tell us about her membership?"

Beni nodded. "The argument Gytha, when you saw me shouting after Mattris, it was to do with…"

"We know," Gytha interrupted her, "there is no need to say more."

"One last question senior librarian. The duty rosters of the lay brothers, the scrolls that they send you, what happens to them?" Steven had returned to his seat, he both looked and sounded quite weary, the youthful vigour he had displayed that very morning seemingly a distant memory.

"They go straight to the archive room, the one you visited before. They are kept for two years and then destroyed to free up space. I never look at them, if you wish to check them all you will see that the seals are all intact."

"Yes, we will want to check them," Steven said. "We will be up to see you about them in the morning."

"In the morning?" Gytha queried. "Why not now, there is still some daylight left, not that there is in the archive room granted, but we…"

"Have other things to do first Gytha. You may go Senior Beneshiel, that is all we wanted to know for now."

Beni stood and started to put up her cowl. "Beni," Gytha felt compelled to say, "I am sorry…for all of this I mean. I never wanted you…questioned like this."

Beni had her cowl up tight now, Gytha could not see her face at all, and the response was delivered in a flat monotone. "I understand, you are a mage after all and what power do any of us wield here?" She sighed wearily, "we are all under great duress at the moment. Perhaps we can speak together, just the two of us, when time allows."

"I would like that," Gytha replied. And no more words were spoken until the librarian and her escort had left the room.

Steven closed the door and went to sit opposite Gytha, the candle flames from the chandelier giving his face a ruddy look.

"That was awful," Gytha said in a matter of fact tone, "I think I have just lost a friend."

"She is still a suspect," Steven pointed out, "and I do not believe that this order is anywhere near as benign as she implies. She could still be punished for past membership."

Gytha groaned.

"But she won't be." Steven added hastily.

She gave him a nod of acceptance. "Why didn't you want to see the rosters now?" she asked him. "I thought we had little enough time as it is."

"Because," he sighed, "her statement means that we should probably be casting a far wider net than we have been. It now seems that someone in this order was responsible for Raiman's death at least, but the order doesn't just include frost mages. The killer could come from the frost school I grant you that, but they could also come from the fire school, the lightning school, the earth school, the healing school, the acid school, the illusionist school, the glamor school, the light school, the vortex school and however many other schools this place holds."

"But the projection spell that killed Raiman, that pushed Caswell off the roof, that killed Lipshin and the knight, that was a frost mages work."

"And did you not just hear? The librarian was sharing information with all of them about frost magic. All it takes is a powerful mage and the knowledge of one frost spell. Before we go and check the rosters I want a list of names from Chief magister Greville of all the top four or five senior mages from each school. Then we will see if Raiman worked for any of them in the days before his death. We had two names, now we have thirty or forty, what the librarian has told us has just made the whole situation worse."

"I don't know," Gytha sounded unconvinced, "the spell is highly specialised..."

"And the caster has had years to practise it."

"But why? Why learn a spell alien to one's latent abilities? Why not just cast a projection spell that one is familiar with?"

"To throw a bloodhound off the scent?" Steven suggested. "The fact is that both suspects have witnesses who say they were with them when at least one of these murders were carried out. Now, we either pull apart the statements these witnesses made, or we widen the search, or we do both, which is of course what we shall do. Let us concentrate on Raiman's murder, look at the rosters in the morning, and take things from there."

"But we are still a couple of hours from curfew," Gytha pointed out. "What shall we do with them?"

"Well I," Steven stretched in his chair, "need to speak to Greville, then to Shadan, then to my wife. I also have to sort out the arrangements for Sir Benet, who leaves a widow and two children. I will also have the chambers of the frost mages searched for this jewel you were talking about, not that we know what it looks like of course, but the effort must be made. Anyway, that will fill up the time nicely. I suggest that you get something to eat, for you are allowed to talk in the refectory again, see your friends and go to prayers, where Lipshin's death will be announced. Then be back here in the morning, fresh and bright, with your lovely blue eyes shining. Agreed?"

He had obviously heard her stomach rumble. She flushed with embarrassment. "As you wish sir knight. See you in the morning with your lovely blue grey eyes shining. What about Lady Fedrica though?"

"We have spoken. And will speak again. That is all you need know."

A most unsatisfactory answer, but there was little else she could ask for.

She left the chapter house and headed downstairs to the refectory; food was the only consolation she could have right now.

39
Fedrica makes a request

"Patrols are to continue to be doubled. The Grand Duke has his own staff, but we will provide him with an honour guard of six, to be present at all times. The ship of his herald will be here first, arriving maybe a day before he does, it could be here tomorrow, or maybe not for a week, there is no way to tell. When the Grand Duke does arrive he will leave his vessel and take our ferry to the harbour under the college. Most of his staff will have to walk between islands, just like we have to do. I want the duty rosters prepared before the sun goes down. This would normally be Steven's job, but, as he is busy I am trusting you as a senior knight to fill in for him. Understood?"

"Yes sir." Sir Edgar saluted commander Shadan after his instructions had been issued. Shadan stalked the confines of his office like a hungry bear, now he turned his attention to the lay brother present, a pallid fellow with a long jaw and pock marked face.

"Now Brother Olroyd, as you are responsible for the accommodation and hospitality for the Grand Duke I expect your staff to be washing every stone in his chambers until I can see my face in them. Fresh rushes, fresh bedding, tapestries and drapes beaten and cleaned; the room fresh and aired. He will sleep with two attendants, so I want the same attention to detail given to their truckle beds. I…"

The man interrupted him. "Sir, with all due respect we have prepared accommodation for his grace before. We know what to do and my staff are working like ants in a hive even as we speak. May I be allowed to leave and attend to my duties?"

Shadan nodded grudgingly, surprised that the lay brother knew his duties better than the Knight Commander did. "Dismissed," he said gruffly. Both Edgar and Olroyd jostled to be out of the door first, Edgar being the successful one. Shadan took his seat and picked up a great sheaf of paper, looking glassily at it whilst wondering where exactly where to start.

But he never got to start. For a slight figure stood silhouetted in the doorway, the hands fidgeting uncertainly. "May I speak with you?" came the request.

He stood in greeting, "Lady Fedrica, always a pleasure, how exactly may I assist you. Please be seated."

Fedrica did so. Her dress was parti coloured, royal blue and white velvet. Her hair was pinned back under a silver fillet studded with tiny sapphires, exposing her snow pale neck. She was making the most of what she had Shadan thought, but she was way too skinny for him, and twenty years too young of course.

"I would just like to speak on the matter we touched upon the other day." Fedrica spoke in cool, precise tones, but Shadan could see the obvious façade, the girl was just a bag of nerves.

"What matter? Oh, Steven's assistant, the red head, the mage. Still not happy with her?"

Fedrica's eyes narrowed, "I caught them holding hands earlier. I fear more than ever that she is exerting an unhealthy influence over him."

"Any evidence that they are lovers?"

Some hesitation. "No. But the looks they give each other are evidence enough for me."

Shadan rubbed his chin in an affectation of concern. "Alas I need more evidence than mere sympathetic expression. But have you really thought this through my lady? You want her sent from here on grounds of promiscuity, but in order to do that I need names of lovers, and because they have been working so closely together your husband's name could easily be dragged into this. I don't want my right hand disgraced, and I am certain you don't want that either."

Fedrica gave a frustrated little cluck. "Can you not just have her transferred somehow, sent away quietly, even swapped for somebody else? Surely the removal of a novice mage shouldn't be that much of a problem?"

"I need a reason my lady. Only mages with talents sought by other colleges can be freely transferred, moving a novice is a waste of time and resources ordinarily. Why are you so concerned with this girl? The arrangement between them is just temporary, she will be back with the other novices as soon as this business is cleared up." Of course what he really meant to ask was what the problem was if he did have sex with her? Were men not to be allowed mistresses anymore? But he decided to avoid that particular matter.

"I am his wife. His loyalty should be mine to command."

"And I am sure he would say exactly the same."

Fedrica cast her eyes downward, started chewing her lip, fiddling with her ear. Her next words, when they came were so quiet he struggled to hear them.

"He...doesn't really like me, you see."

Shadan reached out to her, tilting her head back up, he tried to sound jovial. "An ideal basis for a marriage! I have been with Lady Shadan for thirty years, but we have probably spent twenty-five of them apart. I think she is a vinegar featured old shrew; she thinks I am an outrageous bore. Yet we have still raised a family successfully, she has her life in the city, I have my life here and we both enjoy them utterly." He saw that his words were not helping things, so he changed tack. "Look my lady, I need you cheerful for I am relying on you to charm the Grand Duke in a few days. Have you ever spoken to him before?"

Fedrica shook her head.

"A most amiable fellow, and a great honour for both of us to meet him. Look, as you know your husband is charged with solving the current...problems in the college. If he fails and I pray to Artorus that he doesn't, but if he does, if a killer is on the loose when the Grand Duke is here, then I will need a scapegoat of some sort, someone to blame the failure of the investigation on. Ordinarily it would be Steven who takes the blame but, if he was being, how did you put it, unhealthily influenced by another, then just maybe I will have grounds to get this scapegoat transferred out. Yes?"

Fedrica's eyes brightened immediately. "Indeed sir, I thank you for considering my words."

"Though of course we both want this killer caught as soon as possible."

"Of course." Fedrica stood and made to leave.

"And how is the lady Edith?"

"Improving."

"Good to hear it. Now you must forgive me, I have much to do."

Fedrica gave him a slight curtsey and glided out of the room. Shadan watched her go and picked up his papers again, attacking them with far more relish than he had exhibited earlier.

****

News is both imparted and withheld

Gytha too was another woman who could be extremely light on her feet, she fairly floated down the stairs and pattered noiselessly into the refectory where she was confronted by another example of the resilience of the human spirit.

The fog of noise that hit her as she strode through the entrance was in such stark contrast to the silence of the previous day that it briefly stopped her dead where she stood. Conversation had indeed been allowed again, ostensibly so that everybody could discuss the arrival of the Grand Duke. It was true that people were talking, but they were rarely talking about him. With a sagging heart she realised that they would soon have much more to talk about once prayers had started and the latest casualties were announced to them all.

One good thing though was that Kessie and Miriam were sat at the end of one of the great tables, slightly apart from everybody else. Gytha went and helped herself to a bowl of rabbit stew, an enormous hunk of bread, an eating knife, and a goblet of fragrant ale and sat and joined them.

"Ah! The great investigator joins us!" Miriam said in a mock sardonic tone. "Any news? Can we all sleep soundly in our beds tonight, well as soundly as the cold will allow us to at least."

Gytha shook her head. Her sombre mood was immediately picked up on.

"You all right Gytha?" Kessie asked.

"Still at large then," Miriam assumed.

Gytha nodded. "Sorry girls, but I will not be joining you for prayers, I will take them in my own cell and then try and get some sleep. It has been an eventful day, though the events in question were...well were not the ones we really wanted."

Miriam's eyes creased, she seemed poised to ask a thousand difficult questions, but Kessie forestalled her, seeing correctly that Gytha did not want to be too forthcoming.

"Oh well," she said, "there is always tomorrow if the Gods are willing. I will ask Camille to grant you some of her wisdom before I go to sleep. I was going to ask your advice on something too, something that seemed a little odd to me, but it can wait. Found any rabbit in the stew yet?"

Gytha shook her head and smiled; drinking a draught of the ale she mopped her lips fastidiously with a linen cloth before answering. "You can ask me Kessie, I just can't talk about certain things yet, that is all. I will be able to tomorrow though, though I can't guarantee what mood I will be in."

"A difficult one," Miriam smiled, "I guarantee it. Come on then Kessie, tell us about your "odd" feeling, I am sure a good scratch will get rid of it."

"Well, all that it was," Kessie seemed far more inclined to talk than usual, normally she just let Gytha, and Miriam get on with it, only interjecting when the opportunity arose. Now though she seemed quite keen to direct things. "In the Oval Room today Eubolo said something to Kas. Do you know that there is a separate room next to it with a bed and everything? I had no idea myself. Anyway..."

"You digress," said Miriam.

"I digress. The night the two of you were in the tunnels, in the middle of all that trouble you stirred up Eubolo went to fetch her in that room, and she was fast asleep. Snoring he said, so not just asleep but really, really asleep."

"So?" Gytha and Miriam asked in unison.

"Well that friend of yours Gytha, the librarian. She was in your cell with me jumping around like a summer fly on a still pond. The sense of power coming up through the stone was so strong it almost made her sick. I could sense it too, whether it would have woken me if I was alone I don't know but well, I am a novice, I am not as attuned as a senior. And Soma as well, she noticed it too, so I just wonder why senior Kas didn't."

"Maybe her grief masked her senses," Miriam suggested, "she has taken old Arbagast's death quite badly."

"Maybe," Kessie acknowledged, "but he was only missing then, his death was still to be confirmed. It is probably nothing, it was explained to me that the stone is like marble, it has veins of weakness running through it and the power would seep through those veins. Your cell Gytha is probably at the top of one vein. So that is all well and good, probably Kas was nowhere near a weak spot..." she hesitated, unconvinced by her own argument; "but then again the Oval Room and this sleeping chamber are below us on the ground floor, between us and the harbour, so in effect it is closer to whatever power was flooding the college. So surely the feeling of power should have been even stronger for her. I am sure it isn't important, but I just wondered if I should ask her about it. I like her and I don't really want to upset her, do you think it would? upset her I mean."

"No," Gytha shook her curls, "it is a relevant point you are making. You ask her. Or would you rather I came down and did so? It seems odd to me too and falls within the remit of the investigation."

"No," Kessie said hastily, "I don't want her scared, you can be a bit scary at times. I will ask her in the morning."

"Scary! Me?" Gytha choked on her stew. "The cheek of it. Seriously though let me know what she says, it could be important. Anyway, are you enjoying your powering up staffs...thing?"

"Surprisingly yes. It is rather relaxing."

"Boring," Gytha said.

"Relaxing. Did a senior mages staff today, felt like rather a triumph it did."

"Good for you," Miriam patted Kessie's back and mopped up the last of her stew. "No questions about Warran, Gytha? I have spent most of the day with him."

"Did you seduce him?" Gytha asked tartly, though she was smiling as she did so.

Miriam pulled a face. "He has an examination tomorrow, a serious one, we worked all day on theories of power manipulation and mental attunement with the plane of Lucan. Very dry, very technical and all he talked about all day was you. Why in the name of every God in the skies have you discarded him? He slowly drove me insane with his "Gytha this," and "Gytha that," I am relieved to be free of him tomorrow, though I fervently hope he passes after all the work we have done."

"Miriam," Gytha said coolly; "he discarded me. For the sole reason that I could not say I loved him."

"Couldn't you have lied!" Miriam exclaimed.

"No! Not to him. I can't lie to him, he deserves better," Gytha said firmly, though, for a brief moment, she spoke with a mouth full of bread which rather detracted from her sober tone.

"Look. He was talking about love, he apparently knows what it is, I probably don't. I have read enough books detailing how love affects the soul, how it makes it soar, how every moment apart is a waking agony, how music plays and choirs sing when you are together, how it inspires poetry, how it makes women swoon and men beat their breasts with longing. And I feel none of those things when I am with Warran. I just feel cosy, content, relaxed, when I am with him. He is a friend, with whom I occasionally...well you know."

"Perhaps cosy, contented and relaxed is the very definition of love," Kessie suggested.

Gytha shrugged her shoulders. "Perhaps you are right. There is a singular lack of fire between us at times though."

"Oh you can be such a bitch," Miriam said, "Just speak to him about his exams when you can, he would appreciate it."

"Yes," Gytha conceded, "I will. What will you be doing tomorrow seeing as how you have no one to train, no tutorials allocated, and the elven translation thing seems to have stalled? I have a book you can borrow if you wish, it is in my cell, I think there is a passage in it dedicated entirely to you."

Miriam had acid in her eyes, "I saw it, those strange knights told me about it. The Horn of Murmuur indeed."

Kessie sniggered.

"Anyway," Miriam said, "tomorrow morning I will be going to the House of the Dead, to light candles and make dedications to those we have lost. I will happily do some for you if you want."

"You? Go outside? In the daytime?" Kessie was incredulous, Gytha however was silently chuckling.

"Aren't there knights patrolling the area around there, looking for our escapee priest? And who is in charge of them..."

Miriam went several shades of crimson, Kessie look puzzled.

"Why, it is Sir Nikolaj I believe. And you still haven't told her have you?"

Miriam shook her head whilst Gytha bade Kessie lean over the table so she could whisper in her ear. As Miriam studiously examined the breadcrumbs in her lap before brushing them off Gytha continued to whisper, Kessie occasionally interjecting with an occasional "No!", "I don't believe you!" and, "It's always the ones you least suspect!" When Gytha finished speaking Kessie was staring at Miriam with a degree of wonderment.

"Go on then, get it out of your system, have a good laugh." Miriam spoke briskly but didn't look up, her posture was so defensive all Kessie did was reach out and take her hand. "All I can say is that he is a man with very good taste," she said with a smile.

Gytha too sensed that this was not a time for teasing. "Seriously Miri I am quite proud of you, doing what you wanted rather than being afraid of what others might think of you. And you told us, well me, and you didn't have to. Anyway, I shall have to bid you both goodnight, asking the Gods to give me wisdom in your prayers is probably a very good idea."

She leaned forward again, kissing first Kessie, then Miriam on the cheek before handing her eating knife to a lay brother and leaving the refectory for the evening.

She did not return to her cell immediately, rather she took the right corridor as opposed to the left. The lamps were being lit, small lamps hanging from a central beam by a thin chain, they provided scant illumination outside of a diffuse, fiery glow. Fresh rushes mixed with clean straw had been scattered over the uneven flagstones under her feet.

The cell she wanted was unoccupied, but the door was ajar, all doors having to be open prior to the evening bell, however slightly. She stepped quietly inside and went to the table, which was covered with pieces of loose parchment, many of which had been scrawled upon by a spidery, undisciplined hand.

She found a blank sheet and a pen, scrawled some hasty words on it then placed it on the bolster pillow where it would be easily seen. She then left the cell as quietly as she came, returning to her own room to pray and sleep. Yet it was a fitful sleep for her because she could not get something Kestine had just said out of her mind.

"It is always the ones you least suspect."

The letter she had left was only discovered an hour or so later when the cell's incumbent returned after another tumultuous prayer session in which the deaths of Senior Lipshin and Sir Benet were announced. He picked it up, read it, smiled, then placed it in a fold of his robe. It did not say much, but it did say enough.

"Dear Warran, Sorry I haven't seen you these last days, rather busy as I am sure you know. Anyway, good luck for the morrow, I have faith in you and will be willing you to succeed. Love and friendship as always. G."

****

"Here you are sir, the report on Sir Vargo as requested. I would recommend having a scribe reassigned to me as it took me three times as long to write as to dictate." Steven handed yet another ream of paper to his Knight Commander.

"All needed elsewhere I am afraid," Shadan told him. "The logistics of a Grand Duke's visit are something akin to writing out the entire book of Artorus with your own blood. In fact I would rather do the latter than the former. Have you a name for these murders yet?"

"Not yet sir, hopeful of getting one tomorrow."

"You said that yesterday Steven."

"I did sir yes. We were close too, but our key witness was silenced as you know."

"Well," Shadan said in gravelly tones, "don't make a habit out of it. Make sure your next key witness survives the day."

"I will sir."

"I would assist you if I could, but as you know..." He held up one of the many piles of paper on his desk.

"I know sir, I will leave you to your...logistics." Steven saluted and was ready to go, Shadan however, had one more thing to say.

"Your wife is still very unhappy with your choice of assistant."

Steven gave an exaggerated sigh. "I have spoken to her, is she still bothering you about it?"

"Yes. I may get this mage transferred just to keep her quiet."

Steven's vehement reply caused Shadan to raise an eyebrow, which was tantamount to an outpouring of emotion in such an imperturbable man. "No sir!" Steven declared, "it is completely unnecessary and the mage in question does not deserve it. She is totally innocent in this matter; you have my word."

"Yet the good Lady Fedrica is of a family that is quite influential amongst our order."

"As is mine sir."

"Correct." Shadan conceded the point with a sigh, "I will let the matter pass for now, but I will tell you what I told her. Catch our killer before the Grand Duke arrives and this matter will die a niggardly death. If not, I make no

239

guarantees at all."

"Yes sir." There was an underlying tone in Steven's voice, an exasperated tone. "I will update you in the morning."

"Do so Steven. Oh, and Steven…"

"Yes sir?"

"Try and be nice to her, your wife I mean, I am not sure if I have ever seen a sadder person in the whole world."

"An act sir, but I will comply with your request."

"Good. Artorus bless your investigation."

"And your logistics sir."

A gruff laugh was exchanged, and the conversation ended for that evening.

DAY TEN
40
An enchantress under lamplight

It was a cold night again, but when Gytha opened her shutter in the morning her cell was flooded by bright early sunshine. A cold sun, a dawn sun, but sunshine nevertheless. She waited patiently for her cell to be searched, the same knights, yet the search was getting more cursory by the day, they were obviously getting bored already. They were far more interested in looking at her proscribed book...again, they had read more of it than she had Gytha thought, and yet this day their visit was more welcome than ever, and for one simple reason. They had brought everybody a spare blanket, an old blanket, a blanket that smelled more than a little odd, but a thick blanket and by the Gods did she need one of those.

As soon as the knights had bid her goodbye she headed to the refectory, ate a perfunctory breakfast on her own then skipped upstairs to the library where Beni was expecting her. Steven had yet to arrive and so the two women were alone together for a little while. And to her regret, Gytha could sense a little distance between them.

"Did you see Iska again yesterday?" Gytha asked.

"I did yes. She continues to heal, and her spirits are good. She will be fine."

Silence.

"Steven was harsher on you than I expected, I truly am sorry about it."

"Don't be. He is a man under pressure, and I am a suspect after all."

Silence again.

"Are you sleeping better of late?"

"A little. Things are still patchy, but we are not allowed to share cells anymore anyway."

Somewhere a mouse was nibbling a piece of decaying paper.

"I...I... Gytha faltered, and it seemed Beni was content to let her flounder, fortunately, Steven entered the library just as Gytha was going to submit a completely unjustified and yet grovelling apology for her actions yesterday.

"You have the key librarian?" Steven asked, completely ignoring the resentful stare he was receiving.

"Of course I do," Beni said. "I will need to show you the box you need to examine. Follow me."

She led them out of the library, through the passage in the wall and up the stairs. After unlocking the door to the archive room she led them to one of its far corners, stopping to light the lamps hanging from the double row of central pillars.

"The lamps are shielded by glass," she told them. "For reasons that must be obvious, even to the less educated amongst us." She gave Steven a withering look.

"I am well educated enough librarian," Steven answered her, "and it seems an extensive education does little to cultivate manners anyway."

She used her taper to light another lamp, the sixth in the double row. "Are you referring to the manners that threatened to strip a defenceless woman and drag her naked through the college?" her tone was both acerbic and resentful.

"You are hardly defenceless, but I must concede your point. You have been evasive thus far and I felt I needed to force the issue; however, I would have only done such a thing as a matter of very last resort. One thing you must not do though is apportion any blame to Gytha for my actions. She was as ignorant of my plans as you were and has defended you stoutly whenever the occasion has arisen. She is your staunchest ally should you but know it."

"Oh," Beni said, as though she had been slightly wrong footed. Gytha was surprised too, he had obviously detected something of the strain between both women and was trying to address it, perhaps he was more sensitive than she had given him credit for.

She lit four more lamps, five lights either side of each other. Against the wall, adjacent to the pillars was a small desk, a chair, and a stool. She disappeared for a moment behind a row of cluttered shelves, emerging shortly afterwards struggling to carry a large wooden box in both arms, a box that was stuffed with scrolls.

Steven went to assist her and together they set the box down on the desk. The scrolls were ordered neatly within the box but there seemed to be no end of them.

"I am afraid," Beni told them, "that such sundry records are afforded quite a low priority. All I do is stack them in the box after they arrive though I do write the date received on the outside. The scroll you want is likely to be near the top, but I really cannot guarantee it. Now I will just light the desk lamp and leave the two of you alone, take all the time you need." She gave them a coquettish and knowing laugh.

"Shall I see you later, or maybe tomorrow? we still have to finish our card game," Gytha asked her.

Beni's nod could just be viewed, though she was all but clothed in darkness. "That would be nice Gytha. And good luck with your...research."

They heard her footsteps recede down the stairs, then started to apply themselves to looking through the scrolls, Steven on the chair, Gytha on the stool. Each scroll was annotated by a date written in Beni's unfussy, concise hand.

"This is, in all probability, a complete waste of time." Gytha picked up another scroll, checked the date, frowned, and set it to one side. "We know Raiman saw most of the mages shortly before he died, he could have told any of them he would be in the aquifer that night."

"Well it was your idea," Steven said; "shall we abandon our search?"

"It was my idea," she admitted, "but this stool wasn't giving me a sore backside when I thought of it."

"Shall we swap?" he suggested.

"Erm...well no!" Gytha held up a scroll with a triumphant gesture. "For I have found it, the last scroll had to be near the top I suppose, now let's break the seal and have a look."

Steven went to stand behind her and look over her shoulder as together they pored over the duties Raiman had been assigned on his last day. One name in particular, stood out.

"Eubolo," Steven spoke in a soft rasp; "the day he died the only frost mage he was confirmed to be attending on was Eubolo. There are a couple of other mages there, not frost mages, names that Greville gave me last evening, but Eubolo has to be our priority now. I shall arrange to have his chambers searched again, and thoroughly this time, not some sort of half-hearted inspection. I will do the same with these other mages, we must appear even handed at least. If we can find this soul jewel or the missing elven journal we have our man."

"I still cannot believe there is murder in Eubolo's heart," Gytha said despondently.

"Well look at it this way, here we have proof that Eubolo specifically asked to see him on the day that he died, we also have his name all over the herbal requisitions with the ingredients for blue fire, and we also know that though he was taking a tutorial when Caswell died, he did disappear for a while after setting his students some work. I had that checked again yesterday, your Warran was among the ones confirming it. Also, yesterday, when Lipshin died, he was seen in the refectory for a while but there was also a period where no one knew where he was at all. Unfortunately, we cannot correlate times exactly, he may have been eating when she was killed, he may not, but I think we have enough information to give him an extremely testing interview."

"When you put it like that I suppose you must." Gytha stood, eager to be off the stool. She then started humming to herself before assaying an elegant pirouette which ended with her leaning with her back to one of the pillars.

"What was that?" Steven sounded amused. He WAS amused.

Gytha's head was close to a lamp. Combined with her red hair her face seemed to be surrounded by a warm, coppery halo of soft ambient light. "I was dancing," she said. "Part of the Rite of Renewal, the dance of many spring festivals, you didn't recognise it?" she sounded a little offended.

"It is rather dark in here. If I had better light I am sure I would have known it immediately."

"You are digging a hole, Steven."

"Sorry."

"You haven't seen me dance, have you? I used to quite a lot, a couple of years back."

"No, I haven't. I bet I missed something."

"Not really," she laughed, "but it is a good exercise for stiff joints." She started to hum the same tune again before performing a couple of elegant twirls taking her from one pillar to the next. She was closer to him now; he could see a certain playfulness in her penetrating eyes. "Want to see some more?" she asked.

"Go on," he answered quietly.

And then she really did start to dance, singing softly all the time as she moved lithely and gracefully along the corridor between the pillars. Sometimes she twirled, sometimes she lifted her feet, stretched her legs, willowy arms swaying like smooth branches in a languid breeze. Then she stopped again.

"What is wrong?" he asked. "Why stop?"

"You cannot see me properly. I don't wear this robe when I dance."

His throat suddenly felt as dry as a shallow pond during a drought. As he watched she carefully untied her belt and lifted her robe over her head, leaving her in just shoes and shift. She then hurled the robe behind her, not caring where it landed.

"See my arms?" she said, holding them out to him, "the freckles. I hate my arms."

Before he could answer she was off again, singing in her smooth, husky voice as she spun and swung before him. Sometimes getting close enough for him to touch, sometimes pulling away until she was near covered in darkness. She kicked off her shoes, pointing and balancing on her toes, hair spinning so that it covered her face, for she wanted it covered as much as possible.

Because her head was thudding, blood echoing through it like a drum in a cave. She knew what she wanted to do next but could she? Should she? Guilt was running through her system like a poison but her dance, a dance which she had started with only innocent intentions, her dance had stirred something else inside her. Desire, and it was desire that was burning her skin, making her heart pound like stampeding horse, and it was desire that was proving far stronger than her guilt ever could.

She spun one more time, till she was just a couple of feet from him, and once that was done, in full view of his keen eyes she started loosening the laces at the front of her shift.

She danced a little more, swinging with more vigour and less co-ordination, the laces loosened even more. It slipped off her right shoulder, her breathing became sharper and more urgent.

One more turn, two more sways of her hips and her shift slid down to her feet, surrounding her like a linen puddle. She stepped out of it before kicking it into the darkness. She had no idea where any of her clothes were but that was what she wanted, to be both vulnerable and in control. She heard him swallow, she wanted him to swallow, she needed him to. Reclining against a pillar she stretched her arms skyward, keeping one leg straight, one knee slightly bent. Now she was silent, she wanted him to look at her, only her, top to toe, missing nothing about her. Her mind was in a ferment. "Come to me!" it implored him, "Come to me!" it said again. But as yet he did not move.

She slid her hand over her face, her breast, down to her stomach, down, down....

"Come to me!"

And at last, to her eternal gratitude, he did.

Lips meeting in a burning kiss, tasting each other's breath, tongue against teeth, against gums, against tongue, her hands pulling at his short, tight hair, his hand stroking her cheek, teasing her earlobe, before he lowered it, squeezing her breast with a suddenness that made her gasp. Then he was lifting her, her feet were no longer on the cold stone but playing against air, she had no choice but to wrap her legs around him, laughing as she did so.

"What ARE you doing?"

Steven's turn to laugh. "Want to see what a man can do on his knees?"

"On his knees? You don't mean..."

Such strength! He managed to keep her off the ground as he lowered his head, his tongue running over her breast, sternum, navel, getting closer, ever closer. She threw her head back as she felt his thumbs opening her, parting her, rough hands brushing her smooth thighs, and then finally, unerringly, his tongue found its intended target.

Tingling, sweet tingling fire, nerve ends soaring like an Artoran chorus, mouth opening as she half gasped, half squealed at the darkness.

"Oh you do," she exclaimed.

She gave herself up to him then, wriggling, pushing, grinding, letting him control her. Deep, deep inside her she felt her arousal swelling, growing, living, becoming liquid under his touch. It would happen today she thought, so often it didn't, so often she got so close only to end up frustrated, having to smile, having to lie as gently as she could. This time though time was not limited, no one was looking over their shoulders, jumping at a sudden noise, they had all the time they needed, and the privacy to do what they wanted, she could call out as loudly as her passion allowed and no-one, nobody would hear her.

Then at last he set her down once more, pulling his shirt off, letting her hands play with his torso, his musculature, feeling the same scar she had felt yesterday. He let her explore at her leisure knowing that sooner or later her hands would start fumbling with his breeches, loosening the belt, untying, lowering...

And it was sooner rather than later, his turn to kick off his boots, to send his breeches into darkness. Her soft, gentle, yet urgent hands were on him, teasing, pulling, caressing. She kissed him again and giggled, a girlish, high pitched sound he had not heard her make before. She leaned forward and whispered into his ear. "Now it is my turn to show you what a girl can do on her knees."

And she did, and she made him groan, and she made him forget his guilt, at least for a little while.

****

A novice has an excellent idea

Kestine ambled nonchalantly from refectory, into the cavernously empty great hall, then into the reception room where the great doors were almost fully open. It left the air frigid but the room, normally a room of crepuscular shadow and perma-twilight, was flooded with the exultation of a post dawn sunrise. Its light bathed carpets, doors, stairs, windows, and the effect was similar to that of a man washing his body clean after spending days mining coal. The carpets were not red Kessie realised, they were vibrant orange, the inner doors were not black but deepest stained nut brown, the stone of floor and stairs was not just glassy obsidian but was covered in a patina the colour of pale ash. Everything looked different under this purest of light, so much so that Kestine briefly wondered at the nature of perception, how all the senses could be lied to, and how much of her sensory experience was actually truth and how much was artifice. Could the carpets be both red and orange at the same time? If her eyes told her that glass was transparent as air, but her sense of touch told her that it was solid then could they both be right, or were her eyes being deceived? Well they obviously were because if she put her fist through glass then she would definitely feel it, yet, she had never done such a thing before, what if she put her fist through glass and it actually passed right through it without damaging her? She shook her head dismissively; these were concepts that were not worth dwelling upon on such a fine morning.

Not that she had time to though for of course, just before the great doors off to her right, was the stairway to the Oval Room. She danced down the steps, missing alternate ones, humming to herself as she went. Strange how a freezing, but bright morning could lift her spirits.

They were not raised for long though for as she strolled into the Oval Room she could see that things were not well. Kas was at the table, head slumped in hand, body rocking with soft, barely audible sobs.

Kessie put her arm around her. "What is wrong?" she asked urgently; "can I do anything?"

"No," Kas sniffled, taking her hand in her own. "It is just grief; it is a strange beast. You think you have it controlled, that you have dealt with it, but it is like the ocean, it swells and crashes, rises, and falls. Some days are good, others are…well like this one. Sorry Kestine, I am not much use to you like this, I will try and collect myself, a mentor that is not composed is not a mentor at all, as Arbagast once said to…" she started to cry again.

Kessie waited patiently for the sobs to subside, then suddenly had an idea. It didn't happen often, she daydreamed far too much for ideas to normally intrude, but she had one now and was going to suggest it, Kas could only start crying again after all.

"Why don't you leave the tutoring till the afternoon senior? It is a lovely morning, and you like to walk. Why don't you go for a walk in the sunshine, I am sure there are things I could be getting on with. I was just thinking to myself how sunshine lifts the spirits."

To her surprise Kas seemed to brighten up at the suggestion. She put her handkerchief in her pocket and looked at Kessie with something like gratitude in her brown eyes.

"Yes, yes, you have arrived at something. I shall go for a walk along the southern cliffs, if I do that I can visit the House of Xhenafa first, light a candle and say a prayer for Arbagast." She stood and pulled her robe tight around her. "I will come back around the time of the noon bell and in the meantime you…" she reached under the table and pulled out a couple of small wooden staffs, far shorter than the ones they usually worked on, "can charge these two staffs. The Childs' college has asked for them, they want to start doing sparkfire in a couple of days."

"Oh…great," Kessie said, trying to muster some enthusiasm. She was pleased however that her idea was acted upon with such expediency, Kas had her outer cloak on and was ready to leave within minutes. She wrote a quick dedication to go with her offering and with a final, "back at the noon bell," she was gone.

Kessie was alone. It was deathly quiet, there was not even a sound of waves lapping against the rocks of the harbour below her. She suddenly realised that she had not asked the question she had discussed with Gytha and Miriam the last evening. No matter, Kas would be back in a few hours, she could ask her then.

As for now, well she had work to do, she picked up one of the little staves and placed it gently on the floor, the other she placed centrally on the table, ready to charge. She tied the blindfold round her head and started putting the metal coverings on her fingers. No, wrong way round, she undid the blindfold and started again. She sighed wearily, such a lovely day and she was stuck in here, no windows, little air, it seemed rather a waste to her.

"Gytha was right, this could get very boring, very quickly," she announced to the walls, before starting the chant she had spent these last days learning by rote, whilst the pallid sun continued to rise joyously outside.

****

A release that almost brings meaning

Right now though Gytha didn't care for the sun, nor the clouds, the moon or the stars, she was enjoying herself far too much to trouble with them at all. And Miriam had been right about the stamina of the knights, poor Warran would have been worn to a cinder by now. Steven was testing her, seeing how far she could go, how long, how much she could endure before collapsing. Yet he knew her well enough by now, well enough to know that she would never concede to any man.

She had forgotten the sequence by now. They had started against the pillar, that was where he had entered her for the first time, lifting then lowering, lifting then lowering, sinuous, balletic movement that had sent thrills running through her flesh, transmuting flesh to spirit, earthly body becoming ethereal, almost holy, as sublime as any transcendental experience. Then he had placed her on the floor, then they had swapped, and swapped again, and again, or so she thought, she had no idea in truth. As she was riding him for possibly the third time she started to laugh, letting her long curls trail against his skin.

"Do you laugh this much every time you do this?" he had asked, forgetting that he was laughing too.

"I always laugh when I am having fun." She leaned forward and started to rub her breasts in his face. It was a bit of a stretch, so she sat up again, noting that the rhythm between the two of them had become so natural, the equilibrium so profound that she barely had to consider his pleasure, or he hers, pleasure just followed, it was as simple as eating. "So tell me," she panted softly, "are you my bear right now?"

"Your what?"

"My bear. I am Gytha Bearstrider, am I not?"

He smiled. "No, a bear would work you far more strenuously than this."

"How strenuously? Want to show me?"

"By the Gods, are all Kibil girls like you?"

"I am a mouse in comparison. This might surprise you, but I have probably not made love more than thirty times in my whole life. Most of them with Warran. And he is so...so..."

"So what?" a quick, harder thrust, a surprise that made her squeak.

"Respectful. He treats me like I am fragile and prone to snap, a butterfly in the palm of his hand, he is so gentle. That isn't a bad thing, sometimes I like gentle. But other times I like...like it is now."

"And how is it now?"

"Earthy, primitive...wait, are you stopping on me?"

Steven blew through his cheeks. "Perhaps I am getting a little tired..."

"Don't you dare Steven Aarlen! You bested a knight in combat the other day, what am I in comparison?"

"Ten times more formidable."

She spread her thighs a little more so that he could go deeper into her, then she leaned forward again, breathing on him, softly clasping his lower lip between her teeth. "Don't stop Steven," she whispered, "I want you so badly, and I am so close, really close."

"So what do you want me to do?"

She licked some sweat off his chin, slight stubble, he needed a shave. "Stop teasing Steven, just fuck me, harder than you have so far, harder than you ever have with Fedrica, it is how I want it, I get so few chances to do this, just show me how strong you really are."

He had always found her voice sensual, but now, her words being breathed in his ear, enticing, beckoning words, goading him, pleading with him, he had no choice but to respond. He would make her scream to the stones...

She dug her nails into his shoulders before realising that Fedrica might see the marks and so instead placed her palms onto the floor either side of him. So it was the stone that she scraped as he hammered at her with a hitherto unknown fury, the stone that she pounded with her fist as her orgasm built up to a level she could no longer control and the stone that she splayed her fingers on to as at last it was released, her legs quivering, beyond all control, her thighs slick with fluid, her head crashing onto his chest with a shivering, desperate cry. For it struck Steven then that desperation was at the very core of who Gytha was, an untameable spirit tamed, corralled, trapped by surroundings, trapped by circumstance, trapped by her own gift. A passionate, intelligent, playful woman who could not fully be any of these things. She was a prisoner, and prisoners were desperate, and it was that this moment that he realised that his feelings for her might possibly go beyond what was acceptable, that he didn't just want her right now, but forever. It was a dream, a desire that could never be realised. So, in a sense, he was becoming a prisoner too, he had never longed for anybody as much in his life, yet it was a longing that could never find fulfilment, a longing that was a trap, his own gilded cage.

Finally, she peeled off him to lie next to him, eyes staring at the vaulted ceiling, a ceiling she could barely see for the lamplight could not reach nearly so far. He looked over at her, pale nipples still engorged with blood, then he leaned over and kissed them. "Creamy," he said, "just as I thought."

For Gytha's part her head was still pounding, the pulsing sensation still gently receding. She was thinking back, remembering a tutor in the Childs's College who had once asked her, "What do you want Gytha, what do you actually want, what is it from life that you crave more than anything?" And she could not answer her, she could not answer her even now. Yet, for a moment just then, for an infinitesimally brief moment she had floated free of the ceiling, of the college, she had risen above the calling birds, the fleecy clouds, into a cerulean sky, a sky flecked with eternally bright stars. And there, between the stars, maybe beyond them, there it was; that something.

Crystalline, beautiful, exquisite it hung there. It shimmered, it flickered, something she couldn't fully define but she did know that it held all those answers she was searching for, she could satisfy that tutor at last. It would give everything meaning, love, happiness, fulfilment, to just touch it with a trembling finger would give her understanding, clarity of purpose, exultation of her spirit, reason, certainty, bliss, love, she would have it all. And it was all just there, poised, enigmatic, enticing, exciting, so tantalisingly close, it was just there, and she could take it at last. She reached out with tremulous fingers, closer, closer, till there was but the width of a hair between it and her fingertips. She craved its pulchritude, ached for it, for it could make her beautiful too, it would cleanse her impure spirit, her constantly gnawing self-doubt. She would no longer be riven with jealousy, enmity, pride, anger, selfishness, frustration, loathing, she would touch perfection, that was what she had been chasing her whole life, and it was just the width of a hair away.

And then the moment was gone, her fingers clutched nothing but space, and all was darkness about her once more.

She shut her eyes as the last pulse finally left her. So she would be unchanged then. She would still be Gytha, flawed, depressingly human, Gytha. But she had been selfish even now she realised, she still had something left to do.

"Are you close?" she asked him.

He nodded.

She got on her knees and took him in her hand, he was slightly flaccid, he needed some work. She leaned forward, her lips parting.

"Want to bet I will swallow every drop?"

"That is a wager I shall gladly accept."

She smiled at him, for this was definitely a wager she was not going to lose.

****

A beautiful morning for a walk

Such a crisp morning! Miriam was both thrilled and horrified as she strolled down the steps from the college. Thrilled, because it was true about her, she rarely went out voluntarily and to choose such a bright day to emerge from her cave was serendipity encapsulated; horrified, well because she was outside. Outside! And for all the bright sunshine it was cold enough to turn her nose pink. And her freckles blue. Still she was down the steps now so there was no going back, and the reason she was here was a virtuous one at least.

Most days when she did step outside the confines of the college during daylight hours she was welcomed by a familiar vista, drizzle to driving rain, leeching the colour from the grass, painting both land and sea in a palette of dreary greys and browns, but today, today was an obvious exception. There must have been a slight rain shower maybe an hour or so earlier because the grass was green and vibrant and looked like it was coated by a thousand glassy jewels, each of them reflecting the colours of the rainbow. In the wilder parts of the island where ferns and bracken dominated the sun picked out the stretches of vivid purple on the plants that had not yet died back for winter. The scent of water rich earth, primal, pungent, pervasive, was inescapable. It was a fillip to a fuddled mind. And the sea, the churning, sleepless sea, so often brooding and threatening was today smooth as a baby's skin, quartz blue, peaceful, slumbering, restful as a meditating hermit, she almost wanted to go onto the beach, kick her shoes off and dip her toes in it. Almost. But not quite.

The stones scattered on the muddy path scrunched under her leather shoes as she turned onto the southward road towards the House of Xhenafa. She looked left, to the college, and saw that each tower was flying the blue and white flag of Tanaren. That meant that the Grand Duke's arrival could not be too far away. So that also meant that they would soon be issued with their ceremonial robes, hundreds of warmer, neater, better fitting garments that smelled of lavender and storage herbs, issued only when the Grand Duke was here and snatched straight back off them once he had gone, to the protestations of all. That was all his visit really meant to most of them.

The House of Xhenafa, the house of the dead, was busy this morning, unsurprising considering the death of senior Lipshin. She would light a candle for her, for the poor knight, for Senior Arbagast, for...she was losing track of all the fatalities, three candles would have to suffice for now. They had found Senior Tola too, there was talk of a mass funeral to be held on the beach following the Grand Duke's departure, it would surely be an occasion almost as hard to endure as the execution the other day.

She went inside, took the candles off the priest, presented her dedications and prayed for the souls of the departed, that they had reached their destination safely and that they had been judged fairly for their deeds in this life. It was busy in the house, claustrophobic, heat from warm bodies not all of them as fastidiously clean as she was. In truth she was glad to leave, to stand under the trellis covered walkway outside the forbidding door and inhale the clean air once more.

More people were going into the house as she departed it. She was daydreaming as always and almost bumped into one of them, proffering a hasty apology as she effected a last second evasive manoeuvre. She looked to see who she was saying sorry to and was a little surprised to see it was Senior Kas, she had thought she was spending the day with Kestine.

"Sorry senior," she said, giving the other woman a conciliatory smile. "I should warn you that it is rather busy in there."

"I can see," Kas replied. "Still, I won't be there long, I will just light my candle and be on my walk, it is a lovely morning for it, though those distant clouds suggest the afternoon may be less forthcoming with the sunshine."

"Indeed senior, if walking is something that gives you pleasure then there is no better time to do it than on a day like this. Did you see Kestine this morning, may I ask?"

"Yes, coming here was her idea, I have left her with work, she is not sitting on her hands or anything."

"Oh Kessie is not one to avoid hard work. Did she talk to you about some matter that was bothering her, concerning the night that Gytha and I explored the caves?"

Kas looked at her askance, she frowned and took a step backwards. "No, she said nothing. Do you know what she wanted?"

Miriam tried to sound even more apologetic than she had earlier. "I do yes, it is a trivial matter but isn't really one that can be discussed here, I am sure she will ask you on your return."

"Well that will be some hours away. I am going to sit on one of the benches overlooking the southern cliffs to look at the sea then walk the coastal path for a while, you are welcome to join me should you so desire."

Miriam shook her head. "Oh no, I never range too far from home."

"Not even on a day like this?"

Miriam trod on her heels for a moment. "Well I will think about it," she said finally.

"Well," Kas said breezily, "I will see you when I see you. Good day novice Miriam."

Miriam nodded to her and was on her way, returning to the college the way she had come. As she walked, holding her robe close to her spare frame she thought about the day ahead. Warran would be taking his exams shortly, there was little she could do for him now and, as yet, her daily duties were still suspended, technically she was still assisting Gytha but of course neither Gytha nor Steven had given her anything to do either. She had absolutely nothing to do all day long.

The college sat to her right, an indomitable slab of midnight stone peppered with a hundred windows, some of glass, some just shuttered. It was huge, maybe the largest building in the whole of Tanaren, a home to many hundreds. It was warm...ish, safe, she could bury herself in its bosom and read until her eyes were sore...

The steps were right in front of her, but to her surprise she didn't take them. Instead she made a complete about turn and started to take the path back to the House of Xhenafa again. Of course she wasn't returning there, oh no, there was an alternate route coming up and she would be taking that. Miriam's long, indecisive detour meant that Kas would be ahead of her now, maybe she was already at the cliffs, so she could see her and ask her Kessie's question. And once she had done that maybe she would go on a wander of her own, it was quite hilly around there, lots of places to explore and a few knights exploring there at the moment. And one of them was supposed to be Sir Nikolaj.

She had not seen nor spoken to him since that night. She had in fact tried to drive him as far from her mind as was possible. It had been dark, he couldn't see her, she was the only woman around when any woman would do for what he wanted. He hadn't wanted her for who she was, rather than for what she had, what every woman had...and yet...

And yet what if she was wrong, what if he did in fact have some vestige of feeling for her? In truth she wasn't sure if she had any feeling for him outside of his looks and good manners, but the only way to find out if any of this was pertinent was to speak to him. And on this island they couldn't avoid each other forever, best to get it over and done with..." Sorry Miriam but you were naked and wet, and I just lost control of myself. It won't happen again." It would be blunt, it would be painful, but at least she would KNOW, and then she would be able to get on with her life.

And now she was here. The path, the well-trodden path arced eastwards at this point before finally curving south and leading to the House of Xhenafa, and from there, onwards to the bathhouse. However, there was another path branching off from it. This one was narrower, part overgrown with yellow weeds, and it led south and slightly west. To take this path was to head into one of the wilder parts of the island, a place of small hillocks and hidden dells that drove a wedge between the house of the dead to her left and the gardens, workshops, and animal pens further to the west, on her right. She could hear the cockerels calling over the sound of the sea for the chicken coops were the closest of them all, it made her hungry for an egg. Feeling in her pocket she grasped a rind of hard cheese that she had smuggled out of the refectory that morning, something to nibble when peckish. She shrugged her shoulders, muttered, "I had better find him after all this," to herself and headed off down the overgrown path.

She had not gone far when the path cut between two small hills, each of them clothed in moist ferns and tangles of thorns and rapidly browning bracken. Strolling into this small cut she could suddenly hear the cheery sound of small, dark, songbirds. They chirruped merrily as she walked for there were few places here that weren't totally dominated by the gulls, it was a different sound, a happy sound and it gladdened her heart as she walked.

She knew that there were a few more small hills to negotiate before the path opened onto a flat grassy area, a sward that sloped gently down to the southern cliffs. The cliffs there fell away in stages, almost like a terrace and were fringed by twisted, naked trees, finger-like branches coiling like smoke as they reached fruitlessly for the clouds. Benches had been set in the area for people to sit and stare at the endless ocean and just behind the benches lay the coastal path, broad, muddy, as well tended as the one she was treading right now was not.

Ha! Keth burn it, she almost turned her ankle on that stone! She stopped walking and knelt down, testing the injured area. It was fine, it was the shock of her jolt as she was walking that had rattled her more than anything. She stood once more and looked around.

How strange. She was surrounded by nature. A small, ribbon like snake, grey of scale and beady of eye regarded her for a moment before slipping into a shadowy gap between the tangles of bushes nearby. The sun had not quite fully penetrated here yet, the clumps of dull bracken that clothed the bottom of the hills were still encrusted in thin shards of translucent ice, part melted by the rain but still glistening defiantly at the sun that would ultimately destroy them. The air here was not as fresh as it had been on the broader path, it smelled of damp and humus, cracked resinous wood and bruised leaves, broken spider webs fluttered in the slight breeze, a cricket chirped somewhere behind her, but apart from these tiny sounds all was strangely silent. Miriam suddenly felt quite alone.

And her perennial problem was asserting itself again. She had always been cursed by a weak bladder, something she had always blamed on her nerves and now both these, and the cold were contriving to make her desperate to relieve herself. And there were no facilities near enough for her, she would have to disgrace herself again. She clambered around and behind a couple of bushes, feeling her robe rip and snag on twig, thorn, and branch until she found a level spot she guessed was concealed from the main path. How many times had this problem embarrassed her in the past? She remembered a time over ten years ago trying to conduct a conversation with an old mentor whilst sitting in a bush and watching a dark puddle spreading around her feet. Sex on a cave floor, urinating in public, she would be belching like a man during a concert recital in the great hall next.

Business completed she tried to wash her hands on a dew covered leaf only to end up having her palms covered in a gritty black film. She dried herself with a hand cloth produced from a fold in her robes and simultaneously reminded herself to wash properly when back in her cell, whilst thinking that crisis moments like these were a timely reminder of why the countryside was something of an anathema to her.

Back on the path she turned a corner to be confronted by two slightly higher hills covered in the same scrub as the ones she had just passed. If memory served her right she needed to pass these, then the path dipped a little into another dell before opening right by the cliffs. She started to hum to herself, a reassuring sound whilst in the midst of this mini isolation. Then suddenly, ahead right there was a crack of dry wood, wood hidden under bushes where the rain couldn't touch it and in response a small cloud of those singing blue-black songbirds took to the air before settling amidst the undergrowth of the hill opposite. She stopped her own singing, there was something odd about that broken branch, what had broken it? Something heavy?

She started to speed up, just to get past that disturbing noise. Then though she realised that it was just a precursor to something worse.

"Miriam!"

A human voice, uttered in a low hiss, as though it were trying not to attract attention.

"Miriam!"

She froze and turned her head right to look in the direction of the noise. Halfway up the hill, amidst the tangled wood and broad, yellow-brown leaves, a white face had emerged. A greasy face, the lower chin covered in a rash of spots, it had been presumably hiding under those bushes until it had seen her, at which point it probably couldn't believe its luck.

She stopped and moved towards the face, until the spraying twigs from the lower outlying bushes rubbed at her ankles and calves.

She had come this way in the hope of seeing Sir Nikolaj, but instead had bumped into someone else entirely.

"Gideon!" she called out to him, "Gideon! What in the name of Elissa are you doing here?"

41
Gytha is troubled by an itch

Gytha had Steven's arm around her as she lay on her back, stared at the twinkling lamps, and thought about her current situation. Neither of them had yet bothered to dress, they just lay there, holding each other, each lost in their own personal circumspection. A warm glow seemed to envelop both of them, keeping out the chill airs and eddies of this shadowy room. Gytha felt a welcome sense of serenity, of peace, of tranquillity. However, it was a tranquillity that couldn't last for tranquillity never does and it was Steven who broke it with a laugh that smacked of personal victory.

"Sorry but did we have money on that wager? If so you owe me every penny."

Gytha closed her eyes and rubbed her chin. "You know we have no money here, that we are treated as babies, and besides you were evil back then, I only pulled away for the briefest moment and half of it went up my nose!" She leaned over so he could closely inspect her face. "I have cleaned it all off haven't I? I am not going back to the library with a scaly chin, Beni would spot it in an instant."

"No," he answered wearily, "it is clean as a new born babes and no, you didn't get any in your hair either. So are you going to owe me for your miserable defeat?"

"You can have the same again, if you have the stamina for it."

Steven smiled, "just give me a little longer..."

"Weakling!" she cackled, though her tone soon grew serious. "We have done it now, haven't we? I mean your wife, if she finds out then I will be on a ship to Keth knows where before the day is over."

"She will only find out if one of us tells her, and I can't see that happening any time soon. Besides, Shadan as good as told me that if we find the killer before the Grand Duke gets here he will let the matter die anyway. You will be a heroine and heroines do not get banished, no matter what they have done."

"Then I suppose we had better not linger here, however much I would like to. I do not get too many opportunities just to lie with someone, just to feel close to them. When I had my head on your chest earlier I could hear your heart. I, well all of us mages do not get many moments like that, small memories but ones to keep close. You would not really understand."

"I am beginning to Gytha. As a knight we know all mages grab their chances when they can, but we never consider the furtive, secretive nature of it, and the guilt, the thought that ordinary human experience is somehow wrong for you." Steven sat up and looked around for his clothes, he was beginning to feel cold at last.

She remained lying on the floor. "We are hardened to it. It is hammered into us as children that certain things are forbidden. Then as we get older, and our bodies change we finally realise just how difficult such standards are to erm...uphold;" she grinned at that last word.

"We cannot fall in love or live as other couples do, most of us accept it, but not all." She thought of Warran.

"You believe love exists then?" he asked her.

"Of course!" she said vehemently, "I fervently believe that love exists. I also believe that the Lilac palace in Koze exists, that the statues of the nine women of Svytoia exists, that the divine frescoes of Anmir exists, that the great bridge of Horlock exists. I believe that all of these exist, it is just that I will never experience them first hand. Love is just another thing we have to live without. It sounds cold of me saying that, but we have to devise ways of coping with the impositions of being what we are. Outright denial is my way of dealing with it, I am not sure how successful I will be in the long run."

Steven had found his clothes and started to dress, Gytha finally sat up and looked around for her own. "Right, time for me to move," she sighed; "besides, something is beginning to niggle me, and I won't be able to relax until I give it a scratch."

"Niggle you?" he smiled, pulling on his shirt. "It is not a flea is it? Anything could be living on this floor."

"No!" she snorted, "what sort of slattern do you think I am? Oh Artorus beard, one shoe! Only one shoe! Where in the name of the void can the other one be?"

"Find that shoe and you will be happy is it?" Steven laughed, for apart for the one shod foot she was still wearing not a stitch. "Come on then, tell me, if it is not a flea then what vexes you so terribly?"

"Ah!" she said in triumph, holding up a second shoe. "No, it concerns Lipshin's plan, her escape plan. Now you could say many things about her but not that she didn't have an eye for detail. She had months, maybe years to work on her plan and yet there is a flaw in it, at least as far as I can see."

"Go on," he held out her shift, she had been casting around for it since putting her shoes on.

"Well Mattris said that Lipshin knew a route through the wall passages to take them from the roof all the way down the floors so that when they emerged they would only have to drug the guard at the harbour. Now I just

HARBINGER OF THE DEAD

thought he was referring to the same exit that I used to access the passages, on the ground floor in the reception room..."

So did I..."

"Well if so..." she tightened the laces on her shift and started to look for her robe, "then what about the guard on the great doors? Anyone emerging from that particular entrance, or exit in this case, would be seen by the guard on the doors. How did Lipshin not think of this?"

"Well that is the exit on our map that is closest to the harbour..." Steven emerged from behind a set of high shelves with Gytha's robe, which she accepted graciously.

"Exactly. So what I am saying is that Lipshin did think of it, and that she knew of another exit, one where the door guard could not see her."

"But I know the tunnels; as I said, I have a map, the closest exit to the harbour steps is the one in the reception room, there is nowhere else. To get to the harbour you must cross the reception room. Then you go through the doors, down the stairs, past ...."

"The Oval Room, where they charge the staves, you go past there. It is the only place between the great doors and the harbour guard where there could be another exit from the passages...."

"But there isn't on one the map."

Gytha pulled the robe over her head and started to tighten her belt.

"Forget the map. Brother Raiman dug one hole into the tunnels, the one I climbed through, but what if he dug another? This also ties into something Kessie mentioned yesterday, about how all the senior mages on the ground floor were affected with nausea when the spirit awoke. But there was one exception. One senior mage slept right through it, she had to be woken before she noticed it. Now either she was in a spot that the power couldn't penetrate, or..."

"She was so used to feeling it that it no longer bothered her, so she slept despite it," Steven said quietly.

"And Senior Kas wasn't even on the ground floor, she was below it. And she still supposedly noticed nothing. Now I am not saying that Kas killed Arbagast, she was far too close to him. But..."

"But she still has questions to answer." Steven checked that his clothes fitted as immaculately as usual. "We had better go down there, talk to her and search the Oval Room. Xhenafa curse you Gytha, I was rather hoping for seconds, now it will have to be another time."

"Another time! How utterly presumptuous!" Gytha exclaimed, pulling at her hair so that bore a semblance of order. "You stuck your finger up my arse! I am afraid I will have to think long and hard about giving you the same again, you are leading me down the path of depravity."

"Sorry," Steven mumbled, "I thought you might like it."

"Oh Steven, what kind of girl do you think I am? Just be aware that next time, if there is a next time...."

"Yes?"

"You can lead me down that path just a little further."

****

The strangest place for a vital reunion

"You want me to climb up? To walk through all that...vegetation?" Miriam was horrified at the prospect."

Gideon shook his head eagerly. "Yes. It is not far. And please hurry before you are seen!"

Miriam shook her head. He was right, it wasn't far, but she would have to wade through bushes, bracken, tangled roots and Keth knew what to reach him. But he sounded desperate, oh he was obviously desperate so she couldn't linger where she was. She bit her lip, looked down and started to climb up the hill.

She swore constantly under her breath as her robe was snagged, tugged, pulled, and dragged by the tangle surrounding her. The soil had a lot more stones than she had imagined, hurting the soles of her feet. Eventually she hitched her robe up to her calves but that only meant that she had her legs scratched rotten. She would have so much to complain about once she got back to the college. The warm fire in the common room by the library had never felt more appealing in her life, just so long as she avoided most of the company.

Finally she was there. Gideon was kneeling amongst the undergrowth, eyes wide and fearful, he silently beckoned her to get on her knees too, which she did, though her facial expression displayed her disgust at the prospect. "Follow me," he whispered to her.

And then she saw where he had been hiding himself. Under a weave of overhanging bracken lay a dry, hollow space, floored in soft earth covered in a layer of dead, dried ferns which had been flattened to the contours of Gideon's body. From the path it was impossible to see, unless the knights searching the area took days to systematically explore every piece of scrub one could hide here indefinitely. Miriam was impressed by his ingenuity; she just hoped her charging through the undergrowth like a scalded bear had not left an obvious trail to his place of concealment.

He wriggled along his little hiding place and then patted the earth next to him, indicating that he expected her to lie there. She baulked at this initially, it would be an extremely tight squeeze for two people, but he looked so earnest and so frightened that she assumed correctly that for once, his obsession with her was not the foremost thing on his mind.

So she squirmed into the hollow to lie next to him, staring at the flashes of clear sky visible between the traceries of branches.

"I used to hide here to avoid chores," he said quietly, "disappear for an hour or two then make up some kind of excuse when I returned to the priests. It is dry, it kept the rain out this morning."

"But not the cold," she noted. "Meriel's benison but you are shivering! And pale as milk, you may well have a fever you silly boy! How did you end up here? How did you get out of the caves?"

"I climbed," he said bluntly. "There was a cave that opened out on the cliffs. I got past the knights one evening and scrambled up the cliff. It was sheer at one point, I thought I would have to climb back down but there were some old tree roots there, I hauled myself up using them. Then I came here, I have been here ever since. Do you have anything to eat?"

She absently handed him the rind of cheese she had purloined from the refectory. It was hardly the most appetising treat, but he devoured it instantly with all the gusto of a gourmand. She wondered when he had last eaten. "You climbed the cliffs?" she said, her head shaking, "you were lucky not to have fallen.

He shook his head with a nonchalance that suggested that such an outcome would not have troubled him unduly. But she had more questions for him.

"Did you see the elven spirit in the caves? You were lucky if you didn't, it is supposed to defend against intruders."

"I saw...a light," Gideon said hesitantly. "I saw it a few times, but it was always from a distance. I sensed that I was being...watched, but that whatever was watching me was not necessarily hostile. You know that main cave, the first one you entered after climbing down the ladder, there was a second exit from there, I never went into it, I sensed that this thing watching me did not want me going there."

"That was where Gytha went," Miriam nodded in affirmation, "where she was almost killed, maybe it was just those tunnels that the spirit was sent to guard. I am impressed that you slipped past the knights."

He seemed happy to hear her praise. "At first they just hung around in the cave by the sea. Then though they started to search the tunnels but in doing so they left other side tunnels unguarded. I had already had time to navigate my way around and they were clueless so it was quite easy really, if they had just waited I would have had to come for them, I was so hungry. Instead they came chasing after me, I slipped past them, and they had left some food in the sea cave, so I had a meal out of it too!"

Miriam laughed softly, "ingenious. So you climbed up the cliff and came straight here?"

Gideon nodded.

"But you can't stay here for ever."

"I know. I am hoping to sneak out one night, cross to the other island and stow away on a supply ship," he saw her face fall, "it is a huge risk I know…"

She was now at her no nonsense best. "It is an insane idea. How will you know what ships are in the harbour from here? And they search each ship rigorously in case a mage has the same idea as you and tries to escape. You will be caught in no time."

"But what else can I do?" his eyes were round and pleading.

"Come back with me," she said firmly. "Hand yourself in. What you probably don't know is that you are no longer suspected of murder. Other people have died since you started hiding here like a rabbit, so you are in the clear."

"Oh…" he gasped, there were tears in his eyes, "but what about…"

"Your spying on all of us? The punishment is up to Father Krieg. You might get a good thrashing; you might get thrown out of the priesthood, but you will not face death for these offences."

"But if I am expelled from the priesthood I will have nothing…I would be left to starve."

"A resourceful boy like you? I think not. I have to go and see somebody first but then I will be coming back this way. Wait here, come back with me and I will speak up for you. I will talk to Father Krieg personally if need be. I swear by Artorus that I will do everything in my power to help you. Bear in mind that my friend is working with the Knight Captain, I am sure a word in their ears will help you immeasurably."

There was a silence as Gideon considered her words. A small bird landed on the branches above them, only to see how close those strange humans were and fly away in alarm. Miriam rolled her tongue around her cheek; this day was not panning out as she wanted at all.

"I heard you," he said finally; "you and the knight. In the cave. Together." There was a bitter, resentful tone to his words that made Miriam curl up inside.

"Oh," she said quietly, "what must you think of me?"

Gideon's reply sounded considered, as though he had been dwelling on such a question for a long time. "I think I understand why you behaved in such a way. He is a knight, a warrior, quite handsome and probably older than you. And we all feared death in the caves. It is natural to cleave to a protective figure in such circumstances. Against such a man how must a figure such as myself appear? I was upset at the time, but I understand your reasoning now. At least I think I do."

Reason had little to do with anything that happened that night she thought, but he had obviously come to a conclusion and forgiven her, though of course he had no right to be aggrieved in the first place. It was not a topic she wished to dwell on and in truth this ferny little hidey-hole was proving rather uncomfortable; she wanted to leave and decided that now was the perfect opportunity for her to do so.

"Right," she said, wriggling on to her elbow, "I had better go. I swear that I will be back in a matter of moments, I just want to get to the cliffs, see if the person I want to talk to is there, ask them one question, then be on my way. You just wait here till my return."

He nodded and she smiled in response. She looked at him properly then, he was pale but sweating, his eyes were red and weeping slightly. She decided to chance it and grasped his hand, it was cold as stone. "You cannot stay another night out here," she asserted. "You need to see a healer. A hot posset, some thick blankets and an herbal infusion will see you right in no time. Just wait here, and we will walk back to the college together."

She left the none too cosy den, raised herself on to her knees, looked around with all the furtiveness of a hungry rabbit at dusk, stood slowly, and was away. Gideon saw her lift her robe slightly to look at her calves, heard her mutter, "more perforations than a sea sponge!" and then listened intently as she crashed through the foliage once more to re-join the path.

He lay there for a moment, thinking. Her lower legs were covered in scratches, but they were still her legs, Miriam's legs, shapely and smooth. He had so much to think about lately that the reason for his recent adventures, his love for Miriam had become fogged, obscured. Her antics in the cave had crushed him, humiliated him and for some hours he had actively hated her. She had betrayed him as he sat in darkness just yards away, she was just a harlot, just like all other women, she really was no different to anybody else.

But would anybody else have climbed up into his hiding place as she had, talked to him the way she did, shown such utter compassion in her wide brown eyes? He thought about her face, pert, curious, smattered with light freckles, and her manner, precise, nervy just as he was nervy, perfectly spoken. He thought about her quick hands, the robe that pulled partly off her shoulder as she clambered to join him, the warm gentle hand that had touched his own and he melted once more.

He loved her. He could not be without her. And he would walk to the college with her and do as she advised; she was after all, so much cleverer than him. But he could not stay here, not after she had gone. He needed to see her, to see who she was speaking to, if he was noticed his black robe would give him away in an instant, but he was past caring about such things. Besides, he was handing himself in was he not? What did it matter if a knight intercepted him first?

Slowly he levered himself out of his hiding place. Like Miriam he cast around a good while before being happy that nobody could see him. Then, and with far more grace and far less noise than Miriam had exhibited, he too left the scrub clothed hills to take the path to the cliffs.

****

Gytha's itch gets firmly scratched

Kestine was yawning like one of the great tusked seals of the ice bound north when Steven and Gytha joined her in the Oval Room. Before her on the polished table sat two small mage staffs fashioned out of oak. Her arms were stretched out in front of her, and her head lay between her arms. When she heard the sound of footsteps she emitted the aforementioned yawn, slurred the words "done one, one more to go," turned her head, then sat bolt upright as she recognised these two intruders.

"Sleeping on the job you lazy mare!" Gytha snickered at her, "but it is not boring, oh no, not in the slightest!"

"It is tiring work," Kessie drowsily defended herself, "because we transfer some of our own power into the staff it makes us rather weary. Well known fact." She yawned again, putting her hand over her mouth this time.

"Where is Senior Kas?" Steven asked her, obviously not in the mood to hear conversation between friends.

"Gone," Kessie replied, rolling her shoulders.

"Gone?"

"Yes. She needed a few hours away from this place, she was quite upset this morning, so we both decided she needed a walk, first to the House of Xhenafa, then along the cliffs for a while. Said she would be back around the time of the noon bell."

"Did you ask her?" Gytha enquired, "what you discussed with Miriam and myself at the evening meal, did you ask her about it?"

"Never got a chance. Thought I would do so when she got back. Is anything wrong?"

"No. Yes. Maybe." Gytha wasn't sure herself to tell the truth.

As they were speaking Steven was inspecting the curved walls, touching them occasionally with the flat of his hand. "Well, as we have the combined intelligence of two novice mages present can you tell me how in the name of Artorus beard I am supposed to find some sort of magically concealed entrance in these completely smooth walls?"

"Entrance?" Kessie was astounded. "Are you serious?"

Gytha nodded as Steven continued to search.

"Well you won't find anything magical in them," Kessie continued, "they are warded, they absorb power, nothing gets in, nothing gets out, it means that everything we generate goes into the staff."

"It doesn't have to be concealed by our power," Gytha said quietly; "just some sort of hidden doorway, it could even be in the floor." She looked around, the stone in both walls, floor and ceiling was smooth as glass, anything secret here was concealed by a degree of ingenuity far in excess of most human engineering. How on earth would they find it, did such an entrance even exist?

"Well Kas has never mentioned it," Kessie said, reluctantly forcing herself to stand. "The only way to find it would be by touch, to feel for an irregular edge or something, but I will be amazed if there is anything of the sort here."

The three of them started to feel their way around the room, Steven on the right hand wall, Kessie on the left with Gytha on her hands and knees scanning the floor. The light was not good, but she knew her hands would be filthy by the time she had finished, if they weren't already. They carried on in this manner in complete silence for some time until finally Gytha had had enough.

She stood slowly, making an exaggerated sigh to attract attention. "We are wasting our time. There is nothing here. I just had a notion that we might find...something worth investigating."

"Well there is always the landing outside," Steven suggested.

"And the little bedroom, I have the key if you need it," Kessie added.

"Well," Steven took Gytha's arm, "let's have a look shall we? Do you give up so easily every time?"

"My knees were hurting," Gytha protested.

Steven and Kessie looked at each other and shook their heads.

They went outside for a while, Steven looking over the walls of the landing for any likely spot. "Kestine," he asked, "can you open this bedroom door for us, it might be easier for us to start there and then move outside."

Kessie nodded and started to fiddle with the key. She had never used it before, and it took her a while to manipulate it correctly so that it slotted into the door. There were many utterances of "Artorus nibble my ear," and, "Elissa shrink my fingers," (Kestine never swore), before she was happy with what she had done. Finally though she stood back and pushed.

The door clicked, hinges ground and slowly a dark aperture yawned open before them.

Kessie gave a small whoop of triumph and went inside, Steven following holding a small lantern obtained from the Oval Room. Gytha went last, hearing the splash of water against the pier of the stone harbour down the stairs beneath them.

"Not much to see here," Stephen said to them, holding the lantern up and slowly scanning the walls. "Small room with a bed and a desk with drawers," he set the lamp down on the desk and pulled the drawers open.

"Nothing. Have you slept in here Kestine?"

She shook her head." No. Not yet. I find it a bit...confined if I am being honest. So did Senior Arbagast according to Kas, he hardly ever used it too."

"Really?" Gytha's ears pricked at this; "so basically this is just a private room for Senior Kas?"

"Well I wouldn't put it quite like that, but she is the one who uses it the most."

Gytha did not answer, Steven was touching the walls just as he had done in the Oval Room, she however was thinking hard, her eyes sharp and keen.

She studied the floor as Steven reached the wall the bed rested against.

"Rushes on the floor and a rug?" she mused. "Why use both?"

Steven looked at her, he seemed to be following her train of thought.

"What does a rug do?" he asked quietly.

"Keeps the cold off the floor, hides the dust..." Kessie searched for a third answer, but Steven interrupted her before she could say anything else.

"Hides the dust?" he repeated, "or just hides?"

"Shall we pull it back?" Gytha suggested.

One leg of the bed held the rug in place. Steven went and hoisted that side of the bed into the air as Gytha and Kessie slowly pulled the rug towards them. Steven had to twist his neck to see what the women were seeing, but their expressions told him that it would be worth the effort. And he was not to be disappointed.

On the floor, directly underneath the centre of the bed, where the rug had formerly lain, sat a small, square, wooden hatch secured with an iron bolt. The space it covered was not regular in shape, there were small open gaps that the hatch did not fully conceal, it was a job done as expediently as possible and not properly finished.

"Give me a hand with this," Steven indicated the bed. With Gytha and Kessie taking the other end they shifted the bed to the other side of the room, giving them full access to the hatchway. Gytha tried to draw back the bolt, it was stiff and required some effort but finally it slid clear. She lifted the hatch up, exposing a drop of about five feet and a tunnel that led the way into darkness.

"Right," Gytha said, "who's first? Me?" she went and sat next to the hole letting her legs dangle over the edge. Steven though put his arm on her shoulder, his tone was more than cautionary.

"If this tunnel leads to where we think it leads, it might be best to get some of that blue fire first. I for one am not keen for an elven spirit to freeze me to death."

****

Two women contemplate the world

The weather was changing, the fine morning was becoming a memory. The wind was picking up and the sky was getting dark. Torn fragments of black cloud were starting to cloak the island at some pace. Even Miriam knew what that foreshadowed, rain. She really didn't have much time to look around before the deluge hit her. And this was most apparent as she cleared the last of the hills to look upon the south of the island and the mighty sea that so dominated the view. The wind whipped at her wiry hair and tugged at her robes, alternately wrapping it tightly around her legs then lifting it to her knees, revealing the shift underneath. The Sea of Peace it was called, a more inappropriate moniker she could not think of, and it traversed many hundreds of miles, touching the coastlines of many exotic countries and peoples. To her left somewhere the Sea of Peace merged with the Bay of Mothravia, waters that lapped against the fens of Arshuma and the vast country of bog and marsh that gave the bay its name. And all of it sat right in front of her, the whole world in the palm of her hand. The sea smelled good in her nostrils, it caused her senses to quicken, her thoughts to sharpen and she needed them sharp right now.

Ahead of her was a broad swathe of grass. The path she was treading soon ended as it fed into the wide coastal path running left to right: left to pass the bath house and the House of Xhenafa before fizzling out against the crumbling walls of the college boundaries, right to pass south of the lay brothers' field quarters, the small walled pastures and animal pens where they worked, the latrine where the bodies of Arbagast and Havel were discovered and the stone casting circles before it curved north to follow the island's boundary to the bridge that connected it to the Isle of Healing.

Miriam looked either side of her, hoping against hope to see a wandering figure clad in the armour of a knight coming towards her. Nothing. Of course there was nothing. What were the chances of her stumbling into Sir Nikolaj, here of all places? Granted he was supposed to be patrolling the area, but it was a large area, she could stumble around for hours before seeing him.

She was about to turn to go and collect Gideon when she spotted something further away at the cliff edge. Ahead of her was a stand of spindly trees, one of many that hugged the southern part of the island. To her left though were the series of stone benches that people sat on to regard the vast panoply of sky and ocean before them. And one of those benches was occupied.

The light was so strong and the figure so distant she could not tell who it was by looking. But it could only be one person, with the weather in transition like this few people would remain outdoors, the exceptions included the experienced walkers. And Senior Kas liked to walk.

Should she? Shouldn't she? A quick question wouldn't do any harm, besides maybe Sir Nikolaj would happen along as she talked. Miriam strode purposefully up to the first of the withered, silver barked trees before turning left and following the cliff edge towards the benches.

It was deceptive here, for though it was the cliff edge, to her right, under the cliff there was yet more solid earth, part of a shelf of land that had started to slip into the sea but had been arrested by some earthly or divine force beyond her humble comprehension. The drop was maybe twenty to thirty feet, sheer for the most part except at either end of the shelf, where it sloped steeply but smoothly and could be trod by wary feet. The further part of the shelf, that part under the benches, was all greened over, covered with thick, spongy grass but that part of the shelf directly underneath her was a mass of tangled briar, bracken, and thorn, thick and impenetrable, difficult even for small animals to crawl through. Beyond the shelf was a drop, a long drop, and the sea, which was getting greyer and more threatening by the minute.

She strolled along the cliff edge, looking at the shelf to her right, looking at the sky, feeling the strengthening wind starting to make her shiver. Finally she reached the benches, thick stone coated in lichen, a perch to watch the sea, not one to provide comfort. She passed the first bench, the second, then the third before reaching the fourth where senior Kas was sitting and staring straight ahead of her, her face as blank as the college walls.

Miriam sat next to her in silence, not completely sure of what to say, Kas did not acknowledge her at first, still looking into space, when she did start to talk it was in a monotone, as though she was addressing the sea and sky, rather than the person sitting next to her.

"Incredible isn't it. So much of nothing. Just light and sea and air going on almost forever. The Gods paint in broad strokes but no man has ever come close to replicating such…enormity."

"I was just thinking along the same lines," Miriam interjected as soon as she was able, just to make sure Kas knew she was actually there.

Kas raised her right arm and pointed directly ahead of her. "Imagine we could grow wings, fly in the direction of my arm. We would fly for days and days, maybe weeks before encountering anything apart from the occasional rocky island no bigger than this one. Finally we would run into the Kudreyan peninsula, the Snake as it is sometimes called. If we had flown this way…" she moved her arm to point more to her left, to the east, "then we would land in the country of Fash, a verdant land, my mother's homeland, a country of green heights, sheer cliffs and groves of lemon and lime trees, whose scents are carried many a mile by the warm breeze. Its cities are built from white stone, the shutters of its buildings are fashioned from rosewood, its ships sail to every corner of the world. It is dominated by deep gorges carved by quicksilver rivers and streams, the air is sweet with the scent of herbs and aromatic resin, busy villages cling to the cliffs or straddle the vibrant waterways. Women would be out baking bread or lacemaking under the fierce sun, whilst the men drink heady wine under the shade of the grape vines. My mother told me many tales of Fash, before I was brought to this place. Now fly here," her arm moved further east again, "and you land in the bogs of Mothravia, a country larger than Tanaren yet one barely populated, its villages all have to be built on stilts, so they do not get flooded. Then over here…," she pointed almost directly east this time, "we have the Arshuman basin, ten great cities founded by ten wealthy families fleeing persecution from a mad Kozean emperor, a country that is now our greatest enemy. Carry on and you fly over the Derannen mountains into Chira, the white empire. You would skirt the province of Voykali, fly directly across the provinces of Pladashu and Meyaka until you reach the lakes, each one the size of a small sea. Beyond them you would finally reach the cities of Chira and Anmir, then cross the Dragonspine Mountains into a land few people have ever explored, though those that have all bear testament to its hostility. Fly west, in the complete opposite direction and you encounter even more sea, until you reach the islands of the Sea Elves and the passages that they guard to lands that are completely unknown to us. And I have not even mentioned the lands beyond Kudrey, the Kozean Empire, the heat and the jungles full of strange trees and stranger creatures. Such a vast world, too vast for one human mind to assimilate, one would need to be a god to understand its complexity. And yet here we are, sat in a part of it that is tantamount to a tenth of a grain of sand on a beach with no end. The older one gets, the more knowledge one accumulates, the more one realises that one knows nothing at all."

She still sounded distant, obviously repeating an internal monologue she had run through her mind many times before. Miriam felt she was intruding, that Kessie's question could easily wait. She wondered how to extricate herself from the conversation but in the meantime she could do little else but add her own comment to Kas' little speech. "It just makes you realise how insignificant we all are. Our lives, our deaths, our hopes, desires, all are ultimately meaningless. All that has happened in the college these last days, all the horror, all the fear, what are they to the Gods? I sometimes struggle with my beliefs, my prayers, why should the Gods care for me? For any of us? Thinking about the size of their universe always incites both feelings of wonder and futility in equal measure. So many scholars a hundred times more intelligent than I have pondered the question of meaning, of what and why we exist at all and as yet none have come up with an answer beyond "the Gods have a purpose for us all, one we cannot possibly divine."

"Yet we carry on, day after day, doing the same things, making the same mistakes, or coming up with new ones. We are all so flawed, the ant in the jar who keeps running around in circles thinking that maybe the place he has passed a hundred times already will this time provide him with an escape route. We learn nothing, we are nothing, and all we do is hurt those around us." Kas was still staring, head turning neither left nor right and the conversation was becoming darker than even one such as Miriam, hardly the most optimistic soul, was used to dealing with.

"Yet we have life," Miriam asserted; "however unimportant it is unique to all of us. We may stumble in darkness, yet we do have a path, a path we follow until the Gods deem otherwise."

"I agree," Kas said, "life may be unbearable, but death is many times worse. And death has claimed so many these last days, including Arbagast, and Arbagast did not deserve death, there are many that live that deserve it far more than he."

"We are not the arbiters of justice in such matters though," Miriam pointed out, "I am happy to leave such things to the Gods." She suddenly felt a fleck of water strike her face, time to collect Gideon. "The weather is turning to rain," she said, "it might be better to return to the college before we all get a soaking."

"Ask your question first," so Kas had not forgotten after all; "I will answer as best I can."

Miriam had begun to stand but sat again following Kas's invitation. The stone bench was both cold and damp, she would be happy to leave it behind.

"All it was, was that Kestine wondered why you did not feel the surge in power when the spirit stirred, when I was exploring the caves a couple of days back. You slept through it while other senior mages on the ground floor did not, the power was so strong it made them sick, or so I was told. I am sure there is a simple explanation for it, you can tell Kessie when you get back if you want."

Kas did not answer immediately. Another fleck of rain. Miriam was suddenly starting to feel nervous, though the reason for this was hard to define. She reflexively reached for her mint, only to withdraw her hand, she would keep it for when she walked through the college doors with Gideon.

"I felt nothing at all," Kas finally replied; "these things are notoriously hard to gauge, some people feel certain kinds of power very strongly indeed, others not so much. I had worked hard that day and was very tired as a consequence."

It was a reasonable enough answer, yet Miriam had the very strangest feeling about it. Kas had done nothing but gaze at the sea since her arrival yet this time as she answered she started looking around, at the grass at their feet, at her hands, at a circling gull struggling against the wind. She did not look at Miriam at all, it was the very definition of an evasive reaction.

"I believe it was Eubolo who went and fetched you, did he sense anything? Did he mention it at all?"

Kas shook her head, she still did not look Miriam's way. "Not that I remember."

"Well," Miriam tried to sound cheery, "we can always ask him later."

"Yes, I suppose you can."

Now Kas was beginning to colour. At the forefront of Miriam's mind now was to get away as soon as she could and find a knight, to tell him of Kas' odd behaviour.

"Well, I had definitely better be on my way now. This looks like being a right old storm, the worst since..."

"The night I saw Arbagast die. I...I mean the night that Arbagast died," Kas stuttered.

Miriam's heart froze for a moment. Briefly she looked over to Kas only to find Kas looking right back at her. It was an eye contact that lasted less than the time it took to blink, Kas' hazel eyes meeting Miriam's darker walnut brown, yet it was a contact that told both of them everything that the other woman was thinking, the fear they were experiencing, it stripped all forms of pretence bare.

"That was a silly slip of the tongue..." Miriam gave a forced laugh. "Goodbye Senior Kas, I will see you..."

"The Gods allocate their gifts differently to all of us." Kas was staring ahead once more, "some people are eloquent, vivacious, masters of the spoken word, able to convince people that the sun is the moon, that night is day. Others, like me, are steady, reliable, lacking in imagination, all the qualities needed for a staff mage. The downside of course is that I am relatively honest and have never acquired the ease of manner required to lie effectively. Something that I know you have now realised."

More rain. Miriam blinked it away. She had to clear her throat to speak effectively. "Senior Kas, if you want to talk to somebody..."

"I am talking to you am I not?" Kas said. "If you were to speak to Eubolo he would tell you that he was aghast at the power flooding the sleeping room, that he thought I must be ill not to notice it. That would lead you all straight back to me, only this time it would not be you asking the question, but a dozen knights with swords and armour. I cannot cope with such...scrutiny. So Miriam, do you want the truth?"

Miriam nodded.

"Then I will tell it. But I warn you that its disclosure will benefit neither of us in the hour to come."

42
A new suspect with questions to answer

"This is a natural tunnel, and it is only a couple of feet from the floor of the sleeping room." Steven looked up at the hatchway, squinting against the murk. "So there wasn't a lot of actual digging required from the lay brothers. Now I wonder where we are?"

"Well behind you is a dead end." Gytha was ahead of him holding the torch, its flames were an eerie blue as they flickered against the smooth rock of the twisting passageway. All three of them were standing inside it, Kestine being the last to descend into the labyrinth.

Gytha continued, "so it is ahead we go. The tunnel twists to my left and it is very narrow, expect to graze a knee or elbow as we go. Oh and Steven, I hope you are good at stooping." She was in the lead, her own personal insistence for she felt that she knew the caves better than the other two, being in them all of once and never having seen this part of the system before.

"It is not what I expected," Kessie said, "so cramped and musty, nobody would choose to come down here surely?"

"Well I certainly wouldn't," Steven said. "I have nipped into the one cave, the first cave you enter from the knights' passageway, and I have seen the cave holding the elven artefact…thing. But I have gone no further. Such places are for moles and rabbits, and slavering Agnathi beasts whose jaws can tear a man clean in two. Imagine running into one of them here ladies, eh?"

Kessie looked over her shoulder and swallowed, Gytha just aimed a kick at him, failing to connect but making her point nonetheless.

The tunnel continued to bear ahead and left, narrow, claustrophobic, the herbal fragrance from the fire belonging in another environment completely, one of open fields, of sun and spring rain, of the hospital herb gardens on the other island. Not here, not in this moribund darkness.

There was no noise other than their padding feet and shallow breathing, Kessie found the atmosphere grating, like fingernails dragged along slate, if this went on too long she would have to go back, cave exploration was for braver souls than she.

But she did not have to worry much longer, for Gytha suddenly stopped dead in her tracks, so much so that Steven almost barged her over.

"We need not go any further," she said plainly.

Kessie looked around. A cave, a desk, a couple of torches resting against a wall. And a bizarre and truly beautiful construct fashioned out of glass, or of crystal, something only a true master could ever hope to craft, and then only if the master was not of human stock.

"So that is the artefact," Gytha murmured, "the housing for the Casta'zhana, the soul jewel of the elves, the one that holds the spirit of the elf Sinotaneh..."

"The spirit that has been used to kill all those people," Kessie finished; "it is a beautiful thing."

"It is," Gytha said. "From here Kessie, if you take the exit to the left you get to the entrance cave that can be reached from the knights' passageway. Presumably, if you take one of the other exits you go the way Miriam went until you finally get to the cave that looks out to the sea."

"And the tunnel leading to the house of Havel the pig," Steven pointed out. "From the bedroom we were just in you can travel far out of the college and come back again without any of the knights having an inkling about it. Senior Kas was left alone most of the time, as all staff mages are, she could travel anywhere, anytime. A fair journey to the pig pens..."

"But Kas is a keen walker, the distance would mean nothing to her." Kessie said.

"We need to go back," Steven said, "and find her. There is no point continuing in these caves, we have already found our answers."

"But Kas is no killer!" Kessie protested, "and she revered Arbagast, she would never hurt him."

"She is in the mire Kestine," Steven said. "How far though we can only find out by speaking to her."

"She went to the House of Xhenafa." Kessie was still shaking her head, "but I will say it again. There is no way she would hurt..."

"Miriam was going there wasn't she?" Gytha queried.

Kessie nodded.

"No matter," Gytha shrugged, "the odds of them bumping into each other are tiny and Miriam is far too sensible to barge in and ask stupid questions."

And with that, they returned the way they came.

****

A confession leads to mortal peril

"Raiman had been serving the Order of Jedrael for many years." Kas was staring at the sea again, speaking clearly and calmly, though Miriam could see that her hands were trembling slightly and that her thin lips were bloodless. "Actually, I have too, I was astounded when I received the invitation, why would anybody want me? It was not until a good while later that I realised that a staff mage in this place has a degree of autonomy that no other mage has, that the knights rarely come down to the Oval Room to watch us and so we are the ideal people for any tasks that require a degree of tact or secrecy. I wasn't wanted for who I was, but for what I was. I joined because I was flattered by the invitation despite not sharing any of the order's beliefs, I had never been asked to be part of anything before, it felt good to just...belong to something. Silly really, I have never felt superior to anybody in my life, to those with power or without it, I have always lacked a certain...confidence with people, I have never even lain with a man, for what it's worth.

We were aware that there was a cave system under the college, it is no real secret, it is cited in several sources, but it was only in the last few years that exploring the caves became a priority for the order. That was when Raiman suggested that Havel joined us. Havel was one of the lay brothers who swing from a rope over the cliffs to collect birds' eggs. He knew that there was a cave in the cliffs, he would use it as a place to hang the ropes from, he also knew that there was a blocked tunnel system there, so, following instructions from the order, the two of them set to clearing it. Shortly afterwards they built a connecting tunnel from cave to surface; the location was remote enough for their work to go unnoticed. Havel dug down from one of his pig pens, he thought it was quite funny for such a place to have a secret tunnel. Over the next year or two the caves were explored, the connecting passage from college to entry chamber was built along with a secondary exit into the bedchamber next to the Oval Room. This meant that a mage could pass from college to island and back in total secrecy. The caves have...secrets, some of which are only now being discovered, valuable secrets, to the order anyway.

And both Raiman and Havel knew it. Recruiting Havel had been a mistake, he had a lot of influence over Raiman but none of his discretion and he soon saw that they could use the knowledge that they had to extort money from the order.

Raiman was reluctant to do so at first, but Havel quickly brought him round, Raiman had a young family, he had to think of their futures. Soon, I became the liaison between order and lay brother, I would be given the ensorcelled object, a quill knife in my case, I would visit a secret drop point to find money and instructions, then I would sneak out to a rendezvous point to deliver the money."

The rain was becoming steady now, Miriam pulled her cowl over her head, Kas barely seemed to notice it, she just continued to talk in her steady monotone.

"If the whole system seems ridiculously convoluted, that is because it is. You must remember that just to be part of the order can mean imprisonment or death, we are constantly living in fear of both. The order is an ideal you see, I could not see that when I joined but it is striving for a better world for us, an end to confinement, it searches for a way that we can live relatively normal lives. The risk of exposure is a very real one but the ultimate benefits, not for us but for future generations of mages, outweigh the risks. Nobody in the order knows the names of its fellows, everything is done in secret, if the centuries old Imperial edict against us was relaxed somehow, if we could be treated in the same way that a symposium of priests or philosophers are treated then maybe so many wouldn't have died here."

Kas took a deep breath and sighed, a grief racked sigh that tore at Miriam's heart. Miriam had put her hands into the pockets of her robe as the wind and rain would be chapping them otherwise, Kas though kept her hands out, they were a raw pink now, and still trembling. She sat there still but her internal composure, her dead face was gone now, there were tears in her eyes, true sorrow in her wracked face as she spoke again, her voice higher now, tremulous and unsteady.

"The night Arbagast died I had to make a delivery, go to the pig sty where Havel would be waiting and give him the money there. The reason I had to make such a journey rather than say meeting him halfway was down to the fire of Istraek, the blue fire we use to stop the cave's hauntings. Havel had a flask in his hovel and would use it whilst they excavated the tunnels but the oil for it, the only way they could use it was by lighting an oil we prepared for them you see, the oil was difficult to make, used rare ingredients and so had to be spared whenever possible. So it was I who had to go to them, I am one of two mages who can generate the fire naturally, so there was no need to waste precious resources.

So using the blue fire I navigated the tunnels and reached the sty. I gave him the money. But then he said, "we need to talk." He was an uncouth man, coarse and strong, I hated having to meet him so. I asked him what he wanted but he said, "not here, too cramped, at my place." I refused, there was no way I was going to his tiny house in darkness, so I suggested the stone circle nearby. The order has used them in the past, for urgent business, the senior mages know when it is occupied and when it is empty, and the high walls shut out prying ears. It was further to walk for both of us, but he assented. He went first, I followed a little later, I hadn't realised after travelling through the tunnels how foul the weather was.

I was expecting trouble and I got it. I had not seen him since Raiman's death, and I knew he would think the order responsible for it. I told him that the man had drowned but he just didn't believe me, the rumours of the hand of Xhenafa had reached even him. He wanted money, silence money or he would go to the knights he said. Three times the amount I had just given him to be paid monthly. An outrageous piece of blackmail and one the order would never accept.

He wouldn't have known but recalcitrant lay brothers are a problem the order has in all the colleges from time to time. Once I had reported his words there would be only one outcome, his own silence, a permanent one. He had just ordered his own death as I listened to him speak. A greedy fool, one whose time was nearly up, even if he had outlived the night.

Nevertheless, I did try to make him see sense. I told him his demands were extortionate and they would never be accepted, he laughed and said he wondered what Sir Steven would say to that. There is no other way of putting it, but an argument broke out. He was frightening when angry, he swore and raised his fists to me. I held my ground though; I was very proud of myself at the time. Maybe that was the last time I will ever experience such a feeling."

She noticed her cold hands at last, crossing them over her chest she buried them under her arms to try to warm them.

"And then!" she said, her high voice taking on an incredulous tone. "In the middle of the rain and the shouting in walks Arbagast! We were so wrapped up in our argument we hadn't heard him approach! It was difficult to tell who was more astonished at the presence of the other, but he had heard enough, enough to know my secret and some of the purpose of the argument.

"Why are you here?" I asked him. He told me yet another attempt at charging a staff had failed and that he doubted his powers. He had come to the circle to try and cast, in a safe environment, to see if he really could do it anymore."

"Arbagast was losing his powers?" Miriam interrupted for the first time, a surprise to both of them, Kas visibly started at hearing another voice.

"No," she shook her head, "not really. In the caves there is an...object, a repository of power. When activated it sucks power from any nearby source, the wards we use do not affect it, so it passes through the walls of the Oval Room and takes power from any mage nearby."

"I think I know the object you mean. How is it activated?"

"I do not know the specifics. This "object" is fashioned out of some precious crystal or other, used to house a stone that contains the spirit of a long dead being. It powers the stone, nurtures it, when somebody attempts to activate the stone, experiment with it, it supplies the power and before you ask I have no idea who has the stone or how to use it; it is a secret way above my status in the order. So Arbagast was not losing his abilities, he was just being tapped as an energy source. I knew of course, but I could not tell him. Keeping secrets from him was so hard…" she trailed off into silence. Miriam sat with her for a while, getting wetter and wetter, colder and colder before deciding that she needed to prompt Kas into continuing.

"So," she asked, as politely as possible; "what happened next?"

"Arbagast spoke to me, told me how misguided I was being part of this order and that I must resign from it. I told him that once you were in you could never withdraw, never leave, that you knew too much. He looked so disappointed, his last thoughts of me were ones of disappointment…" She stopped again, putting her hands over her face as she sobbed loudly.

But she didn't remain silent for long, she seemed keen to finish this story of hers, to relieve herself of the torment of secrecy. "Then Arbagast strode up to Havel, told him he should be ashamed for berating a woman so and that he would face justice for it. Havel countered by saying he knew too much, that no mage could do anything to him any longer. Arbagast said he would see about that. He started to move his hands, to generate power to attack Havel, it was so out of character for him to show aggression like that but then I realised, he was doing it for me, he wanted to protect me.

But Havel was too quick for him, he lashed out, struck him. There was a brief struggle as I watched, trying to generate my own power against Havel but I was too late. Havel was so strong, one blow and Arbagast struck his head against the stone wall and collapsed. I knelt over him, tried to revive him but it was no use, he was dead, Havel had killed him.

I was too numb to cry, in too much shock to comprehend…but Havel wasn't. "We need to get rid of him," he said, as though Arbagast was one of his pigs slaughtered for Winterfeast. He put Arbagast over his shoulders and strode off, me running impotently behind.

I think he was going to take him to the cliffs and throw him into the sea, but in the darkness he went the wrong way, he walked to where the land rose in a steep slope to the sea, where carrying a man, even one as old as Arbagast, would be a burden in such weather. Havel finally stopped and set him down. "I have a better idea," he said. There was no sorrow in his voice, no regret, no compassion for the dead. My grief was great, but my anger was beginning to swallow it, even before seeing what Havel had planned next.

I realised that we were at the outdoor latrine. I remember thinking to myself, "no, no, no, he surely cannot be contemplating doing what I think he is going to do." I refused to believe it, to believe that he would do such a thing even as I saw him untie one of the securing ropes for the latrine shelter and pull the cover back, exposing the trench. The stench was unimaginable, finally I came to my senses. "No!" I shouted, "no, you mustn't!" But he did. He picked up Arbagast's body and threw it into the trench. There was a horrible soft sound as the body landed in...in...well, you know. And then Havel looked up at me and he laughed. "Shit landing in shit!" he said in his horrible scowling voice."

Despite the rain and their wet faces, Miriam could follow the trail of tears on Kas' face.

"I just snapped," she said. "I had just seen the man I regarded as a father treated in such a vile way, with such disrespect by this...animal, that I just snapped. I cast, no focus, no discipline, just an outpouring of naked power. I heard bones snap as Havel was lifted off his feet and it was with a great sense of satisfaction that I saw him thrown into the trench himself, shit landing in shit indeed. I had killed a man and I felt good about it.

I briefly thought about lifting Arbagast out, but I had not the physical strength and the trench was too deep, I would have to climb in it myself. So I just took the rope, replaced the shelter over the trench and tied it up. Then I heard Havel groan. He was dying for sure but was not yet dead. I could have tried to save him, found a rope or some wood, lowered it down to see if he could pull himself up but I didn't, I left him to drown in that muck, a just end for a terrible man.

As I went back to the tunnel I remembered the flask of oil for the blue fire that he kept in his hovel. I found it but in my confusion, my fear and grief I left the ensorcelled object behind. I left the flask in one of the caves, thinking that no one now could connect the order to the crime and returned to the sleeping chamber next to the Oval Room. I slept there, waiting for my clothes to dry and returned to work in the morning."

Miriam was thinking hard as Kas related her confession, there was so much information to absorb but one obvious question leapt out at here.

"The others, the other deaths, did you...?"

Kas shook her head. "Not me, someone else in the order maybe. But then that is the point isn't it, I cannot prove that I am not the person they are looking for, if I am imprisoned for one death why not link me to the others? It would be very convenient for the investigators would it not? Besides, kill one person, kill two, kill a hundred, the punishment is still the same."

Miriam felt a chill at these words, a chill not borne of the weather. "I know Steven and Gytha..." she spoke in hurried tones; "they are fair, they will want the truth. I..."

"I have killed." Kas's composure had returned but now her voice had an icy quality to it, a cool dispassionate tone, one that Miriam noticed all too readily. "I have killed," she said again, "my punishment is already known to me."

Then, for the first time she turned and looked directly into Miriam's eyes. "I wanted to die, after losing Arbagast, I so wanted to die. I was not afraid of being caught, of execution. But then I saw one, I saw senior Oskum die on the beach, we all saw it, the coldness, the cruelty, a mage paraded like a performing monkey for all to gawp at. I do not fear death, but I do not want to die for the entertainment of others. And so I must fight on, to try and live if I can, which does of course raise something of a problem..."

Miriam sidled away from her, she half stood, her mind started to freeze over as she realised the meaning of Kas' words. "Come in with me..." was all she could say.

Kas shook her head firmly. "I told you earlier that what I was about to say would benefit neither of us in the hour to come. I have told you the truth, a truth you had guessed at already and now you realise that only one of us can return to the college, only one of us can see this hour out alive. I have thought of taking my own life, but I lack the courage to act in such a manner. So I am left with just one way out. I like you novice Miriam, you are clever, perspicacious, but I cannot feel the blade of the knights and die in that manner, I just cannot. I cannot be the sacrifice that proves your own innate intelligence. I am sorry, truly sorry that it has come to this, but I really cannot see any other way."

Miriam was standing now, slowly backing away from Kas, then Kas stood, and Miriam could sense the power she was drawing up inside her.

"It is you or I Miriam, one or the other and my powers exceed yours greatly."

Miriam turned, she could see the stand of trees, they looked so far away but if she could just reach them...

She broke into a run then, legs that had barely run in their life starting to pound underneath her as her lungs tore at her in their terror.

Kas spoke once more, her voice partly masked by the gathering storm. "Run novice Miriam run! For nothing else will avail you now!"

****

The alarm is raised

Steven and Gytha had reached the House of Xhenafa just as the rain had changed from a distraction, to an irritant, to a confounded nuisance. Soon they both knew it would be a deluge nobody wanted to be stuck underneath. The crowd at the house had long since dissipated and the two of them strolled into the room of offerings entirely on their own.

Father Krieg was there of course, he proffered them the votive oil and candles, which they politely declined.

"Senior mage Kas," Steven asked him, "has she been here today?"

"Yes sir knight," Krieg gave an affirmative nod. "She was here before the weather turned but she left us quite a while ago now. Actually, I saw her on the path as she left, through the window here..." he indicated a tiny window of thick glass next to where he was standing, the only window in the room. "She was talking to your friend sister Gytha, she was coming in as Senior Kas was leaving."

"Miriam?" Gytha started, her assumption that Miriam would not involve herself in matters was suddenly on less than secure foundations. "She was speaking to Miriam?"

Father Krieg nodded.

Steven and Gytha thanked him and walked out into the foul weather. Sir Nikolaj was there with a huddle of other knights stood nearby.

"The southern cliffs," Steven told him; "get your men to scout them, Senior Kas should be there. She is to be apprehended immediately."

"For what reason sir?" Nikolaj asked him.

"She is involved in these murders somehow; she may even be our murderer. We need to..."

Just then though they were joined by Kestine. She had been running hard, was out of breath, her cowl was down and her yellow blonde hair stuck to her face like it had been glued there.

"No one has seen her," she gulped in lungsful of wet air. "Checked her cell, the library, everywhere. She was last seen in the refectory having breakfast but that was a long time ago now."

"Who is missing then?" Nikolaj asked her.

"Miriam."

Nikolaj and Gytha exchanged glances. He had not been informed that Gytha knew of him and Miriam, but instinct told him enough, and the looks they gave each other confirmed that instinct. He turned on his heels and shouted over the wind at the group of knights, who by now were rapt with attention.

"Southern cliffs. Now!"

He broke into a run and the knights following him soon did likewise. Steven, Gytha and Kessie were walking at first, but soon they were running too, towards the southern cliffs to find Senior Kas and to confirm that Miriam was not in the trouble that they all feared that she was.

****

An unlikely rescuer, and redemption at last

And she was in trouble. She had never been in so much trouble in her life. She was running pell-mell now, her feet kicking up mud and water from the sodden path and the trees still seemed as far away as ever. She wasn't even sure why she was so desperate to reach them, she just thought that the scant cover they afforded might just give her a sliver of hope of survival. Get there, try and hide, wait for Kas to come looking for her, find a branch or stone or something and then hit her with it, that was the only plan she had, and it sounded more and more pathetic every time she ran it through her head.

She looked behind her, trying to see how much distance she had put between the two of them. At first she couldn't see Kas at all and for the briefest of moments hope soared in her breast, perhaps Kas had just been joking, perhaps she had just walked off in the other direction, perhaps...but no, one more look and that small, flickering hope was snuffed out as easily as thumb and forefinger quell a candle flame.

Kas was not behind her at all, she had circled around and had been running in the same direction so that she was almost level with her but some way off to her right. Of course, Miriam thought, Kas was extremely fit, she walked miles almost daily and she had caught Miriam up in almost no time. But why had she veered off to the right? It took a few moments for her to grasp the reason, but when she finally did Miriam's throat almost seized up in her fear.

Miriam was now between Kas and the cliffs and beyond them, the sea. If Kas tried to hit her with a bolt of magical force she could be pushed over them, to plummet to her death on the rocks below. And she could sense it, could sense Kas was drawing power from the magical plane, a lot of power, far more than Miriam could manage herself. All mages had an innate sense of the shifting tides of energy held within the so-called Plane of Lucan, that realm of energy from which mages siphoned the power to create their spells. If a mage was doing this nearby then other mages could perceive it, could almost see into the mind of the casting mage and, because of this, they could sometimes interfere with whatever that mage was trying to attempt.

Of course! She could try at least, try and drain the power Kas was summoning through her own body. It was the sort of skill any warrior mage pitted against one of her own kind would find routine. It just required a temperament that was calm and collected under extreme pressure, and Miriam needed to eat mint before having a slight difference of opinion with a tutor. Yet now she had to focus, to think, to try, to attempt, and blind terror was just the incentive she needed.

She tried to empty herself of all other thoughts, the jarring of her feet on the uneven ground, the by now driving rain soaking into her drenched and heavy robes, the bilious sense of panic, the taste of vomit at the back of her throat, she had to empty herself, become a vessel, a conduit, to invite the power Kas was sucking from the other plane to enter her instead of the other mage.

And then suddenly it happened. A crackle of blue energy spat from her forefinger to strike and blacken the grass next to her. She yelped in surprise as a plume of smoke rose from the scorched ground. She had read the theories of course, how to dispel and disperse unwanted energies, in fact it was a topic she was studying right now, but to date she had never seen it put into practice. It was a shock, in more sense than one. A staff of course was really what was required, to channel the power into a staff was a far safer option than using her own body, but she had no option than to risk damage to her mind. She looked ahead of her again. Futile. The trees were still too far away and Kas would be ready long before she reached them.

Long before, because she was already prepared. Miriam was still drying to drain the energies from her erstwhile killer when she heard the dread word, "Ptaressas!" The spell was cast, now she could do nothing but scream.

And scream she did as her feet were lifted off the grass and into the air. She heard a crack of bone in her shoulder as the bolt of power struck her fully on her side and then she was flying, twirling, spinning through the air. She saw the leaden sky, the ferocious clouds, then she was looking at the trees that she had never reached, though oddly enough it seemed that there was a figure moving amongst them; then she saw the sea, grey and dull as iron, obscured by a haze of rain and fear, She shrieked blindly, she was going over the cliffs to be smashed to pieces, there wouldn't be enough of her left for a gull to fill its beak. But no, for finally she saw the undercliff, that strip of land beneath the main cliff that had been sunk by tide and erosion, and she saw the great thicket of bramble, thorn, and bracken on its eastern side, and it was getting bigger, bigger, ever bigger.

She plummeted into it with a crash sending a spray of yellow and brown leaves, pieces of dead wood, shrivelled and withered berries, and bits of furze and thorn flying into the air. She lay on her back on a bed of bramble and spines, pierced in a hundred places, but she was alive, alive. The cliff edge was but a matter of ten feet to her right, she could taste the salt spume generated by the storm tossed seas, but she wasn't under the sea, she was not drowning or being dashed against slimy rocks, she had avoided that fate by the narrowest of margins. Maybe she had drained off just enough power to save her life.

Or rather, to grant her a reprieve only. For suddenly, and with a great unlooked for rush the pain, the blow to her shoulder, the cuts and scratches from the thorns, finally hit her. She howled in her agony, she was not good with pain, not good at all and right now she had never felt more pain in her life.

She had to get free, get clear of her bloody bower. She kicked with her legs, they were cut and scored but they were loose. She then tried to lever herself up on her left elbow, her right arm being limp and useless, full of shooting pain for it had borne the brunt of Kas' power. Again, some success. Now all she had to do was crawl out of the thicket, she would be cut a hundred more times but there was nothing for it, she crawled out or died where she was.

She travelled a few unsteady feet before it got too much for her. She stopped and vomited her morning oatmeal over the bushes and the front of the robe. The pains were enough to make her faint: despite the rain, wind and driving cold she was beaded with perspiration, she couldn't do it, it was too much for her. She stopped and looked over the undercliff, past the thicket it was just a sward of thick, tangled grass. Running down to it from the cliff above was a thin dirt track, used by those lay brothers that harvested bird eggs no doubt. It trailed a winding route before reaching the undercliff at the opposite point from where Miriam was now scrambling. And as she looked at the track her heart froze in place.

A figure was clambering down it, a blue robed figure, a senior mage; Kas was coming for her.

And she was trying something else, her hands were held out in front of her, palms open facing each other. And between them Miriam could sense rather than see a tiny ball of flame. She was summoning mages' fire, she was going to burn Miriam alive, amongst the sopping wood and wet leaves, but a mages' fire required no kindling to fuel it.

All mages had a fear of fire, the fate that they had to be rescued from as children on the mainland and Miriam's cold fear and nausea became a blind white terror when she saw what Kas had planned for her. She redoubled her efforts, robes and skin tearing as she pulled her limbs free of these thorny fetters, her pain screamed with every movement, but she ignored it, she needed her nerves to be numb and unfeeling, Kas was going to burn her alive.

But she wasn't going to get free in time, Kas was half walking, half running towards her and the fire between her hands was now a ball the size of her head, Miriam screamed in anger and fear, her arms and legs exposed by her torn robes, all of them coated in blood, she didn't want to die like this, not like this, not like this, why had the Gods done this to her?

Then, to her left, a scraping sound, stones and mud cascading down the slope in a shower. She turned her head as much as she could, the slope there was almost sheer, but somebody was sliding down it, risking grazes, risking fractures, risking all sorts of injuries, someone was sliding down it, someone who obviously had little care as to what happened to him.

Gideon.

His black robe was caked in mud from his slide, his face was pale as fog swirling over snow. He landed amongst the tangles of wood and fern, stamping on it, pressing it down with his hands as he came over to her, eating up the space in no time.

"Let me help you," he said to her.

Without waiting for a reply he dragged her clear of the mesh entrapping her. He put her left arm round his shoulder and half dragged her clear of the thicket, both falling free of it to land on the spongy grass with a soft thump.

Miriam rolled clear of him. "Get out!" she pleaded with him, "she wants me, not you, get clear Gideon! run while you can!"

And then, despite the rain, the buffeting winds, the woman closing on them with murder on her mind they looked at each other. And connected. He looked different to her now, older, his chin was firm, his expression one of calm resolve, that of somebody who had faced fears all his life and was, for the first time overcoming them. A boy becoming a man as Miriam watched him.

"She is not going to hurt you anymore," he said to her, his voice level, almost soothing.

And then, as Miriam struggled to her feet, her right arm hanging uselessly at her side, he strode away from her to face Kas.

Kas was only yards from both of them, close enough for Miriam to hear her words over the sloping rain. She was dully surprised to realise that Kas was crying, that she was forcing her speech through her tears.

"Out of the way boy! Understand that I have no choice in this! I don't want to hurt you, either of you but I...have...no...choice!"

"Leave her alone!" Gideon shouted back, stalking towards the woman, heedless of the ball of flame she was cupping between her hands. Miriam started to hobble after him, but she was too slow, in too much pain to gain any ground. She realised though that Kas' emotional state was affecting her casting, her power was dissipating, losing focus, yet she was still a senior mage, and her power would still be enough for her deadly purpose.

"So be it!" she screamed at Gideon, hurling the ball of flame at him.

Her aim was not good though. It caught Gideon on the shoulder but most of the fire scattered wide of him, plummeting over the cliff and into the sea. Gideon still burned though, his hair and shoulder were caught in the flames, they billowed in the wind as he patted them out. Yet he did not scream, he displayed no fear, instead he started to run at Kas, head down, charging her like an angry bull.

"Ptaressas!" Kas screamed at him, Miriam saw a blue bolt of force smash into the boy's chest. She could imagine the splintered bone, the ribs spearing into his lungs, Gideon stopped then, staggering back under the blow, yet he stayed on his feet, and a moment later he was running at Kas again.

Kas had not expected this, this naked defiance of her powers. Her shoulders sagged as this boy demon, this man child who had brushed off her most fearful spells got closer and closer to her. Now she could see the blackened flesh on his face, smell the burning blood that spilled over his shoulder and chest, her plans had gone awry, her powers were spent, now it was her turn to run.

But Gideon had the momentum. He was on to her in moments. There was the briefest struggle as he crashed into her, burned shoulder first. Miriam saw a whirl of wild, flailing limbs, heard a shriek of alarm and horror, then watched as Kas went over the cliff, her wailing cries soon swallowed by the crashing sea and dolorous wind. Gideon though did not follow her over the precipice. He stopped at the edge, staggered on unsteady legs before falling onto the grass, flat on his back to stare blankly at the roiling sky.

Limping, staggering, loping on her bloodied legs Miriam finally got to him, sinking onto her knees as she brushed the hair out of his eyes with her good hand. She leant over him so that their faces were just inches apart.

He was in a bad way. No. He was dying. His hair on one side was scorched or burnt off entirely, the skin of his face and cheek had shrivelled, exposing a glint of bone, and he was coughing up blood that was leaking into his punctured lungs, his lips and chin being coated with it. Despite his undoubted agonies though he recognised her, his lips moving as though to speak.

"No," Miriam said, "do not try. Just let me thank you for what you did. I would be dead without you Gideon, dead."

Gideon's breath came rasping and uneven yet he somehow managed to smile at her, he almost seemed happy, happy that he had finally earned her gratitude rather than her opprobrium.

She had to do it. What choice did she have? She pressed close to him and gently kissed him on his lips, the first kiss he had ever received in his short life, a gentle kiss, light as gossamer but a kiss nevertheless, a kiss from Miriam, from the woman he had so worshipped, when she pulled back her own lips were flecked with his blood.

"Thank...you," he said in a rasp so faint she could barely hear him. Bubbles formed in the blood around his mouth, bubbles that rapidly declined in frequency, then stopped for good as his eyes finally glazed over. His body relaxed as life finally left it, and Miriam and her large, tear rimmed brown eyes were the last thing he ever saw.

He had gone. He had found redemption. Miriam closed his eyes with her hand, though she knew that rigor mortis would soon open them again. She wanted his eyes closed, she wanted him to look peaceful, that done she too collapsed onto her back next to him, it was now her turn to stare upwards at the tormented heavens.

Fear had been coursing through her blood, numbing her, keeping her pain at bay. Now though it was over, she was soaking wet, tired beyond reason, cut and torn like an animal carcass in the shambles and her shoulder had been smashed by Kas' spell, pain flooded her like a tide spilling over a gravel beach.

Her eyes started to lose focus, everything was in a haze, shapeless grey forms floating in front of her. She was dying wasn't she? She felt she was just drifting, floating. There was no time anymore, she may have been lying there for hours, days, years, she had no idea. But it didn't matter, she was going, going, going.

Finally something different did loom over her, something with black in it, something scarlet, like a knight's tunic. There was a face, it looked like Sir Nikolaj, but it couldn't be Sir Nikolaj, she had looked for him earlier and she couldn't find him then. She had read somewhere that Xhenafa did not appear to the dying as the withered, black robed form he was often depicted as, rather that he took on the appearance of someone familiar, a friend or a loved one now passed on, a sop to ease the panic of those souls who were called from this earth forever.

So that was it. He was Xhenafa. She wanted to speak to him, to say that she was not afraid, that she would travel with him gladly. That she did not fear judgement, that she had strived so hard to do the right thing in her life, that if she had hurt others that it was not by design, that she had made friends, that she had loved, though perhaps she had not been loved in turn. Yet the only words she could utter, faint, tiny words that they were, were, "Havel killed Arbagast. Kas killed Havel. I...need...a...wash."

She was ready. Her senses were fading fast but that just meant there was no more pain. She felt Xhenafa lift her like she was made of goose down, felt him carry her in strong arms, and as blackness finally took her she knew she would awake in a better place than this.

And finally her eyes closed and embraced the darkness to come.

43
One disaster follows another

"Havel killed Arbagast. Kas killed Havel. That is what she told Nikolaj." Steven pulled his cloak tightly around his shoulders, but it still did little against the rain. "Strange, I was beginning to think of a different perpetrator altogether."

Gytha just stood there, her mouth open, pale eyes fixed on the limp, lifeless figure Sir Nikolaj was lifting gently onto the wagon they had taken from a nearby barn. "Miriam!" she gasped, "sweet Meriel, Miriam, what did I get you involved in? What have I done to you?"

She sprinted to the wagon, just as Nikolaj set Miriam down gently, ready to be taken to the Isle of Healing. Gideon was not with her, the priests of Xhenafa had already claimed their own and were returning him to the house of the dead. Miriam too looked dead, robe torn to ribbons, exposed skin on arms and legs lacerated and bloody, complexion...well her complexion was always pale but now it was so white as to be ghastly, the pallor of a cadaver. Gytha looked at her and pulled at her dripping hair in desperation, "is she…," she asked Nikolaj, "is she…. like to die?"

"I do not know." Nikolaj's voice was thick, he was trying to give the outward impression of a man who, though concerned, had seen death many times and was no more affected by this occurrence than by all the others. Gytha though noticed the slightest of inflections in his voice, of emotion being forcibly suppressed. "She breathes and that is good, but she is cold, and her shoulder has a fracture I think. I will put the cover on the wagon and will wrap her up with my cloak. A little comfort is better than none at all. Are you coming?" he offered Gytha a hand.

And she was about to take it, had not something else happened at that moment. A knight came running up the path to intercept them, he had come from the college and was quite breathless as he stood before Steven.

"What is it Leuring?" Steven asked wearily.

"Bad news sir, concerning you…"

All heads turned, "go on," Steven spoke in cut glass tones.

"It is the lady Edith sir. They are calling it a secondary infection. She is…not good. The healers are saying the next few hours are crucial to her…"

"Survival?"

Sir Leuring nodded.

Steven nodded at the messenger and briefly chewed his lower lip. Gytha knew him well enough by now, he chewed his lip in that fashion when trying to control his emotions, especially in front of his men. "Meriel, bless us," he muttered under his breath before hailing Sir Edgar, who was nearby.

"I have to go back to the college, Nikolaj is taking the injured girl to the healers so you will be in charge of the knights here. Go and see Greville, tell him that we may have found our murderer, and tell Shadan too, I will not be available for some time. Understand?"

Sir Edgar, unflappable and phlegmatic, merely saluted. Gytha however was not experiencing such mental stoicism. Miriam needed her, yet she knew, she just knew that Steven wanted her around too. Fedrica would probably be in all sorts of disarray and Steven would have to comfort her while his daughter possibly lay dying next to him. She did not know what to do, which way to turn. Fortunately though, Kessie came to the rescue. The youngest and quietest of the three friends she might have been, but she often displayed more maturity than any of them.

She took Gytha's hand and looked at her closely. "I will go with Miriam," she said, "somebody else might need you more now. I will come back with news when I can."

Gytha nodded then walked the short distance to where Steven was still talking to Edgar. "Shall I come with you?" she asked him.

His expression was one of eternal gratitude. "If you so wish," he said, "at least we will be out of this rain at last."

"I am rather bedraggled," Gytha noted her lank, dripping hair. "I shall just go to my cell and change first. I am fed up with looking so dowdy next to your lady."

Steven sucked in air, deflating his cheeks. "Yes, dry yourself out first, but don't worry about dowdiness, I doubt that Fedrica is in a state to notice anything right now."

****

Fedrica's turn to make a confession

And he was right. As a slightly drier Gytha entered Steven's office in the chapter house Fedrica was on her knees, hands clasped in front of her, praying to a silver icon of Meriel. Her face was beetroot, her hair was untied, snot and tears were mingling under her nose, never had Gytha witnessed a more distraught or fractious sight.

Steven, pale as wax, was standing next to her. He turned to face Gytha as she made her entrance, Fedrica continued to pray.

"Is my presence unwelcome?" she asked tentatively, wondering whether or not Fedrica would just throw her out. To her surprise though it was Fedrica who answered.

"No, you know Edith, she knows you, the lady that sang to her she called you yesterday. She was fine yesterday, doing well, it was just this morning…," Fedrica was forced to stop as she both sobbed and sniffed simultaneously. "She just started sneezing and couldn't stop."

And she still was sadly. The coughing of the distressed child could be heard in Steven's private chamber, even through its door of solid oak. It was a sound to rend a much harder heart than Gytha's, who coloured a little further each time a fresh bout of it filtered through to her ears.

Fedrica then stood and stared at both of them, her eyes were huge and appeared to stand out of her scarlet face, her hair hanging in straggly clumps over her narrow shoulders. For one of the first times in her life Gytha almost believed in the possession of a soul by a malevolent god.

"But you see, you don't understand. It is all my fault, the Gods are punishing us for my wayward behaviour, my aberrant lust. It is all my fault Steven, and since I have been here I have tried to transfer my own guilt on to the shoulders of another. On to you Gytha, I tried to paint you as a harlot but there is only one harlot in this room, and it isn't you. How can either of you ever forgive me, especially if Edith…if Edith." She buried her head in her hands and started to sob violently, her entire upper body shaking uncontrollably.

Gytha and Steven exchanged a quick look before he spoke. "What are you talking about Fedrica?"

Fedrica's hands stayed firmly over her face as she half spoke, half sobbed her words. "I am an inconstant woman Steven. And I cannot keep this from you any longer, not now the Gods are torturing me so. I must confess my guilt to you, to both of you, listen and judge me as I deserve."

"Go on," Steven said softly, remembering at last Sir Vargo's barbed words on the night of their duel.

Fedrica put her hands to her sides. Now she let her hair part cover her face as she spoke, whether it was to obscure her from them or to obscure them from her none of them could say. When she spoke it sounded like a confession given to an Artoran priest.

"The knights' tower, built into the city walls of the capital is where I have lived these past years, indeed all of the time since Edith was born has been spent there. And most of the time I have been on my own. There is no reproach from me to you Steven, I know the lot of a wife of a knight, I know what it entails, and I accept it. Many of the wives of higher ranking knights live in the tower, they have their own community, their own circle. It is just that I have never felt part of it. Most social gatherings revolve around Lady Shadan, she is

291

much older than me and I find her very...stern and intimidating. Even her husband the Knight Commander agrees that she is a very severe presence, and to be honest I spend a lot of time trying to avoid her. So I tend to spend a good deal of time on my own, reading, embroidering, playing those sort of board games that one can attempt solo. Most of the time I cope well enough with solitude but there are occasions where I do have a little cry, I miss you Steven and sometimes tears are the best way to deal with things. Well one day whilst having one of these episodes of weakness I was noticed."

"By whom?" Steven asked, though he suspected that he knew the answer.

"I think you know him. His name is Sir Dylan, one of the younger knights, newly promoted. I thought I was alone, in a corridor next to my chambers, but I was not. I was dabbing my eyes with my silk handkerchief, the one decorated with butterflies that my uncle gifted me, when Sir Dylan came up to me and asked if there was anything he could do. And Artorus forgive me, but we went into the reception room in my chambers, and I unburdened myself in front of him. My tears poured from me as he listened. We talked till it went dark before he left, it would not be prudent for him to remain at such an hour after all. Then the nurse brought in Edith, all the children had gone to market that day, and that was that."

"Except that it wasn't!" she started to sob again. Steven, sitting next to her, let her fresh bout of tears work themselves out, though they were not loud enough to drown out the bout of coughing from Edith next door.

"Dylan had conducted himself so honourably, with such a sense of decorum that I started to look out for him, to inveigle my way into his presence, into his conversations whenever I could. We started to meet in the common room, in the hour before dusk, to play the board game Knight and Blade. I knew the rules a little and expressed a desire to be more proficient at it, a desire he was happy to fulfil. This went on for a few weeks until one night when the common room was closed for redecoration. They were taking down, cleaning, then re hanging the tapestries. I suggested that we played that evening in his chambers, he was surprised but did not refuse me. Oh but Steven you can guess at my motives at suggesting such a thing! I had developed a sort of infatuation with him. He is a good looking man, almost a younger version of yourself, and I had a longing for him to...to approach me in a manner that did not befit his status, nor mine. And now the Gods have seen through me and are punishing me so. Punishing you too."

"What happened?" Steven was beginning to sound interested.

Fedrica shook her head before continuing. "There was a storm that night, Uttu's lightning struck a building nearby, briefly starting a fire. I pretended that I was afeard of such things and suggested that some wine might help. So we started to drink, then, soon after we started to gamble on the outcome of the game, as it went on, the odds went higher and higher and I in particular became more and more inebriated."

"You?" now he was surprised, "I have never seen you drink anything other than watered wine and small ale."

"I do not," she said pointedly, "but the wine that night was not watered, and it affected me greatly. Dylan suggested that we postpone the game till the morrow, but I used the storm as an excuse to continue, saying I did not want to be alone. I of course contrived to lose the game and then, when I counted up the money I owed him I again expressed surprise that I did not have enough. Of course I had known such a thing a while ago. So I told him I would forfeit my dress."

Gytha's ears pricked at last, Steven's surprise had finally become shock. "Your dress? Seriously? What did he say?"

"He dismissed the idea with a laugh, but I was so heady, the wine had affected me so that I did not see his embarrassment. He said that there need not be any money changing hands at all, that the wager was for fun only, but I said that a bet was a bet and that I would not renege on it. I gave him the key to my rooms, told him where he could collect the money still owed. I did not go myself because I felt a little unsteady on my legs. Reluctantly, he agreed and when he had left me alone I...I...," she hesitated, her face going an even deeper shade of red...," I undressed in his room. I was still wearing my shift you understand but that was all. I wanted him to come back and see me, no, I wanted him to do more than just see me. Could my shame be any greater?"

Steven and Gytha said nothing, letting Fedrica compose herself before continuing.

"I wanted him to take me as a husband takes a wife. May the Gods help me, that is what I wanted. It has been a long time Gytha since Steven possessed me in such a manner, hardly at all since Edith was born, I am not as comely to him as other women might be."

"Enough Fedrica," Steven was irritated now; "your assumptions about such matters just aren't true, but we will discuss that another time. What did Dylan do when he finally saw you?"

"Turned his back. I obviously did not have enough about me to charm him either. He asked me to dress and shamefaced, I agreed. I was so agitated though, drunk, or embarrassed I do not know, that I spilled wine over my shift before I could put my dress on. He said that I should take it off and he would get it cleaned, he then went back to my chamber for a spare. I dressed fully then, though I was too drunk to tie all the laces and fastenings I at least resembled a respectable woman once more. He kept his back to me all the while, then when I was done I collapsed on one of his couches, fell into a sleep so deep that the next thing I remember was waking up the following day feeling very ill."

"He let you sleep there?"

"There was little else he could do apart from put a blanket over me. When I awoke I was sick, so he arranged some medicine for me. He behaved with the utmost sense of chivalry; I just wish I had done the same."

Vargo had mentioned Dylan cleaning clothes and buying medicine for her, Fedrica's tale was matching this perfectly. "Have you dined with him since?" Steven asked her.

"Yes, a meal and a game, on several occasions. No wagers, no repeat of my disgraceful behaviour, though I know that once was quite enough. And he returned the money that I insisted he take; I somehow knew that he would."

Steven gently cradled her stooped shoulders. "Fedi, I have heard many worse things than that, of people who have committed far greater indiscretions than you, and any divine punishment they have received was much less severe than this..."

She pulled away, raising her voice in anguish. "Can you not see? Intent is everything, the Gods see everything, they know what festers in my heart. I wanted Dylan that night, and on other nights too, I wanted him more than I wanted you, my stomach ached with desire for him. I would lay abed at night thinking of him doing...doing...such things that I am sure you can imagine. I am no better than a Rose district whore!" The timbre of her voice changed then, there was a bitter edge to it, and an equally acrid smile crept over her face. "And the irony of it all was that I had tried everything in my power to draw him close and failed, yet just days before I left Tanaren, just before Edith fell ill, his head was turned in one hour by a mage from this very island. She stayed one night with us, and that was all it took for her."

"Cheris?" Gytha enquired, biting her lip to stop a wry smile creeping over it, "shorter than me, black hair cut just so, grey eyes?"

Fedrica nodded, "you know her?"

"I do." Gytha was not surprised, one thing Cheris had in abundance was charm. She would never be short of male company if she so chose. Steven however was far more interested in his wife's behaviour than that of a mage he

294

had never uttered a word to.

"Be that as it may," he said gravely, "I can forgive you for one night's drunken foolishness, and as for the intent, well you are young, we have been married for nearly four years and I have maybe seen you for three months of it. You made a mistake Fedi, we all make mistakes, the true folly comes from not learning from them."

Fedrica did seem a little heartened by his words, though only briefly for she then stood and turned her teary gaze to Gytha. "There was no real threat in my words to you. I could see from the very first moment, from the way Steven talked about you, from the way the two of you addressed each other that you were natural friends, similar people who understood each other. And I was jealous for I find cultivating such friendships difficult and Steven does not have the ease of manner with me as he has with you. My sins have been ones of lust and envy, the Gods must look dimly on one such as me, hence this terrible punishment."

Gytha said nothing, her mind was working too quickly. Instead she just stepped forward and embraced Fedrica, bony little Fedrica of whom she had had such venal thoughts. She let the younger woman cry into her shoulder for a little while before she finally spoke.

"Our animosity is forgotten my lady. And if you both can forgive me I shall leave you to be alone together. I wish to go and pray for Lady Edith, to go and ask them to forgive too, for if they are doing this as punishment then maybe they are punishing the wrong person, for how can a three year old child bear the brunt of such ire?"

She held Fedrica close but looked over at Steven to see that he was thinking the same thing.

Guilt. Tearing at her as an eagle tears at the body of a helpless pigeon. Guilt ripping at her flesh and cutting her sore nerves. She released Fedrica, bowed to them both and was gone.

****

Gytha's pledge to Syvukha

Guilt.

Guilt.

Guilt...nausea constricting her stomach...heart sinking...shame...all of it coming back to...

Guilt. The Gods saw all did they not? and though their attitudes to sex were fairly liberal for a single, unattached person, they were far more censorious for those that sought comfort in the arms of a married man. Under normal circumstances Gytha did not believe in divine retribution for matters that the Gods would surely see as too trivial to interfere with, but normal circumstances had never put her at the heart of the situation before. When she had lain with Steven Edith was stable, the weather was fine and clear, and Miriam was merely going to the House of Xhenafa to make offerings to the dead. Now the world had changed completely and the possibility that it might be her fault was growing in her heart as she climbed down the steps and strode through the reception area and great hall.

Steven had lain with her. Now his daughter was very ill. Gytha had lain with Steven. Now one of her closest friends was very ill. Coincidence, or punishment? Perhaps spending some time in the House of the Gods would give her an answer.

Between the arched doorway to exit the great hall and the doorway to enter the refectory stood a narrow corridor. She entered it and turned south, for at its end stood the arch that led to the holy house. It was a poorly lit area, just a couple of high chandeliers sporting two or three wanly flickering candles, the reason given for the lack of illumination was that it gave one a chance to empty one's mind before the period of spiritual contemplation to come. Empty your mind, so that the spirit and love of the Gods can fill it entirely. But right now Gytha was finding it very hard to empty her mind at all. Her mind was raging, a ferment of confusion, having said that it did suddenly occur to her that the blank wall to her right held the secret passage she had travelled through prior to exploring the caves that night. The night Tola died. She winced inwardly as she remembered.

Walking from the corridor into the holy house was just as walking from darkness into radiance. The building was the highest in the college, covering a full two storeys of college space. Its vaulted roof lay just beneath the windows of the college's top floor, where Greville had his chambers and the knights their chapter house. Set in its southern wall, the wall facing her, were six great windows, each maybe half the height of the entire wall. They were leaded and their borders held many images of stained glass inspired by the holy books. At their centre though the glass was clear, flooding the house with luminosity even on such a stormy day as this. The message was obvious as those entering blinked away tears of light blindness; this was a place of illumination, a place to enrich the soul with the wonder of the Gods, a place to learn, to understand how the divine shaped the mundane, how faith inspired knowledge, how one's place in this world could be discovered, one's purpose known. The preceding corridor was the path of the pagan, a world of murk, of stumbling ignorance and the house represented how such ignorance could be banished forever. "Enter ye and understand," as the holy book stated in its first chapter. And Gytha needed to understand, more than at any other time in her life before.

She knew that the holy house, along with the adjoining kitchens and lay brother's dormitory were newer buildings than the rest of the college, built a mere four hundred years ago as opposed to seven, replacing the original wooden structures. The stonework was cleaner, better finished, less eroded, built with love rather than haste in mind. She walked in, looking briefly at the engravings on the flagstones at her feet "Artorus, strength with reason," "Sarasta, bringer of fruitfulness," "Elissa, progenitor of mankind," before turning left and walking towards the pulpit and altar standing next to the east wall. Behind it were the kitchens, the heat from whose ovens penetrated the walls, keeping the holy house warm even in the bitterest of winters. A few pews stood before the altar, reserved for the elderly, infirm or those of high importance. Most people though stood to hear the service of which there were two a day, one just before breakfast and one just before dusk. Attendance was never compulsory, but few people ever missed services, even the highly educated amongst the Artoran believers knew the importance of the nourishment of the soul. Behind the west wall, in a chamber of its own stood the great bell, through which most of those here timed their daily activities. Finally there was the north wall, the wall that bordered the refectory, and it was that wall that Gytha turned to face.

This wall had been whitewashed and over this wash had been painted many frescoes. Alcoves were set in the wall at regular intervals, within them stood pale marble statues of the major Gods, one god per alcove and before each statue stood a small altar and a frame to hold the votive candles and dedications that worshippers chose to leave. A couple of the alcoves, though holding the altars, had no godly statue. These were left that way in case a devotee of one of the lesser gods wished to bring their own icon to worship. Gytha went to one of these and gently placed one such icon at the alcoves centre. No more than six inches high and fashioned from simple wood many of its features had been worn smooth by years of rubbing from finger and thumb. It could still be seen that it was a man, that it bore an axe in each hand and that it had a long, forked beard. Gytha went and collected two candles and a taper, set them upon the altar, lit them and kneeled.

Before praying she looked at the fresco surrounding the alcove. For her it had always been the most disturbing of those on the wall. It depicted Xhenafa, the withered one, travelling through the void. In each claw like hand he held the hand of another, the hand of a man and a woman taken from this earthly life and now embarking on a journey to the seat of the Gods, before which they were to be judged. Just underneath these figures though were something else. Long, thin, ghostly shapes, barely recognisable as humanoid. They were white of skin and emaciated, bulging pink eyes brim-full of malice, clawed fingers almost as long as their arms reaching outward, upward. Reaching to snatch those hapless souls from Xhenafa's grip. Keth's pale demons doing their masters bidding. These demons, though rare were even more feared than those borne of fire hammered from his anvil in the underworld. For these demons were not confined to the underworld, they could traverse the void, some said that at certain times, when the will of man was weak they could even enter the corporeal world. If these demons took the souls from Xhenafa they would be brought before Keth for his own warped judgement. The bad, his own kind, would work at his furnace, the good, those he despised, would be changed, warped, twisted by his power, and once this process was finished another pale demon could be sent forth into the void.

Gytha knew the beliefs of the ignorant and the non-educated too. That the pale demons were not just created from the souls of the good, but from the souls of mages too. Keth spawn they were often called, and to prevent their inevitable corruption in death they would be burned in life, purified, for by doing this they could not be transformed into a demon, they could not claim the souls of the innocent, they either laboured in the underworld or sat at the seat of the Gods if judgement was kind. Country folk who therefore sent a child to the pyre mistakenly believed that they were actually performing an act of mercy, saving that child from becoming a demon. Many priests and knights had laboured long and hard to disabuse the rural folk of such a terrible notion but with limited success. Deep rooted beliefs were not something that could be dispelled by a glib tongue.

Gytha saw the fresco as if for the first time and shuddered. Even the kindest and fairest amongst them could end up serving Keth. A life of good works was no guarantee of an eternity in paradise, not if a demon could tear you from the grip of Xhenafa. She shook her head and started to pray.

"Syvuhka," she entreated, "please show me the light, the reason for your actions. Please tell me if my misdeeds have angered you so. And if that is the case why is it not I that have been punished? Why punish a child and a woman whose every action in life honours you? Please show me the sense in punishing innocents for the actions of the guilty."

Gytha still did not truly believe that she had called the wrath of the Gods down on Miriam and Edith. But if they died, if just one of them died then she knew that she would only blame herself, and that she could never forgive herself either. She had involved Miriam in the hunt for the killer and because of that Miriam lay on a bed on the Isle of Healing. And she had not brought Edith here but hearing Fedrica's confession, hearing her belief that one night of mildly embarrassing behaviour had caused her daughters relapse had made Gytha feel culpable also (to seduce a man, Fedrica, just dance for him whilst removing your clothes, ask an expert in such matters). If Edith died she feared for Fedrica's sanity, Gytha now cared for a woman who was her sworn enemy just one day ago.

She repeated her prayer over and over again, changing the words slightly, mixing up the sentences but keeping the meaning the same. She heard priests bring out the step ladders behind her and light the great double row of hanging wrought iron chandeliers (even the light from the windows was deemed insufficient for this place it seemed). Then she heard them go to the incense burners, fill them with dried sticks and herbs and light each one in turn, filling the house with a pungent blue smoke. Time was passing, it must be late afternoon now and still Gytha prayed.

"Something troubles you, young Gytha?"

She stood and bowed. Father Ambrose had been standing at her shoulder, Gytha was always impressed with his ability to recall the names of everybody in the college. "I am troubled yes, Father, my friend Miriam is seriously ill, and Sir Steven Aarlen's little girl Edith is fighting a fever that threatens her life. I just do not see how the Gods send such terrible trials for the innocent yet leave the guilty unpunished."

"You are saying that your sense of justice exceeds that of the Gods?"

"No, of course not, I am just struggling to understand how a three year old child "deserves" that which is being meted out to her. Is she being used as punishment for the sins of the parents? Or are we just talking about some random cruelty, and she was just unlucky enough to be in the wrong place at the wrong time? It is true after all that children suffer far more from the privations of sickness and disease than adults do. My own family has experienced such tragedy as have many others."

Father Ambrose nodded gravely. "The answer to such a question is both long and complex, for we are not talking about the actions of just one god here, but of many. Divine they may be, but they too exhibit jealousy and envy and they do act sometimes to spite each other. Children are the provenance of Elissa yet say Elissa has angered another god in some way, by favouring an enemy or hindering an ally. This god may act against Elissa's interests and targeting a child is an easy way to do such a thing."

"So a child, or any person afflicted in some way is not necessarily being punished for the sins of others."

"We cannot say for certain. If a mortal displeases a god then that god has a right to punish him and it is that god alone who chooses the form that the punishment shall take. The motivations of the Gods are manifold, they are complex, the Gods together act like the weave of a blanket, many threads bound together, each following a different path yet all mutually dependent on each other. If a child sickens, it may be for a thousand reasons and unless one can read the minds of the Gods, or the Gods choose to impart the reason to us through signs or dreams as some in the south believe then we can only speculate, many hands scrabbling in soft mud to find the diamond buried there."

Gytha gave him a deferential smile. "It is said is it not, "never ask a priest for advice for though one will end up enlightened, one will also end up knowing less than when one first asked the question."

Father Ambrose raised his gaze to the heavens. "I fear you are right. Matters of theology are torturous even for those that have studied them for decades, such as I. And even the most learned of us can have disputes that lead to war and tragedy I fear."

"You have an example Father?"

"I have many, sadly. I suppose one of the most famous concerns a dispute long ago over a couple of lines of holy text that refer to the "God home, high above the clouds...,"

Gytha briefly forgot her inner turmoil to interrupt excitedly. "The wars of the Holy Mountains, that is what you mean, is it not Father?"

"It is," he nodded. "The early founders of Chira simply assumed that the Gods lived at the top of the Dragonspine Mountains far above them. But then, as the empire grew, and the faith spread other regions thought it was their mountain ranges that held the home of the Gods. The text is like that, many parts of the empire interpret passages so that they think they are referencing them in particular. Tanaren I am afraid to say is as guilty as anywhere else in thinking that Artorus refers to their country specifically, a view endorsed by many priests, shame that it is on the order. Anyway soon we had the people of Chira city saying that the Gods lived with them, the people of the Hagasus saying that the Gods lived in their mountains and some peoples living along the vast stretch of the Derannen Mountains saying that the Gods were with them. Three completely irrevocable viewpoints. Things got nasty, pilgrims from the lakes were attacked in the capital, the lakes raised an army, the imperial soldiers prepared to meet them, the people of the Derannen closed their borders..."

"There were a couple of pitched battles were there not?" Gytha asked.

"There were, though none of them were decisive. Finally, his Sublimity the High Lector called a symposium to interpret the words of the holy book and finalise exactly where the Gods did live."

"A classic compromise, was it not Father?" Gytha smiled.

"Well I would say that they interpreted the words correctly, that the Gods do not live in the mountains but above them, far above the clouds indeed. None of those contesting the matter were particularly happy, but they contented themselves with the knowledge that, if the Gods did not live with them, then they lived with nobody else either. And this has been the accepted doctrine ever since."

Gytha nodded with him and prepared to kneel before the alcove again, a brief flash of lightning caused her to start momentarily. "Thank you Father. So you are saying that we can never know the true motivations of the Gods..."

"Just that we can guide them. If you live a just and honourable life, if you obey the tenets of the holy book, then the Gods have no grounds to punish you on any matters. Living such a life is not easy, there is no man or woman living or dead that has ever lived without breaking one of the tenets I would say, but we can but do our best and hope the Gods are kind in their judgement of us."

He was about to leave her to resume her prayers and Gytha was happy for him to do so. There was just one question remaining, one she didn't really want to ask but felt compelled to.

"Father, can you just explain the great discrepancy to me, why Lucan gifts us with our powers and yet Elissa and Artorus still bestow upon us all human needs and desires. Why do we all crave love or affection, call it what you will when our magical gifts render them obsolete to us? If we cannot marry, cannot bear children, cannot even lie with another person why give us the hopes and dreams of those that can? Why force us to live a life of denial?"

Father Ambrose sighed deeply, "I wonder how many times I have been asked this question in my long life, especially by the young. There is no easy answer. Firstly, as I explained earlier the Gods act independently of each other, Artorus knows that Lucan will bestow his gifts on the select few of us, but he does not know who will receive them, so he creates all people equally. The most important thing though is that you are human, and to remove a large part of what makes you human changes you into something else, a beast of another name entirely. To use your powers wisely, you have to be like the rest of us; take away love, or empathy, and would you have any qualms about murdering a child if it got you something that you needed badly? To be a mage you need to be human Gytha. It gives you great benefits, but the price admittedly is high. You have to endure a range of challenges and trials many of us cannot possibly imagine. You need to be strong of character to wield your power sensibly and just maybe, the strength given to you by enforced abstinence helps reinforce that character. Now I am afraid I will have to leave you, the next service is not far away, and I have to prepare, I pray that Artorus, or in this case Syvukha, shows you the way forward and gives your mind the clarity that you seek."

He left her, feet padding softly on the rush lined floor and she knelt to resume her prayers. Her conversation with the priest, though interesting, had done little to resolve her internal dilemma, whether Edith's and Miriam's current travails were in some way her fault. She smiled wryly at his words concerning character, it illustrated to her that priests did not know everything. There was a certain strength of feeling amongst the clergy that a celibate mage was more powerful than a libertine, in her experience though some of the most proficient mages of her acquaintance spent as much time with their robes above their waist as around their ankles.

Still, she had much to ponder, according to Father Ambrose people did get punished for the indiscretions of others, it was just impossible to know specifically who was being punished for what. She, in her own heart did not believe that everything was her fault, did an hour of passion with a married man constitute such a flagrant breach of the tenets (it was a breach, but hardly a major one, surely?) that others had to die to illustrate her error to her? No. The odds on such a thing being true were one in a thousand. But just imagine that that tiny fraction was the pertinent one, if Edith or Miriam died there would not be enough oceans in the entire world to wash away her contrition.

She had character flaws; she knew that. She could be stubborn, prideful, and most of all, selfish. Sometimes she would follow her own interests only and be blind to any consequences there might be for others. She was reminded of an allegory in the holy book, the woman for whom the world ended at the tip of her nose. She lived in a rural village, surrounded by a stockade and there were many hazards to life there. One day a fire burned down some of the houses, killing several people and rendering them homeless. Other villagers rehomed them, but she did not, for they were fools building too close to each other so that the fire spread easily. Sometime afterwards the river burst its banks drowning some people and again leaving others without homes. She did not help them for what fool built next to a river? Then there was a famine, many people went hungry, some even starved to death, but she did not share her food, for these people foolishly produced children they had not the capacity to feed, they should have turned to celibacy.

Finally though the village was overrun by a giant pack of slavering wolves. She sat in her house, hearing the screams but disregarded them as the cries of hysterical simpletons. And she stayed where she was as the villagers ran to the manor house and barred the doors and windows. Eventually she did look outside to see the wolves gathering nearby waiting to feed. Realising her danger she ran to the manor house, beating on the door and begging them to let her in, but they called back to her, "we would let you in, but only a fool would run here so slowly when surrounded by such peril. Look to yourself and no one else, this is what you have always told us; for you the world has always ended at the tip of your nose. Save yourself for we shall give you such aid as you gave us when we were in need. None." And then, as she turned to flee the wolves set upon her and tore her to pieces.

Perhaps, Gytha thought, she was like that too. She had wanted Steven; it suited her needs to hate Fedrica because it partly justified her actions. Yet without Steven and Edith Fedrica had nobody, Gytha knew this but did not care. And Miriam, well she had always teased Miriam who always took it in good part. Yet what if it was a front? What if the things Gytha said really hurt her but she didn't dare show it? Miriam had never told her this but then again, Gytha had never asked her. It was a one in a thousand chance that Gytha had brought the wrath of the Gods down on Miriam and Edith, yet a one in a thousand chance was still a chance. Gytha had fought against the idea all afternoon but now she knew she would have to concede the matter and alter her prayer.

"Syvukha, wisest and most powerful of the Gods." Gytha murmured the words, ensuring nobody else could hear them. "If my actions have brought down misfortune upon Edith and Miriam then I ask you to forgive me, and to make them both well. My contrition will be that I forswear Steven once and for all, let Meriel restore them both and I will never seek carnal pleasure from Steven ever again. You have joined him with Fedrica, and I understand and accept that, let Meriel restore them, and I will abide by your will."

Over and over again she prayed, her knees sore with the kneeling. She barely noticed the light fade in the windows or the easing of wind and rain. She took little heed as the congregation formed in the hall behind her, eager for the evening service, for it was not unusual for those possessed by a swelling of the faith to pray at the alcoves and ignore the world around them. She took only a passing interest in the beauty of the singing or of Father Ambrose announcement that all was well within the college again, that the killer had been found and was now awaiting their own judgement from the Gods. She noted all these things, but they mattered little to her, her prayer was all that mattered now.

The service ended, the crowd began to disperse, soon only a handful of gossiping stragglers remained. But Gytha did not look up, her knees were raw, her back was stiff but she continued to pour everything she had into her entreaty, everything she had, everything...

"Gytha?"

She turned (oh how she ached!) to see Steven standing there. His skin was ashen pale, his eyes grey and exhausted, he appeared to have aged in hours. She stood, bit her lip, and came towards him. "Is Edith...?"

"The fever has broken. She sleeps. The healers have said that the worst is over, that she is a little fighter and that I should be proud of her."

Gytha put her fist to her mouth to stop the tears coming. "That is wonderful," she choked. "Just wonderful. Praise..."

"You," he said. "You have been here for hours, your eyes are red from incense smoke, and your prayers have been answered."

She wanted to hold him, she could tell he wanted to hold her, but they both held back, just standing, looking at each other. His thought processes had followed hers; she could see his guarded expression. There was a barrier between them now, perhaps there should have been one from the start.

"Not fully answered," she said, "I need to know how Miriam is first."

He half smiled at her, "Sir Nikolaj returned just moments ago. She rests, she is peaceful. I will not lie; she has been given constant soporifics for the pain, but her cuts have been bathed and dressed and her arm is in a sling. Nikolaj will be going back tomorrow, he does seem awfully fond of her."

So Steven had guessed about Nikolaj and Miriam. She felt no need to confirm it for him. She just beamed at the news and swallowed hard as she could. She hated crying women, though she herself had been brought to tears on a few occasions these last days, but she didn't want to cry right now, too many things fighting for space in her head.

"I will go over there at dawn tomorrow. It will take a couple of hours to walk there and maybe I can get the ferry back. Perhaps we can meet and talk about things then."

"Yes. We are both too emotional right now. Still there may not be too much to discuss now the killer has been found."

Gytha bit her lip. She was nowhere near as certain about things as

Steven appeared to be, but she was too tired to argue. Besides why upset him when he must be so happy and relieved at this moment? "Give my love to Fedrica, tell her I am so happy for her. And hug Edith for me."

"The singing lady. That is what she calls you. Now go and get something to eat. And rest. You look so tired."

"I am," Gytha said, "Gods bless you and your family. See you tomorrow when I return."

She stopped at the refectory, ate a little lentil broth, and walked slowly back to her cell. She had done the right thing. She had given up Steven to save her friend and a little girl. She had done the right thing. When she had been praying she had convinced herself that her feelings for Steven revolved solely around cementing a physical relationship with him. Now though it was dawning on her that the bond between them was stronger than mere lust. She had an understanding with him, could speak freely before him, she could argue, criticise, laugh, and confide in him. He was far more than a friend to her; their relationship had been going for a matter of days but the intensity of experience that had occurred in that time had led to them learning far more about each other than they would have under ordinary circumstances. Friendship leads to understanding and understanding leads to lo... No. She dared not think of that word. She was tired, emotional, she needed sleep. She climbed into bed, put her head in her hands and let out a long sigh of pent up frustration.

Miriam and Edith lived. She had done the right thing. And the pain tearing at her insides was almost too much to bear.

DAY ELEVEN
44

An invalid visited, and a journey by sea

She was good as her word. Rising before dawn she washed, dressed, put on her thicker shoes and ran her comb through her hair until it was free of knots. Then, as the first light of day kissed the college towers and shone the colour of blood on the flags of Tanaren she made her way to the Isle of Healing.

There were great standing puddles of muddy water on the path leading there, a legacy of yesterday's storm. She tripped lightly between them; her mood lighter than it had been when she went to bed. Miriam yet lived and she was going to see her, her own emotional confusion could be set aside for a few hours at least.

Miriam's room was one of the more basic ones at the hospital, a bed, a tiny window, a couple of stools for guests, little more than that, but it was clean, warm, and smelled of fresh herbs. Kessie was there, she stood and embraced Gytha as she entered and Miriam was awake, flashing a wan smile as Gytha took her seat.

"That is the last time I act on my own initiative," the patient said weakly, showing Gytha her arm, bound tightly by a bandage of white linen. "If this is what being adventurous does for you then I will leave it to bolder souls than I."

"She slept till this morning," Kessie said to Gytha. "Drugged up to her eyes she was, ranting and raving...and the language! Fit to burn the ears of a Tolmareon blood warrior!"

Gytha and Miriam stared at her. "Only joking," she added sheepishly.

"Don't you start teasing me." Miriam blew a wisp of wiry hair away from her nose, where it had been tickling her. She noticed that it was disturbingly grey. "I have enough of that to put up with from the red head next to you, and Cheris, when she is here."

"I wanted to talk to you about that." Gytha spoke, and she was all remorse and contrition. "You do know that when I tease you it is never out of malice, I never mean anything by it. It just that it occurred to me the other day that I have never asked if my words upset you. If they do, just tell me and I will stop. I would never knowingly hurt a friend."

Miriam looked taken aback for a second, then a wicked gleam shone in her eye. "Well I never thought I would hear such things off you. Are you that spirit in the old tales? Have you killed the real Gytha and stolen her skin?"

"Cow," Gytha poked her tongue out.

"I see not," Miriam said.

"A week ago I would have said frigid old cow, but that is something I have to revise, is it not?"

"Trying to embarrass me. Won't work. Can't turn time backwards, what happened just happened. And I doubt it will happen again. I don't think the man in question has any further interest in me."

"But he brought you here," Kessie said.

"He did?"

"And he stayed here until it started to get dark. You slept the entire time, or rather you were drugged the entire time."

"Oh," Miriam said quietly as memories started to come back to her. "He picked me up. I thought it was Xhenafa, but it was him. No matter, he was probably just the first man to see me. And poor Gideon, but alas it was too late for him to be saved, physically that is. I think he was saved spiritually; I would be dead without the poor lad's sacrifice. I must light a candle for him when I can."

"And poor Kas," Kessie added, "I cannot believe she was the killer. She just seemed too placid, too quiet and docile to commit such...acts."

"Oh she wasn't the killer," Miriam stated bluntly. Gytha started and looked at her, intensity returning to her pale blue eyes. "She told me," Miriam continued, "she killed Havel but that was a crime of passion, after what he did to Arbagast, oh and she was in the Order of Jedrael, but that was the limit of her crimes. They were bad enough to see her run through of course, that was why she tried to silence me, but she didn't kill Caswell, or the other lay brother, Meriel's benison but my arm is beginning to hurt."

Soon afterwards a healer came in with a draught for her to drink. The three women then played dice games for a while; Miriam as always, lost frequently and Gytha was almost as bad, Kessie it seemed was making it look easy. "Blame my time with Soma," she said. As they played Miriam recounted, in a rambling manner, all the events that led up to Kas and Gideon's death. "He was not a bad boy, just a misguided one, and he saved my life in the end at the cost of his own. To think I would end up feeling sorry for a boy that used to spy on me in such an unpleasant manner."

Finally Miriam slept again. A healer came and told them that she would be able to return to the college in a couple of days, just so long as she rested and drank the healing draught regularly to numb the pain. As the healer bid them goodbye another person entered the room.

"She sleeps, Sir Nikolaj," Gytha said, "and she might be sleeping for a while."

"I will wait," he said breezily; "I have a couple of days without duties. You two on the other hand had better leave soon, it is getting dark out there. The sea is mild today, leave now and you should catch the last ferry."

Gytha leaned forward and gently kissed Miriam on the forehead. "Sleep now Miri, I cannot tell you how happy I am to see you well...alive and recovering."

"Have you seen her legs?" Kessie asked, lifting the sheet to show her. Miriam was covered in a tracery of cuts and scratches up to her thighs, most were superficial and the worst of them were bandaged but there were enough angry, red, and sore ones still exposed to make Gytha wince.

"Just to remind you that a man is present in the room," Nikolaj had turned his head away. "Perhaps you should cover her up until I leave."

"Sorry Sir Nikolaj," Kessie pulled the sheet down.

"It is nothing you haven't seen before." Gytha looked at him cheekily.

He looked slightly exasperated, "that isn't the issue. Giving a lady some dignity is."

"Well spoken sir knight. You are rather fond of our Miriam are you not?"

Now the man just looked embarrassed.

"Well so am I," Gytha continued, "there is a lot to love about her. I beg you to treat her well, she is a far more sensitive soul than she pretends to be."

"Your words are heeded. If you see Sir Steven tell him I will be back in the morning."

It was nowhere near as dark and threatening as Sir Nikolaj had told them it would be, rather reinforcing Gytha's opinion that he just wanted her and Kessie gone so he could have some time alone with Miriam. Still, it gave both women a chance to take a leisurely stroll along the path to the harbour. The air was fresh and clean, the breeze brisk without being fierce and the grass and heather were moist and fragrant. It was a good walk and so much more enjoyable than her last trip this way, where she saw the duel between Steven and Vargo.

The harbour was decked out with flags and the wooden piles supporting the planked wharves had been painted blue in honour of the Grand Dukes imminent visit. The ferry, a single sailed skiff with four oars took its leave as soon as they embarked. Gytha and Kessie were not alone, sailing with them was a mage delivering herbs from the medicinal gardens for Senior Frankus and a lay brother whose hands and robe were spattered blue, obviously the man who had just done the painting. The crew of four consisted of Mergil, a craggy man of middle years with a face weathered brown by the elements and his three sons, all in their mid or late teens who spent a lot of their time fishing when the ferry wasn't needed. There was some light, friendly conversation as the boat pulled away from the wharf, everyone was on first name terms with everybody else after all but once the Isle of Healing was firmly behind them talk soon tapered off as the sail was unfurled and they were all subject to any vicissitudes the sea might have in store for them.

Gytha probably travelled between islands on foot most of the time, unlike many others who preferred the ferry to a walk that could take several hours depending on fitness and the weather. When she did take the ferry though her usual reason was to look at the Isle of Tears from a fresh perspective, not from atop it, but alongside it, a rare opportunity to see it as others might see it, traders and travellers to whom this was just a place to stop off rather than a home. The ferry skirted the islands north side, the opposite side to where Kas, Miriam, and Gideon had fought their deadly duel the day before; as they travelled Gytha was struck by the height of the stark, stygian cliffs, their smooth yet rugged nature, indomitable in the face of wind and rain, never broken by the ire of the storm tossed sea. Several spiky outcrops of glistening stone jutted out from under the surface of the frothy ocean, jagged teeth of an undersea beast, not all of which were visible to the naked eye. Many dangerous shoals lurked just out of view and only Mergil, his boys, and a few others knew the best route to avoid them. Gytha looked up to the thin green crown of the island, she saw the kissing rock, the stone benches mages sat on to witness the temperamental waves and the gulls that made their homes on these frowning cliffs, then finally she saw the college itself.

It always looked smaller than she expected from here. Granted the angle between ferry, clifftop, and college meant that a good part of the ground floor was invisible to her, but she had still expected it to be bigger somehow, hundreds of people lived, and unfortunately died there after all. Did not their lives deserve something grander, something to celebrate the great sweep of human experience that dwelt within rather than appear to diminish it? Perhaps not. Perhaps people were just not that important, perhaps the sense of self was exaggerated, perhaps people overestimated their true worth, seeing it as how they would like it to be rather than what it was. Did any of them, did any of their hopes, fears, joy, tears, triumphs, and despair ultimately matter? In a hundred years who would remember any of them after all. There would not even be any children around to cherish the memories of their parents and grandparents; the life of an island mage had as much substance as air.

Her gloom and inner reflection did not last long, for after passing rather too closely one of these weed encrusted, barnacle clad outcroppings they saw the mouth of the cave that held the harbour. Minutes later they were tying up inside the cave, a tunnel between cave mouth and harbour having robbed the sea of most of its fury. Climbing off the ferry they walked along a broad shelf of smooth stone that served as the landing, even here Gytha noticed flags and pennants bearing the colours of the Grand Duke fluttering in the swirling breezes the cave funnelled in from outside. Passing several torches in sconces and the knight on duty there they went through a narrow archway and up a steep flight of spiral steps. This opened out onto another landing, the one that housed the Oval Room where the mages staves were charged. One solitary torch flickered wanly there, but aside from that the Oval Room was in darkness. One more flight of steps and they were at the great doors and reception room. Home at last.

Here Gytha bade farewell to Kessie and went to seek out Steven. She found him after climbing even more steps, for unsurprisingly he was close to his family at the chapter house. His hair was combed, and he was dressed immaculately in an expensive black shirt trimmed in silver, he had both time and inclination to take care of his appearance. By contrast, her hair was stiff with salt, her face was tinted pink with exertion and by the weather, she did not look anywhere near her best. So inevitably the next person she saw was Lady Fedrica, but this was a different Lady Fedrica, one bursting with joy and happiness. She even embraced Gytha as she walked into the room, the same room Gytha had left them in far more harrowing circumstances the previous day.

"Edith is well," Fedrica told her, "she sleeps, she is a child after all, but she is well. I hear you prayed for many hours for her successful recovery, and for that I wish to thank you. Once winter has passed the three of us will be travelling to Crown Haven, the knights have an estate there. Steven will serve with the chapter whilst the climate should be conducive to a full recovery for Edith. Steven will then return here for the autumn, Commander Shadan has authorised everything." She pressed close to Gytha as though imparting a confidence. "And as I will be alone with Steven for a far longer time than I am used to, I am hopeful that in the following winter or spring Edith will have a sister or brother to play with! Wouldn't that be wonderful! I will pray to Elissa this very night so that she makes it so happen."

So Steven would be leaving her. For a half of a year. Crown Haven was an island, a large island far to the south, a sea voyage of several weeks would be needed to get there. It was a warm, wealthy country, the sort of place Gytha would love to see herself. But such thoughts had to end there.

"That sounds delightful. I will add my prayers to your own," she said, with a beautifully disguised lack of sincerity.

"Gytha!" it was Steven. "Come into my office, we cannot talk long, people are gathering in the great hall for a celebration, and I am honour bound to join them."

Gytha curtsied to Fedrica and did as Steven requested. Once there he shut the door so that they could talk freely.

"Crown Haven?" she inquired.

"Yes. Shadan has been there a couple of times and cannot speak highly enough of the place. It is supposed to be a curious mix of cultures and the Mage College is small and easy to run. Most importantly it should be good for Edith's health. And I cannot take any more chances with that."

"Any more chances," Gytha thought. He has been thinking along the same lines then. No chance of him wanting to continue as they were. Over. It was conclusively over. A green shoot trampled before it could fully bloom, but then, what other outcome could there ever have been? His mistress perhaps, she would happily have continued as his mistress when Fedrica had gone but his tone told her otherwise. A thousand to one chance was still a chance, and she was wrong to even consider jeopardising Edith's health in this way. "I will miss you," was all she could think of saying.

He nodded, "same here. I will be back though, it's not that easy to get rid of me."

"Bring me back some exotic foodstuff or spice, something to flavour oatmeal with."

"Thinking of your stomach again?"

"I never stop. So they are celebrating the demise of our murderer then?"

"Indeed. Music and an impromptu feast laid out on trestle tables. The Chief Magister has even sanctioned the use of your power on the chandeliers. Those magical glass orbs you use instead of candles were placed in readiness for the Grand Duke, but, they have been lit for tonight as well."

"Nice," She said tartly, before taking a deep breath to finish her sentence, "especially when our killer is still at large."

His eyes did widen at her words, but she got the impression that he was nowhere near as surprised as he pretended to be. "And why do you say that exactly?"

"Two reasons. Firstly Miriam told me. Kas confessed to killing Havel but denied everything else."

"Kas may have been lying."

"Why?" Gytha shrugged her shoulders. "Kill one person and you face the

311

death sentence, so why admit to killing one person but deny any other murders? There is no point."

"Maybe as she reflected on the enormity of her crimes she found that she couldn't confess to them all."

"Yes, of course," Gytha could not but sound derisive. "" I want to confess, and I shall start my confession by not confessing to anything." Please be magnanimous enough to allow a little scepticism on my part."

He had to smile, "and how is Miriam?"

"In pain but recovering. She should be back here soon with her arm trussed up and Sir Nikolaj to support her."

"Are those two...?"

"No more than you and me," she winked at him.

He seemed slightly embarrassed by that; "and your second reason? For thinking the killer is still free that is."

"A simple one. Kas was not a frost mage."

He shook his head, "now you know I don't agree with you on that one..."

But why?" she said cuttingly, "what know you of our power? You are trained to fight with sword and shield yes?"

"And mace and lance."

"Fine, fine. So would you willingly march into battle with a spear or bill hook? Would you use an axe? Maybe yes if you had to but given the choice you would use a sword. To do what our killer does, to have the mental facility to control a spirit must be very taxing, so why complicate things by using powers that you are not familiar with. A frost mage killed those people Steven, on that I am emphatic."

He gave her a resigned sigh. "Very well, what are you going to do about it?"

"Proceed as we had planned yesterday morning. Speak to Eubolo again. Raiman worked for him the day he died, I will just ask what he did and what they talked about. Perhaps I will learn something."

"And perhaps you will not."

"I have to try. Do you really want the Grand Duke here and a killer on the loose? Especially if he is the killer's ultimate target, though I fail to see how killing the man would benefit any mage on this island."

"Very well, ask your questions, I am still pretty hopeful that we have found our killer already though. Try and give the impression that you feel the same. A murderer who thinks he is home and dry may make a mistake of some sort."

"That is very shrewd for you." Gytha gave him an arch smile.

"I have my moments. Now will you accompany me to the great hall? There are people there who I am sure will want to congratulate us on finding the killer we haven't actually found. According to you that is."

****

An old man says his piece

The great hall was busy, but not frenetically so. People, as they so often did on such occasions gathered together in small groups to talk, reflect, share news and gossip and try and make light of any cares that the day may have put upon them. Gytha soon heard that the searches and other restrictions imposed after Oskum's small rebellion had been lifted and that the ceremonial robes worn for the Grand Duke's visit had been delivered to every cell. A quick look round told her where the food was, four low trestle tables at the other end of the hall piled high with pewter bowls containing cheeses, hot and cold sliced meat, bread, and flavoured oils to dip it into, sweet and savoury oat cakes, honey cakes, wine and weak ale amongst other things. The kitchens had done well given such short notice. There was more light than usual in the hall too, the candles in the chandeliers had been replaced by a series of small crystal spheres each of which glowed with a soft, diffuse light, magically powered, as Steven had said earlier. In particular they illuminated a series of painted religious icons situated on the east wall, chief and largest of which depicted the holy pantheon; Artorus at the centre with the sun, his sun, shining above his head. Rays from the sun spread out to strike both the other Gods and a human man in the lower part of the painting, a stylised depiction of the Grand Duke himself. A man favoured of the Gods indeed, though Gytha did note that all leaders under the Artoran faith had such things commissioned on their accession and some of them went on to have very short reigns indeed.

Both she and Steven were hailed several times, people wishing to do exactly as Steven had suggested, congratulate them on their success. She happily let Steven do the talking, she rather felt that she had achieved little or nothing these last days and was happy to let him accept any plaudits. Which he did, with a humility that suggested he felt the same way she did. Neither of them wanted to spoil the mood however, for she soon noted the palpable sense of relief amongst those talking to them.

Eventually they ended up talking to Eubolo and Goodbern. Goodbern was walking stiffly with a clean white bandage around the crown of her head, covering the nasty cut she had received there when Lipshin died. With them was an old man. He would have been quite tall in his youth but now was so stooped he barely came up to Gytha's chin. He had a short, white, pointy beard but little hair on his head, the bald pate being covered only by a few silver, spidery wisps. His eyes were watery blue but keen as a warrior's axe, sitting aside a long, bent nose that reminded Gytha of those water birds that fed by dipping their beak just under the surface of a shallow lake or low tide. He walked with the aid of a stick in his right hand and grumbled incessantly under his breath as Gytha enquired after Goodbern's health.

"Sore," she affirmed, "especially my back which was cut in several places. I get by though; I am not one to sit and mope after being surrounded by catastrophe. I am dividing my time by finishing off Caswell's little herb harvest on the roof. And organising! So much organising!"

"What Senior Goodbern is trying to say," Eubolo interrupted smoothly, "is that the frost school has been rather decimated by recent events. They wanted me to go on duty charging our staves following the deaths of Kas and Arbagast, but Goodbern here dug her heels in and refused to let me go. Mattriss is still surrounded by an alcoholic cloud so toxic it kills insects and so she has persuaded Senior Halpin here to ease himself out of retirement and help with some of the lectures that need to be done. Mages have to be taught after all, no matter the circumstances."

"Persuaded." The old man fulminated in a voice reminiscent of cracking twigs, or a swirling wind picking up dead, dry leaves." Like a stallion gets "persuaded" to have its bollocks cut off."

"As you can hear," Goodbern beamed, "Senior Halpin was more than enthused about assisting our cause."

"I am pleased that you are teaching us again," Gytha said sweetly, flashing him a faux grateful smile. "I always found your tutorials utterly stimulating."

"Did you novice Gytha, did you?" He turned to face Steven, "what do you think of her sir knight? A fine figure of a woman indeed, many a place for a man to rest an eager hand. If I were but five years younger..."

"Thirty years at the least, surely." Goodbern spoke with eyebrows raised as far as her injured head would allow. "And you should not be lusting after young novices anyway, it is very unbecoming."

"What else can I do at my age?" he said. "I am that kind of a man that can no longer prove that he is a man at all. I am as flaccid as one of those salad leaves on that table over there and have been this last decade at the least. But I have my eyes, I can look, and no number of stern reproaches are going to stop me. So I say it again Gytha. You are a fine figure of a woman. Your ceremonial dancing is the closest I have been to having him standing to attention in a long time."

"Oh stop embarrassing the girl," Goodbern scolded him.

"It is all right senior," Gytha said, "I am almost flattered that my performance can elicit such a reaction, maybe it even affects other men so too. " She gave Steven a sideways look.

"Your dancing was supposedly in praise of the Gods only," Eubolo laughed. "It was probably not intended to give starchy old men the sort of thrill they would normally get in the Rose district."

"My dancing was always performed with the sole intention of praising the Gods," she pointed out to him; "yet I cannot be held responsible for the reactions of others."

Halpin shook his head so hard flecks of spittle shot out from the corners of his mouth. "Getting old Gytha, Getting old. You probably hear a load of cow dung about it bringing wisdom, respect, and dignity. Dung I say, dung! Wisdom? I am no wiser now than when I was a boy, I still feel like a boy, despite looking like a ravaged and dry old snakeskin, long shedded and very scaly. My arse cheeks resemble a couple of chestnuts these days and are about the same size. Two chestnuts at the back, two walnuts at the front and everything as shrivelled as a month old grape. And respect? Who respects an old fool that cannot keep his dribble inside his mouth? A man that walks into a room, recognises nobody in it and cannot even remember why he walked into it in the first place. And dignity? I am not there yet but what dignity is there in having your arse wiped by a healer, your piss stained robes being washed by a lay brother? Growing old is a curse I tell you. I want to run around the island's perimeter singing the song about the dowager and the blacksmith, I want to drink such ale that my head will be in two different places in the morning and a want to hammer a woman so hard she would be barely able to walk in a straight line afterwards. Can I do any of these things?"

"You couldn't do them when you were Sir Steven's age," Goodbern pointed out.

"Maybe. But I could at least try. Now climbing a flight of steps is an achievement, even if I have to sit down to breathe afterwards. Getting old is horrible, only mild mannered milksops like Rebdon enjoy it, people who never knew what being young meant. People like me, like Caswell though, hate it, hate the infirmity that it brings. At least Caswell is out of it now, Gods keep her. I still have to shuffle here and there not knowing what day it is, where I am, or what is on my dinner plate. Why are there so many kinds of bean anyway? What purpose do they serve? Age Gytha, a curse on all men it is, a curse!"

"Well, whether you think otherwise or not," Goodbern answered him, "we do respect you, age brings with it a status you should be proud of."

"What!" he was frothing again. "Like old Margery the healer? Best thing ever to happen to that island she was in her youth. Everything was clean, the herb gardens doubled in size, discipline was almost military. She transformed the place, made it better and richer than ever before. Now all she does is sit in her room shouting out, "Hamley, I'm peeing myself!" Hamley being her lover and with the Gods these last thirty years. Pick the dignity out of that lady Goodbern. And now I have mentioned it, I need to make water too, both you and Eubo...something will have to guide me to the latrines, or I will end up relieving myself in the wine bowl over there. Might make it taste better if I did mind. Age Gytha, age! Live your life when you are young and die long before you end up like me!"

****

Gytha wants to retire but has to speak to people first

After taking their leave, Steven pulled Gytha to one side.

"Wasn't he one of our suspects?"

"In your eyes," she smiled, "you mentioned him, I put you straight on the matter."

"In my defence," he said, "I don't think I had met him. I am glad you corrected me in this case at least. Were his lectures stimulating then?"

"Yes, unfortunately," she shook her head wearily, "and probably will be more so in the days to come. He was as like to talk about the soup he had that morning as he was about our powers, either that or the bounteous beauty of fresh young womanhood. Anyway, if he does end up lecturing me I will keep my robe firmly over my knees, don't you worry. And now I think I am going to retire, I am tired, sea travel always exhausts me no matter how short the journey. It is getting dark, and I need a wash, I am covered in mud and salt, after that, prayers and sleep, I don't think I am capable of much more."

"Do as you feel. I will retire soon also, I would like to see the family, see that Edith continues to recover. Tomorrow is all about preparing for the Grand Duke I am afraid, wearisome in the extreme, but Shadan is a stickler for preparations."

"I will see you after I have spoken to people," she nodded in the direction of Eubolo. "At least I will if I learn anything. If not I will leave you to your...preparations. Meriel's blessing on Edith, on all of you."

They parted with a smile and Gytha left the great hall to stroll to her cell.

She had reached the library, had passed the common area and was amongst the bookshelves when she almost bumped into Soma, who was walking in the opposite direction.

"Oh hello," Soma said casually, as though Gytha was the last person she was expecting to see. "Not celebrating in the hall? I thought you were one of the heroes of the moment."

"Tired," Gytha said with a toss of her curls, "and a bit of a headache."

"Then I will not detain you." Soma though made no attempt to move out of the way. "Though maybe I could ask one quick question."

"Well it appears I am a captive audience." Gytha could not get to the door unless Soma moved, so she affected a wan little smile and let Soma get whatever matter she had on her chest, off her chest.

"You have triumphed, you have your murderer, though I must say in my brief meetings with her she did not seem much of a murderer to me. But then that is the trick I suppose, appearing to be one thing when you are actually something else entirely. Anyway, you have returned order to this place, you just have one more thing to do."

"Which is?"

"The spirit. The one I have been sensing so strongly. What are you going to do with the spirit? Leave it free to roam the caves again or release it? All you have to do is smash the Casta'zhana after all. Will you do so?"

Gytha pushed her hair from her face, it did so need a wash. "We have yet to find it and the knights are too preoccupied with the Grand Duke right now to want to help me retrieve it. I hope to look around Kas' chambers tomorrow, hopefully it will be there and yes, I made a promise, I will release the spirit if I can, though if I do that the artefacts that it guards, many of which we probably still have to discover, will be open to plunder."

"She no longer cares. Her people are dead and forgotten by all except her. All she wishes now is to join them." Gytha could barely see Soma's face under that impenetrable mass of wild hair but there was a certain wistful quality in both her voice and eyes that struck her as odd and reminded her that Soma was still something of a mystery to all of them.

"How can you possibly know what she wants?" Gytha asked.

Soma licked her thin lips and took a step backwards, Gytha could now access the doorway should she so choose. "It is a feeling rather than a certainty," she said; "my power is different to many of you here. It is based far more on instinct and emotion, I do not try to control the forces that run through me, say rather that I guide them and that sometimes I let them guide me."

"I am not sure that is an answer," Gytha smiled, "but…"

"You have an element of that in you too," Soma interrupted. "Emotion guides your power more in you than others here. I told you before, you are stronger than many here tell you that you are, your strengths are just different to theirs, maybe you will discover this one day. Anyway, I have prattled away enough of your time, I want to find Kessie, show her some card tricks, may the Goddess grant you a fruitful sleep."

Gytha had no idea which goddess she was referring to nor was she in the mood to ponder whatever allusions Soma was making to her. She just wanted the sanctuary of her cell and sighed audibly with relief once she finally got there. Even better, she had enough water for a good wash. Pouring it into her pewter washing bowl she undressed, soaked her washing rag and proceeded to rub herself vigorously, letting rivulets of icy wetness drip over her bare skin, cleansing her pores and dissolving the salt and mud spatters that clung to her so irritatingly. It was rejuvenating, energising, it revitalised her mind and for the first time in hours she felt like she was thinking properly again. But it was not to last.

The door creaked open. Gytha hurriedly tried to cover herself with her hands and was prepared to let loose a stream of invective at the intruder so foul, it would make the stone walls blush.

It was Warran.

He saw her unclad state and immediately covered his face and half turned his body away from her. "So sorry," he mumbled, "I will come back later."

She dropped her hands to her hips. "Come in and sit down, there are hardly any surprises in what is standing in front of you. Oh, but close the door as much as you can first, the last thing I want is anyone else barging in and staring at me."

Warran pushed the door to so that it was less than an inch ajar. Then he walked fully into the cell and was about to sit, but then Gytha had another idea to badger him with.

She turned her back to him. "Can you wash me please? I cannot reach everywhere behind me." She handed him the rag.

He started to dab her tentatively, "I am not sure I should be doing this…"

"You are helping me. Surely there is no harm in that? Anyway, to more important matters, your exams, did Miriam's tutelage work for you?"

"Indeed," he smiled for the first time. "The best marks in the group apparently. I think I shocked senior Dollan, "I had never expected to see such cogent theorising…from you," she told me."

Gytha spun round and planted a firm kiss on his cheek. "Well done," she told him, "all you needed was belief. I am proud of you." Then she turned once more and continued to let him wash her back.

"I need to talk to you," she said finally, as he moved down to her thighs and calves. "Serious talk. About us. Not now if you don't mind, I am too tired, over the next couple of days, if you are still willing to listen to me."

"All done," he said, handing her the rag. She went down onto her knees, ready to wash her hair. "And of course I am happy to listen, see me whenever you are ready."

She looked up at him, eyes wide, one hand holding her hair. "I still find you attractive Warran, I hope you can say the same of me."

He laughed at that. "You are kneeling in front of me with barely a stitch on, reach under my robes if you want the answer to that question."

She hesitated. "Warran, and I am getting ahead of myself here but, setting the love thing to one side for the moment, if we were to...resume certain aspects of our former relationship..."

"You mean..." he was blushing, his blushing infuriated her, why did he always get so embarrassed with such matters?

"The...physical...side, yes," she said. "Can you not be so...nice with me next time."

"You want me to disrespect you?" he half spluttered. "If there is a next time that is."

"No, of course not. But respect does not always equate to gentleness..."

"I don't understand."

She sighed. "I mean, next time, if there is a next time, if you ever want me again, can you do the things I ask, even if what I ask seems a little...surprising to you." Now she was blushing, and that was even more infuriating. What was more, Warran didn't answer immediately, she half expected him to storm out in disgust. But he didn't. Instead a sly smile spread slowly over his face. "I like surprises," was all he said. He started to walk out but stopped at the door and turned around. He was still smiling.

"So, what is the Horn of Murmuur exactly?"

She sniggered, "ah, so you have heard..."

"It is common gossip. Those knights that search the rooms have told everybody."

She sighed, then stood and picked her proscribed book off her desk, opening it at the relevant page. "Read about it there. Take the book with you. Actually, read the chapter before that one, about the lady and her rather muscular gardeners. If you follow what she tells them to do you won't go far wrong."

He took the book. "Really? So it is an instructional manual."

She gave him a knowing wink, "don't let it shock you."

His smile broadened, "I am far less shockable than you think."

Then he did walk out, but his steps were light and airy, happy even, disgust was the last thing Gytha saw in them. He shut the door as tightly as he could, and she took a deep breath and shoved her head in the bowl. The shock of the cold water made her yelp but once that yelp was over, to her surprise, she found that she was smiling too.

****

Miriam's pain is eased, and not just by drugs

Elsewhere, on the Isle of Healing, Miriam finally awoke with a drowsy yawn. For a moment she was confused; this was not her cell, it was warmer, there was a small window of glass through which the receding light of a pale dusk shone wanly. It illuminated the comforting embers of a glowing brazier against the far wall, and the silhouette of a man in a chair sitting close to her.

A man in a chair?

She sat up with a start and a strangled cry. Or rather she tried to, her shoulders barely lifted off the bolster before she sank back into it again, the pain making her wince before she could speak.

"Who are you? What is...owwww!"

"It is Sir Nikolaj. I have just seen the healers; they will be along with another draught to help with the pain soon. They can't give you too many apparently because you could go mad or become addicted to the stuff or something."

"Oh." Recollection finally hit her, where she was and who she was with. "I have slept till nightfall. Gytha and Kessie have gone then. But...but why are you here? Have you no duties?"

He leaned forward a little so as not to raise his voice. "I have been given a little time away from them, ostensibly to investigate exactly what happened to you."

"Of course," she said, her manner becoming business-like. "Well you see I left the House of Xhenafa...."

He placed his hand over her good one. "No, no, you don't have to say anything now, you can rest, I can always hear the tale in the morning. Steven knows about what happened between us, that was why he gave me the task of coming here."

"He knows!" she suddenly felt unaccountably afraid. "Then we might be punished! I..."

"No," he sounded reassuring; "he will do nothing. If he punished every knight that did such a thing he would lose a good part of his garrison. You are quite safe, never fear."

She sighed with relief. "Oh good. Well, I suppose it was only once..."

"It doesn't have to be Miriam, unless that is how you want it."

Whatever did he mean? "You are a very smooth talker, or at least you were that night. I believed every word."

"Perhaps I meant every word."

"See. You are doing it again."

"Or maybe I am just being honest."

"Oh." Her head hurt. Her arm hurt. Everywhere hurt. Yet she didn't care. "So you want us to...go on, I mean like in the cave?"

"Only if you want to."

"Seriously?"

"Seriously."

"Oh." A brief silence. "My arm hurts."

"Anything I can do?"

"Not really. Though talking helps."

"Then talk Miriam, talk to me about something."

"About what?"

He shrugged, "that night in the cave, you were mentioning Abo, the first Lector of Artorus. Tell me about the second. Then the third."

"Wouldn't that be a little...tedious?"

"You talk. It helps with the pain. I listen. And get to hear your voice. Nobody loses then, do they?"

"Right," she sighed cynically; "my last admirer died saving my life."

"And this one is happy to do the same. Now go on, tell me about Abo the Second."

Miriam shook her head. "You are handsome Sir Nikolaj, maybe your features are a little sharp and your nose is on the large side, but you are handsome, there are many younger, prettier girls out there for you. And I can be such trouble, I worry about everything, obsess about trivialities. I..."

"Look Miriam," he clasped her good hand a little more firmly, "can we just enjoy the moment? Maybe in two weeks I will tire of you, maybe in three weeks you will tire of me, maybe in four weeks we will be sick of the sight of each other. But if any of that happens, it happens in the future, not right now.

Let us just enjoy the evening, and the following morning, there will be time enough afterwards for things to go sour, if indeed they even go sour at all."

A small laugh. "You need to see the brain healers while you are here, there is something going very awry between your ears. Still, as you ask, Abo the Seconds' real name was Utash of Cold River. He was elected by his fellow adherents, the first election by the first sanctified followers of the pantheon of Artorus. It was an auspicious occasion, thousands travelled for many miles to be there..."

And she talked. And Sir Nikolaj listened. And as she talked the night fell and the room became dark, all apart from the glowing coals and the merest twinkle that glimmered in Miriam's eyes.

DAY TWELVE
45
Eubolo displays some foresight

As it was almost everywhere else, life in the college started at dawn. The lay brothers sleeping in the dormitory or outbuildings outside the college walls were woken by the cries of competing cockerels, for those inside the college though it was, as ever, the church bell that stirred them from slumber.

Gytha was not a light sleeper, neither was she renowned as someone whose countenance at early hours was bright and airy as the morning breeze. She often overslept. She often overslept on purpose. She often made a point of being one of the last people at prayers or the refectory, as though this small act of insouciance marked her out as some sort of rebel against authority. It was good to fight back sometimes, as long as there were no long term consequences, Gytha was all too aware that the college system would always triumph in the end.

This morning though, she was up and ready whilst the sky was still a wash of cool indigo spotted with tiny and fading stars. She had had time to think. Now she felt she had to do something, however ineffectual that something might be. She alone here seemed to realise that Kas' death did not end things, that the Grand Duke was coming, and that he may still be a part of somebody's nefarious schemes. Even Steven seemed happy to let the matter rest, people were too eager to accept the easy answer, if that answer allayed any fears they might have. But Gytha knew differently, if something happened to the Grand Duke while he was here then the interrogations and punishments that would follow would dwarf anything they had all seen so far. So she would spend the morning talking to the senior frost mages once more, those few that were left, hoping that the guilty party would finally let something slip that could be used to condemn them.

She left prayers early, and ate her breakfast at pace, having to wipe a streak of milky porridge from her chin as she left the refectory. Then she went to the reception room and climbed the stairs to the senior mages' chambers.

Eubolo's door was open. She rapped it sharply just to alert him to her presence. There was no need for he was standing behind his desk counting a number of small wax tablets stacked high upon it and saw her immediately.

"Come on in Gytha, come on in. Take a seat. You can see," he gestured at the tablets, "that I am tutoring some youngsters this morning, fresh out of the Childs' college. There is a good reason why we do not yet trust them with precious parchment. Remember the fire in Senior Aubrey's rooms? Guess how that started."

She went and sat the other side of the desk to him, wondering exactly how to begin.

"You have not yet had breakfast?" Was the feeble way she chose to do so.

"No, not yet, for if I had then you might not have had this opportunity to speak to me. I will go and dine once your questions have been satisfied."

"My questions?" She frowned. "You sound like you were expecting me."

He pushed the tablets to one side, sitting at the desk so his eyes firmly met hers. "That I was is testament to both our intelligences," he said cryptically.

"Can you explain, senior?"

"Of course. I can speak freely I take it, there is no knight lurking in the shadows with the finger breakers at the ready?"

"You have spoken to Beni."

"That I have. And I knew you would come. And the reason I knew is that I knew that you knew that senior Kas, Artorus be merciful to her, was about as capable of cold calculated murder as a chicken here is capable of flying to Tanaren."

"And your reasoning is?" Gytha shifted uneasily on her seat.

"Kas herself. I knew her fairly well. A nice woman, moderate intelligence, yet hardly any self-esteem and shy as a maiden on her wedding night. Furthermore she was utterly devoid of ambition, and somebody who invokes a spirit to kill for them must surely reek of it."

"Kas was shy?"

"Horribly so," Eubolo nodded. "The reason she spent so much time in that darkling room charging staff after interminable staff was because she preferred that to having to talk to people. Is that a murderer to you?"

"No," Gytha assented. "She killed Havel the lay brother, but that was a crime invoked by grief and anger, I do not believe she killed anybody else."

Eubolo clapped his hands together. "See! I can foresee things when I try. This however leaves you with a rather obvious problem does it not? That somebody is out there, somebody dangerous, somebody who, even as it stands now is pulling all the strings and remaining just that little bit ahead of you. And that somebody is a frost mage, a senior frost mage and though our numbers have been thinned there are still a few of us out there. And we are all suspects, and you have come to me first which rather suggests to me that I am suspect number one. Am I right?"

324

"Not entirely." Gytha sighed and rubbed her chin. It was sore, did she have a spot? "You are a suspect but the reason I came to you first was that lay brother Raiman was scheduled to do some work for you on the day that he died. He must have spent some time here; you must have spoken at length with him. I just wonder what form any such conversation took."

Eubolo swallowed, then stifled a cough. "I was not with him all the time, but yes we did talk and about several things. Come with me."

He stood and made his way to the door that led to his private rooms. Gytha hesitated to follow at first, partly out of a novice's respect for a senior's personal space, partly because of a creeping unease. Would not a murderer want to commit his crime away from prying eyes?

He seemed to read her mind. "Come on through," he said quietly, "I assure you that you are quite safe."

He held the door for her as she stepped through. He then went and wedged it so that it remained open. His room was simple enough, a bit like Beni's, bed, straw on the floor, a chest of drawers, a couple of wall hangings and two bookshelves on the far wall just under the tiny window. The top shelf of the bookcase on the right was only secured on one side, the other had slipped and was resting on the books underneath it.

"He was building me a bookshelf." Eubolo spoke in a tone that managed to be both carefree and deadly serious. "I have been having problems with both of them for some time, worm eaten wood, rusting nails, whatever. So he agreed to repair and reconstruct them."

"He didn't quite finish." Gytha pointed at the errant shelf.

"No. He had to see Goodbern after me, he had to work to schedule, he insisted."

"Then I will speak to her next. What did you talk about anyway?" Eubolo though was slapping his forehead in frustration.

"I am a dolt, my saying her name has reminded me. Goodbern wanted me to check for resistances in the warded rooms, to see for how long they could hold back that elven power, my head has more holes than a Vylantan cheese. Oh well there is always tomorrow. As for what Raiman was talking about it was his children mainly. It was also the prospects for the harvest on the mainland, the difficulty in getting clean straw for the floors, the best nails to use for different jobs, oh and the war against Arshuma, he had cousins fighting in it, I told him we had sent mages to help them out. It was all very convivial. He was in a very good mood, told me that the Gods were about to change his luck for the better. He obviously did not have my gift of foresight, so it seems."

"No he didn't. I wonder what cheered him so."

Eubolo shrugged his shoulders. "No idea, foresight it seems only stretches so far. He still moaned long and hard about having to work in the aquifer that night though. He hated it more than any other job on the island."

Gytha bit her lip. "He told you about his duties that night?"

Eubolo smiled, flashing his white teeth. "He hated the job so much I imagine he told everybody that came within ten feet of him."

****

The beast gnaws at Steven

When he was a boy, Steven's religious tutor had once told him about a pagan belief that inside every man or woman lived a beast. No one knew what the beast looked like for it dissolved upon the death of its host, but it was known that it fed upon the emotions of the host and that in turn, it excreted doubt, malice, and mischief. When one took secret delight in another's misfortune, that was the beast, when one wished a friend to do well in some endeavour, but not as well as oneself, it was the beast again. The beast fomented mistrust in others and sophistry in oneself, and it gnawed constantly, purposefully trying to sully moments of happiness or pleasure by instilling feelings of uncertainty or guilt. Well it was certainly gnawing at Steven right now.

The mood amongst his fellow knights and most importantly with Knight Commander Shadan was one of joyous relief. The Grand Duke was nearly here and the murderer, whose activities were so threatening to both the Duke's person and to the image of the knights protecting him, was supposedly dead. Steven had spent the last day or so trying to instil a sense of urgency into his colleagues, to tell them that they needed to stay alert, to keep their eyes to the shadows, but he had only been met by dutiful nods and blank faces. If he had told them that the killer was still at large they would not have believed him.

Of course he had never really believed that Kas was the killer, the beast had been gnawing at him from the moment they had found Miriam and the dead priest together (Kas' body was to wash up on the beach a day or so later). When Gytha had conveyed Miriam's words to him it was only giving solid foundations to his own vague uncertainties. He thought of Gytha again, the redhead with the fierce blue eyes, the laughing blue eyes, the passionate blue eyes, the gentle blue eyes, the woman that played upon his thoughts like a master musician plucking at the strings of his brain, a musician who plays by instinct rather than by design. Her voice, her laugh, her smell, her graceful movement, her intensity, they never left him, would they ever leave him he wondered? Such indelible thoughts were not for now though, if indeed they were for any time, he had to purge himself of them if he could. A Grand Duke was on his way, a fiend was on the loose, he was walking barefoot on smoking coals, and they were getting hotter by the second.

And now Shadan wanted to see him in person. He made his way to his superior's office, stopping only to admonish a couple of his men for lounging against a wall hanging, before finding himself standing proudly before a commander who, should caution not warn him against assumptions contrary to former observations of his character, could almost be described as happy.

"Steven!" the man boomed at him. "An auspicious day is it not? Nearly all our preparations completed and an eagle off our back with the death of our killer!"

Steven shifted uneasily. "About that particular matter sir. I do not think…."

"Tell me later man, I have brought you here for a specific purpose, to tell you something, something to your honour and profit indeed. Care to hear?"

"Of course sir."

"Very well. The Grand Duke will be here for what, three days to a week. Anyway, when he leaves I will be on the ship with him."

Steven was genuinely startled. "You sir? But what about your command? Why would you want to return to the mainland?"

"Because Steven, I am going to retire. Thirty-five years of service is enough for anybody. I need a rest, even if that rest is to be shared with Lady Shadan. I have maybe only spent six months of my life at my manor in the country. I plan to spend my latter years enjoying it there, riding in the forest, hunting with horse and falcon, and any other form of pursuit…."

"That keeps you away from Lady Shadan?"

"The nail had a broad head, but you have struck it like an expert smith. My replacement, when he is decided upon will be here early in the New Year, before your voyage to Crown Haven. Wonderful place Crown Haven, fruit orchards that smell so sharp and fragrant it makes your heart sing. Just avoid the olives. Anyway, you will see that between my departure and my replacements arrival there will be an interim period, a period with no one of my rank in charge. So Steven, are you ready to take command for that period, even if it is only for a few months?"

"Me sir? Are you sure?"

"Of course. An ample reward for your perspicacity. The men look to you in most things anyway, command will not be such a terrible burden to bear. Oh, and you are to be granted a manor, Riverholme, near the Erskon. Nice place, your good lady will love it. Now, if you will forgive me I wish to check the stairs and the harbour once more, if any knight has a trace of tarnish on their armour then they will wish they were facing an eternity on the furnace rather than five minutes of me, and this silver fruit knife."

A minute later Steven was walking back to his chambers to check on his daughter and give his wife the news that would surely complete her joy. At the door though he stopped. The beast was gnawing him again and it was Shadan's own words that were the cause.

An interim period. A period of transition. What was it about those words that tugged at his sinews so? What was it? What was so important about an interim period? What? What? What?

And then with a mental flash that replicated the flare of a sun clearing a bank of cloud he knew and understood. He turned and walked away from the door before leaving the chapter house entirely. He had a question to ask, one question of one particular person. Then he could return to his duties.

The only problem was that that person would be about as pleased to see him as a honey farmer in a bath would be to see a swarm of vengeful bees.

****

A curious bookshelf

Gytha was getting a distinct sense of déjà vu. Senior Goodbern's door was, just like Eubolo's, slightly ajar. So, just like she did with Eubolo she rapped loudly on the door and called the senior mages name. This time however there was no answer. She knocked again. Called again.

Nothing.

Gytha sighed and pushed the door wide enough so that she could see the entire room. She half expected Goodbern, like Eubolo, to be stood behind her desk, preparing for the day to come.

But she wasn't.

Her desk though was occupied. Upon it rested several broad wicker baskets from which the fragrance of lavender and mint was arising. Of course, Goodbern had told her so much yesterday, she was finishing off Caswell's little harvest, cutting herbs and flowers from the garden on the roof. That must be where she was now. The only question was should Gytha go after her or take a seat in the room and wait.

Go up on to the roof or wait? Go, or wait?

She decided to wait.

She perched herself on a low bench near to the desk that appeared to be covered in green satin cloth. It was not the most comfortable seat, but novice mages were quite used to such petty annoyances. Several senior mages believed that discomfort enhanced concentration and that a padded chair strewn with cushions only led to somnolence amongst the students. Senior Goodbern obviously adhered to such views.

Gytha looked around. She was a frost mage, Goodbern was a frost mage, but Gytha had rarely had tutorials in her room. Goodbern tended to teach those closest to graduation, give them a final push, that extra little bit of grounding in the subtleties of their art, enough to please the assessors, those who determined whether a mage was ready for graduation to senior status. No doubt in a couple of years Gytha would be sitting here on a regular basis but for the moment, much of the room was unfamiliar to her.

The room was rather like Goodbern herself, cheerful and no nonsense. It had a curious absence of dusty corners and idle clutter. Everything was clean, no books leaned at odd angles in their shelves, no piles of half-forgotten papers protruded untidily from half opened desk drawers. Everything sat where it belonged, order triumphed over chaos, Miriam would love this room.

In the north facing wall there was a window, leaded with thinner glass panes than the norm. An expensive window some three or four times larger than the one Eubolo had, Goodbern was after all, the head of her school and Eubolo's superior. Easing herself gratefully off the bench Gytha went up to it and peered through.

And saw the sea. Keth take her but what else did she expect? She looked down a little. The Childs' college was just under her and to her left, she could see its yard from here, the yard she had played in so many times as a youngster herself. Now though it was deserted, prayers, breakfast, and study all came before recreation, that yard would not be filled for some hours yet.

She stepped back from the window and pulled strands of rogue hair from her face. There was no sound in the corridor outside, no bustling footsteps as Goodbern returned to her rooms. Nothing. Gytha sighed, she had to admire the spirit of the woman returning to her duties so soon after receiving the injuries to her face and back. She would be stiff and sore for some time yet Gytha surmised, maybe she would not be bustling quite so much right now.

She was about to turn and sit back on her bench when she noticed the door just a few paces to her right, close to the window. That would lead to Goodbern's bedroom and from there, there would be another door leading to a tiny sluice room, like the one Beni had.

The door to the bedroom was right there and there was still no noise from the corridor outside. Was she bold enough? Just a little peek, what harm could it do? If she heard Goodbern outside then she would have ample opportunity to shut the door and return to her seat. Just a little peek, hardly excessive boldness from Gytha the bear strider.

The door swung open on superbly oiled hinges to reveal a room every bit as tidy and precise as the one behind her. Bed with covers neatly arranged, small cabinet next to the bed, carpet instead of straw, smaller window at the north wall under which was a small wooden seat, wall hanging between the washroom door and the north wall....

No books. Odd. The books used for teaching purposes were kept in the main room, but all senior mages had a private collection of books of their own, books they used for research or just to broaden their knowledge of their pet subjects. Yet there were none here. Gytha was perplexed for a moment before realising her error and smiling to herself.

They were behind the wall hanging. Where the edge of the hanging exposed the wall she could see some dark spaces, recesses of some sort, the perfect place to store one's books. The hanging itself was quite off-putting though entirely appropriate for the rooms of a frost mage. It depicted the mage god Lucan in his aspect of cold. A long, thin humanoid figure with skinny jointed limbs and bulbous aquamarine eyes, a prowling cadaver shrouded in a pall of icy mist it reminded her of the fresco surrounding the alcove where she had prayed for so long the other day. Lucan as a pale demon? An interesting inference. The hanging was certainly a sinister thing to behold. But then, Gytha concluded, was there any aspect of Lucan that was not sinister?

Again she went to shut the door and return to her bench and again she was being pulled in another direction. All scholarly professions, and mages were nothing if not scholarly, had a healthy curiosity about books and especially about books owned by other people. Gytha bit her lip, she shouldn't she thought but what harm would there be in a quick look? The knights would have searched Goodbern's rooms too and anything proscribed would have long since been removed.

Just a quick look then. Gytha opened the door behind her wide, all the better to hear any tell-tale footsteps, then she took a few steps forward, pulled the wall hanging back slightly and, being delighted that her suspicions were confirmed, and books were in the recesses, started to have a quick scan of the titles....

****

Illumination in a darkened room

"By all the thunders of Uttu, it is not you again! What can you possibly want with me now? The size of my feet, the length of my fingernails, what is left for you to know about me?" Librarian Beneshiel's response to seeing Steven stroll in and stand before her was nothing if not predictable.

"I promise I will not take up much of your time."

"Good," she said emphatically; "I am very busy this morning."

"So I see." Steven looked around the library, there were just two mages present, both with their noses in books, one of them was yawning. "You are positively buried by the press of flesh today."

"Do not be facetious sir knight. A librarian has many duties that do not involve interacting with those that attend this facility; besides, many mages are still at prayer."

"But not you."

She gave him a look of disdain, "I pray privately thank you."

"And the Gods obviously listen for here I am." He gave her a breezy smile, she gave him a low scowl, tipping back her cowl to give it greater emphasis.

"You have been seen on the ground floor a couple of times lately," he continued. "A rare thing for you, any particular reason?"

Beni stood and made a pretence of sliding scrolls neatly onto a nearby shelf. "A favour for Gytha. She asked me to offer words of comfort to one of the mages you had whipped. A young girl who will be permanently scarred, Gytha just thought that with my experience of such things I might be able to help her, and I am happy to do what little I can."

"This is Iska, the girl with the broken nose?"

"It is yes, she is recovering, walking about now, not that you have any interest in such matters."

"On the contrary librarian, I take an interest in the welfare of all mages here."

"Do you," her voice was still sour, "except for the ones you execute."

Steven's tone darkened at that. "He murdered two of my men, what would you have done with him?"

Beni remained silent.

"Anyway, I wanted to talk of another matter, is there somewhere we may speak privately?"

Her brown eyes met his, she saw their sombreness and nodded. "My rooms, but please be brief."

"I will, have no fear on that account."

Once in her room she sat on the bed and gestured for him to sit on the room's solitary chair. He stretched his legs out in an exaggerated manner before speaking again.

"My Knight Commander is retiring soon, once the Grand Duke leaves. There will be a replacement but until he arrives I will be assuming his duties."

"Congratulations." Her tone could not be flatter.

"Thank you. So you see I will be in charge for an interim period. Yet such an arrangement set me to thinking about another time such a situation may have been in place."

"What other time?" Beni yawned, her attempt to cover her face being utterly half-hearted.

"Well the librarian before you, erm Cob, Coba..."

"Cobbert."

"Yes Cobbert. She ended up with the healers yes? And you became the new librarian. Now did such a thing happen seamlessly or was there an interim period where no one was in charge?"

Beni looked at him questioningly. "Yes there was a gap, two to three months if I remember it right, but there were people in charge here, the day to day duties of the librarian, the filing of reports, the dealing with requests, all the sundry other duties, they were covered."

"By whom?"

"All the various schools of power nominated a representative, each one of them took turns to be responsible for the library for a few days."

"And the frost school, did they nominate a representative?"

Beni was looking thoughtful now. "They did yes."

"Do you know who it was?"

"Yes," she nodded at first, but then shook her head. "You do not think Kas was the killer?"

"No I don't. Can you give me the name?"

"I can, yes." She screwed her face up, her vexation obvious. "I had been thinking about such matters myself. But after recent events it makes no sense to suspect..."

"The name please," Steven spoke gravely. "Who was it, that for just a precious few days had free rein of the library? Who was it that could look at all its dark corners, embrace all its secrets, search the archive room at their leisure, maybe pick up a few precious elven documents and keep them till this day? Who was it that could take an impression of the keys and have them copied on the mainland, maybe by a loyal, well paid lay brother? Who was it in all the years since who could use those keys to access the archive room via the tower on the

332

roof, without giving you the faintest idea they were there, though maybe they wandered in here first, just to check your whereabouts before creeping into the archive room to study, or to steal? Who was it that has had years to study the missing parts of the elven journal, to learn the secrets of manipulating the spirit, to use it to kill for their own ends, who was it librarian Beneshiel? all I want is the name."

Beni stood, her shoulders were shaking slightly, her eyes were wide, her pupils dilated as the shock of Steven's words and the slow dawning of realisation finally hit her.

"Of course Sir Steven. Though I can scarce believe it. Though it makes no logical sense."

"Please!" he half-growled, half pleaded with her.

"Yes, yes," she swallowed to slake her dry throat, stood as tall as she could and met his gaze for the second time, though now her expression was one of both concern and growing alarm.

"It was Senior Goodbern."

46
A book finally reveals the truth

Gytha was rather enjoying this. She had pulled the wall hanging fully to one side now keeping it there through judicious use of both hip and foot. To keep her hair out of her eyes she had tied it with a small piece of string, that she kept with her for just such a purpose. Her reading string, she called it and the ponytail it had created fell over her shoulders and down her back in a silky russet plume. But the books were worth far more of her time than the surreptitious glances she could presently afford to give them.

In the current age, some three books out of five were printed. Most of the great monasteries of Tanaren and beyond had a near monopoly of printing presses, meaning that most books produced had some connection to the Artoran faith. The mage colleges had long argued that they too should build presses but as yet the church had successfully resisted such ideas, meaning that the colleges had to pay to get what they needed in print. Consequently, a lot of important works by mages for mages had to be replicated by hand, a job for the less magically talented graduate mage. Senior mages such as Goodbern would therefore commission certain works to be copied for them with the result that her private library consisted of an almost even balance of written and printed works, it also meant that it was a very eclectic collection indeed.

There were many books on history on the top recess, which was, of course, the thing that had drawn Gytha so successfully to the collection in the first place. Not all the titles were written on the covers, so she had to pull a few out and open them to see what exactly their topic was. Many were about Tanaren's early history, its foundation, and the part the noble Mesteia and Hartfield families played in it. There were some more about the bloody fifth century, a hundred years of civil war and kin strife. There was a thin tome entitled, "The migration of Kibil", about her own ancestors Gytha presumed and a more substantial work about the evolution of eastern Tanaren, often the most war torn part of the country and the place where the breakaway Artoran sect of the Fracht brotherhood had its most enthusiastic support. Some had illustrations, she was chafing to have a proper look at them all but was still acutely aware that there could be approaching footsteps in the outer corridor at any time.

The second recess consisted mainly of books discussing faith. She skipped through them quickly; after her possible punishment and subsequent delivery by the Gods just two days ago she was in no mood to glance at matters of theology. Amongst them though she did spot a tome on the pagan religions of the south where many people revered the Emperor of Koze as a God; interesting, but she had no time. There was also another, thinner work on "The beliefs of the Wyches and their devotion to Zhun, the one God", elven religion then, she was surprised that the work wasn't proscribed.

Finally, she had to crouch to look at the final recess and here, at last, were the books concerning all matters arcane. The recess was, unlike the others, chock full of books of all sizes with little empty space to speak of. Also unlike the other recesses, they were not put away neatly. In fact, it struck Gytha that this was the only untidy part of Goodbern's entire chambers. Some books were stored with the spine facing outwards, others with the pages facing her, some were even stored at an angle with corners poking out. The books here were either looked at frequently or just thrown there as an afterthought.

She looked at those where title or author was on display; the titles, "Expansion of the mind", "The power of prestidigitation", "Thaumaturgy and the Plane of Lucan", "Mastering the power of the mage God", "The frost mage in battle", didn't Beni have a copy of the last one? And the authors, Kurak of Belspina, Clavelly of Ygfal, Clantar of Krans, all redoubtable Chiran mages, but there were others too; Spanisgraza of Hashgeth, Ran-Katoul of Drecabensis for example, who had practiced their art well outside the empire. Gytha knew that most of the works here would be way over her head. It was time to leave.

She stood up stiffly and went to stretch and replace the wall hanging. As she did so however her leg caught one of the protruding book corners and in less than a moment a small pile of books slid from the recess into an untidy little heap on the floor.

"Shit," Gytha hissed through her teeth. She knelt, picked up the books and made to stuff them back where they came from, hoping that Goodbern would not notice that a new state of disarrangement had replaced the old.

She glanced quickly at some of the newly revealed titles, "The power within, how one mind can control another", "Mages as agents of the Gods", "The Arcane Wych, power lost to civilisation", "Lorens of Kibilchira, the greatest frost mage ever to stride this earth." Gytha grinned, Lorens of Kibilchira, his deeds and abilities were told to every budding frost mage as soon as they had left the Childs' College. She remembered the time…

Hold on, what was the book on top of it? She had replaced it where? Ah yes, there, she put her hand back into the recess and retrieved the tome, thin, handwritten, bound in leather, it was one of the older books in the collection.

She re read the title.

"The Arcane Wych, power lost to civilisation, by Immel of Anmir."

A vein in her temple started to pulse.

"The Arcane Wych, power lost to civilisation, by Immel of Anmir."

She tried to swallow, but her throat was suddenly very parched.

"The Arcane Wych, power lost to civilisation, by Immel of Anmir."

Suddenly a vague recollection was transformed into one of absolute clarity. This was the missing book. When both she and Beni had trawled the library looking for works that might shed light on the creation of blue fire this was the one book they couldn't find. Beni had said that there had been a fire in the archive room, and she presumed that this was one of the books that had been destroyed. But it hadn't been destroyed. It was here. And maybe the secret of blue fire lay within its pages. And if that was the case it meant that Goodbern…

No, no, no. That made no sense. Goodbern had been badly injured when Lipshin had died, and wasn't she with Kessie when Caswell had died too? That was the reason Gytha had never seriously considered her a suspect. Kessie said that Goodbern had walked in to see both her and Soma and that shortly afterwards Soma had collapsed because she had sensed the presence of the spirit. But perhaps Soma had been deceived somehow. Yes, of course, hadn't Eubolo just told her that the warded rooms might just hold the power back, delay it awhile? Come to think of it Tola had told her exactly the same thing in the caves; an apocryphal tale he had said, about a mage and a light spell, light that passed through a warded room after a few minutes giving this mage a chance to settle down to read first. Tola had said it was fanciful, so she had dismissed it as some sort of fable. But maybe she had done so rather too readily. Which would mean that Soma may have only sensed this power some time after it had been used. So Goodbern could have summoned the spirit then rushed to see Soma just as the power was seeping through the wards. And perhaps when Goodbern had gone in to see Lipshin in her cell all those papers she carried were only there to conceal something else. Something like a soul jewel….

"Oh Artorus preserve us," she breathed to herself.

Gytha shoved the remaining books back, released the hanging and made for the door. The book would not be on a proscribed list if it was thought destroyed, maybe there was nothing in it that controversial anyway. Also, if any other mage had seen it they would think nothing untoward about it, it was rather an obscure work in truth. The only mages who may have asked questions about it were Caswell, who was nearly blind, and Beni, who rarely left her library. It was effectively hidden in plain sight. Her mind was thumping, thumping so hard she only realised at that moment that she had ceased to listen for footsteps in the corridor.

She walked back into the main room shutting the door behind her.

A second later Goodbern entered the room through the external door.

Gytha had to think fast. She had no idea whether or not Goodbern had seen her in her private room, but she decided to tough it out and pretend she had never been there. She feigned a look through the window before turning to the senior mage with an expression that she hoped was one of shocked surprise and not, as she suspected, one of red faced embarrassment.

"Senior Goodbern, "she blustered, "your door was open, I thought I would wait here to…"

"Yes, yes," Goodbern said in her bustling manner, "help me with these first."

She was carrying three good sized baskets stacked on top of each other which, because of her relatively diminutive stature, reached right up to her nose. Gytha, who was almost a head taller than her superior rushed over and took the top two baskets, placing them gently on the main desk. They were both full of mixed green leaves and sprays of cut herbs of various colours. It would not be long before the aroma filled the room.

Goodbern did the same with the last basket before stretching her shoulders and grimacing.

"Do you need a rest senior? Is your back troubling you?"

"A little," Goodbern winced, "but two more trips should see everything gathered safely; actually no, if you assist me then we may be able to finish it in one. I take it you are here to ask me something?"

"Yes senior. I was just making enquiries as to what…"

"No matter, you can ask me on the roof. Behind the desk you will find the last of the empty baskets. Follow me with them, there's a good girl."

Gytha could hardly refuse. She found the baskets easily enough and started to traipse behind Goodbern out of her rooms and down the corridor, heading for the same hatchway on to the roof that she had gone through the day Caswell had died. Did Goodbern suspect her she wondered? Had she seen her in her room? If she had, then getting the two of them alone on the roof would give her the perfect opportunity to… Caswell had fallen off there had she not and Gytha did not have the ability to resist any force bolt that her powerful superior might fire at her. Gytha resolved to stay as far away from the edge of the roof as she could, and to keep Goodbern between her and the precipice, that way she could not be blasted over the edge by surprise. To do that she would have to get on to the roof first, ordinarily she would defer to the senior mage but just for once etiquette could go to the furnace. Picking up pace she soon ensured that she was a couple of steps ahead, an easy thing to do for Goodbern was labouring a little with her back.

On one of the benches lining the corridor, slumped with his head resting in his right hand, was Senior Mattris. He had red, rheumy eyes and had not shaved for some time. His robe too was stained with dark patches, possibly wine or some other equally potent liquid. It did seem that he was waiting for Goodbern to approach though for he hailed her and even stood and bowed slightly as she stopped in front of him.

"Senior," he said, his voice was tired, bleary, defeated yet he still seemed keen to talk. "I would just like to say that I am ready to resume my duties, I can start again tomorrow if need be."

"Good. We are rather desperate for your help, anybody's help. The new intake from the Childs' college arrives within the week and a few of them are said to have potential in our field. How is your head?"

"Throbbing. But I have drunk everything of note in my room. It has not helped; I miss her far more than I ever thought possible."

Goodbern nodded, "we all do. She will be hard to replace."

Mattris clenched his teeth. "She will be impossible to replace. At least she will for me. I will just sit here a little longer, let my head clear, then I will start preparing tutorials; for what year might I ask?"

"Three and four, I will let you back in gently, you can do the tens and elevens like Gytha here once you are fully back in the fold."

He whistled tunelessly; his teeth still clenched tightly. "Back in the fold, how appropriate. Just like a sheep indeed, do you not agree Gytha?"

Gytha just shrugged her shoulders, feeling a little awkward at the question. Mattris gave her a wicked grin before easing himself back onto the bench. "See you both later," he drawled.Gytha stepped forward, took his hand, and gave it a squeeze. She couldn't think of anything to say but it turned out there was no need. He looked at her again, this time his eyes were watery with tears. "Thank you," he said, in a halting, choked voice.

Gytha turned and sped after the retreating Goodbern, soon she was two steps ahead of her again.

And, just as she had planned she was first on to the roof, not an easy feat when hurrying and carrying baskets. Once up there she set the baskets down and offered Goodbern her hand, which was accepted. Her hand was much colder than Gytha's. The ascent then complete Gytha gathered up the baskets and hurried over to the pots that were sitting under their flapping awnings with all the disinterest of a bunch of soldiers on sentry duty. Goodbern joined her a moment later and as she busied herself in picking up one of the baskets Gytha looked at the distance between herself and the edge of the roof. It would take power of godlike dimensions to topple her over there now.

"Caswell so enjoyed her bit of gardening. I always think of her when I come up here." Goodbern was stood right next to her and in her hand was a knife fully capable of eviscerating Gytha with one deft slice. Gytha took a step back before realising that if Goodbern was the killer, then she would not use a method of execution that would mark her out as so obviously guilty. "It is not the best tool for this," the senior mage admitted, mistaking Gytha's fixated stare, "but it was the only one I could find. Right, I shall start over here, you hold the basket while I cut, then you can ask me your questions."

Gytha obeyed as Goodbern moved to a place where the herbs were still unlopped, fronds swaying in the breeze. It was a mild day, bright and clear with apologetic streaks of cloud splashed over a pallid sky. Gytha held the basket low as Goodbern began to cut, all the easier for her to place the harvest in the basket as she worked. Goodbern hummed tunelessly to herself, obviously waiting for Gytha to ask her questions, Gytha therefore had to oblige.

"All that it is senior," she spoke, hoping against hope that her nerves would not show in her voice. "Is that I am trying to reconstruct what Brother Raiman did, who he spoke to on the day he died, before he went into the aquifer."

"Any particular reason? I thought these matters were long put to bed."

"They have been," Gytha said hastily. Too hastily. "It is just that Sir Steven wanted me to tie up the ends of any open threads remaining. I have to write a report you see, so all these little details have to be pursued."

Cut, cut, another frond in the basket. "And you think he spoke to me?"

"Senior Eubolo told me as much."

"Yes." Goodbern stopped for a moment, her face vague. "Yes, that is right he did come and see me. I used to give him quite a lot of work I suppose."

"What job did you have for him senior? It was not on his schedule. And did he talk about anything? Any subject at all?"

The cutting resumed. "The chandelier in my room. I wanted it taken down and polished, all the spider webs and caked in soot removed. He said he would do it in the morning, but of course he never got the chance. And I still need the work done. As for the job not being on his schedule, I had only badgered him about it earlier that morning, so there was no way it would have been written down."

"Yes, that makes sense. And what did he talk about?"

"His family, his lack of money, the usual subjects for him..."

"He had quite a lot of mouths to feed I believe."

Chop, cut, chop. "Yes, five or six. Most of the time they lived on the mainland, but they did come to see him once, he even introduced them to me, lovely children, clean and polite, I had a ball made from Wanysai rubber that I gave to them. They loved the way it bounced. So sad, for the children I mean, I hadn't really thought of it that way before." She stopped cutting again, looking almost wistfully at the sky. "The lay brothers lack education, but they can have families. Have you ever wanted children Gytha?"

She had not expected that. "I... well..."

"I wanted children. Lots of them. I had a man once, but he died. I was pregnant too, a long time ago, just like you were..."

Now Gytha was startled. Was there anybody who didn't know her "secret"? "You know about that? I thought..."

"Yes I know." Chop. "You were fourteen, I was a little older. Same outcome for us both, and the same abortionist. I was the first one Caswell... attended to in that manner."

More herbs in the basket. It was beginning to get heavy. "I had not realised I was so young," Gytha mused, "and Caswell, it sounded like..."

"I never fully forgave her? Yes, you could say that. I believe you were grateful for what was done to you. I was not. I had mine administered at the point of a knight's sword."

Gytha felt feverish, hot, and shivering cold by rapid turns. Could she dare voice her thoughts at this juncture? It could put her in so much danger, but then, maybe she already was.

"Is that why Caswell was selected senior?"

Goodbern stopped then. She turned and gave Gytha the strangest of looks. "Whatever do you mean girl?"

"I," hesitation, "I only regretted what Caswell did to me because of my age, a year or two later and I am sure I would have resented it more. I came from a large family, having children around feels natural to me, so yes I would like children if that answers your question. And yes I understand the role that Caswell played in that regard, and I see that it is a necessary one, but..."

"Is it really? Why can we not have children?"

Goodbern was looking at her appraisingly, it seemed to be a discussion she was profoundly interested in. She set her knife down next to one of the pots.

"Well senior," Gytha said slowly, "a parent with the gift..."

"Taint. Many outsiders call it a taint."

"Well a parent with our powers has a greater risk of passing it on to their children."

"Granted. It is a greater risk but even then it is still only a small one. Research done in Koze of all places show that the chances of passing our powers on to our children is less than one in five. One in five Gytha, and because of that we are forced to abort that which is formed by the most natural instinct a woman can possess, the need for a child. I am too old now by blessed Elissa, but it is still an issue I can keep fighting for, maybe one day things will change, for your generation perhaps or the generation after you."

"Fight for?" Gytha asked. "You mean through the Order of Jedrael."

"Ha!" Goodbern roared. "So you know about that! You are a smart girl, frost mages are always the smart ones, Steven chose you well indeed. The order is the only way mages can fight for what they want, and of course the order has been declared illegal for that reason. Resentment is like a bucket that collects rainwater, the longer that it sits on the ground, the older that it gets, the more water that collects in it. I am fifty now and my bucket is brim full, just as yours will one day be."

Gytha swallowed. She too set her basket down and flexed both hands into balls to get feeling into her fingers. "Senior Goodbern, we know Kas did not kill Brother Raiman, Senior Caswell, Senior Lipshin, and Sir Benet."

"Oh I know that!" Goodbern said dismissively. "It is why you are here is it not, to accuse me of those crimes. I did see you coming out of my bedroom Gytha, guilt and fear written all over you in letters of fiery divine ichor, I know the book you saw, and I know you must have drawn your conclusions over it. You think I am the killer, that I command the spirit to my will. Please answer me honestly, you have acted creditably, and with no little acumen up till now, please do not spoil it with evasiveness."

Goodbern was fixing her with the sort of stare a snake uses to mesmerise its prey. "Yes senior," was Gytha's dry throated response; "I think you killed those people, and now can you show respect for my seemingly astute behaviour and answer me with the same measure of candour. Are you the murderer we have been seeking these last days?"

"Yes." Goodbern said, with the lightness of voice people used to discuss the weather, or the harvest, or the price of bread made from poor, damp grain. "I am that person. And now I suppose you have many more questions?"

Gytha could not feel her legs, her throat was dry as wind blasted sand. "Yes senior, I do."

"Then ask them quickly, for I obviously have little time for idle words."

Gytha nodded acceptingly, then she began to ask.

****

Drip theory explained

"Why do you want me to come with you?"

"Because I do not know where Gytha is, so until I do you can be mage liaison officer."

"But I don't want to be!"

"Neither did Gytha."

Beni emerged from her room, keys in hand, Steven following just behind her, she was shaking her head at him, he was just shaking his head.

At the library door though she stopped and turned to face him. "Do you really think it could be Goodbern? I mean after the injuries she sustained?"

He shrugged his shoulders. "Who knows? Only she can tell us, and it is not just Lipshin and Benet's deaths that remain a mystery. When Senior Caswell died Goodbern was with the mage Soma, who detected the magic being used through the walls of a warded room. How could Goodbern summon this spirit in front of witnesses?"

"A warded room?" Beni peered at him; her dark eyes were inquisitive. "Yes."

"You are unfamiliar with drip theory? It has been proposed by several eminent mage scholars, the possibility that power travels at different speeds through different mediums, just like water or any other liquid."

"Well can you give me a brief overview?"

"You wish me to adumbrate it for you?"

He looked at her caustically, "Senior Beneshiel, I am well aware that in both intelligence and learning, you are far ahead of this humble soldier, so can you just go ahead and tell me exactly what you are talking about."

She fluttered her eyelids and smiled at him, "would you have guessed that I used to be a terrible flirt?"

"Used to be?"

She pulled her cowl back up. "Sorry, I forget how I appear sometimes. Now, imagine you have a piece of porous rock, chalk or limestone for example, and a large bucket of water. If you hold the rock up and start to pour the water will pass quite freely either side of the rock whilst, at least initially, the rock itself acts as a barrier to it. You think it impervious but then suddenly the water starts to seep through, and then it starts to pour through. That which you thought was a barrier was in fact something that could only resist for a while. Now Soma has an affinity for this spirit power, and she reacted when she finally felt it. You thought that it passed straight through the wards but what if the wards were like the piece of limestone, that it held the power back for a while before finally it flooded through the stonework. So Soma did feel the spirit rise..."

"But not at the time it actually happened."

Beni nodded.

"Keth's fire. Goodbern cast her spell, killed Caswell then went to see Soma, and Soma reacted in all innocence thinking that the spirit was abroad at that moment, when in fact..."

"It had been summoned and had killed some minutes before."

Steven gave a low, tuneless whistle." Would Gytha have known about this drip theory?"

Beni shook her head. "As I remember it is only taught in the months before a mage tries to graduate, so probably not."

They left the library and stood in the corridor, Steven put a concerned hand on the mages shoulder, Beni did not try to pull away. "Lock the door and wait here for me, I will be a matter of moments."

"Where are you going?"

"To strap on my breastplate and get my sword, I have a horrible feeling they might be needed."

****

A logical explanation for madness

The vein in her temple was pounding as Gytha spoke. She could sense the power in Goodbern and though the senior mage seemed not a jot concerned by her own confession Gytha knew that something was going on in her mind, that a plan had formed and was just waiting for its moment.

"So senior, I take it Raiman was trying to extort money from you." All her attempts to keep her voice as neutral as possible where failing by now, her words were as tremulous as a fledgling's wing.

"Not from me, from the order," Goodbern corrected her. "Raiman was a good man, a faithful servant for many years, it was Raiman that got the library keys copied for me. Unfortunately, he fell under the influence of Havel, who was a beast. Involving him was a terrible mistake. We needed a strong man to excavate the tunnels but should have given more thought to the type of strong man to recruit. He was obviously marked for death but Kas, Gods give her peace, got to him first and did the job for us."

"So after fixing shelves for Eubolo, Raiman came to you, demanded money, then told you he would be in the aquifer that night?"

"Yes. He wanted payment the following day but when he told me he would be in that cave, alone, for a good part of the night I knew exactly who my first victim would be."

Goodbern's tone was so casual, so conversational, it would have been easy for Gytha to think she was having a one on one tutorial, as opposed to being alone, with a murderer, on the college roof. "So tell me please, why now, why pick these last days to start this spree of killing? I am guessing you must have seen the elven journal a good while ago and copied the parts you needed so what prompted you to murder in this way and at this time?"

"Now that," Goodbern pointed a pudgy finger in Gytha's direction; "is a complex question. You see, before Beneshiel became librarian a group of us took turns to look after the general business of the library. I was in charge for a meagre six days, but they were six days that would change many a life here."

"Or end it."

"Sadly, yes. At the time the order was tasking me to research matters related to elven power in Tanaren so naturally when I was given the library keys the first subject I looked to was just that. I found the book that detailed the creation of blue fire on my first day, I found the elven journal in the archive room on my last. I was enthused when I saw it so I quickly made a mould of the keys I needed so I could return at leisure. We were searched you see, the temporary librarians, the temptation to spirit away a book of particular interest is strong in us all, so I couldn't steal anything.

Once the keys were copied though it was a different matter. I could access the archive room through the south east tower door, here on the roof, without ever broaching the library floor. Whilst I had charge of the library I hid the book in the archive room along with some others of little value or consequence. When I had the keys though I started a small fire, burnt those inconsequential tomes and smuggled out the book on blue fire over the roof. That way Beneshiel, who was inexperienced back then, would never know what books were missing and what were destroyed, as far as she knew, the book on blue fire had gone up in smoke.

The elven journal though was stored in a trunk and catalogued, so I could not fake its disappearance. Instead I contented myself with stealing parts, translating them, then returning them at my leisure. The only original part I kept, and it is still hidden in my rooms, was the part giving details on how to summon and bind the elven spirit protecting the caves far beneath us. I did not want to share that knowledge with anybody, not even the order."

"So the Order of Jedrael is not involved in the spirit murders?"

"No. I acted unilaterally, and not for the benefit of the order. You see, in the intervening years I acquired another benefactor, one who shared my vision on the way the spirit could be used. I wrote to him you see, because I believed that the spirit had great potential, military potential, and he agreed with me. But he wanted proof, two demonstrations of its use. Raiman and Caswell were those demonstrations. You see I only mastered the technique, only acquired the ability to control the spirit quite recently, after years of research. That was when I wrote to this person."

The wind was picking up. It swirled around Gytha, making her shiver, she pulled her robe tightly about her shoulders. "So you killed Caswell because of what she did to you in the past? That was the sole reason that you selected her for death?"

Goodbern shook her head. "No. Not just that. One of my victims had to be a mage you see, that was specifically requested. I was going to choose Halpin as he was the oldest, but Caswell had spent many hours with me as of late moaning about her eyesight, the loss of her faculties, her growing helplessness."

"So you put her out of her misery, like a lame horse?"

Goodbern nodded. "Also, and this was something quite out of my control, she had found the elven journal herself and wanted to research it, but before researching it she wanted to discuss it in depth with me. I obliged her but after we had talked, when she left me alone I realised that I may have compromised myself. Some of my answers were too specific, too pertinent, too relevant to a journal I had purportedly never seen before. Caswell thought slowly, but forensically, I knew that in due course I might get some awkward questions off her, so I did what I had to do. Then, when she was dead I rushed to her room and stole those parts of the journal which, to my memory, mentioned blue fire and spirit binding. I didn't want to give the investigators such obvious clues after all."

"I see," Gytha was thinking hard; "now I understand why she wrote down a comment about the arrogance of mages, I think it may have been beginning to dawn on her that you knew more than you were telling. But the thing that always pointed to your innocence was that Kessie swore she was with you when Caswell died and Kessie doesn't lie. Was there something wrong with the wards in Soma's room? I have heard from a couple of sources that wards may not be the impervious barriers we novices are told they are."

"Novice Kestine didn't lie. But she was mistaken. I summoned the spirit from my room, then when that business was finished I rushed as fast as I could to see her and Soma at the warded room. And you are right about our wards, elven power can seep through them like water through a sponge. So there was a delay you see in my summoning the spirit and Soma sensing it, only a few minutes, but it was enough. It was pure serendipity on my part, it could not have worked out better for me. The wards held the power away from Soma just long enough for me to have witnesses as to my innocence!"

"You were fortunate."

"Say rather that the Gods were with me."

"The dark Gods maybe."

"But why Gytha, why? For you have yet to ask the most important question."

Gytha tried to swallow, to slake her arid throat, but with little effect. "You mean, who is your benefactor?"

"Exactly."

"I will ask in a moment. Firstly though, why Lipshin? You had your two victims already so why? To me it looked like a killing arranged in haste and in panic, so what drove you to it?"

A spasm of what appeared to be regret briefly passed Goodbern's face.

"Sometimes when you start things the consequences are difficult to foresee. Like kicking a stone off a mountain top, a stone that starts an avalanche. I knew about her escape plans, that she was sending letters to Old City for she was using the infrastructure of the order to do so. Now, I knew that at some point you would hazard the caves, oh and by the way I thought the guardian spell I set down there would stop you or even kill you. I had put it there to stop Havel plundering the elven treasures, most of which we probably still have to discover, and I thought no one could breach it. I had not reckoned on you taking Tola with you. His death was not my doing either, the spirit was fulfilling its original purpose in defending itself and the secrets of its people, I did not summon it. I still wonder why it left you alive too, perhaps it thought you not powerful enough to bother with."

"Perhaps," Gytha admitted. She did not tell Goodbern of her exchange with Sinotaneh, it had long been noticeable to her that she had yet to call the spirit by her true name, "anyways, you were talking about Lipshin."

"So I was, so I was. Whilst she was teaching or rolling around with Mattris somewhere I took one of her "secret" letters and placed it in a cave I knew you would access. A diversion for you, one to keep you off my scent. And it worked did it not?"

Goodbern took up her knife again and began ferreting around in the soil held in the pots, digging out the roots of some plants, cutting them and transferring them to a nearby basket.

"However, after the execution of that young fool Oskum she came into my room and confronted me angrily. Several schools of magic were composing letters to Greville to protest about mistreatment she said, why were we not doing the same? I, for obvious reasons, did not want to draw attention to myself in such a manner and tried to calm her down. A next to impossible task. Her arguments became more general, her grievances wider. Finally, she told me someone was pilfering from her room, though obviously she did not say what was being pilfered. Now, I am not the best at hiding my emotions and she must have read something in my expression, some tic of some sort for she screwed up her face and asked; "was it you?" I denied it then, but I could see she was unconvinced. Then, shortly afterwards she was arrested and sent to the cells. Given time to think, just like Caswell, she may well have come up with some obvious conclusions, especially when you confronted her about that self-same letter and told her where you had found it."

Gytha shook her head. "You were wrong, senior, she thought the letter was still in her room. Whatever she thought was being pilfered, it wasn't that."

Goodbern grunted, "now that is annoying, maybe she was referring to her hidden stash of coin then. No matter, after our argument I could sense she suspected me."

She was about to talk," Gytha nodded sadly. "We were going to see her again after you had spoken to her. She would have told us everything."

More roots were thrown into the basket. "So I did what I had to do, not what I wanted to do. You accused me of acting in panic earlier and you were absolutely right, I was desperate to silence her. As soon as she was imprisoned I tried to summon the spirit but the wards in the cells interfered with my mage sight, I could not control or direct the spirit from afar like I had before. This task had to be done face to face. So I tried to see her immediately afterwards, but the knights stopped me, said that she would be interviewed in the morning. So I asked them to notify me when you were going to see her and to my immense relief, they did. I bundled up the necessary papers and hid the soul jewel in my robes along with a sharp stone. The plan was to kill Lipshin, then draw the stone across my forehead where the blood produced would far exceed the severity of the wound. I would say that the spirit had hurled me against the wall before disappearing, but things did not quite go to plan. Firstly, a knight was stationed with us, so he had to go too; secondly, I had to talk to Lipshin, distract her whilst simultaneously summoning the spirit."

"Is summoning the spirit no easy task?"

"Oh the summoning is easy enough, you just stroke the gem and transfer a little of your power into it, it is the control afterwards that is the problem for the spirit has its own will and it struggles against you constantly. So I summoned it and ordered it to kill both of them quickly, which it did. However, because my thoughts were also on other matters, because I was taking a risk and was stressed, I did not have full control of it, and so it turned on me. It killed the others expediently because it wanted to devote itself fully to my demise. I had to do something quickly.

I had already cut my head with the stone as the knight died. He was brave, he conquered his obvious fear and tried to defend Lipshin, I do regret what had to happen to them. Anyway, when I first summoned the spirit I sensed a crackle in the wards in the cell walls and door. The power I had used had stirred them, but it was not enough to set them off. So it gave me an idea. As the spirit came for me I turned my back and called a lot more power to me. It set off the wards then alright, my back is still feeling the effects. More importantly it made the spirit banish itself without taking my life. To control it properly you need full concentration, you cannot do two things at the same time."

Gytha took a moment to ponder Goodbern's words. "So Raiman and Caswell were demonstrations, Lipshin and Sir Benet died to keep us off your scent. Yet senior, there is one thing that still makes no sense to me at all."

"Go on, I thought I had explained my motives with clarity."

"You have. Yet your thinking seems flawed. For however slowly the investigation progressed, however many times Steven and I stumbled down paths with dead ends, ultimately we had to find you. This is an island, there is nowhere to run here, nowhere to hide. A great many of our initial suspects are dead, we had to get to you in the end. For all your subtlety we were bound to find you."

The next plant she pulled up had little roots to speak of, Goodbern wrinkled her nose in annoyance before discarding it. "Oh I know you had to find me eventually, I just had to delay it long enough, that is all."

"Long enough for what?"

"For the Grand Duke to arrive. I was so close too, he might arrive today, he might arrive tomorrow, I just had to keep you off me for one or two more days. I thought Kas' death might have done it for me but alas, we are having this conversation just a little too early."

Gytha put her hand to her mouth. "So you are going to kill the Grand Duke!"

Goodbern stopped her gardening. She set down her knife again and looked at Gytha with both incredulity and no little exasperation. "Oh and you were doing so well, to get so close and be so wide of the mark at the last moment. Kill the Grand Duke? And bring the wrath of a thousand armies down on our heads? Granted the Order of Jedrael might wish for such a thing, a war to assert our power over the non-gifted, but as I told you, all this was not done for the order but for myself, for my benefactor and ultimately for my country."

And then Gytha realised. And her head pounded with the realising, and her breath became short, and her skin became flushed. "You are saying that your benefactor and the Grand Duke…"

"Are one and the same yes. Everything I have done here has been done on royal command."

47
Waiting

"She is not here. Disappointing." Steven stood in Goodbern's room looking idly through the same window Gytha had regarded the world from not long earlier.

"Well no, but you can guess where she is right now surely?" Beni asked, "the baskets on the desks..."

"And the smell yes. Lovely fresh smell. I presume she is on the roof gathering more." Steven turned to look inwards again, to look at Beni who was picking through the contents of the basket with interest, "so that is where we had better be headed. Come on."

He made for the door, but Beni stiffened as he passed her. He stopped. "Problem?"

"You know there is. This is where we part company. You know I cannot go onto the roof."

"Cannot is the wrong word librarian. Will not is more apt I feel."

She shook her head. "You are wrong. I just can't do it. I have been to the ground floor several times these last days and each time the effort of will required causes me actual physical pain. The roof is a stretch too far for me. I am sorry, you will need another mage liaison for this."

He seemed to accept her protest. He sat at the low, uncomfortable bench and stretched out his long legs. "Well in that case we had better wait here, I am sure she won't be too long."

"Thank you," Beni said. Finding a well-padded stool she perched herself daintily on it, facing Steven from a distance of several feet.

And together they waited for Goodbern to return.

****

A chilling proposition

There was a somewhat brief, but very shocked silence. Goodbern took a moment to sense Gytha's discomfiture before continuing to speak.

"Let me give you some background regarding all this. A lot of my family have been caught up in the war with Arshuma. I had two younger brothers, there were just four years between all three of us. When the war started a lot of Tanaren was quickly overrun, including the town where they both lived. They fled with their families but subsequently both of them joined the muster to fight back and regain their homes. Now they are both dead, killed in battle by an Arshuman axe or spear, no funerals, nothing more than food for worms. Even worse, a nephew, one I had never got to see was burned alive when they razed his village. Now, a lot of us here want to join the war effort, want to fight back but thanks to the mage college treaties only a tiny amount of us will ever get the chance to do so at any one time, and only then if the government treasury pays the enormous fee. The only way I would get to serve would be if I had an idea to give us an edge in the war."

Gytha looked perplexed. "You would use the spirit? But how exactly would a spirit be able to defeat a whole army?"

Her basket was full, Goodbern moved to where Gytha had placed the others, picked one up and resumed her work. "Imagine two armies at camp, facing each other the night before battle. Say the Arshumans had their king there, or a general, or a mage. The spirit could be summoned, seen by nobody, and made to assassinate this person in the dead of night. When dawn came all they would see was a dead king planted with the mark of Xhenafa. Soldiers are far more superstitious than mages, imagine the effect on morale, their army would be on the run within the hour."

"But your actions would violate every treaty ever drawn up by the colleges," Gytha protested. "Even I know that using the spirit of a dead being would be classed as necromancy and necromancy is illegal, well... everywhere."

Goodbern nodded sagely. "It would have to be kept secret, if anybody found out then we could well end up with the Chiran empire and half the known world fighting us. Nevertheless, when I wrote to the Grand Duke he was receptive to the idea, it would after all be near impossible to prove that unsanctioned magic had been used by us if the only person to see the spirit was dead. As to why I only wrote to him recently, well, it took me years to perfect the control technique, so many of my free hours were spent in warded rooms practising, getting frustrated, barely escaping with my life at times. But it was all worth it."

"But you have been caught now, and if the Grand Duke's letters to you were found..."

"Burned, all burned. None of this can be traced back to him. He never signed them anyway, nor did he use his seal."

"I see," Gytha sucked at her lip; "so his visit here, purportedly to see Greville, is actually to see you and check that your... plans are viable."

"And before he leaves," Goodbern said gleefully, "he will announce that another mage will be joining the war. Furthermore, when I get back here afterwards the Grand Duke will encourage Greville to stand down as Chief Magister..."

"And you will succeed him," Gytha finished the sentence.

"I will. There are presently about half a dozen men in line for the job before me but if the Grand Duke commands, then that job will fall to a woman. You yourself must surely see the benefits of that."

Gytha nodded, how could a murderer be so plausible? She had expected a maniac, not somebody explaining their crimes away with calm reasoning. "So my discovering your misdeeds has scuppered things for you?"

Goodbern continued working, not even looking Gytha's way. "Maybe. Once the Grand Duke arrives of course you would never make any charges count against me. He is bringing sealed letters of protection with him, meaning I could never be tried for the murders here, Kas will get the blame and the whole affair will be quietly dropped. Until he gets here though I admit I am vulnerable. So, I am going to make a proposal, one you would be wise to accept, if you love your country that is."

Gytha decided to be awkward. "The war really isn't in my part of Tanaren..."

Goodbern laughed uproariously at that. "I see you still cling to the beliefs and traditions of your long annexed country. Think girl, think. There is no "right" part of Tanaren. Lose the east and sooner or later it will be the turn of your people to feel the bite of an Arshuman blade. Our cause is the same in this matter, as well you know."

"Very well. What is your proposal? What do you want me to do?"

"What do I want you to do? Why nothing. You help me carry these things back to my rooms, then you return to your cell and forget about everything that has happened. As far as everybody is aware the killer has been killed in turn. You are a hero. Let me proceed with my plan. Let me help win this war. Let the Grand Duke come here and let me speak with him. That is all."

"And what of Sinotan...I mean the spirit?"

"I will destroy the jewel when the war is over. In truth I will have no further use for it anyway."

"Why do you say that?" Gytha queried.

"Because every time I summon it I have to undergo a mental duel with it. It is acting against its purpose you see. Its role was to protect the caves from plunderers. It has been quite successful in that; many secrets still remain to be discovered. Its role was not to kill those against whom it holds no enmity, those people who have never attempted to despoil the legacy of its people. I have to force it to kill and every time I do so I alter it slightly, change it from its original form, turn it into something...darker. When I called it forth to kill Lipshin I barely recognised it in truth. It used to sing...but there was no song last time. I have maybe half a dozen more uses from it, after that it will no longer be viable."

This didn't sound good. "Viable? Why ever not?"

"Because eventually it will cease to have consciousness, the memory of what it was. It will become a mindless wraith, a spirit of malice and spite, and then it will no longer respond to my commands. Destroying the jewel then will banish it from this world forever."

"But she will have no memory of her people, she will never be able to re-join them. All those she loved, fought for, all that has sustained her this whole time will be taken from her."

Goodbern was dismissive. "But it will have no mind. There will be no "loss" as such because it will have nothing to remember, you cannot pine for that which you cannot recall. As I said, all it will be is malice. Sad, but just think of it as another victim of this war, maybe even its final victim."

"I see," Gytha whispered, "and what if I reject your proposal?"

"You are no fool girl," Goodbern snorted; "try and arrest me and I will be forced to defend myself, a novice against the head of a school of magic, think about that if you have to. Now what do you say, is my proposal accepted or not?"

Goodbern was looking at her as though her answer was a foregone conclusion. Gytha caught her breath. So much of what Goodbern had said made sense, albeit in a detached, cold, ruthless sort of way. Refuse and Goodbern would probably kill her, though any knight finding Gytha dead up here, murdered by frost magic would probably arrest Goodbern as a matter of course. So perhaps she was bluffing. Yet, perversely, and because of Goodbern's lucidity, Gytha started to think about accepting the proposal. The war was indeed a terrible one, a lot of people in the college had lost family to it over its ten horrific years, and if indeed the east of Tanaren fell the rest of the country could well collapse too, Goodbern was certainly right on that matter. All Gytha had to do was walk away. All she had to do was let one of the mildest, most inoffensive mages on the island be remembered as a mass murderer. All she had to do was break an oath she had sworn to an elf that had been dead for seven centuries. That was all she had to do. War had many casualties and perhaps her conscience would become one of them, sacrificed out of necessity, out of a desire to win this terrible conflict. Gytha thought long and hard, fixed Goodbern with one of her more intense stares.

And finally she gave her answer.

A drunkard brings terrible news

"So it is called drip theory then." Steven was in a playful mood.

"Yes it is." Beni was not in a playful mood.

"Does the word "drip" refer to the properties of magic or to the person who formulated the theory?"

She gave him a sideways look. "Several people have postulated similar works on the nature of resistances, I am sure that not all of them have attained your measure of muscular pre-eminence. Though I am not sure if it is a good thing when muscle starts replacing brain, as has clearly happened in your case."

"But isn't the brain a type of muscle?"

"No."

"But there are similarities, if you do not use your muscles they shrivel and atrophy and if you do not use your brain…"

"Well, you would be far more of an expert on that subject than I."

Steven flashed her a toothy smile. "You know; I am still struggling to find what it was that used to make you so irresistible to men…"

"I never used to say "no". That was about it."

"You are exaggerating."

"I wish I was," she said sadly.

At that moment the door started to creak open. They both looked up, expecting to see Goodbern struggle in carrying baskets laden with greenery. Instead it was Mattris who stared at them with red, overtired, eyes. "Oh, I heard voices, I thought Goodbern was back, I wanted to ask her a couple of things regarding my tutorials tomorrow."

"Oh Matt," Beni sighed, "you look terrible, like you haven't slept in a while."

"Come closer and smell my breath, you will get your answers there. Anyhow, when they both come back can you let me know? I will be in my room moving papers about, by that I mean I will be picking them up off the floor, the ones I haven't vomited on at least."

"Both?" Steven asked, "someone was with her?"

"Yes, Gytha. They went up onto the roof together. Just let me know, if it is not too much trouble. Wouldn't mind a chat Beni, later on, if you don't mind. Need to say sorry and stuff, who says alcohol doesn't make you a better person?" and with that he was gone.

Steven half leapt out of the chair. "We need to move, Gytha might be in trouble!"

Beni though remained seated; her expression was suitably anguished.

"The roof Steven... I... Please, just take Matt with you."

"He is pissed!" Steven half roared at her. He came over to where she was sitting and knelt in front of her, putting out his hands and gently holding her face, forcing her to look at him. "Librarian, you have told me on more than one occasion that Gytha is a friend. Now that friend might be in serious trouble. I cannot do this alone; I need a mage with me. I need you. Gytha needs you. If you want me to say it, I will say it, that I rather admire you in an odd sort of way but that I feel sorry for you even more, all those years a prisoner in that candlelit gloom. But now you have no better cause to try and free yourself at last. Help us both. Come with me, I am happy to help you in return if I can."

She stared at him for a moment with wet, startled eyes. Then she slowly stood and curled her slender fingers around his open hand. "Don't let go of me," she whispered.

"I will not."

And hand in hand, they left Goodbern's chambers and headed towards the hatch leading to the roof.

****

Sinotaneh

"What you are saying." Gytha spoke very measuredly, very deliberately, for she knew the importance of every word she was about to utter, Goodbern after all could probably kill her with ease. "Is that we are in a war and that the people you have killed were casualties in that war. War after all demands sacrifice..."

"Yes," Goodbern agreed, "four victims, lives lost to save many more, I just wish it had been two, Lipshin was too shrewd for her own good."

"You say that there were four victims, senior, but I think you are not seeing everything as you should. You see, once Caswell was dead people started to see Xhenafa in every shadow; they were frightened, and fear leads to irrationality. Without Caswell's death there would have been no escape attempt and so Sir Beverley, Sir Welton, Senior Oskum and Dicken the healer would all be alive now too. We would not have attempted the caves so Tola would still be with us. Arbagast died because your experiments were causing that strange artefact to drain power from him and led him to believe his abilities were fading. He stumbled upon Kas and Havel and so indirectly the deaths of Arbagast, Kas, Havel and young Gideon the priest can also be attributed to your summoning the spirit. And let's not forget the spirit too, for she will become another victim if things continue as they are. That is over a dozen dead Senior Goodbern, a dozen

355

that would still be with us if it were not for your grand plan. Furthermore, though I agree with you that sacrifices are necessary in war, those sacrifices have to be willing ones, if people wish to give their lives for a greater cause then it is their choice to make. None of these people had a choice, none of them shared your vision. They were murdered plain and simple, they are dead people crying out for justice and you would deny them that justice. So, while I agree with much of what you have said, I cannot accept your proposal, you must come with me and hand yourself over to the knights. Laws cannot be disregarded because any individual feels that they are above them. So please, leave your gardening, place your hands behind your back and lead on. I will be right behind you."

It was a bold speech; a novice mage would never normally speak to a senior that way and Gytha struggled to keep her voice calm. She watched Goodbern like a hawk, wondering what she would do next.

To her surprise Goodbern continued gardening, shuffling over to another pot and digging in the soil with her knife. "Disappointing." The senior mage said, "very disappointing for such a bright girl. You know I cannot go quietly as you suggest."

"You have no choice senior," Gytha was keeping her fear under control. "Your plan has been discovered and your guilt is known to more than just me. Finding that book was just the last link in a very long chain, Sir Steven and I have suspected you for a long while. If you use your powers to attack me then all that it will avail you is to give Steven final proof as to your guilt. He knows it isn't Mattris, or Eubolo, or Beneshiel; if he finds me with the mark of a frost mage on my body he will know it is you immediately. Surrender senior, and the knights might still be merciful."

It was a colossal bluff of course, as far as Gytha knew Steven was happy accepting Kas as the killer and was probably right now putting some Tanarese flag over his door for the Grand Duke to see on his arrival. But she had to try her utmost to get Goodbern to come quietly, if the senior mage attacked her she could use her own powers to defend herself for a while. But only for a while, Goodbern had probably forgotten more things about their art than Gytha had yet learned.

"You are right novice," Goodbern reminded her of her rank for the first time. "I cannot use my powers against you, my guilt would be obvious. So maybe I should just summon Xhenafa one more time."

"But you do not have the jewe..." Gytha's words died in her throat. She suddenly realised why Goodbern was digging so avidly amongst the soil of that particular pot. After loosening the earth, she had set down the knife and plunged her hand into the dirt. When she withdrew it she was holding something. She placed it into the palm of her hand so Gytha could see it clearly.

Gytha had long wondered what the soul jewel actually looked like and her reaction upon seeing it at last was an odd one, a mix of both wonder and disappointment. At first it just looked like the sort of gem a noblewoman would have set in silver and displayed in a necklace or in a brooch pinned to her breast, expensive but unremarkable; then though she realised that it was filling most of Goodbern's palm and so was the sort of gem even most noblewomen could never truly afford. As to the colour, at first she thought it a dull topaz, then the light caught it and it reflected back as a glittering emerald. Then she saw it as an opal, then a jacinth, then a corundum, then a sapphire. Gytha was unsure as to what power was affecting her eyes so, but it seemed to be a thousand different colours at one and the same time, it reminded her of the eyes of a wise old man, knowing, thoughtful, reflective, a fitting gem to house the soul of someone who truly knew the meaning of the word sacrifice.

She looked closer, then closer still and finally she saw it, a tiny pinprick of white light, not a reflection of daylight but a tiny, intense light that shone from the very heart of the stone. Gytha realised what the light represented, an essence of a life, one preserved long past its natural span. So that was what a soul looked like she thought, in a rather detached manner.

So mesmerised was she by the beauty and strangeness of the thing she did not at first realise that the light was growing in size. She did not begin to stir until it blazed like a dying star with the jewel radiating a thousand facets of shifting colour. And it was at this point that she realised that the light was no longer housed in the jewel but had left it and was starting to float above it.

And it was still growing.

It was wondrous yes. It was dazzling indeed. But it was being controlled by someone who only wanted to see her dead. Gytha finally felt life in her legs, turned tail, and ran.

She did not head for the hatchway, it was too close to the edge of the roof and Goodbern even now could use her abilities to try and hurl her over it, to have her body smashed far below them on the hard earth, exactly like Caswell. Instead she headed for the doorway of the northwest tower. The tower was partly ruined but the door opened onto a viable passage that led to the floor of the senior mages. Perhaps she could get to it before the spirit fully materialised. Then all she had to worry about was the door being locked and the spirit being able to follow her down the steps.

Gytha was a fit, long legged girl and sprinted like a gazelle over the slightly uneven flagstones lining the roof. She was nearly there, nearly at the door but to her growing alarm she could sense a power behind her, a terrible malign power. She decided to chance a quick glance behind her for the door was close now, ten paces at the most.

So she did look over her shoulder.

And her steps faltered and died.

For she knew now that there was no hope for her.

She stopped, turned to face the menace, and screamed in terror.

Sinotaneh was less than twenty feet away from her. And yet it was not Sinotaneh, it was certainly not the image of the fair elf maiden she had seen in the cave far beneath her. Goodbern had said the spirit was being corrupted but it was not till now that Gytha realised the extent of that corruption.

This Sinotaneh was a coiling, writhing serpent, a seething, sinuous, twisting viper. In form she was as a thick, oily smoke, black as pitch, and that form was constantly shifting. At times it resembled something humanoid, it was possible to distinguish limbs, a body both slight and slender, but it was a shape that would only be maintained briefly. Thereafter it would change, dissipate into a coiling, churning, hissing plume, redolent with malevolence, spite given form, hatred given presence, an asp of the pit, a cobra of the furnace it stood before Gytha and yet cast no shadow upon the stone.

Only one aspect of the creature remained constant, it appeared to have a head. In outline it resembled the head of a woman and yet it possessed no facial features save the eyes. And they shone with a fell light, a basilisk's eyes, the eyes of a hungry, devouring beast, a coalescence of all the evil and iniquity of intent channelled through it by Goodbern's naked ambition. For this was Goodbern's creature, no spirit of elven sanctity this, for she had twisted it entirely, corrupted it into a demon of withering death. And its eyes were solely on Gytha.

And Gytha knew not how to respond. She backed away from it until she felt the clammy stonework of the tower pressing into her back. The door was there but she was too numb, too unfeeling to even try and grasp the iron ring that served as its handle. The last time Sinotaneh had hovered before her she had talked, and the spirit had listened. This spirit though was another matter, Gytha could feel the hatred pulsing from it in waves, would a creature such as this give her faltering words any heed at all?

Perhaps reminding her of her name would work again. "Sinotaneh!" she cried out to it. "We have spoken before! I am your friend, I want only to help you, to free you from this bondage. Spare me and I will honour the promise I made you before!"

And the creature did stop momentarily, almost as if its true nature was trying to reassert itself. Its shape became humanoid again, an elven shield maiden trying to wrest itself free of its shackles. But it was only a brief interlude for soon the serpent was back, authority was restored. It advanced towards Gytha and as it did, so an arm appeared from its roiling, incorporeal body, it was stretched out toward Gytha and there was a hand there, and the hand was clawed, the fingers long and withered, white with the smoke of an intense, searing cold rising from it. Gytha realised that it was Goodbern's hand, she was projecting it into the form of the spirit. And it dawned on her that it was this, and not what she had seen in the cave, this, this vision from the void, this conjuration of the furnace of the damned, that this was the last thing that Raiman, that Caswell, that Lipshin and Sir Benet had ever seen.

And then it started coming towards her.

"Goodbern! Hold right there! I am detaining you on charges of murder! Banish that creature or it will go ill for you!"

Gytha recognised the voice. It was Steven. So transfixed was she by the terrible shape looming before her she had not noticed him climb the hatchway and stand on the roof. He was marching purposefully toward Goodbern with sword drawn. And behind him was somebody else, smaller, slighter, the cowl of the robe had been blown backwards by the wind revealing a woman with long, dark, silky hair.

"Beni?" Gytha breathed.

The spirit had stopped again. The arm and hand disappeared. It was as though Goodbern had had to relinquish full control to face this new threat.

But face it she did. With a word of command, a streak of fierce white light sped from her upturned palm to strike Steven fully on his breastplate. He was dashed to the floor, sent spinning backwards over the stone to crash against the low parapet of the roof. It was a violent impact, but the parapet saved him from falling over the edge and to his doom. He lay there, unmoving, it seemed that Goodbern was again free to make the spirit do her bidding.

****

Beni looked up at the sky with a sense of horror. It was enormous. It sat high above her as though eating up the world. She shrank underneath it, cringing in palm soaked terror as she was reduced to the size of an ant, or a worm squirming its way through rank, oozing mud. It would eat her, chew her up, grind her bones and spit her out like a piece of gristle. It was a monster, and there was no escape from its implacable gaze.

There was a noise, close by, clattering metal, ringing stone. She looked behind her. Steven was prone, groaning. There was blood on the ground. She looked around again and saw Gytha, Goodbern, and the spirit for the first time. Suddenly the sky was forgotten.

She heard Gytha call her name, regarded the terrible spirit that once again was reaching out its arm towards her and saw Goodbern orchestrating matters, the jewel that caught the sun glittering in her left hand.

****

Gytha watched as Beni performed an incantation, the words being too softly spoken to reach her ears. Between both her and Goodbern a thin wall of swirling, translucent, crystalline energy had materialised with at its centre, a small sphere of utter darkness that seemed to be consuming the light surrounding it. Gytha realised that it was a vortex, a storm of raw power caused by two mages attempting to nullify each other's abilities. The more mana that was used, the larger the vortex would grow and if neither mage backed down or submitted to the dominance of their rival then the explosion of magical energies could flatten anything that happened to be in the vicinity, human or otherwise.

Gytha looked at the spirit again. It hung there limply, uncertainly, the aura of anger surrounding it had ebbed slightly. Of course! Goodbern had told her herself about her murder of Lipshin, about how difficult it was to maintain control of the spirit if otherwise distracted and how dangerous it was for the summoner. This was her chance. She had to take it.

"Sinotaneh!" she said, as evenly as she could manage, trying to make sure her enunciation of the elven language was as perfect as she could possibly make it. "Listen to me. I know you have been commanded to kill me, but I am asking you to disobey that command, to free yourself of that voice that compels you to act so against your nature and your purpose. She that has summoned you has been weakened for she is engaged with fighting another who too wishes to aid you. Now is your chance! Now is your time to assert your authority over she that has forced you to kill those against which you had no quarrel. I beg you to both spare me and to seize that chance for yourself, for this could be the hour in which you are finally freed of that which binds you to this earth! Aid me, aid yourself and then you can re-join your people!"

Gytha prayed to every god and every saint that her eloquence would serve her well, this one time when it was truly needed.

The spirit hand was withdrawn, but the creature hung there still, silent, unmoving. Gytha licked her dried, cracked lips and prayed some more, willing with every drop of blood in her body that Sinotaneh would, or rather that she could, listen to her.

Then the spirit turned, its shape reverted to humanoid again and it started to move towards Senior Goodbern.

****

By the Gods this was tiring, Beni thought as she tried to enter Goodbern's mind again, neuter her power and force her to submit to her own will. Actually though, she considered again, it was not as tiring as she had imagined. She had plenty of reserves left, she could keep this up for a good while yet; it was Goodbern who was tiring, Goodbern who was being beaten down, if she did not banish that spirit and concentrate fully on their duel she had no chance at all. And she would have to move fast for the spirit was moving towards her. Then Beni realised, perhaps Goodbern was trying to banish the spirit, but the spirit was refusing to go, Goodbern, fighting on two fronts was weakened irrevocably, one battle at a time, and you could win it, two battles, and you would probably end up losing both.

Then the shimmering vortex between the two mages collapsed in a second, swallowed into the tiny sphere of utter dark that had stood at its heart. Goodbern slumped to her knees; both Gytha and Beni walked slowly towards her. Steven too, for he was standing again, his scalp bloody, but his sword was back in his hand once more.

But no one approached Goodbern faster than the spirit.

She held the soul jewel in her hand uttering the same elvish phrase over and over again, but nothing was happening. Goodbern looked up at the approaching menace, her eyes white with terror and called out in high pitched fear, "I banish you!", "I banish you!"

But Sinotaneh remained unbanished.

She had retained her humanoid form too, it had been thus since she had left Gytha and now she was looming over Goodbern, who just knelt there and whimpered.

Sinotaneh extended her arm again, stretched out her impossibly long fingers towards Goodbern's skull. Then both fingers and hand passed through the skull until they were inside her head. And it was inside her head that they remained.

Goodbern did not scream, rather her mouth stayed open as she gargled and spluttered incoherently. Spittle fell from her lips to fall upon the ground, then that spittle started to become flecked with blood.

And it was not just her mouth that was bleeding.

Streaks of it started to run from the corners of her eyes, from her nose, even from her ears. Then those streaks became rivers, and those rivers became torrents. Blood, an impossible amount of blood started to gush from those same sources, her white eyes became entirely red, swelling as they did so until they finally burst, showering fluids and jelly over her robes. Blood from her nose and her fleshy eye sockets melded together until her face, her features, her teeth, her still open mouth, disappeared under this scarlet deluge and only the hair atop her head was visible. Then that too twisted and cracked as her skull imploded under the spirits' vengeful torment. Only then, as fragments of bone and brain spat from the opened suture did she cease her bloody gurgling. She keeled over backwards, her body twitching and jerking in the dance that only death can perform. And from her open palm the soul jewel slipped quietly onto the gore slicked stone.

It was over. The harbinger of the dead would haunt the college no more.

Beni and Steven stopped where they were after witnessing this gruesome spectacle, reluctant to get too close to the still present spirit. Gytha though continued to walk forward until Sinotaneh was again just feet away from her.

And now it was Sinotaneh, not the black horror that had threatened Gytha's life.

As life had slipped from Goodbern so it had returned to her and she had transformed, by slow degrees, back into the fair, yet mournful elf maiden Gytha had first seen in the caves, and it was to Gytha that she was now looking.

"Destroy the stone, for I cannot. Destroy the stone human and let me fly to my people."

Gytha just nodded. Walking over to where the bloodied remains of the dead mage lay she stooped and picked up the stone from the sticky, glutinous pool that surrounded it. Her shoes and fingers were now dark with blood. Gytha shuddered and stepped clear of the gory mess. She regarded the stone which seemed duller than it was when Goodbern had revealed it to her, probably because part of the life force it contained was currently floating free of it. Then Gytha realised she had a bit of a problem, how exactly does one shatter a gem?

"Erm, Steven, Beni, how are we going to destroy this exactly?"

Beni was at her shoulder within a few seconds. "Beautiful isn't it, imagine what we could learn if we researched its properties…"

"We are going to destroy it Beni, take it up with the elven lady if you disagree."

Beni cleared her throat. "Of course, of course. Well there are spells, potent freezing spells known to shatter the hardest stone. All we need is some silver, some liquid metal and Pasitano's "Properties of the glacial heart" though the incantation from it can take several hours. If I might suggest…"

"Artorus melt my benighted ears," Steven snatched the stone from Gytha's hand, though one wary eye constantly kept Sinotaneh in view. "If you want a week long symposium on basket weaving, invite a few women, if you want something done quickly and without fuss, ask a man."

"How dare you!" Beni protested, "if you want something done slapdash and improperly ask this lumbering ape! Gytha, what do you see in him?"

"He is teasing you," Gytha smiled, "and me. He likes to be provocative because he enjoys the outrage. Just ignore him, though I too would like to know what he is up to."

Steven had returned to the gardening area. Setting the stone down on the ground he waited for Beni and Gytha to join him. Slightly more unsettlingly a silent Sinotaneh also drew closer, her undying eyes keen to witness whatever he had planned.

Steven swallowed nervously. "Look at these great earthenware pots here. Full of soil, see how these tables struggle to support them, drop one on your head and you would soon be floating through the void."

"So what exactly are you trying to say sir ape?" Beni asked caustically.

"That this jewel is not a true gem, it might even be hollow and so is more fragile than you imagine. And also that these pots are incredibly… heavy." And with that, and indeed with some effort he tipped one of the largest pots off its table so that it landed squarely onto the jewel underneath.

There was a loud crack, Steven leaped backwards as he was showered by a spray of flying soil. The pot shattered into many shards, but it was not the only thing destroyed by the impact. For there was a brief, blinding flash of pure, white light as a thousand, a hundred thousand tiny fragments of what appeared to be glass flew many yards in every direction. Some struck Gytha and Beni's feet and they yelped and jumped, not in pain but in shock as tiny slivers of the stone's power were discharged into their bodies. Then the flash was gone and there was just spilled earth and smashed terracotta.

The soul jewel too was no more.

From behind Gytha came a great sigh, a sigh that spoke of relief and of gratitude, of release from an eternity of torment, of approaching peace and serenity. Gytha turned and beheld Sinotaneh for one last time.

"I am… released! I can leave here!" the spirit almost sounded tearful. "I am free, you have freed me red hair, you, your companions will forever be counted as friends of my people."

"Thank you," Gytha replied, "and my name is Gytha."

"Then Gytha, please know this. Upon my departure many aspects of what I am now will no longer be needed. I choose to pass them on to you before I go. A gift from the elves, a parting gift of thanks from one who will soon be amongst those she loves. Will you accept it?"

Gytha was not quite sure what Sinotaneh meant, but to refuse her now seemed churlish in the extreme. "I accept," she replied hoarsely.

"It will change you in some ways, maybe many ways but the changes will be subtle and may take a goodly while to manifest themselves. And so Gytha red hair, let us merge for this brief moment, for the time to re-join my people is nearly upon me. What songs we shall soon sing!"

And then, before Beni or Steven could move or react in any way Sinotaneh came forward until she occupied the same space on which Gytha was standing, almost as if she was swallowing her whole. Gytha stood still, her face shocked, her arms spread either side of her as she suddenly started to glow. Her hair, her body, her eyes, her feet, all of her was both surrounded and consumed by a nimbus of clear, pale light. For a moment the two onlookers saw the veins pulsing underneath Gytha's skin, they saw her heart pumping in fury, they saw the outline of her bones, her muscles, her organs, they saw all that she was in one fleeting second. Or maybe it was all that she was now becoming. Gytha fell to her knees and gasped. "I see them! They are there for you! Farewell friend, may Zhun grant you eternal happiness!"

And then, suddenly as it appeared the light died around her, the daylight replacing it seeming a poor substitute for its dazzling radiance.

Gytha, still on her knees, leant forward and placed her hands on the stone of the roof. Steven and Beni ran over to her, concern on both their faces.

"Are you alright?" Steven asked her. "What did the spirit do to you?" were Beni's words.

Gytha was silent for a second before she eased herself into a standing position, breathing heavily as she did so.

"She is gone," she said. "I saw... something, and she has gone to join it. And yes I am fine and no, I have no idea what just happened to me. All I know is that I feel a little strange and a little weak."

"Then let's get you off this roof," Steven said in a no-nonsense manner. "I will get some of the knights and the priests of the dead to clear up this... mess. A fitting end for such a cold killer."

Gytha shook her head. "You are wrong. She was not evil as such. She wanted to achieve good in fact but became possessed of a mania that destroyed her reason and her more human feelings. She lost what she was in trying to achieve a truly worthy goal."

"Well no matter. You can tell me more when we are out of this wind. Come, take my arm, I will help you to the hatchway. Can you walk unassisted librarian?"

"I can, yes," Beni told them; "though I would also rather be downstairs, my first taste of clean air in years has been exhilarating but perhaps I should keep the dose small for now."

"Thanks, both of you," Gytha said. "You both saved my life."

"No," Beni corrected her, "I believe it is you that has saved mine."

"Well my breastplate saved me," Steven smiled. "Whatever she hit me with should have crumpled my ribs into powder, so at least I can confirm that the anti-magic powers of my armour actually do work!"

"Better than your brain does at any rate," Beni told him.

"Poke all you like witch, I am in too good a mood to let you verbally wound me right now."

They laughed together until they got to the open hatch. Steven signalled to Beni to go first. She was about to do so before chancing one final look at the sky.

And she was glad she did so. For she pointed at something there and exclaimed. "Look at that gull! It is so beautiful! Its feathers shine like finest pearl!"

"Really; gulls?" The other two spoke in an unimpressed monotone but by now Beni had disappeared. Gytha followed and then Steven and so soon there was nothing alive on that roof save for those birds taking an interest in Goodbern's corpse.

As for the gull Beni had pointed to, it had other things on its mind and no regard at all for the babbling humans it had just flown over. It was hungry, it wanted to fish and to that end it flew westwards, leaving the college behind it. Swooping low it passed over the cliffs, the gardens, the animal pens and grain stores, the kissing rock and the stone circles, the entire theatre where the events of these last days had played out, until it was over the connecting bridge to the Isle of Healing. Soaring high on a thermal it looked afar at the hospital, at the people tending the expansive herb gardens before finally descending, swerving slightly north, towards the sea.

However, before starting its daily hunt it decided to take stock. Its height dropped, dropped, slowly dropped until it was at the harbour where it finally alighted on a blue painted wooden post supporting the wharf. It was however surprised by the bustle, the mass of humans running hither and thither and so took off once more, leaving behind it the great ship that had moments before moored there, a ship whose flags fluttered blue, white, and gold in the sunlight. The ship that told all watchers that the herald of the Grand Duke had finally arrived.

48
Aftermath

The Grand Duke's visit lasted for four days and was a riotous display of pageantry. Flags flew everywhere, cornets and drums sounded at his approach, everyone was bedecked in their finery, wherever the Grand Duke went a joyous cacophony inevitably followed. On his first night a sumptuous banquet was held, tables were set up in the great hall for his retinue and the senior knights and mages, everybody else made do with the refectory. Gytha was actually invited to sit with Steven and Fedrica on a table next to the Grand Duke, but she politely declined; Goodbern's confession and his culpability in the whole affair had already soured the occasion for her. As far as the food was concerned, the cooks had come up with the novel idea of dyeing the food unusual colours so that the diners had to guess what each dish was. It was the first time Gytha had tried green chicken in broth and blue pears in wine and by the end of the feast, with everybody's lips stained black by the mix of several competing dyes, she fervently hoped it would be the last.

Thereafter his schedule, though it involved tours of various parts of the island and the Isle of Healing, saw him mainly in the company of those of high status. The novice mages only saw him again on one night where a concert was held, Emonie being one of many to perform for him; and on his departure, where he regaled all present with a rousing speech, praising the part they were playing in the Arshuman war. After this speech, and with a great sense of theatre, he surprised his audience by opening a small chest next to him and spilling its contents, gold coin after gold coin onto the white linen covered trestle table before him. This, he had said, was another payment to the college, payment made to secure the services of another mage to fight the just cause. And that mage would be... Mikel of St Brenetta. Those hearing this nodded in approval, it was a sound choice for Mikel had gone to the mainland to fight on prior occasions and had always acquitted himself with distinction. Those who knew the Grand Duke well though observed, as he took ship to return home, that there was a certain tightness to his features, almost as though he was disappointed with the way things had gone on the island even though everybody else thought his visit a resounding success.

And he had company for his return voyage. Apart from Knight Commander Shadan and Mikel the mage the Lady Fedrica and her daughter took sail with him. The Grand Duke had found her company utterly delightful and with the Lady Edith's continuing improvement there seemed to be no reason for her to remain on the island any longer. Fedrica, still euphoric at her husband's promotion, their new manor house and Edith's improved health was now beside herself with happiness, especially when the Grand Duke extended an invitation for her to be a special guest at the next Winterfeast ball. Steven's expression as he waved her off was all but inscrutable.

Following the visit, life on the island finally returned to something like normal. There were, however, a great many funerals held over the ensuing days and at long last many there could grieve properly for the fallen. So much death in so short a time had numbed almost everybody to some degree, inured them to the sense of loss they should have felt at the departure of friends. Now though, with the whole terrible situation resolved there were many tears as the flames consumed the bodies of the dead. Lipshin, Tola, Kas, Oskum and yes, even Goodbern, all had friends who could weep openly for them at last. The souls of the lost commended to the Gods meant catharsis for those who remained, Xhenafa would now have to wait a little longer before claiming the rest of them.

Miriam returned to the college whilst the Grand Duke was visiting, her cuts and scratches healing well, though, with her right arm in a sling, it meant that writing would be difficult for her. She saw Mikel, briefly, before he left for the mainland, it was as convivial a meeting as those between former lovers could be. He was friendly, she polite, and a brief kiss on the cheek ended their conversation. She told him that it was time for her to move on, something that, unsurprisingly for her, he completely agreed with. And that brought their relationship to a close.

What alarmed her a little more were the enhanced prospects for early graduation for both Gytha and Kestine, something she was still a little way from herself. Though she was happy for both of them the thought that they might actually graduate before her had never occurred to her before. She was the eldest after all and the most hardworking. But things had changed. For Gytha, the loss of so many members of the frost school meant that Eubolo was now at its head and that to fill all the vacancies created by the loss of tutors he was obliged to promote some mages before they were truly ready, enhancing the prospects of all who followed that particular discipline. As for Kestine, she was still seconded to work one or two days a week as a staff mage, furthermore, a supply ship bringing brazier coals for all brought something even more welcome to some novices. Senior Aidan, all the way from Old City, a new graduate and now the head staff mage at the college, the man Kestine would be working under. He was in his early thirties, six feet tall, blond and blue eyed with a firm, clean shaven jaw and a line of patter that was already sending many hearts a fluttering. Being a staff mage's assistant was now a position to covet, with possible early graduation and the prospect of spending hours in the company of Senior Aidan. Kestine was suddenly the envy of many of the novices, and some of the seniors too.

As for Gytha, it would still be some weeks before she ceased to be a mage liaison officer. Steven wanted a full report on every aspect of the investigation for, in his mind, there were many mistakes and oversights that he hoped to learn from should such similar tragedies strike again in the future. Once Lady Fedrica had left she was moved up to a room in the chapter house again where she could use its library for her writing. Also, a stone by stone search of Goodbern's chambers had at last uncovered the missing pages of the elven journal, something that Gytha was required to translate, though Miriam too sat with her when she could, and it was primarily this that dragged Gytha's report out by some weeks.

Steven saw her little, his promotion was keeping him busy so he said but Gytha could not help but feel that he was avoiding her. She was saddened by this, the need to finalise things between them, to talk things through properly was strong with her but she never seemed to get the chance to pin him down. But, as she had to admit, he was very busy. He, and some of his knights had tried to access the caves again but to their surprise had found everywhere but the entry chamber, and the cave housing the artefact, blocked by rubble. There was much alarm at first for it was feared that the college foundations might give way, but further investigation saw that the passages had not actually collapsed, but that rubble had actually pushed up from the cave floor. Also, the beautiful artefact that had so transfixed them all had shattered, probably when the soul jewel had shattered. Tiny fragments of it had embedded themselves into the rock, when the knights entered the chamber with torches it had glittered like a thousand multi-faceted stars. Senior mages were told, and they were all in agreement, that the power released by the shattered artefact had pushed up the cave floors, a final line of defence from the long dead elves.

No magic guarded the caves anymore, just the rubble. A few days, or weeks of concerted labour could probably clear the passages once more, but Steven decided that it was not worth it, that his men had more important things to do with their time and so the elves would retain their secrets for some years yet. He had the tunnel to the caves resealed, the slabs re-laid, and, as far as he was concerned, the matter was considered closed. Steven had given Gytha a wink when he had told her and she knew that he was abandoning the caves for her, and for Sinotaneh, it would be left for other knights to plunder, a long time in the future, if they so wished.

And of course there was something else, questions upon questions that Gytha could only evade for so long. Beni had asked her about it, Eubolo, Miriam, and many others, what had the spirit actually done to her? What had it imparted? How had she changed? And, so far, Gytha could only give the same answer, that it had altered her not a jot. Her abilities remained the same, the way she thought, felt, the way she perceived the world around her, there was no difference at all. Nothing. If she had been given any sort of gift at all it was proving all but impossible to unwrap.

And now she couldn't sleep. It had been days, weeks, since Goodbern had died and for every night since she had slept heavily and peacefully. Until now. She lay on her comfortable bed in her room in the chapter house turning this way, then that way, then this way again. She had kicked the blankets off her, then pulled them on again, she had lain on her back, then her front, then on her side. Nothing was working. The room had no window but outside she knew it was the dead of night, a moon that was near to full would be casting a strong reflection on a sea black as pitch, and it would be cold.

She sat up, knees to chin, arms around her legs and blew noiselessly into the cool air. The candle that had provided the only source of light had long since sputtered out, its wick totally consumed. There was nothing but stillness, and silence.

Why was she so restless? What was making her feel so uneasy? The murderer was caught, peace once more reigned at the college so why was her stomach all acid and bile? Something was wrong, she knew something was wrong, but what? As ever, when she was riddled by doubt and uncertainty she started to play with her hair. She had combed it before bedtime, it was sleek and silky as she ran it through her fingers, though she did wish it was a different colour. She wanted it to be golden, like corn during harvest, she remembered helping with the harvest years ago, as only a child could help, and she remembered that soon there would be a ceremony in the house of Artorus to commemorate the Goddess of the harvest, the Goddess...

Sarasta. It was Sarasday, Sarasta's day and it meant something, she knew it meant something. She scratched her head for a moment, both her brain and body craved sleep and so were working slowly, but they would not get sleep, at least not yet for Gytha finally realised why this night was significant.

It was one of the nights for Lipshin's escape attempt. The ship she had paid for would be out there, at sea but close by, waiting for a signal. The ship did not know that Lipshin was dead, and it would be poised, ready to whisk a mage away from here, a mage they wouldn't know by sight...

She was out of bed in a moment, somehow pulling on her robe and shoes at the same time. Who knew about Lipshin? She realised that she had told several people herself, as Lipshin was dead she had not been judicious with her tongue. Yet there were guards everywhere, at the great door and the harbour specifically, surely nobody would have the nerve to try and appropriate Lipshin's plan for their own? Maybe Mattris still wanted to try but on all the recent occasions she had seen him he gave no indication of ever wanting to leave here, he was still a broken man, yet perhaps this was just a pretence. Who else would risk their life this way? Someone with far more to live for on the mainland than here.

And then she knew. Speeding out of the chapter house she passed a few knights whom she forestalled with the words, "mage liaison business, just ask Steven." Then she was in one corridor, and another, running all the while. Finally, she was at the hatch to the roof, a place she had not visited since that fateful day...

She pushed at it and mercifully it was not locked for it opened with a slight creak. She pushed her head through, feeling a chill breeze redden her ears and nose. She looked around and realised that she need not go any further.

Resting against the northern parapet of the roof, just a few yards away were two brushwood torches. They were both alight and yet they blazed with a flame displaying a shifting array of colour, deep blue to turquoise, turquoise to sunflower yellow, to shy pink, to verdant green...

Sparkfire.

The signal to the waiting ship had been given. Gytha climbed down from the hatch and sped down the corridor, fleet as a deer. Down the stairs she went to the great doors and the stairwell that led all the way down to the harbour where a ship might be heading at that very moment.

****

Broken vigil

He had lost at dice and was paying the price for his failure. Sir Kennet pressed his back against the moisture coated stone, shut his eyes and listened to the soft echoes of water lapping against the cave walls. Beaten by three twos. Three twos! It was unconscionable. Not only had he lost because of his pathetic luck he had staked his two crowns against Sir Beech's guard duty, three nights watch, in the harbour. What an Uba touched idiot he was. He had lost his money and was standing here, on the stone wharf, counting the iron mooring rings till dawn. That was the last time he would ever play Killer again, at least until the stakes were interesting anyway.

He opened his eyes again and looked around. A thin shaft of moonlight glistened on the choppy waters of the entrance tunnel, other than that it was only the torchlight that provided any illumination. It was an eerie place at night, the water filled caves, all echoes and soft, sibilant waters lapping against unyielding rock. One was completely alone and yet one never actually felt alone for the water was whispering, beckoning, almost as though it was hosting a hundred spirits of the sea and they were inviting him to join them. It was enough to turn his skin cold.

Fearing a fall into sleep and disturbing dreams he eased himself off the cave wall and started to pace the length of the harbour, his studded boots clopping metronomically, creating an answering echo of their own. Finally, he reached the archway and the steps leading up to the landing that housed the Oval Room of the staff mages. His remit was to patrol there also, and he decided to do so, anything to be free of the lure of the sea spirits for a while.

It was a spiral stair, lit by tallow candles in cressets and he climbed slowly, pulling his cloak around him to mitigate the chill sea airs that constantly floated upwards here. Once on the landing he yawned theatrically, though he had no audience to perform to.

Or did he?

The landing was lit by a single torch, it was almost in total darkness save for the pool of soft tangerine light cast by that torch, yet just beyond that light there was a shadow that was a darker shadow amongst shadows. It was a shape, a female shape and it moved ever so slightly as he watched.

He loosened his sword and started to half pull it free of the scabbard.

"Who goes there?" he demanded; his voice was strong, yet it sounded jarring among the velvet sounds of the night.

The figure advanced till it stood illuminated by the torch. It was a woman, and she was smiling at him, a toothy smile sweet as a honey cake.

"I am terribly sorry; I seem to have become lost. I am new here you see and have yet to learn how to find my way around properly." She advanced past the torchlight and was now stood close enough so that he could see her clearly. Small, almost scrawny, mid to late thirties with a shock of curly hair that almost covered her entire face.

"Never you mind about that," he said, eager to assert himself. "You have a novice's robes, and the cells are back up the stairs and through the doors on your left. It is way past curfew; I don't know how you got here without being stopped but it is time you were off. I will forgive this transgression if you are new but see that you don't do it again."

"Oh I won't," she said, her tone was soft, almost mocking. "I sleepwalk you see; it has led me into all sorts of trouble in the past."

"And it will again if you do not go back to your cell. Now be off with you!"

"Of course sir knight, of course, but can I just ask you one thing before I go?"

He huffed, but if it got rid of her..." all right, ask and be on your way."

Soma took one more step forward, hands together, palms facing upward, there appeared to be a light radiating from them. She gazed at Sir Kennet with her warm brown eyes and spoke almost seductively to him.

"Do you like butterflies?"

****

A moving shadow

Gytha careered down the stairs at full pelt making as much noise as a knight's charger during a joust. Someone was bound to interrupt her sooner or later and the man to do it was Sir Edgar, who was on duty at the great doors, the entrance to the college.

"Hold it Gytha, you could break your neck on those stairs and wake the whole college in the process. Is anything wrong?"

She slowed down at last, trotting gently up to him, talking while gasping for breath.

"Sorry Sir Edgar. I... was... just wondering... if you had... seen... anyone pass... through here lately. Maybe... heading for the stairs to the... harbour."

Edgar shook his head before turning to look at the strip of night sky showing through the partially open doors. It was shimmering with tiny stars.

"No," he confirmed, "just me here tonight, me and the silence, until you turned up at any rate."

"Oh good." The relief in Gytha's voice was easy to discern. Maybe she had got it wrong. This was the only way to the harbour now, the tunnel under the bed in Kas's room was another that had been blocked by rubble, but still... the sparkfire.

She had better check the harbour all the same. She started to amble quietly to the stairs in the north wall that led there when Edgar interrupted her again.

"Actually," he said, "it is odd you should mention it."

She stopped, ears pricking, and looked at him. "What do you mean?"

"Because I have just remembered, strange that it has slipped my mind, but I did hear something earlier, like soft shoes padding across the room behind me. I mean I turned and looked, then I left the doors to search the room and the stairs..."

"But you saw nothing?"

Edgar scratched his head, "no. I wouldn't say nothing. There was like a shadow, close to the torches, a shadow that moved but when I went up to it, it just disappeared. How is it I am only remembering this now?"

"What sort of shadow?"

"Oh a woman's. A slim woman, half crouching as she crept along the wall."

"Thank you Sir Edgar. I am just going to check the harbour."

"Shall I come with you? Strictly speaking a mage isn't allowed out..."

"Business for Steven. He will explain everything. Bye!"

She was running again, down the spiral stairs to the Oval Room. Once there she headed for the next flight leading down to the harbour. But the top of the stairs was blocked. It was a knight, cloak wrapped around him lying prone and unmoving. For a moment, Gytha feared the worst. She sank to her knees and pushed her face close to his. Then she smelled his less than fragrant breath.

He was asleep. And he was snoring.

She briefly wondered if she should try and wake him but soon thought better of it. Stepping over him she continued down the stairs to the harbour, through the arch and onto the jetty, wondering exactly what she would see there.

****

Departure

There was a ship. A small single masted cog bobbed gently next to the jetty, ropes securing it were pulled through the iron rings set into the stone. A couple of bearded sailor types were putting out a gangplank for somebody. A slight woman covered in wild, curly hair. She had a small cloth bag in one hand, they seemed to be all the possessions she was taking with her.

Gytha took two steps on to the jetty, even her light footsteps echoed here. Without turning to look the woman raised her voice to call to her.

"Hello Gytha. You are a little earlier than I expected. Do you want to chat? Or are you coming with me?"

Soma did turn then. Smiling at Gytha she headed down the jetty towards her, Gytha too, started along the damp stone, the two of them meeting halfway.

"You knew it was me?" Gytha asked.

"I did," Soma nodded, "only you could sense my escape. But I am glad you are here. Firstly, are you coming with me? It will be quite an adventure."

Gytha's lips were dry. Escape? Her? "These men are expecting Lipshin and a man," she said, "and they are sailing to an island in the south somewhere. And they are expecting money..."

Soma put a finger to her lips. "Shush; they were expecting somebody, they had no idea what the mage paying them looked like. As for the rest, they will go where I ask and accept whatever money I give them, which in this case will be no money at all. Their will is not strong, and I can be very persuasive..."

"Your powers. That is what you can do? It is very unorthodox."

"I know. But I am good at it. So, are you coming?"

Gytha was stunned by the request. How many times had she thought of her home village, of her family? How many times had she stared at the blank ocean wishing she was anywhere, anywhere at all but here? And now a chance to leave it all behind had landed in her very lap. She could sail away, land in Tanaren somewhere, live like a fugitive, go days without food, have knights and vengeful village folk hunting her at every turn...

"No," she said, hating herself for even uttering the word. "I have been here too long; I would not know what to do...out there."

"I could help you in that," Soma said brightly; "but I understand. The wider world can be frightening, especially for one so unfamiliar with it. Anyway, I once wanted you to leave here so that I could unlock your latent powers, powers that the college here do not fully appreciate. Now though I no longer have to, somebody else has got there first."

"Somebody else?" Gytha frowned, "oh, you mean the spirit."

"I do."

"But I feel no different at all."

"Give it time Gytha, give it time, besides things are starting to work already."

"How so?" Gytha was perplexed.

"How did you know I was here?" Soma asked.

"Oh I just couldn't sleep, then I remembered the day..."

"And why couldn't you sleep?"

"I...don't know," Gytha faltered, "something just kept me awake, that is all."

"Something indeed," Soma smiled, "something that could recognise me, and tell you about me. As I said, give it time."

"But why would whatever gift the spirit gave me recognise you?"

Soma looked serious for a moment, she swung her bag a little, something inside rattled. "Icons of my children," she said. She sighed deeply before continuing. "To answer that question I first need to ask you a favour."

"Ask it."

"I will. Before I left I pushed a note under Kessie's door, a letter of apology…"

"I thought you couldn't write."

"I can, a little, and that is the problem. The letter is badly written with terrible writing, I just wonder if you could give her my apology instead."

"I will Soma. But what do you need to say sorry for?"

Soma looked sheepish. "For lying to her. Twice. I had to you see, to protect myself and to protect others. When I lied it was just not me and Kessie alone together. The woman, the murderer woman was there too. I was telling them both of my past and was honest for the most part, saying just enough without saying too much…"

"Did you know," Gytha said haltingly, "that Goodbern was the murderer?"

"No idea. I just saw a figure in authority, and I am very uneasy around figures of authority."

"Oh." Gytha said, "it was just that you always seem to be a step ahead of us, so I just wondered…"

"I would have told you if I had known. I wouldn't just let people die, however annoying they may be."

"Of course. Sorry. So how did you lie to Kessie exactly?"

"Well there was one smallish lie and one slightly bigger lie. Which one do you want first?"

Gytha shrugged her shoulders. "The smallish one?"

"Certainly, though I cannot talk for too long for obvious reasons. I told Kessie that my village and the priestesses of Jhuna that served it all hated the Wych folk, that they were the enemies of our blood…"

"And they weren't?"

"Well yes they were. The villages hated and feared them though they had never seen one in their lives. The priestesses though, that was different, they feared the Wych folk yes, but they didn't hate them. They respected them you see, and it served their interests to keep the villagers frightened. That way the two communities would likely never meet and accordingly would never destroy each other…"

"But why would the priestesses care about elves?" Gytha asked.

"Oh do catch up," Soma raised her eyes in exasperation; "the one god of the elves is called Zhun, the priestesses' worship Jhuna. The two gods are pretty much one and the same. So where do you think the priestesses got their beliefs from?"

"From… the elves!" Gytha said in surprise. "They must have had contact with the elves at some point."

"Good Gytha, you are learning. But the contact wasn't just something that happened a long time ago, it is happening now. The priestesses and the elves still meet in secret."

"They do?" Gytha gasped in shock, "but why?"

"I cannot go into details, but the two peoples exchange information, the elves learn about any dangers the humans might pose, where they are hunting and the like and the priestesses are given secrets of the elves in return. And sometimes they are given even more than that."

Gytha shook her head, "now you are losing me again."

Soma's voice had become earnest, her breath shorter. "I told Kessie that I spent my youth living between the priestesses and my family. Truth is, even though I had cousins in the village most of the time I was with the priestesses. Why? because my mother was not a villager, she was a priestess herself, and she had been visiting the elves since her teen years. And one time she returned from such a visit carrying more than just information. Ever wonder why I never cut my hair? Why I let it cover my face and shoulders so completely?"

Gytha smiled. "Because you are mad?"

"Maybe!" Soma laughed, a laugh that reverberated throughout the cave. "But there is this as well, look and understand." With that she turned the left side of her face away from the staring sailors and lifted her hair, over her cheek and finally high over her ear. And at last Gytha did understand, wondering why she hadn't realised the truth a long time ago.

"You are an elf!" She gasped hoarsely.

Soma let her hair drop once more. "No. My mother was very human, and my children all look human too. My father is elven that is all. It is a common belief that an elf and a human cannot have children. It is mostly true, but there are very rare exceptions, and I am one of them. The only thing elven about me are my ears and a certain lack of body hair. The priestesses covered my head as soon as I was born, a common enough practice and they let it be known in the village that my mother had been despoiled by bandits, so the village remained ignorant of the truth about me. And now I come to my second lie, I told Kessie that I had never met an elf in my life…"

"Well, seeing you are part one yourself…"

"Exactly Gytha. I have to protect them. They are my people too. A hybrid child is seen as special by the priestesses, one who can maybe bridge the gap between both worlds. It is probably too late for me to do anything about it now, but my children..."

Gytha tried keeping her voice down so the sailors wouldn't overhear her. "So you have seen these elves many times?"

Soma nodded. "It is a tiny community, less than a hundred strong. They live in caves under the Wild mountains, not wet, dark holes but places full of warmth and light. Wondrous places where they can still live free. They move from cave to cave to keep the humans off their backs, I have had three of my children in these caves, I learned my skills from their loremaster. And they are part of the reason why I must leave here."

"I thought you wanted to find your children..."

"I do," Soma nodded, "it is my first priority. But once I find them and take them away from the knights... You see I used to spend about three quarters of my time with the priestesses and the rest with the elves. One day though I had to make a choice, to live with one people or the other. I was a young girl; I was in love, and I wanted to see the big city. So I turned my back on the elves and chose a human life. I was quite happy with the way it all worked out, until of course I was sent here. Now I hope to rectify my mistakes."

"But how?" Gytha asked. "Especially once you have your children back."

"But they are the key Gytha. I will go and take them to the elves, we can live there and then, when they are old enough they can make their own choices on whether to stay or leave. Then maybe both myself and the children that remain with me can go and see the humans, offer a truce, offer friendship, make them realise the benefits of an alliance. Co-operation would strengthen both communities for they have more in common than they suspect. Perhaps, when the time is right I can teach them that."

"That is... laudable," Gytha spoke with no little admiration; "but Tanaren is a big place, how can you hope to find your children there?"

"I did not say it would be easy. But at least one of them has the gift, that will help. I could trace them the same way you traced me tonight. Please, tell Kessie all of this, I hated lying to her, she is a good girl with a true heart. I hope you can make her understand."

"I will, have no doubt of it. I am just shocked you managed to conceal your ears from us all."

"The long hair helps, yet a strong wind can lift it and your murderer washed it when I first arrived here. So sometimes I have to use a little trick, convince any witnesses that my elf ears appear normal and human."

"Your powers of deception again? Like you are using with these sailors?"

"Similar, my elven mentors taught me well.

Gytha smiled. "You are very clever. The sailors are looking at us though. So, if you are going to go…"

"Then I had better go now." Soma leaned forward, embraced Gytha and turned towards the gangplank and the restive sailors glaring at her. "Gods protect you Gytha, you and Kessie, and let your gifts develop at their own pace. Do not force them, it is instinct not technique that is the secret to your power."

"And Jhuna keep you Soma. I pray you find your children and bring peace to your people!"

Soma turned and waved at her, before striding up the gangplank and taking her place on board.

Gytha watched the ship cast off, the sailors pushing it clear of the jetty with poles. She wrapped her arms around her sides as it cleared the tunnel and lurched into the world outside. She saw its sail unfurled, translucent in the moonlight and fancied that she saw, silhouetted by that same moon, a slight female form, standing near the prow, arm raised in a farewell salute. Then the wind caught the sail and the ship, and Soma passed out of Gytha's sight forever.

49
Heartbroken

Gytha waited there a while, shivering a little for the breezes off the sea carried the chill of night with them. Then she went and gently woke Sir Kennet, who told her he was dreaming about being seduced by a hundred naked water nymphs before finally seeing Sir Edgar and telling him that she was unsure whether she had seen a ship through the cave mouth, sailing away from the island. Then she went to bed.

Soma's escape did not cause the shockwave that somebody like Lipshin's would have. She had only been on the island a little while and knew very few people. It was felt that she didn't really belong here anyway so what matter was it that she had gone? Steven sent Edgar and three other knights to take ship to the capital and search for her, as was his duty, other than that the matter was considered closed.

Two days later though Gytha finally managed to have the meeting she had been hoping for. She had left the college and had walked the self-same path that Miriam had taken when she had had her final encounters with Gideon and Kas. And there, sitting on one of the benches overlooking the southern sea, was Steven. He had suggested this rendezvous that very morning, they needed privacy he had said, somewhere to talk freely and his choice was an apt one for, as Gytha took a seat next to him and they both gazed at the sea and the wider world beyond, there was no one else around save the wheeling gulls and the odd curious rabbit.

There was silence, an aching silence between them, one that Gytha had to break somehow. She chose to do so by talking about her work for him. "The elven journal is all but translated. It does explain how the spirit is bound to its jewel and how that spirit can be controlled but I confess, most of it goes completely over my head. No wonder it took Goodbern years to understand it."

"So your report is nearly complete?" he did not look at her.

"Yes. Give it two days, three at the most. Then it is all yours."

"Thank you. Now about Soma…"

"You will never find her. Try all you like, and I know you have to try but she will always evade you. She is too clever, and her powers lend themselves to concealment. She is gone and in truth it is for the good that she is gone. This was never the place for her."

"So you did see her before she went…"

Gytha was tight lipped. "Do not press me on this I beg you. Say just that she was long gone when I got to the harbour. Then let the matter die."

"So be it." He still wasn't looking at her.

"Is that why you asked me here, to talk about Soma?"

"No," he shook his head, "I have something to say to you, but the saying will not be easy for me."

"Oh," she looked down at her shoes, "If it is difficult then perhaps you…."

"I am going with my family to Crown Haven, when the spring comes and the anger of the sea eases. You know this already I believe."

"I have been told yes, by you or your wife I believe."

"And do you know why I am going?"

"For some sun. For Lady Edith's health surely."

"One reason yes, but not the only one. I am going there to get away from you."

She half spluttered at that and put her hand to her face. "From me? What have I done to you? have I hurt you in some way? do you hate me or something?"

"No, no, no. I have to get away because I was, I am, getting too close to you. I fear that I am falling in love with you Gytha, if I am not there already. And it is a love that can never truly happen. I think you know why. I made a vow you see, while Edith was lying there stricken with fever…"

"That if Meriel saved her you would abandon me and return to your family. I spent most of the afternoon uttering similar prayers in the house of the Gods. And then Edith and Miriam were saved."

Steven nodded in affirmation. "It could be a coincidence. But…"

"We cannot take the chance of it happening again. I understand Steven. I really do."

"And the longer I stay here the harder it will be for me to tear myself away from you."

Gytha laughed bitterly. "Well I am rather irresistible."

Steven looked at her at last, his eyes were piercing. "Well both me and novice Warran seem to feel the same way about you. Are you back together yet?"

She nodded, "tentatively. I don't know why he came back to me. I treat him abominably at times, but I do care for him. He is more like a friend though than a, well whatever the alternative is. Whatever it is, was, that I had with you."

"Perhaps it is a friend that you need right now."

"Maybe." The wind was playing with her hair again, loose tresses kept tickling her nose. "He is a good man; he is…" she trailed off not knowing exactly what to say next.

"Have the two of you been together since we…."

"Has he bedded me you mean?" she asked bluntly. "Yes. Once. At the kissing rock, it was like trying to relive old times. I gave him some tips, all learnt from you of course, it all went quite well."

He flashed her a wicked smile. "Did he put his fingers everywhere I put mine."

"That would be telling," she laughed, she had quite the slattern's laugh when she tried. "Never you mind."

Another pause, Steven started to shift uneasily on the admittedly uncomfortable bench, "I cannot stay much longer, I am commander now, the knights need to know where I am."

She put out her hand and took his. "A little longer, please."

He sat again. "A little longer. I do have to see Greville though, he is still hopping like a flea over the choice of songs at the performance for the Grand Duke."

"Why?"

"Well it was just one song, novice Emonie sang it, "The song of Ysabel and Garth", do you remember it?"

"I remember it being sung. What is the problem?"

"Well it tells the story of Ysabel and her lover, Garth. They meet in the garden, away from her violent husband. She tells him to go off to war and leave her for she fears for her life if he stays. He agrees, they kiss but the pain of departure is so great they collapse in a faint. Shortly afterwards the husband happens across them, thinks they are dead and consumed by jealousy and rage drops dead on the spot himself. The lovers then awake, see the body, rejoice in happiness and run off together."

"So why is Greville upset?"

"Because Ysabel is the name of the Grand Duke's older sister. Greville is worried that he has inadvertently offended the Grand Duke. Of course he hasn't. Ysabel, the real Ysabel has a bit of a dark past herself and these days is even seen as a rallying point for those who oppose the Grand Duke. So any song that names an Ysabel and questions her morality is fine by him. I…"

"I love you Steven," she blurted it out, "I had not said it, I do not know if you were aware of it, but I love you and when you leave I do not know what I will do with myself."

He squeezed her hand in return. "I will be back you know, count on it."

"I will," she stuck out her chin. "You mentioned a questionable morality, then that is what I have too. I am selfish you see; I have a good man in Warran,

382

but I want more, I always want more. I see a honey cake, and do I think of breaking it up into pieces and sharing it? Do I think that perhaps there is another more deserving of it than I? No, I just stuff it into my face and feel guilty about it afterwards. I am selfish, hot tempered and plain, and I will never change, it is a miracle anyone sees anything in me at all."

"Ah now, I am familiar with this trick," he said knowingly. "You say bad things about yourself hoping that I will reply by saying, "no, no, no Gytha, you are wonderful and beautiful". You need reassurance you see; you need compliments, it is a common thing in women with low self-esteem."

She snorted at him, "and you are a pampered, primped up, posing, big head, totally absorbed with his own legend."

He nodded slowly, "that is probably true."

"And you have tiny genitals."

"Oh now come on! That hurt..."

She leaned over on the bench and kissed him. A long, lingering kiss, a kiss that somehow contrived to be both one of unrestrained passion and limpid tenderness. He held her close, her breast crushed against his. She wanted it to last forever, that when they finally parted their lips she would be old and white haired and that she would die at the moment of their parting. She had loved like this once before, in the bath house, but that had been a child's love, the amour of a silly girl. This, she knew was real and that she could only have it for these fleeting moments. Then it would be lost, maybe forever.

Then they did part, and she lived, and she was not old. And she noticed the cold wind for the first time.

"Maybe," he said; "maybe we can be together again, once Edith is no longer my responsibility."

"You mean when she marries. Steven she is three years old."

"I know, I know, but love should endure..."

"She can marry when she is twelve."

"My Edith," he said emphatically, "is not marrying at twelve."

"So how many years are we looking at then?"

"I don't know, maybe fourteen."

"I will be in my mid-thirties then. I might have no teeth or be bald."

"You will still be Gytha."

That choked her a little. "Thank you Steven. Then I will wait. I have nothing but time in this place anyway."

"In the meantime you can always take Warran up to the archive room."

It was her turn to be emphatic. "No. Not there. That will always be our place. And I am not ashamed of what happened there, I loved every moment of it..."

"Then in fourteen years, if Beni is still librarian, I will meet you there again." He stood finally, and he was staring at the sea again. "In the meantime, that report..."

There was a lump in her throat. And it hurt, really hurt, but she forced the words out anyway. "Two or three days as I said. Then I will no longer be a mage liaison officer, I will be a novice once more and return to my cell. And you will be Knight Commander and there will be no reason for us to speak again, I never spoke to Shadan after all."

"No, I suppose you didn't. Goodbye then my love, my bear strider, thank you for everything, for changing my life. And you are wonderful and beautiful, and forever will be, I have never said such honest words in my life before. But I really have to go now. Wait a little while then leave after me, we shouldn't really be seen together in this isolated spot."

Then he strode off, she could hear the clump of his boots and the clinking of metal against metal as he trod the path back to the college.

She did not look behind her, to see him walk away, she just let the sound recede, for now it was her turn to stare out at the sea, her turn to think, her turn to hurt, her turn to wonder. But she was a girl of Kibil, and she would not cry, though her lungs were tearing at her insides and her throat was constricting the very air she breathed, she would not cry. Pain could be a good thing after all, happy memories could bring pain, and now she saw that love could bring it too. How was it she wondered, that somebody who spent every day surrounded by dozens of people nearly all of the time could ever feel so lonely? How could she ever feel such a sense of gnawing isolation cutting deep into her bones? What sort of anomaly was that? It made no sense. No, she would fight this, she had to fight this. She would control herself, at least until that night. Then it would be only her cell, her bedroll, her books, and any gull that passed her window that would see how she really felt. Gytha stood, patted down her robe and headed slowly for the path back to the college herself, wishing that the walk would last forever.

****

Into the sunset

She needed company, she needed to tease somebody and be teased in return. She needed a fillip, stimulation, something to take her mind off things. She hauled herself up the great stairs to the college noting how clear the sky was and how restful the sea, something that did not happen often during storm season. She made her way through the reception room, through the great hall and into the refectory and was relieved to see Kessie sitting alone, absently chewing on a piece of bread. She went and sat next to her, but Kessie's glazed eyes told her that she hadn't been noticed. Gytha had to wave her hands in front of the other woman's face before she got a reaction.

Oh, hello Gytha. Sorry, I was miles away then."

"Why was that?" Gytha was already feeling better just in talking about matters not related to herself.

"Just thinking about Soma. She has probably made landfall by now; I wonder what she will do next and how she will find her kids. And whether the knights will get her, it can't be easy being a fugitive. How can you sleep easily at night when being hunted like a deer?"

"I think Soma sleeps without any fear at all." Gytha was shrugging her shoulders, "it has been like that for her all her life. As for stealing away her children, I will wager you that it will take her no more than six months before they are back at her side, and they have all vanished like that." She snapped her fingers. "She already has a plan in mind, I am certain of it."

"I hope so," Kessie said in a wistful tone. "I miss her mind; she was so different to the rest of us. We are all far too well behaved, me especially."

Gytha had told Kessie about Soma's true lineage, but they had agreed not to mention it in public, lest a prying ear pick up on it. "That is what she liked about you, your good heart and honesty. As for being well behaved, well, with Senior Aidan showing you his staff every week you have ample opportunities to change that."

"Don't," Kessie flushed pink. "He isn't actually like that anyway; he is quite a gentleman. You know he is just about the only man I have met who, in one hour of conversation has not mentioned these things," she indicated her chest. "That means something, I don't know what, but it does. If you get my meaning."

"So you are still saving yourself."

"I am; the Gods will tell me when the time is right."

"Bless you Kessie, you are a little saint, and you always make me feel so inadequate. Now, let's go and get some food."

She got up and soon returned to the table with a bowl of stew, a slice of pie containing rabbit and leeks, a hunk of bread, and a cup of small ale. And it was not just Kessie who was sitting there for Miriam had joined them, nibbling her bread like a fastidious bird, with her left hand of course, her right still being in its sling.

"And where have you been madam?" Gytha mimicked the tone of a disapproving tutor. "I haven't seen you all day."

"Oh, I have been here and there." Miriam's evasiveness was easy to discern. "Here and there?" Gytha asked. Kessie though already had the answer.

"A certain knight has been promoted and given Steven's old office. Miriam here has been helping him move in because obviously the knight in question cannot occupy a very private room without female help."

Gytha sniggered, Kessie sniggered, Miriam attempted to clarify things though she knew from experience that her cause was already lost. "He needed his papers sorted…"

"And someone to sit on his knee while he did so?" Gytha chirruped.

"No. We actually had an interesting disagreement on the matter of what constitutes an abuse of the knight's powers of surveillance over us."

"Oh! So he gave you a right good surveying then." Gytha and Kessie were laughing again.

"No," Miriam insisted, "we just had opposing points of view."

"So, did he hammer his point home till you were too weak to resist?"

"Gytha…"

"Did he force his erm, opinion, down your throat?"

"I have a damaged arm."

"One arm is all you need dear. Did you thrash it out over his desk until you saw where he was coming from?"

"Saints preserve us, am I in the Childs' college?"

"Did he polish his sword in front of you and hold it upright?"

"Did he assay a thrust with his mighty weapon?"

That last remark came from Kessie. Miriam stared at her with eyes wide, a good friend was siding with the enemy.

She pointed a stentorian finger at Gytha. "Her, I expect it from," then at Kessie, "you, never. It is just wrong."

"But did you win your argument?" Gytha asked sweetly, "or did he vigorously power…"

"Enough!" Miriam's good arm went up into the air, fragments of brown bread were sent showering over them all. "I saw Sir Nikolaj, I helped him arrange his office, we had a discussion, the gist of which I gave you earlier. That is all."

"So there were no roving hands at all, no indiscreet touching, no probing fingers…" Gytha's face was all curious innocence.

"Well," Miriam confessed, "maybe just a little…."

"Ha! Got you! He had you at his mercy in there, didn't he?"

It was Miriam's turn to feign naivety. "And who said that the roving hands came from him?"

Gytha laughed at that till there was stew over her chin, Kessie too, covered her mouth in surprise, Miriam sat back again in triumph. "If you cannot quiet them, then take them on and beat them at their own game," she said. Then she lowered her voice a little. "Anyway, what about you and Steven's roving hands, there is some…" Gytha shook her head firmly. "No. Whatever there might have been, there is nothing now. It is for the good, it could not continue as it was."

She could not keep the hurt out of her face, Miriam looked pained at the reaction her words had elicited. "Oh Gytha, I am sorry, I didn't mean to be cruel."

"You weren't. You couldn't know. It was finalised less than an hour ago."

"We are here for you. Both of us."

Gytha swallowed some ale, wiped her chin with a cloth and nodded. "Yes. And I thank the Gods for that."

"Let me tell you something," Miriam said firmly. "These last weeks I have been trying to come to terms with the fact that I have no close family left on the mainland. For I while I felt lonely, bereft, like an animal that realises for the first time that he is the last of his kind left in the whole world. I think maybe that was why I responded to Nikolaj in the way that I did. I needed closeness, I needed comfort, I needed a shield against the world. Then it dawned on me that I had been stupid, that the truth was staring me in the face. A family isn't solely about blood ties, it is about having people around that care for you, that look out for you. I blundered into a situation that nearly killed me because I wanted to help those that always help me. Ask me to do it again for either of you and I would, gladly. You are my family, the closest I have ever been, or ever will be to other human beings in my life, and I love you and would gladly die for either of you. If you need a good cry Gytha, come to my cell afterwards, we will both be there to hold you. We will always be there, as you two will be for me."

Now Gytha did almost break down. Wiping a smattering of tears off her face she leant forward and embraced Miriam as closely as she could. Then Kessie did the same, and her tears were far less abashed. "I never really had a family, apart from my poor mother, not till I came here," she said haltingly.

They returned to their stew, for their throats were still too raw for bread or pie. Their reverie was soon broken though as a dark haired figure approached them with just a merest hint of trepidation. It was Iska.

"Do you mind if I join you?" she asked. "Or is it a bad time?"

"No," the three of them said in unison, "please sit with us."

Iska did so prompting Gytha to say something about their rather obvious display of emotion. "Sorry about what you just saw, the three of us can get rather oversentimental at times, the Gods only know what others must think of us. I suppose we are a bit of a clique really; we have been very close for a long while. If you feel the need to vomit none of us will blame you..."

"Just do it over Gytha's dinner, not mine," Miriam said.

"Call that a dinner, Miriam?" Kessie smiled. "I have seen a sparrow eat bigger meals. Anyway Iska, we are all being very rude, how are your injuries, if you don't mind me asking?"

"Fine. They still hurt occasionally, and the scars will never go but I have no complaints. My voice has changed a bit with this nose, I sound a bit nasal at the best of times, but I am fine, Meriel has seen me heal without infection."

"What about the others?" Gytha asked. "The ones who had to go through the same thing as you?"

"The others? Well the boys are shrugging it off, pretending it was nothing though nobody believes them. As for the girls, Brytta has become a good friend, she always keeps an eye out for me. Karel had an illness already, some sort of chest problem so the whip did not help her. She came back from the healers a day or two ago and seems to have recovered. And Asitaigne has had a total change of personality, she has gone from being a total bitch to just a bitch. Whenever she gets high handed with others though the boys remind her that they have seen her breasts and the girls tell her that they saw her wet herself. That soon shuts her up. The worst thing for me I suppose have been the nightmares. I was next to Dicken the healer you see, when he died so horribly. I saw it all and it keeps coming back to me at night, at quiet times. I hope it will pass."

"I did not know that," Miriam said, "there are tonics available that can aid sleep..."

"Thank you but I have them already."

"Then stay with us." Gytha spoke next, "we will do what we can for you, they may even allow you to share a cell with one of us till these things ease a little. I will have a word with someone..."

"Thank you again. Actually I came over here to ask you something."

"Ask away."

"It is just that a couple of seniors have suggested that because I have an affinity with lightning and such that Senior Cheris could be my mentor when she returns here. I know that she is a friend of yours, I just wondered what you thought about it."

"Cheris as a mentor." Gytha started to giggle.

"Cheris with responsibility," Miriam too could not contain a snigger. Iska's face fell a little. "Is it really that bad?" she asked. It took Kestine to mollify her, at least a little.

"Ignore those two," she said; "they are too close to her to answer properly. Cheris would be an absolutely brilliant mentor for you. She is only a few years older than you, has a good sense of fun, is really clever and is horribly powerful. Scarily powerful. You will flourish, mark my words."

Both Gytha and Miriam had to concede. "Kessie is right," Miriam said. "It is just that I remember her putting dead beetles in the cook's ale when he refused to serve anything other than meat."

"And the day the two of us took on the boys at pitch and toss," Gytha added. "They haven't played us since, not after the bruises we gave them when they refused to accept they had lost. Cheris will be good for you; you will be good for each other."

"I hope so," Iska sounded enthusiastic at last. "Especially with the news we are hearing about her."

"What news?" Gytha and Miriam asked together. "We have heard nothing."

"You haven't?" Iska was even more enthused, imagine knowing things before the older girls. "There has been a great battle in the war. The Arshumans were sent running for their lives and Cheris was at the heart of it. They say she summoned a great storm that landed on the heads of the enemy and burned them all to cinders where they stood!"

Gytha clucked her tongue. "Artorus help us, she was always scared of her power."

"At least she is fulfilling her potential," Miriam pointed out, "something she could never do here. She would be very ambivalent about hurting others with it though."

"Not if they were trying to hurt her," Kessie said. "Try to hurt her and she would hurt you right back, just like Gytha would."

"I have not her power though," Gytha reminded them.

"Not yet," said Miriam, "but that spirit gift might change things."

Gytha shifted uncomfortably at the idea. "Time to change the subject I think. What do you all think about us goi...by all the Gods, I never thought I would see the day."

For somebody else was walking up to them. Her face was shrouded by

HARBINGER OF THE DEAD

her cowl, which kept her features in total darkness, but her height, figure, her manner of walking told Gytha who it was immediately. "Senior Beneshiel," she said quietly; "would you like to sit with us?"

"I would. Thank you." Beni set her food down on the table and sat opposite Gytha. Then, to everybody's surprise she eased the cowl off her head to reveal her face. Granted her hair was styled so that a lot of it fell over her wounds and concealed them but the fact that she was sitting, with them, in the refectory, was a revelation in itself.

"I have passed through here a couple of times of late," she observed; "but it is not until you sit down to eat that you appreciate the "aroma" of the place."

"Boiled cabbage?" Gytha suggested.

Beni nodded.

"Sprouting lentils?" Miriam asked.

She nodded again.

"Ale that has... strange objects floating within it?" Kestine added

"That too," Beni answered. "They really should open a window here now and then."

"I like it," Iska said breezily; "well, it is better than miasma row."

They laughed together, then set to their food. Gytha, never one for impeccable manners then spoke before she had fully swallowed her pie. "Oh that journal Beni," she said. "It will be library property soon; it is all but translated now. It answered a question for me too, about how the spirit could appear so quickly, so far away from the jewel that held it."

"And the answer is?"

"Well, speak it quietly but it is apparently not unlike demon summoning. Goodbern could use the jewel's power to envision a place in her mind and the spirit would materialise there, like in the aquifer for example. Anyway I shouldn't really be blabbering like this, it is probably restricted information."

"Oh, I am sure it will be," Beni smiled. "Though the library may not be my concern for too much longer."

"How so?"

"Well it seems that Senior Oskum's death was not entirely in vain. Greville and some others are looking at setting up Sunbank Island as some sort of research facility. They want to rebuild the tower, repair the well, move some goats and chickens over there. They are thinking of maybe a dozen people there at any one time, say three lay brothers, four knights and five mages or something and the research carried out might be secret or experimental, pushing the limits of our knowledge. The knights are unsure about it, they use the place now you see, but there are other islands where they can do whatever they do there. And I have been asked if I want to go, when it is ready, and I am seriously thinking about it."

"But I thought you had had enough of playing with dangerous forces, after your accident," said Gytha in surprise, "and you hate open spaces so if there is only one tower to live in..."

"I said I was considering it," Beni reminded her. "You are correct with both your assertions of course, but do I really want to wither and die in that dark room upstairs? I am unsure. Maybe moving islands is too radical a step but I do need a change, I have been living in shadows for too long."

"And sharing a tower with a dozen people? You hate people."

"I have reservations about that too, but as I said, a change might be good for me."

Gytha nodded at that, she could hardly disagree after all. So in fourteen years there would be a different librarian Gytha thought. She and Steven would have to find somewhere else for their tryst, if such a tryst was ever to happen. After all, one of them might be dead by then, they both might be, or maybe they would just have fallen out of love with each other. Their romance had been so short after all, though she knew she would never forget it, at least she knew now why so many poets described love as an agony, and its ending as a thing of such anguish and torment.

They finished their meal at leisure. Miriam, as was her wont, started gathering up everybody's bowls and putting them together when Beni spoke again.

"Can I suggest something? You are all free to say "no" if you want."

"No," said Gytha. "No," said Miriam. Kessie answered with a shake of her head. "Suggest away, and ignore those two, I usually do."

"I wondered if any of you wanted to see the sunset? It is due soon."

"Good idea," said Miriam, "I am all for it, though the balcony does get rather cramped."

Beni shook her head. "No, not on the balcony. Outside, where the benches on the north cliff are, at the bottom of the great stairs."

Gytha smiled at her. "Of course. It should be a good one, the day has been cold, but bright and clear."

And so all five of them made the short journey to the cliff, standing behind a bench as the swaying grass lapped at their calves and ankles.

And they looked west, where high in the cobalt sky ragged, fragmentary clouds were backlit until they turned sugar pink; with the reason for their shift in colour lying under them, brooding and torpid it sat there, the sun. Bloated and corpulent like an elderly merchant sated by too much wine it was near the end of its life and so was sinking, heavy with excess, into the equable embrace of the quiescent ocean; an ocean which in turn greeted it with the same warm cordiality that it always had, since the day Artorus had fashioned them both, aeons ago. And the gulls flying above them became silhouettes as the sun slipped lower, dying in shades of indigo and magenta, its fiery edges gilded, its cooling heart turning ochre as it was gradually swallowed, sliver by tiny sliver, consumed by water and by night, sliding away into the nameless void. There it would rest, a beast that was somehow both heavily squat and powerfully virile, waiting to burst forth into luminous dawn, so ensuring that the cycles of the Gods, night into day, autumn to winter to spring, would begin once more.

And as the five of them watched it depart in all its boiling fury they all reflected upon many unrelated things. Iska saw it as a sign, that she too could renew herself, that her indolent past could be moulded into a future with purpose, she could become curious about the things that affected her, that she could become inquisitive, speculative, enquiring, all the things that her tutors had hoped she would be. Her punishment had opened her eyes, given her a second chance and she would be such a fool if she did not take it.

Beni, by contrast, thought little at all for thought was of limited importance right now, experience was everything. With little effort of will she gladly allowed herself to succumb to a blissful anoesis. And so she felt the icy fingers of the night air stroke her bare skin, she shivered with delight at its chill caress, and she inhaled, smelt the grass and the soil and the damp mud, the salt and the ozone, even the rank stench of seaweed and the rot of the death of a thousand tiny creatures, and she exulted in the senses that were being awakened after so long. So she just let it happen around her, let the world play with her as a child plays with a wooden doll, she let it embrace her for the first time in a decade or more, she just watched the death throes of the sun and she remembered, just silently remembered.

Kestine was in a form of wonder too, as she always was when she gazed at sky, stars, sun, or sea. To her the purpose and design of the Gods was everywhere. She craned her neck backwards till it ached just trying to see it all, such a panoply! Such all-encompassing vastness! Man thought he had achieved perfection when he created great buildings, like the Grand Duke's palace or the golden tower of St Kennelth's cathedral, which she had glimpsed but once, just before they sent her to the island but compared to all this! It was as an ant standing next to a great ox and that was the largest animal she had ever seen. And the Gods had been good to her by and large; she had known true terror in her childhood, a terror that had struck her dumb for a long time, but the Gods had saved her from the fire, and they had put her here. Here she had friends, here she could be a staff mage, or a scribe or a researcher, it didn't matter. For her life and prospects had moved inexorably upward and now she had never been happier with herself. She was content, and few people ever truly attained such contentment.

Miriam meanwhile could appreciate the beauty of the thing but there were always caveats with her. Not for the first time she noted that both sea and sky occupied almost equal space, she had seen so many illustrations and paintings where the sky dominated the horizon, and the sea was reduced to a tiny portion of the page or canvas. And it wasn't true! It so annoyed her! One of the illustrators on the island had embroiled himself in an argument with her on this very subject, he had defended the privilege of the artist to interpret things as his own vision demanded, she defended the naturalistic approach and ultimately the discussion had descended into little more than name calling. And she was not an unimaginative little shrew, no matter what he thought. And the sun was almost gone now, and tomorrow she hoped to catch a glimpse of the elven journal before the library swallowed it forever. And she was due a visit to the bath house, and her hair needed cutting, and... she was doing it again, worry and clutter fogging her mind, this was not the time or place for either. She shook her head, blew through her teeth, and looked again, she saw the sun weaken and the light burn over the sea and finally she felt that rarest of things, relaxed. The fresh mint in her room would remain untouched this night.

And Gytha regarded the sun with sadness. It was going, taking her heart, her hopes, and dreams with it. Her lover was no longer her lover, he had done the right thing, the thing her head told him he had to do, and her spirit wilted like a rose in the southern deserts. Whither next for her? What was she to do with herself? She had loved and lost, maybe she never would love again. And yet...and yet there were ways to counter her despair. She would see Warran tomorrow and she would tease him and laugh with him. One day she might even tell him about Steven, when time had dulled the hurt for all of them.

And then she thought about Soma, the night in the harbour and the ship that bore the half elf away, that could have carried her away too. She could have gone, but she didn't. She could be lost on the mainland somewhere, but she wasn't. At the time she had chided herself for being weak but now she was not so sure of herself. She had dreamed a thousand, thousand times of her home, her mother, her brothers and sisters and each time she had yearned to be with them again, see them again, touch them again. But now they were fifteen years distant, and that time had made them an illusion, they were no longer as real to her as she had surmised. The truth was that the longing for reunification with them was not as strong as the thought of being parted with the ties she had forged here. In fifteen years she had created her own life, her own identity. She was no longer somebody's daughter, somebody's sister. She was Gytha, sorceress, apprenticed to the school of cold and frost, and she knew that many, many miles away, though they would never see or hear each other again, there were two parents who felt nothing but pride in their daughter.

And then, though all their thoughts had been separate, suddenly they were pretty much the same. The sun died before them, blazing it sank beneath the sea, defiant and beautiful. And as they watched the sky deepen to vivid streaks of violet and crimson and the stars assert their own power over the heavens they all thought of their former lives, how they had got here and of the many times they had all considered the possibility of escape, of leaving here forever. But now, as the gloom descended with a swish of fragile, shivering air, they all felt as one. That, no matter where in the world fortune could have had them live, right now, at this juncture, at this brief and transitory moment, here was the only place that they wanted to be.

It was cold, and the hardier night insects were starting to call. As one they turned and headed for the steps, returning to the torches and fires of the college in silence.

50
One final surprise

"I will be with you in a moment. I just want to swill my face!" Gytha called to Miriam from the door of her cell. Miriam nodded and turned the corner to her own cell, leaving Gytha alone.

She pushed the door open and went inside, nearly closing it behind her. To her pleasant surprise, the brazier was already lit, in a safe place, where it could not ignite paper if it fell. She warmed her hands over it for a moment before passing her desk and picking up her washing bowl. She started to pour water into it, enjoying the plashing, metallic, sound when she suddenly stopped.

Her desk was not as she had left it. Poking out from under one of her books was a folded sheet of parchment, and it looked as if it was sealed. She lit a candle and a rushlight with the brazier fire, placed them on the desk and extracted the parchment from under the book using thumb and forefinger.

She examined the seal, but it bore no insignia. So she then broke it and started to read.

"Hail, Gytha, novice mage of the college of Tanaren. It may interest you to know that you have been observed these last weeks, that your progress has been noted. Most importantly of all though has been your bonding with the spirit of the elves. As far as we know you are now unique amongst our brethren, a hybrid of a kind yet unseen, and one whose potential is worthy of much study. We could learn much from each other Gytha, we could teach you and you could teach us. Your future, the path upon which you have been set could be a thing of wonder. Accordingly, you are being invited to join the Order of Jedrael, a brotherhood in which your talents could only flourish..."

The longer that Gytha read, the more her jaw slid slowly open so that when she finally reached the end her mouth resembled that of a hungry amphibian. She set the parchment down, then picked it up and read it again, and again. Now her hand covered her face and her mouth closed. She started to laugh, a laugh that was one part mirth, one part shock, and a hundred parts naked astonishment. She stopped laughing and ran into the corridor, expecting to see some shadowy phantom lurking in a dark corner. But there was nothing, just one bored knight and a dozen candles flickering in their cressets. She returned to her cell and actually shut the door, pressing against it with her back.

"What in the name of all the Gods..." She half croaked to herself.

She dashed back to the parchment, picked it up, then set it down again, sitting on the bed and shaking her head.

"Who are you?" she wondered. "What is your name? Where are you hiding?"

She stood again and tousled her hair. "Who are you?" she asked again, though only the walls and the furnishings heard her. Then she picked up the parchment one final time and laughed, though this time the laugh was mostly mirth with just a small added element of hysteria.

"Then it is true," she said, "and I still don't know your name, or what to do about you."

It took her a couple of minutes to compose herself. Finally, though she stood, smoothed down her robe and exited her cell, heading to Miriam's and her promised assignation there. Behind her, the bowl, and the water it contained, remained unused.

And the parchment, it lay, still opened on the central part of the desk. There Gytha had left it. Though her head was swimming with fear, confusion, excitement, and sadness she had left it there on purpose, without fear of discovery by any passing knight.

For by now the writing on the parchment had completely disappeared.

THE END

By The Same Author

The Forgotten War

The Fangs of the Fen Snake

The Beasts of Midnight Lake

Printed in Great Britain
by Amazon

22352363R00229